W9-BUY-632

I LOVE YOU, BETH COOPER

I LOVE YOU, BETH COOPER

LARRY DOYLE

An Imprint of HarperCollinsPublishers

This book is a work of fiction. Any resemblance to actual persons, living or dead, businesses or events, is legally coincidental. The village of Buffalo Grove depicted herein is the product of a faulty memory and sloppy research, and should not be relied upon by anyone planning a vacation there.

HarperCollins books may be purchased for educational, business, or sales promotional use. For information, please write: Special Markets Department, HarperCollins Publishers, 10 East 53rd Street, New York, NY 10022.

FIRST EDITION

Library of Congress Cataloging-in-Publication Data is available upon request.

ISBN-10: 0-06-123617-9
ISBN: 978-0-06-123617-4

07 08 09 10 11 RRD/WC 10 9 8 7 6 5 4 3 2 1

For my Mom and Dad

IT IS MY LADY; O! IT IS MY LOVE:
O! THAT SHE KNEW SHE WERE.

ROMEO DEL MONTAGUE

ERIC VON ZIPPER ADORES YOU.
AND WHEN ERIC VON ZIPPER ADORES
SOMEBODY,
THEY STAY ADORED.

ERIC VON ZIPPER

I LOVE YOU, BETH COOPER

1.

THE VALEDICT

JUST ONCE, I WANT TO DO SOMETHING RIGHT.

JIM STARK

DENIS COOVERMAN WAS SWEATING more than usual, and he usually sweat quite a bit.

For once, he was not the only one. The temperature in the gymnasium was 123 degrees; four people had been carried out and were presumed dead. They were not in fact dead, but it was preferable to think of them that way, slightly worse off, than contemplate the unbearable reality that Alicia Mitchell's ninety-two-year-old Nana, Steph Wu's overly kimonoed Aunt Kiko and Jacob Beber's roly-poly parents were currently enjoying cool drinks in the teacher's lounge with the air-conditioning set at 65 degrees.

Ed Munsch sat high in the bleachers, between his wife and a woman who smelled like boiled potatoes. Potatoes that had gone bad and then been boiled. Boiled green potatoes. Ed thought he might vomit, with any luck.

Anyone could see he was not a well man. His left hand trembled on his knee, his eyes slowly rolled, spiraling upward; he was about to let out the exact moan Mrs. Beber had just before she escaped when his wife told him to cut it out.

"You're not leaving," she said.

"I'm dying," Ed countered.

"Even dead," said his wife, at ease with the concept. "For chrissakes, your only son is graduating from high school. It's not like he's going to graduate from anything else."

Tattoos of memories
and dead skin on trial

the Sullen Girl sang, wringing fresh bitterness from the already alkaline lyrics, her wispy quaver approximating a consumptive canary with love trouble and money problems. She sang every song that way. At the senior variety show, she had performed "Happy Together" with such fragile melancholy during rehearsals that rumors began circulating that, on show night, she would whisper the final words,

I can't see me loving nobody but you

then produce an antique pistol from beneath her spidery shawl and shoot Jared Farrell in the nuts before blowing her brains out. Nobody wanted to follow that. Throughout the final performance, Mr. Bernard had stood in the wings clutching a fire extinguisher, with a vague plan. Although the Sullen Girl didn't execute anyone in the end, it was generally agreed that it was the best senior variety show ever.

BEHIND THE SULLEN GIRL sat Denis Cooverman, sweating: along the cap of his mortarboard, trickling behind his ears and rippling down his forehead; around his nostrils and in that groove below his nose (which Denis would be quick to identify as the *philtrum,* and, unfortunately, would go on to point out that the preferred medical term was *infranasal depression);* from his palms, behind his knees, inside his elbows, between his toes and from many locations not typically associated with perspiratory activity; squirting out his nipples, spewing from his navel, coursing between his buttocks and forming a tiny lake that gently lapped at his genitals; from under his arms, naturally, in two varietals—hot and sticky, and cold and terrified.

"He's a sweaty kid," the doctor had diagnosed when his mother had brought him in for his weekly checkup. "But if he's sweating so much," his mother had asked, him sitting right there, "why is his skin so bad?"

Denis worried too much, that's why. Right now, for example, he was not just worried about the speech he was about to give, and for good reason; he was also worried that his sweat was rapidly evaporating, increasing atmospheric pressure, and that it might start to rain inside his graduation gown. This was fully theoretically possible. He was also worried that the excessive perspiration indicated kidney stones, which was less likely.

I hope you had the time of your life

the Sullen Girl finished with a shy sneer, then returned to her seat.

Dr. Henneman, the principal, approached the lectern.

"Thank you, Angelika—"

"Angel-LEEK-ah," the Sullen Girl spat back.

"Angel-LEEK-ah," Dr. Henneman corrected, "thank you for that . . . *emotive* rendition of"—she referred to her notes, frowned—" 'Good Riddance.' "

THE TEMPERATURE IN THE GYM reached 125 degrees, qualifying anyone there to be served rare.

"Could we," Dr. Henneman said, wafting her hands about, "open those back doors, let a little air in? Please?"

Three thousand heads turned simultaneously, expecting the doors to fly open with minty gusts of chilled wind, maybe even light flurries. Miles Paterini and Pete Couvier, two juniors who had agreed to usher the event because they were insufferable suck-ups, pressed down on the metal bars. The doors didn't open.

People actually gasped.

Denis began calculating the amount of oxygen left in the gymnasium.

Dr. Henneman's doctorate in school administration had prepared her for this.

"Is Mr. Wrona here?"

Mr. Wrona, the school custodian, was not here. He was at home watching women's volleyball with the sound turned off and imagining the moment everyone realized the back doors were locked. In his fantasy, Dr. Henneman was screaming his name and would presently burst into flames.

"Let's move on," Dr. Henneman moved on, mentally compiling a list of janitorial degradations to occupy Mr. Wrona's summer recess. "So. Next. Yes. I am pleased to introduce our valedictorian for—"

JAH-JUH JAH-JUH JAH-JUH JAH-JUH

Lily Masini's meaty father slammed the backdoor bar violently up and down. He turned and saw everybody was staring at him, with a mixture of annoyance and hope.

JAH-JUH JAH . . . JUH!

Mr. Masini released the bar and slumped back to the bleachers.

"Denis Cooverman," Dr. Henneman announced.

AS DENIS STOOD UP, his groin pool spilled down his legs into his shoes. He shuffled forward, careful not to step on his gown, which the rental place had insufficiently hemmed, subsequently claiming he had gotten shorter since his fitting. Denis had been offered the option of carrying a small riser with him, which he had declined, and so when he stood at the lectern barely his head was visible, floating above a seal of the Mighty Bison, the school's mascot. The effect was that of one of those giant-head caricatures, of a boy who told the artist he wanted to wrangle buffalos when he grew up.

Denis looked out at the audience. He tried to imagine them in their underwear, which was easy, since they were imagining the same thing. Denis sort of smiled. The audience did nothing. They were not excited by, or even mildly curious about, Denis's speech, merely resigned it was going to happen. He met their expectations.

"Thank you, Dr. Henneman. Fellow Graduates. Parents and Caregivers. Other interested parties."

Denis had left a pause for laughs. It became just a pause.

"Today we look forward," he continued. "Look forward to getting out of here."

That got a laugh, longer than Denis had rehearsed.

"Look forward to getting out of here," Denis repeated, resetting his meter before proceeding in the stilted manner of adolescent public speakers throughout history.

"But today I also would like to look back, back on our four years at Buffalo Grove High School, looking back not with anger, but with no regrets. No regrets for what we wanted to do but did not, for what we wanted to say but could not. And so I say here today the one thing I wish I had said, the one thing I know I will regret if I never say."

Denis paused for dramatic effect. Somebody coughed. Denis extended the pause to rebuild his dramatic effect.

He blinked the sweat off his eyelashes.

Then he said:

"I love you, Beth Cooper."

DENIS COULD THINK of no logical reason why he should not attempt to mate with Beth Cooper.

There were no laws explicitly against it.

They were of the same species, and had complementary sex organs, most likely, based on extensive mental modeling Denis had done.

They had both grown up here in the Midwest, only 3.26 miles apart, and could therefore be assumed to share important cultural values. They both drank Snapple Diet Lime Green Tea, though Denis had begun doing so only recently.

And while Beth was popular and good-looking—Most Popular and Best Looking, according to a survey of 513 Buffalo Grove High School seniors—Denis did have the Biggest Brain and wasn't repulsive, exactly. It was said that he had a giant head, but this was an optical illusion. His head was only slightly larger than average; it was the smallness of his body that made it appear colossal. He had the right number of facial features, in roughly the right arrangement, and would eventually grow into his face, his mother predicted. She also said he had beautiful eyes, though in truth, one more than the other. His teeth fit in his mouth now, and he did not have backne.

Denis could imagine any number of scenarios under which his conquest of Beth Cooper would be successful:

if Beth went to an all-girls school in the Swiss Alps, surrounded by mountains, hundreds of miles from any other guys except Denis, son of the math teacher, and Beth was failing algebra, for example;

if Denis was a celebrity;

if Denis had a billion dollars;

if Denis was six inches taller, and had muscles.

Any one of those scenarios.

One also had to consider that there were 125 to 200 billion galaxies in the universe, each with 200 billion stars. Using the Drake equation, that meant there were approximately 2 trillion billion planets out there capable of sustaining life; the latest research suggested that one-third of them would develop life and one-ten-millionth would develop intelligent life. That left 1,333,333 intelligent civilizations created across the universe since the beginning of time, surely one of which was intelligent enough to recognize Denis and Beth were meant for one another.

Alternatively, if current string theory was correct, there were a google google google google google universes, all stacked up with this one but with different physical properties and, presumably, social customs. In one of these, odds were, Denis Cooverman not only bred with Beth Cooper but was worshipped by ravenous hordes of Beth Coopers. Unfortunately in that universe

Denis had crab hands and inadvertently snipped each Beth Cooper to bits as she came ravenously at him.

This was but a small sampling of the thinking that went on in Denis's Biggest Brain prior to Denis's sweaty lips declaring his love for Beth Cooper in front of 3,221 hot, testy people.

For all its obsessive analysis, Denis's Biggest Brain had neglected to consider two relevant facts. Big Brains often have this problem: Albert Einstein was said to be so absentminded that he once brushed his teeth with a power drill. But even Einstein (who, according to geek mythology, bagged Marilyn Monroe) would not have overlooked these facts; even Einstein's brain, pickling in a jar at Princeton, would be able to grasp the infinitudinous import of these two simple facts, which now hung over Denis's huge head like a sword of Damocles—or to the non-honors graduates, like a sick fart.

The two incontrovertible, insurmountable, damn sad facts were these:

Beth Cooper was the head cheerleader;

Denis Cooverman was captain of the debate team.

THERE WAS A MOMENTARY DELAY in the reaction to what Denis had just said, because nobody was listening. While the adults contemplated cold beer and college tuition, and the graduates contemplated cold beer and another cold beer, their brains continued routine processing of auditory input, so that when Denis's mother yelped *Oh no,* they were able to rewind their sensory memory and hear, again:

"I love you, Beth Cooper."

Mrs. Cooverman had been following right along, syllable by syllable, and she knew something was up at syllable ninety-four, when Denis went off the script they had worked so hard on. Her *Oh no* was the release of tension that had accumulated in the subsequent twenty-nine errant syllables, building suspense for her alone. She did not know who Beth Cooper was, but she knew this was not appropriate for a graduation speech, and probably worse. Mr. Cooverman had been enjoying the speech until his wife yipped.

The bleachers echoed with confused murmurs, while down on the floor the graduating class retroactively grasped the tragic nature of what had transpired, and laughed. Dr. Henneman had been calculating how many dirty, dirty toilets required Mr. Wrona's lavish attention and had not noticed anything wrong until she heard the laughs; they seemed genuine, and that was not right.

Everyone who knew who Beth Cooper was—the entire class and several hundred adults—craned their necks to stare at her. She was near the end of the third row, next to an empty chair, the seat Denis himself was to return to once he was done humiliating her.

He wasn't done.

"I have loved you, Beth Cooper," Denis went on, his eyes clinging to his notes, "since I first sat behind you in Mrs. Rosa's math class in the seventh grade. I loved you when I sat behind you in Ms. Rosenbaum's Literature and Writing I. I loved you when I sat behind you in Mr. Dunker's algebra and Mr. Weidner's Spanish. I have loved you from behind—"

This got a huge laugh, one Denis should have expected, being a teenager. He also should have anticipated that Dr. Henneman would be looming up behind him, about to put her hand on his shoulder, but he did not and continued at the same measured pace.

". . . in biology, history, practical science and Literature of the Oppressed. I loved you but I never told you, because we hardly ever spoke. But now I say it, with no regrets."

DENIS MADE A NOISE, a dry click, as if resetting his throat.

"And so, let us all, too, say the things we have longed to say but our tongues would not."

He had returned to the approved text. His mother exhaled for the first time in more than a hundred syllables. Dr. Henneman decided intervention was no longer worth the effort, and sat back down. Denis also felt better, having disgorged his annoying heart, and so proceeded more confidently, with the well-practiced cadence of a master debater.

"Let us be unafraid," Denis preached, "to admit, *I have an eating disorder and I need help.*"

Fifty-seven female graduates, and six males, glanced around nervously.

"Let us," Denis chanted, "be unafraid to confess, *I am so stuck-up because, deep down, I believe I am worthless.*"

There were at least seven people Denis could have been referring to, and another four so low on the social totem their conceit was meaningless, but the clear consensus was that Denis was talking about Valli Woolly. Valli Woolly acknowledged the stares by baring her teeth, her version of a smile.

"Let us"—cranking now—"be courageous, truly courageous rather than simply mindlessly violent—"

Greg Saloga. He was definitely talking about Greg Saloga. It was so obvious that even Greg Saloga suspected he was being talked about, and this, like most things, made him angry.

"Let us stand up and say, *I am sorry for all the poundings, the pink bellies, the purple nurples . . .*"

Denis had received seven, sixteen and dozens, respectively.

"I'm sorry I hurt so many of you. I am cruel and violent because I was unloved as a baby, or I was sexually abused or something."

Greg Saloga's big tomato face ripened as he erupted from his chair. He had not fully formed a plan beyond *smash* and *head* when something tugged the sleeve of his gown. He wheeled around, fist in punch mode, and came very close to delivering some mindless violence into the paper-white face of the diversely disabled and tragically sweet Becky Reese.

"Not now," Becky Reese said in a calming wheeze.

Greg Saloga felt stupid. She was right. He could kill the big-head boy *later.* He grinned at Becky Reese, much like Frankenstein's Monster grinned at that flower girl before the misunderstanding.

"You should sit down," Becky Reese said.

Greg Saloga sat down.

"In your seat," Becky Reese clarified.

DENIS MISSED his own near-death experience. He was busy expressing the regrets of fellow classmates who started *malicious, hurtful and totally unfounded rumors* (e.g. Christy Zawicky and her scurrilous insinuation that semen had been found in someone's fetal pig from AP biology) or who *chose indulgence over excellence* (e.g. most of the class but specifically Divya Gupta, Denis's debate partner, who drank an entire bottle of liebfraumilch the night before the downstate debate finals and made out with both guys from the New Trier team, revealing the entire substance of their argument even if she did not recall doing so). And Denis was just getting started, or so he thought.

"And let us not regret," he said, "that we never told even our best friend"—pause, then softer, slower—*"I'm gay, dude."*

Denis looked right at Rich Munsch, his best friend. This was unnecessary; everyone knew.

Rich Munsch, however, was flabbergasted. He mouthed, somewhat theatrically: *I'm not gay!!!*

Denis was about to respond when he felt four bony fingers dig under his clavicle.

"Thank you, Denis," Dr. Henneman said, leaning

across Denis into the microphone. "A lot to think about."

For a bright kid, Denis was not quick on conversational cues.

"I'm not done," he said.

"You're done." The principal moved decisively to secure the podium, driving Denis aside with her rapier hip.

She heard a *splish*.

She looked down and discovered she was standing in a puddle.

THE AUDIENCE SPATTERED ITS APPLAUSE as Denis shuffled off the stage.

"As I call your names," Dr. Henneman was saying, "I would appreciate it, and I think everyone would, if you came up and accepted your diploma quickly, with a minimum of drama."

The applause grew.

Denis felt good about the speech. He had let Beth Cooper know how he felt, after all these years, and had made some excellent points about other classmates besides. He wondered what Beth would say to him when he sat down beside her. He had prepared two responses:

"Then we agree"

or

"It's my medication."

Denis suddenly had a scary thought: *What if she tries to kiss me?* Would he politely demur, deferring such action to later, or would he accept the love offering, to the thunderous applause of his peers?

So Denis did not see the dress shoe that belonged to Dave Bastable's father that Dave Bastable had stuck in his path. Denis tripped, lurched forward, stomped his other foot onto the hem of his gown, dove across his own chair and sailed headlong into Beth Cooper's seat, where, fortunately or unfortunately, she no longer was.

2.

THE 10-MINUTE REUNION

YEAH. WE GRADUATED HIGH SCHOOL.
HOW . . . TOTALLY . . . AMAZING.

ENID COLESLAW

DENIS GRABBED a Diet Vanilla Cherry Lime-Kiwi Coke from the cafeteria table. He forwent the selection of Entenmann's cookies that was also available for graduates and their families, because his stomach hurt. He could not tell whether this was because he was overheated and dehydrated, or because he had not defecated in the week leading up to his speech, or because he had just done either the single greatest or most imbecilic thing he had ever done in his life.

In any case, the Diet Vanilla Cherry Lime-Kiwi Coke didn't help.

As he had every thirty seconds since he arrived, Denis surveyed the cafeteria. Fresh alumni, a few still in caps and gowns, most in caps and jeans, caps and cutoffs, caps and gym trunks, or, in the case of members of Orchesis, caps and orange Danskins, clustered in the same clusters they always had, in almost the exact spots they once ate lunch, even though none of the tables were there. Yet they all talked about how hot it had been in the gym and what they planned to do that evening, which was pretty much the same, only in different clusters.

She was not there.

ON THE REFRESHMENT TABLE a silver cube blasted the platinum thrash rap of Einstein's Brain,

> *Fuck this shit*
> *Nuff this shit*

The song captured the essence of adolescence and expressed it in easy-to-understand language, while simultaneously managing to aggravate adults, no mean feat these days. (Sales of the clean version were poor, however.)

What you can do wit
All this shit
Just fuck it!

Although Denis didn't like thrash rap, he was feeling a little outlawish and this song, he decided, would serve as his own personal theme song, saying in rhyme what he had said in rhetoric. He moved closer to the table to facilitate others in making the connection.

"Oh, dear God," Mr. Bernard said, rushing past Denis and picking up the music box, searching for a way to turn it off, or failing that, destroy it. Mr. Bernard did not like modern music or its devices, his primary qualifications to head the Music Department. He shook the box, but it only seemed to get louder:

Fuckitfuckitfuckitfuckitfuckit

Mr. Bernard started to raise the box over his head.

"Let me, Mr. Bernard," Denis said, taking the cube from his twitching fingers. He pressed a nonexistent button on the metallic surface and the music changed to that Vitamin C song that wouldn't go away. Momentarily lulled by the classical string opening, Mr. Bernard wandered away.

He could have at least said *Thank you*, Denis thought, or A*wesome speech*.

And so we talked all night
about the rest of our lives

Denis did his reconnaissance. He did not know what he would do if he found her, only that he needed to do it.

Closest to the exit were clumps of parents who hadn't been dissuaded from attending (Denis's own parents seemed only too happy to wait out in the car, where the Sunday *New York Times* was). Mothers chatted up the teachers, hoping to squeeze out one last compliment about their children, while fathers checked their Treos for weekend business emergencies.

Rich Munsch fidgeted beside his parents as his father interrogated Ms. Rosenbaum, his English teacher.

"I mean," Ed Munsch said, gesturing with his third complimentary Coca-Cola beverage, "is it really worth all that money to send him to college?"

"Everyone should go to college," Ms. Rosenbaum answered.

Ed Munsch chuckled. "Well, not *everyone*."

BETH COOPER WAS NOWHERE.

Denis began strolling, ostensibly checking things out but also providing an opportunity for the things to check him out. He was prepared to accept the accolades of his peers with good humor and a humble nod he had been practicing.

He stopped at a twenty-foot orange-and-blue banner hanging on the wall. It read "Congrats to BGHS CLASS OF '07" and featured a Mighty Bison painted by Marie Snodgrass, who would one day go on to create Po Panda, star of *Po Panda Poops* and *Oops, Po Panda!*, two unnecessary children's books. The bison wore a mortarboard and appeared to be drunk. Other graduates stood around the banner, signing their names to heartfelt clichés and smartass remarks.

No one took note of Denis.

Denis pretended to read and appreciate the farewell

messages while searching for his name. The only entry that came close was:

I'm Gay, Dude, signed Richard Munsch

Just below this was affixed:

stuK

This was Stuart Kramer's "tag"—which he used exclusively in bathroom stalls and on his notebooks—placed there to ensure proper credit for this witticism. Denis was annoyed; that was *his* line.

Denis considered seeding the banner with a few anonymous hosannas to his *awesome speech*, just to get the ball rolling, but he was afraid he might get caught, and he didn't have a pen.

WHERE WAS SHE?

Denis was thinking about just leaving, and then he was thinking about just staying, when he felt those familiar authoritarian talons dig into his soft upper flesh.

"Mr. Cooverman." Dr. Henneman had snuck up on him again.

"Oh, Dr. Henneman," Denis said, with hopeful bonhomie. "Or I guess now I should call you Darlene."

"No," Dr. Henneman said. "You should not."

She fixed Denis with the look, the look she had fixed many thousands of times before, but which she had never imagined she would have fixed on this particular boy.

"Mr. Cooverman," she lectured, "I've never known you to do anything so reckless. At *all* reckless."

And then came the part of the upbraiding familiar to legions of Buffalo Grove High School malefactors, jokers, and stunt-pullers, an interrogatory also familiar to disobedient children and husbands throughout the English-speaking world.

"What," Dr. Henneman inquisited, "*what* were you thinking?"

DENIS COULD NOT THINK of what he had been thinking. He knew that what he had been thinking had been carefully thought, and would surely satisfy Dr. Henneman. But he was having trouble accessing his brain. Every time he tried going in there, the view of his vast hypertextual data matrix was obscured by one insistent memory. All he could see was the replay of a few minutes in his room a week before, when he decided to go ahead with the speech. It was the image of Rich Munsch bobbing around in front of his face.

"You gotta do it!" Remembered Rich was saying, in full dramatic flower. "It'll be like—"

Rich puckered his lips and scrunched his nose, and began yelling in a nasal and New York-y accent.

"You're out of order! You're out of order! The whole trial is out of order!"

Denis said what he usually said when Rich went into another of his inscrutable celebrity impressions: "What?"

Rich's response, in the standard format: "Al Pacino in . . . *and Justice for All,* 1979, Norman Jewison."

Rich bounced up and down a couple of times.

"Unforgettable speech. Like *yours* is going to be!"

There was nothing there to quench Dr. Henneman, Denis decided. He also concluded that the sociology of alien civilizations and implications of infinite universes might be too esoteric for the discussion at hand. And he probably shouldn't bring up *mating*. He began composing a creative plausibility, what in debate they referred to as *bullshit*, when Rich's face came bobbing across his brain again.

"You will *never* see her again!" Rich declared with awful finality. "*Nunca*. After graduation she will be *gone*! Until like maybe the tenth reunion, if you both *even live that long*."

Rich enjoyed having an audience, even of one, and took a little strut before delivering his next, tragic line.

"And she'll be so very pregnant—baking someone else's DNA—she'll have this big cow grin and *she won't even remember who you are!*"

"She'll remember me," Denis said. "I sat behind her in almost every class."

"*Behind her. Behind* her. Be-*hind* her," Rich incanted, like a poorly written television attorney. "She never *saw* you."

Rich stepped back for his close-up.

"You don't exist."

This was a persuasive argument. Denis knew what it felt like to not exist, and didn't much care for it. He doubted it would hold much sway with Dr. Henneman, whose existence nobody doubted. He scanned his memory again, for even the slightest scrap of logic behind this monumental blunder, and there was Rich again.

"If you don't do this," Rich said, pausing to imply quotation marks before croaking out of the side of his mouth in a quasi-tough-guy voice:

"*You will regret it, maybe not today, maybe not tomorrow, but soon and for the rest of your life.*"

"What?" Denis said.

"*Bogart*, dude!"

"I DUNNO," Denis told Dr. Henneman.

Denis had upon his face that sheepish but supercilious grin only found on a teen male in trouble. He had never deployed it before, but Dr. Henneman had certainly seen it, and she was trained to wipe it off. "Not the behavior I expect from someone going to Northwestern University." And then, oh so coolly: "You know, one call from me and you're going to Harper's . . ."

That smirk wiped right off.

"Oh. Don't do that."

Harper Community College, located just five miles away in once lovely Palatine, offered credit courses in:

Computer Information Systems;

Dental Hygiene;

Certified Nursing Assistance;

Heating, Ventilation and Air Conditioning;

Hospitality Management; and

Food Service.

It was where young lives went to die.

"That would be . . . *unimaginable,*" Denis said, even as he was extravagantly imagining it. "I, I don't know what I was thinking . . . I was . . . I was under an influence!"

The phrase *under an influence* triggered a series of autonomic responses in Dr. Henneman: check eyes, arms, grades. But wait, this was Denis Cooverman. Valedictorian, debate champion, meek, quiet, perhaps too quiet, socially isolated . . . She studied Denis for Goth signifiers: pale, check; pasty, perhaps; eyeliner, no; hair, ordinary; piercings, none visible. His gown: there could be any number of semiautomatic weapons or sticks of dynamite under there.

But, c'mon: *Denis Cooverman.*

If Dr. Henneman had been one of those evil robot principals you keep hearing about, she would have started repeating IRRESOLVABLE LOGIC CONFLICT as smoke poured from her optical sockets and her head unit would have sparked and then exploded, just like in Mr. Wrona's sweet custodial dreams.

Instead, she bowed her head and whispered, "Drugs?"

"Oh? *No*," Denis flustered, "not drugs. They're whack," quoting a health education video that could use some updating. "No, by influence, I meant my thinking process was influenced, negatively impacted, by which I mean . . . Rich Munsch."

Dr. Henneman smiled. This would be perfect for her blog, The Uncertainty Principal, the twelfth most popular high school principal blog in the state.

"You really shouldn't be taking romantic advice from Richard Munsch," she said.

Denis—and this will be a recurring theme—didn't know that this would be a good time to shut up.

"But he was *right*," Denis insisted. "I had to do something. I would have been forgotten. Not even. I'm not there." Denis pointed to his head, and because he was Denis, he pointed precisely to his hippocampus. "She has no memory of me. No dendritic spines in her cortex that whisper: *Denis*."

(Denis knew that dendritic spines did not whisper, but he could be poetic, too, in his own way.)

"So I *had* to," Denis continued his pleading. "To *stimulate dendrite growth*. I mean"—and this is where he thought he had her—"Dr. Henneman, haven't you ever been in love?"

Dr. Henneman had been in love, and was in love, with her husband, Mr. Dr. Henneman, who was standing not more than fifteen feet away but remained invisible to all of her students because it required them to acknowledge that she had feelings and plumbing. The plaintiveness of Denis's cry, however, rekindled in

Dr. Henneman the heartache of Paul Burgie, the brown-eyed demon who took her to second base (then above-the-waist petting and not a Rainbow Party) and reported back to the other seventh-grade boys that Dr. Henneman's nipples were "weird"—*as if he had a representative sample!*

Dr. Henneman caught herself crossing her arms tightly across her chest, as she had through junior high. Such silly, everlasting pain. She answered Denis with something approaching empathy.

"There's another Beth Cooper out there," she told him. "One just for you. The world is full of Beth Coopers."

Dr. Henneman began to walk away, already filing Denis under STUDENTS, FORMER and composing additional summer projects for Mr. Wrona. *The grooves between these floor tiles could use a good toothpicking* . . .

"Dr. Henneman?"

"*Yes,* Mr. Cooverman?"

"You won't call Northwestern."

Dr. Henneman chuckled. "As if I have any actual power," she confessed, as she often did to graduates. "Denis, with your SAT scores, you'd practically have to kill someone to not get in."

ALONE AGAIN, Denis decided to assume a cool pose against the wall, in case anyone chose to reference him while discussing his now infamous speech. It was a pretty good pose: casual yet defiant. But no one was talking about his speech; few even remembered it. At the end of the ceremony it had flown out of their heads like trigonometry, gone forever.

Denis canvassed the room, a cruel smile playing across his lips, he thought.

Rich's father was at the snack table, filling paper

napkins with cookie remains. Rich was performing for his mother and Ms. Rosenbaum, both laughing despite obviously having no idea what he was doing. Miles Paterini and Pete Couvier, the junior ushers, were acting like they were already seniors, scoping out where their lunch table would be, temporarily forgetting how unpopular they were. And there was Stephen Gammel guzzling a Coca-Mocha, the horrible new carbonated coffee beverage, and Lysa Detrick showing off the chin she got for graduation, and:

There she was.

BETH COOPER WAS less than thirty feet away. Twenty-seven floor tiles. She was chatting with Cammy Alcott and Treece Kilmer, fellow varsity cheerleaders and Table Six lunchers. Chatting about *him*, Denis suspected. Remarkably, he was about to be correct.

Cammy, who had a preternatural sense for when she was being stared at, noticed Denis first. Denis jerked his face to the side—universal body language for *Yes, I was staring at you*—while maintaining his casual yet defiant pose against the wall. It made him look like a male underwear model, except not. Out of the corner of his rapidly darting eye Denis saw Cammy point. Treece, and then Beth, turned in his direction.

Denis considered yawning to underscore his indifference to the attention, but he was afraid a scream might come out, undermining the effect.

Cammy made a short remark, with either a slight smile or a slight frown. Treece whinnied like a frightened mare, a thing she did in situations where other people laughed.

Beth Cooper began walking toward Denis.

WHEN DENIS WAS EIGHT, he read a story about a boy who discovered he could render himself invisible by turning at a precise angle. Young Denis spent several days systematically rotating himself until he, too, knew the exact angle of invisibility.

Right now Denis could not fathom how he could have forgotten such important information.

3.

HERE SHE COMES

"HOLY SHIT! IT'S THE MOTHER LODE!"

TOMMY TURNER

"HERE SHE COMES," as it so happens, was playing on the iCube as she came.

This was not the "Here She Comes" by the Beach Boys or the "Here She Comes"es by Boney James, Bonnie Tyler, Dusty Springfield, Android, Shantel, Mardo, Joe, the Eurythmics, the Konks, the Mr. T Experience or any of 238 other bands. Nor was it the Velvet Underground's "Here She Comes (Now)" or U2's "Hallelujah (Here She Comes)" or Hall and Oates's "(Uh-Oh) Here She Comes," which is actually called "Man Eater."

Had any of these "Here She Comeses"es been playing when Beth Cooper came it would have been a spooky coincidence (especially "Man Eater"); the fact that this "Here She Comes" was also Denis and Beth's unofficial song (pending Beth's notification and approval) made it, well, also a spooky coincidence, but spookier and more coincidental.

Beth Cooper's coming was accompanied by the latest and therefore greatest song to be called "Here She Comes," by Very Sad Boy,* off his new album, *Third Time's a Charm*, a reference to his upcoming suicide attempt.

Here she comes
But no, not for me

Denis tried to retract his entire head into his body cavity but it wouldn't go.

Graduation cap set at a provocative angle, Beth Cooper came. She seemed to be moving—nay, *sashaying*—in slow motion, as all around her blurred and the song became a sound track.

Here she comes
No never for me

*Née Judah Weinstock.

In the music video Denis spontaneously hallucinated, a sudden breeze kicked up. Beth's long brown hair flew about her face promiscuously.

Here she comes
Oh, she comes for me

Her gown clung to her skin like a damp nightie. It was apparently quite cold in the cafeteria.

Here she comes
And there,
there I go

BETH STOPPED. She was twenty inches from Denis, and, for perhaps the first time, facing him. She was about his height, and this for some reason both startled and delighted Denis. They could walk down the hallway with their hands comfortably tucked in each other's back pockets. They could wear each other's T-shirts. They could kiss ergonomically.

"You embarrassed me," Beth said in the flat, midwestern voice of an angel.

Denis's mouth went dry.

It hung open a bit.

Death was imminent.

Then she smiled.

"But it was so sweet, I'll have to let you live."

Only a fool would have read this gesture as anything other than kindness. Denis was such a fool.

"Great," Denis said, clarifying: "That's great."

Then, a pause. A terrible, multisecond pause.

Denis panicked.

Beth didn't notice.

"So," she said, "Henneman must've given you major shit."

At that moment, Denis realized he hadn't planned for his plan to lead to conversation. Violence, sex, either way he had a plan (both defensive). But *chitchat.*

So, Henneman must've given you major shit.

RESPOND.

"Some shit," Denis responded, with simulated indifference. "Little shit. A modicum of excreta." That didn't come out as cool as his brain told him it would. Before he could damage himself further with *a fecal smidgen,* Beth changed the subject.

"Was it like eight hundred degrees in there?" She scrunched her brow, as she did all things, intoxicatingly. "Like boiling?"

Denis chuckled dryly. Or that was the general idea. He kind of snorted.

"Actually, the boiling point—of water—is two hundred and twelve degrees. Fahrenheit," he said, adding casually, "One hundred Celsius."

Denis instantly knew that was hugely geeky, what he said, and further he knew his brain knew how geeky it was even before he said it; he suspected his brain was out to sabotage him, perhaps fearing that an exterior life would cut down on his Sudoku time.

Fortunately, Beth wasn't listening.

"I am so hot," she said.

Right there, inches from Denis, Beth did this: She bent over and lifted her gown over her head. She was not naked underneath, as Denis imagined, but somehow even better, she wore tight cutoff jeans and a sweat-soaked belly shirt. The shirt pulled up with the gown, revealing the underside of a lacy, clean, perfect and pink brassiere.

It was the first time Denis had ever seen a brassiere, live, on a girl.

"Yes. I, too, am hot," said Denis, also bothered.

"I'M NOT GAY, DUDE."

Rich interloped, oblivious, it seemed, to the historic presence of Beth Cooper.

Rich was more than a foot taller than Denis, which always gave their conversations a cartoonish cant. Now, with Rich's flamboyant indignation and Denis's twitchy anxiety, they constituted a bona fide classic comedy duo, like the ones on those black-and-white DVDs Denis's father insisted he watch.

"I am so *not* gay," Rich snipped, hands perched on his hips.

Denis kept flicking his head in Beth's direction, in long and short flicks. Rich didn't know Morse code but eventually got the gist.

"I didn't realize there was a line."

Beth, on the other hand, was a master of the segue.

"That's okay," she said. "I have to get back—"

"Wait," Denis blurted.

Beth waited.

Two hundred and fifty million nanoseconds passed.

Denis formulated a plan. Quite a good one, considering the quarter second that had gone into it.

"I'm having a little soiree at my house tonight," Denis said with tight suavity. "Of course, that's redundant. *Soirée* means 'evening.' In French."

Rich was mad at Denis, but he wasn't going to leave his friend hoisting on his own petardness like that.

"A party," Rich translated. "More of a party than a soiree. Music. Drinks. Prizes. Drinks."

"That sounds fun," Beth said with merely anthropological interest.

"You're invited," Denis ejaculated. "It's 706 Hackberry Drive. Zip code 60004 if you're Mapquesting—"

"Wow, thanks," Beth responded, her voice dripping courtesy. "We do have this other thing we have to do, but maybe we can stop by . . ."

Denis nodded the Cool Nod, the mere feint of a nod,

but too quickly and too often, making him look like a bobble-head doll.

"That's coo–"

A mammoth paw engulfed Denis's face and slammed his head against the cinderblock.

THE PAW WAS HUMAN, Denis surmised, from the way its thumb was opposed deeply into his throat.

Greg Saloga, Denis thought. *This has to be Greg Saloga, killing me.*

And yet these did not smell like Greg Saloga's fingers, of Miracle Whip and Oscar Meyer all-meat bologna, a reliably pungent bouquet that sophomore year had temporarily rendered Denis a vegetarian. Denis hypothesized that Greg Saloga must have washed his hands for graduation, a minimum of one thousand times.

Unbeknownst to Denis, Greg Saloga's bologna fingers were miles away. After the ceremony, Becky Reese's family invited him out for ice cream. Greg Saloga liked ice cream. It was cold and creamy.

Denis could not see whose hand was buckling the plates of his skull. One eye had a clear and intimate view of the cafeteria wall, which was not beige at all but white with a fine misting of yellow grease. The outward-facing eye had a forefinger in it, doubling whatever image was unobstructed, and so all Denis was able to make out was a slab of angry red meat with at least one orifice.

"You wooed my girl," the angry red meat said.

Denis did not recognize the voice, or the accent, a brassy southern drawl with swampy undertones. But he deduced the *gull* to which the voice referred had to be Beth Cooper, since she was the only one he had ever wooed. That would make this extremely humungous furious person . . .

Impossible.

Beth Cooper did not have a boyfriend. She had broken up with Seth Johansson in November, after he hit a deer with his car and refused to take it to the hospital. Since then, she had not been seen with any other guy on more than three successive occasions. Jeffery Pule, her prom date, had been a Make-a-Wish type situation; even though there were reports that Pule had felt Beth up under the guise of a fit, he was dead now and so completely out of the picture.

Beth Cooper did not have a boyfriend.

"YOU MUST BE BETH'S BOYFRIEND," Rich said brightly, extending his hand in hopes of tricking the meat into releasing his best friend's face.

The meat swiveled in Rich's direction. Its jaw was massive and appeared to have extra bones in it.

"I have to go to the bathroom," Rich excused himself.

The meat returned its attention to Denis. A slight shifting of its grip allowed Denis a better, albeit more terrifying, look.

The meat was a handsome young man whose army green jacket and army green trousers and army green beret and assorted patches, pins and epaulets suggested he was somehow affiliated with the United States Army.

The Army Man leaned in, putting his full weight on the hand clamped to Denis's face.

"Are you prepared to die?" he asked.

"Not really," Denis smush-mouthed.

"Kevin!"

Denis would not have guessed Kevin. Animal, Hoss, Bull or Steve. Not *Kevin*.

"Kevin, stop!"

Kevin turned to Beth, casually leaning on Denis's face.

"Return to your friends, Lisbee," he said, courtly like. "I will rejoin you shortly."

Beth made a petulant, defiant sound. Then she did as Kevin requested.

Denis called after her: "Eight o'clo—"

Kevin squeezed Denis's head, silencing it. He moved in very close. Steam vented from his nostrils, hot beer vapor and a lemony smoke Denis could not immediately place. His lips brushed Denis's cheek.

"You demean her," Kevin drawled all over Denis, "and insult me."

Guys much braver than Denis would have simply apologized here.

"Actually," Denis countered, "she said it was 'sweet.'"

Kevin began choking Denis, just a little bit.

"You move in on my girl," he said, squeezing ever so slightly more, "even as I am fighting for your freedom and safety with my very life."

"Appreciate your sacrifice," Denis squeaked.

"Now over there," Kevin twanged on, "a moral transgression of this order would dictate the severing of your head. Or some other relevant part."

Denis quickly ascertained the relevant part.

"But we're a civilized people," Kevin said, abating his strangling as evidence. "So I am going to give you ten seconds to convince me I should let you live."

"You mean persuade, not convince," Denis said.

Denis was about to discover if the human head could pop.

"IS THERE A PROBLEM HERE?"

Dr. Henneman delivered her catchphrase with Rich standing to her left. Behind and to her left.

Kevin released Denis.

"No, ma'am," Kevin said. "My hand slipped."

"We were just discussing my speech," Denis explained, rubbing his throat. "Kevin here felt—"

Dr. Henneman ignored Denis and addressed Kevin.

"I can't allow you to kill him on school grounds."

Kevin nodded and walked away.

Dr. Henneman contemplated Denis. Half his face featured a port-wine stain shaped like a giant hand.

He wasn't her problem anymore, Dr. Henneman decided.

"Good luck in all your future endeavors, Mr. Cooverman," she said. "You too, Rich."

She left.

Denis checked for his Adam's apple.

"On the bright side," Rich chirped, "Beth Cooper talked to you."

DENIS DID NOT SEE ANY BRIGHT SIDE. Beth Cooper had a boyfriend, and he was going to kill Denis. Neither of these were promising developments. The very best Denis could hope for was that Kevin would only *almost* kill him, causing Beth to break up with Kevin in disgust and, overcome with guilt, visit Denis in the hospital every day, discovering what a tremendous person he was and, perhaps, sponge-bathing him.

The fantasy quickly collapsed in a cascade of hospital regulations and other improbabilities.

Denis watched horror-struck as, across the cafeteria, Kevin was introducing Cammy and Treece to two of his army buddies.

Oh no.

Beth and Kevin were being officially inducted into a social circle. Soon they would become Beth & Kevin, then Beth'n'Kev, and eventually Bevin.

It did not look good for Deneth.

Denis's woebegoneness somehow penetrated the penumbra of Beth's happiness. She turned in his direction. She crinkled her upper lip, tilted her head approximately fifteen degrees, and then, quite clearly, mouthed:

Sorry.

It was the most beautiful word that Denis had ever seen.

The gesture also attracted Kevin's attention, unfortunately. He pivoted, evil-eyed Denis, and then, using the hand not cupping Beth Cooper's silky belly, made a slicing motion across his pelvis.

Denis's testicles ducked into his abdomen. They huddled there, trembling.

Rich was puzzled. He imitated the crotch-chopping gesture.

"What is that," he asked, "an army thing?"

4.

WHAT THE FUN

MAYBE I'M SPENDING TOO MUCH OF MY TIME STARTING UP CLUBS AND PUTTING ON PLAYS. I SHOULD PROBABLY BE TRYING HARDER TO SCORE CHICKS.

MAX FISCHER

A MOTLEY COLLECTION of serving dishes were arranged in some intelligent design on the kitchen table:

a large cornflower blue plastic bowl,

a stainless steel mixing bowl,

an old ceramic ashtray, and

a chip bucket from the Ho-Chunk Casino in Baraboo, Wis.

They contained, respectively:

Natural Reduced-Fat Sea-Salted Ruffles,

Jays Fat-Free Sourdough Gorgonzola Pretzel Dipstix,

Triple Minty M&Ms, and

Quattro Formaggy Cheetos.

Denis sat at the table, very still, and Rich sat opposite him, rolling his chair back and forth.

This was the party thus far. It was 8:30 p.m.

"She's not going to come," Rich said.

"She might. She said she might."

"I'm still mad at you."

"I know."

Rich reached for a chip. Denis was upon him.

"Let's save the snacks."

DENIS HAD BEEN OBSESSIVELY PLANNING this party ever since he'd told Beth about it that afternoon. He made his parents stop at the grocery store on the way home from graduation. They were only too happy, since Denis had never hosted a party before, and only had that one friend.

Denis's mother even allowed crap into the house she otherwise forbade. For someone who shunned anything processed, preserved or tasty, she seemed to know a lot about the relative merits of the various brands of crap.

"Sea salt!" she exclaimed. "Yum."

His mother did nudge him toward the more sophisticated crappy snacks, contending they would train his palate. She had been training Denis's palate since he was a baby, spiking her breast milk with pureed asparagus and later serving him *croque-tofu*, like grilled cheese only terrible, and homemade chicken nuggets made from actual chickens. Denis was the only toddler on his block who referred to *basgetti* as *bermicelli.*

Years later, Denis's mother felt guilty when she read in her alternative health magazine, *Denial,* that junk food was linked to an early onset of puberty. At fourteen, Denis's puberty had yet to onset, and his mother feared his trans-fatty-acid-and-bovine-growth-hormone-deficient diet was to blame for his pubic postponement. Denis's doctor assured her that boys mature much later than fat girls, and that the stool sample she had cajoled out of her son was unnecessary, and extravagant.

Speaking of which, Denis spent forty-five minutes in the bathroom when he returned home, evacuating seven days of excess stress and its biochemical byproducts. A MacBook perched on his knees, Denis diagnosed himself with post-traumatic stress disorder and irritable bowel syndrome. He was half right.

Denis spent another half hour in the shower, deep-cleaning the entire assembly, going back to hit the trouble spots again and again. He rinsed, lathered and repeated, and for the first time in his life, put conditioner in his hair and waited the requisite two minutes.

During his final rinse cycle, Denis set the showerhead to PULSE and let the rhythmic jets massage the same three inches of his scalp while he replayed the best minutes of his life so far.

"You are so sweet," she says, smiling. "I guess I'll have to let you live."

"I guess you will."

"Henneman must've given you major shit."

"Little shit," he coos in a suave French voice.

She giggles.

"Was it like 800 degrees in there? I was so hot."

"You're still hot."

The blood rushes to her cheeks, and elsewhere.

The human brain is an amazing organ, versatile

and loyal. Denis's five-pounder, which could recall Klingon soliloquies with queasy accuracy, could also creatively misremember recent events if it felt its owner needed a break. Rest assured, the brain had an unedited master of the scene in question and could evoke it at will, as it would later that night and seventeen years from now, with Denis walking down the street feeling pretty good about himself until his brain sucker-punched him with evidence to the contrary.

Denis's brain also had Big Green Kevin tucked away in the dark recesses of its Reptilian Complex, with the other monsters. It was keeping sight and smell samples on file in case it needed to activate the system's Fight-or-Flight Response, or as it was known around Denis's brain, the Flight Response.

With Unpleasant Memory Repression set on FULL, Denis tilted his head back and let the hot water ripple over his eyes and lips, like in a soap commercial or an otherwise not very good movie on Cinemax.

His memory fogged over with steam.

"Hey," he says, so cool. "I'm having a little thing later. Music. Drinks. Prizes."

"Wow, that sounds fun!" She bites her lip. "I have this other stupid thing I'm supposed to go to . . ."

A mischievous glimmer in her eye.

". . . but maybe I can stop by for a few minutes."

He cocks a brow. "We won't need more than a few—"

"DENIS, ARE YOU OKAY IN THERE?"

Denis dropped the conditioner.

"Just getting out, Mom."

Denis dried, rolled on some X-Stinc Pit Stick, followed up with several clouds of his father's deodorant powder, brushed his teeth and gargled with X-Stinc Breath Killaz, formulated for the male teen mouth. He tried on some corduroys, some cargo pants, brushed his teeth again, and pulled on a brand-new rugby shirt that was pre-grassed and muddied to look as if some serious rugby had already been played in it.

"You look cute," his mother squealed. "Supercute."

Denis was devastated.

"She doesn't mean that," Denis's father said. "You look fine. You might want to pull the waist of those pants down a bit."

THE STREET LIGHTS CAME ON outside Denis's house.

It was 9 p.m.

Denis sat, hands folded on the kitchen table. Rich continued rolling back and forth, in longer and longer swaths.

They had spent much of their lives this way, at this kitchen table, in front of the TV, lying around in Denis's room, not saying anything. Of the more than 20,000 hours they had logged since bonding in kindergarten over their mutual ostracism, Denis and Rich had spent perhaps 8,500 of those hours, almost an entire year, doing nothing at all, except being together.

Rich picked up the conversation exactly where it had left off a half hour before.

"I should punch you."

"Please do."

Rich was not going to punch Denis. Every time he did—when they were five, nine and thirteen—he was the one who ended up crying. Instead, he decided to agitate Denis, something he had become exceedingly good at over the past fourteen years.

"Hey," he brought up in casual conversation, "what if she comes and brings her Army Man and he kills you?"

Denis's Reptilian Complex scurried under a rock.

"Not a very good party," Rich observed.

"He wasn't really going to kill me."

"Or maybe Party of the Year."

"She won't bring him."

"She might. She said she might."

Denis touched his neck, tracing the raspberry thumbprint on his windpipe. He gulped, and gulped again, but the cold, hard loogie of dread stubbornly inched up his throat.

Rich grinned.

Then felt awful.

Those two seconds neatly encapsulated their entire friendship.

RICH LOOKED FOR SOMETHING to get Denis's mind off what he had just put it on. He reached across the table and plucked an iPod from its cube.

"New?"

"Graduation present," Denis hocked out.

Rich fingered the smart new design and interface that made all previous iPods look like gleaming turds.

"I hear this one vibrates for her pleasure."

Denis snatched the iPod back.

"*You* vibrate for her pleasure."

Rich laughed. "That's not even an insult, dude."

Denis returned the iPod to the dock, rotating the cube seven degrees counterclockwise, then two degrees clockwise.

Sensing something had gone awry with his party's feng shui, aside from the total lack of guests, Denis began fiddling with the two-liter bottles of soda on the kitchen island, or "bar area." He harmonized the carbonated beverages with a plastic bowl filled with ice and a box of Dixie Krazy Kritter cups.

"You know what I got for graduation?" Rich said, swiveling in his chair. "A bill. My dad says I owe him two hundred and thirty-three thousand, eight hundred and fifty bucks."

(Rich's father was a dick.)

"*A quarter of a million dollars?* They don't even buy you *shoes*."

"That includes fifty grand for 'wear and tear' on my mom," Rich said, acknowledging, "She is pretty worn and torn."

Denis reached out to put his hand on Rich's shoulder, but misjudged the spinning rate and had to settle for his friend's ear.

"I'm sorry your dad sucks."

Rich seemed philosophical about it. "It *was* completely itemized. Very detailed."

He looked up at Denis.

"Who knew he was paying attention?"

THEY WERE QUIET AGAIN. Denis began to rearrange individual pretzel sticks in the casino bucket.

"You shouldn't be so nervous, dude."

"I'm not nervous. I'm particular."

Rich occasionally claimed to know things about the opposite sex. Such as: "They can smell fear."

This terrified Denis. "No, they can't."

"*I* can smell it."

Horrified, Denis sniffed his armpit.

"Oh, no," he cried. *"Fear."*

Denis headed for the sink, removing his shirt.

"Why didn't you tell me?"

"What are you talking about? That was *me*, just now."

Denis ran water through a sponge and shoved it under his arms, bitterly.

"Puberty has done nothing but screw me."

THIS WAS TRUE. Puberty had come late to Denis Cooverman, but it had come with a vengeance. Thick curly hairs and sebaceous secretions everywhere. Virulent erections in organic chemistry, mysterious in origin, certainly not attributable to his lab partner, Martha Warneki, whose breath smelled like dead things (Denis suspected she was hitting the formalin). His own smorgasbord of odors, unresponsive to traditional cloaking methods, so ghastly they sometimes awoke him in the middle of night, forcing him to shower just to get some sleep. Robust and succulent acne that in his junior year required medications so mutagenic that the packaging warned Denis not to touch any woman who was pregnant or thinking of ever becoming so. (This was not a problem.)

In the past six months, Denis had gotten his adolescence more or less under control—he could often identify why his erections wouldn't go away, though he remained powerless to stop them—but his hormones still reserved the right to rage at inopportune moments, such as the present one.

"Goddammit," Denis said, twisting a freshly soaked sponge into his pits, hoping to drown the fear.

"Don't worry," Rich said. "She can't smell you. She's miles away."

Denis sniffed his rugby shirt. Perspiration, not the sexy kind. He began flapping the shirt in the air, keeping his elbows up in order to dry his armpits. One might say he looked like a frenzied chicken, but even chickens have their dignity.

This was the kind of moment when Denis's parents would usually walk in, and they did.

"Looks like this party is well under way," Denis's father remarked cheerfully.

Denis clutched the shirt to his bosom.

"Spilled . . . something colorless."

Denis's parents were accustomed to finding their son in awkward poses like this, and let it pass.

Rich swiveled to Denis's mother, who resembled Denis but in a much hotter way.

"*Hola,* Mrs. C."

"Don't call me Mrs. C," Mrs. C said. "I mean it."

She turned to her son, by now mercifully reclothed.

"How many guests are you expecting?"

"Not too many," Denis said.

"None," Rich clarified.

"Well," Mr. C said, prolonging the joshing thing, "don't trash the place or commit any major felonies."

"We'll be home at eleven," Mrs. C said.

"And not *one minute before,*" Mr. C further joshed, opening the refrigerator door. "And it wouldn't be a graduation party without . . ." He withdrew a large bottle in a festive CONGRATS gift bag. ". . . champagne!"

"Whoa!" Rich exclaimed, and meant it. His own father once let him have a sip of his beer, but that was only to get him to take his nap.

Denis looked to his mother.

"You sure?"

This was an argument Mrs. C had lost. She was magnanimous in defeat. "*One* glass per guest. And nobody who drinks, drives."

"And," Mr. C said, "I know exactly how many bottles are in my wine rack. Twenty-three." Denis's father had become a wine enthusiast after watching an award-winning film about a couple of drunks who drank fine wine. Denis's father drank the finest wine that Jewel-Osco carried and placed on sale.

Denis's mother gave Denis the disaster drill she gave any time she left the house.

"Here are our numbers," she said, pointing to the well-pointed-at sheet on the wall next to the phone, "if . . ."

She could never bring herself to complete the conditional, for fear of giving it life.

"If someone's dead or on fire," Mr. C added, "call 911 first."

Mrs. C fixed her husband with a look that said, *You've just killed our son and set him on fire.*

"What?" Mr. C responded. "Bad advice?"

"I'll be in the car."

She kissed Denis on the cheek.

"Have fun. But not too much fun."

"Not much danger of that, Mrs. C," Rich said.

"Watch it," Mrs. C said with a smile, though what she meant was, *Soon my son will be on to better things and you will be gone.*

DENIS'S FATHER DROPPED the joshing shtick the moment his wife was out of earshot. He only did it to annoy her, and to seem cooler than she was. For some reason this was important to him, even if the only witness was his son's loser friend.

He sat down next to Denis, suddenly extremely earnest.

"Son," he said, "this is your last summer before college. That accelerated program isn't going to leave much time for toga parties . . . or whatever. So I want you to enjoy this summer—"

"I know, Dad."

"As a reward for all your hard work."

"I'll do my best."

Denis was a great kid. Perfect, according to the Educational Testing Service. His father couldn't help feeling this was his fault.

"You know," he said, slipping a paternal arm around Denis. "It's okay to just have fun sometimes. Sometimes, you just have to say, *What the F.*"

"Curtis Armstrong in *Risky Business*," Rich cut in. "1983, Paul Brickman. Except he didn't say 'F.'"

"Fuck," amended Mr. C, under cross-generational peer pressure.

"Yay!" Rich mini-cheered.

Mr. C squeezed his son's upper arm and rose. He stood there, allowing his message to sink in. Then he said:

"There's condoms in my bedside table."

"Do you know exactly how many there are?" Rich asked.

Denis's father alarmed himself by responding in a completely uncool and absolutely fatherly fashion.

"They're not toys," he said.

5.

THE L WORD

IF YOU GUYS KNOW SO MUCH ABOUT WOMEN, HOW COME YOU'RE HERE AT LIKE THE GAS 'N' SIP ON A SATURDAY NIGHT COMPLETELY ALONE DRINKING BEERS WITH NO WOMEN ANYWHERE?

LLOYD DOBLER

IT WAS HALF PAST NINE. Little had changed. Denis was currently standing, scratching something on his pants. Rich fingered Denis's new iPod.

"Hey, so: I'm not gay, dude."

The iCube began playing "Girls Just Wanna Have Fun." Rich danced to it momentarily. Realizing this did not support his argument, he turned it off.

"It's okay if you are," Denis said, trying to determine whether the crusty crud he was scraping had come from inside or outside his pants. "Really."

"Well, really, I'm not," Rich insisted. *"No soy homo."*

"Okay."

"What makes you think I'm gay?"

"Everybody thinks you're gay."

"They don't know me. You know me. What makes *you* think I'm gay?"

Denis gave it some thought.

"Everything," he concluded.

He elaborated: "I mean, you just, I don't know, you seem gay to me."

"Is it because of drama club? Because you know, a lot of actors aren't gay. More than half!"

This was a difficult subject. They had never seriously discussed Rich's sexuality before, even when they were eleven, after Rich had the idea to reenact the climactic light-saber battle between Luke Skywalker and Darth Vader using their boners. Especially after that. But Denis felt he owed Rich a fuller explanation, having outed him and all.

"Rich, all during high school, and before, you've never once had a girlfriend."

"Neither did *you*."

It was going to get ugly.

"I *tried*, at least," Denis argued. "And I did . . ." His voice trailed off. ". . . have one."

"Patty Keck!" Rich yelled. "Your secret shame!"

Rich had agreed to never mention Patty Keck, Denis's secret shame.

"Yeah, well," Denis grumbled. "My point is. I had one."

"Making out with a girl like that—" Rich shook his head with deep sadness. "I'm not sure that's not gay."

This brought about a lull in the conversation. Rich plucked a pretzel from the bucket. Denis did not stop him.

"You know she's not going to come."

"I can construct at least six scenarios where she comes."

"Stop constructing scenarios, dude. School's *out*."

"1)," Denis enumerated, "her 'other thing' gets cancelled; 2), it's too crowded and loud . . ."

"She'd hate that."

"You don't know her."

"Yeah, I don't have six years' experience smelling her hair."

It was ugly.

THEY TOOK TURNS glaring at different parts of the room, anywhere but directly at each other.

Rich's glare roved to the festively wrapped bottle that was still sitting on the table where Denis's father had put it down.

"Or maybe she'll hear we have a whole bottle of champagne."

"You mock," Denis said, "but you know nothing of chaos theory." Denis wasn't sure how chaos theory applied here, exactly, but he knew that Rich did know nothing of chaos theory, or much else, unless it was in a movie. Denis often used his superior intellect to score points on Rich, but like here, they were hollow victories.

"*Nobody's* coming," Rich said. "They're all going to

Valli Woolly's. Maybe we could go there. Oh, no, wait—you called her a stuck-up bitch in front of the whole school."

"*You* wrote that."

"I didn't say it in front of the whole school."

"That was *your* idea!"

"It wasn't my idea to gay me!"

Denis was unrepentant. "It was in keeping with the theme."

"Theme." Rich snorted. "Even when you're breaking the rules, it's through assmosis."

Another lull.

"You know," Rich said eventually. "Gay guys don't say, 'dude.' "

"Lame gay guys do," said Denis, still mad about the Patty Keck breach.

"So what's that say about you?" Rich asked sarcastically. "Your only friend is a lame gay guy."

Lull.

"Which I'm not."

WITHOUT APOLOGIZING or even acknowledging they had fought, forty-five minutes later Denis and Rich were friends again. They sat at the table, glumly crunching the fancy crappy snacks.

"You know," Rich was saying, "when we go to college we won't have to be this way."

"What way?"

With thumb and forefinger, Rich branded an *L* on his forehead.

"We're not—" Denis started to protest.

He conceded the point.

Rich was working himself into one of his production numbers.

"Nobody else from B-G is going to Northwestern, and U of I is a huge school. We can reinvent ourselves!"

He sang:

I can be whoever I want to be.

Denis did not recognize:

"Leslie Ann Warren in *Rogers and Hammerstein's Cinderella,* 1965, Charles S. Dubin, director."

That's not gay, Denis thought, but did not say.

"First," Rich said, balancing a pretzel on his lip like a smoking French guy, "we gotta change your name. Denis is . . . unfortunate."

"Not as unfortunate as *Dick Munsch.*"

"D-E-N-I-S? You're a vertical stroke from penis, dude."

Rich drew a *D* in the air and appended the stroke.

"I'm well aware of that," Denis said.

"And my name is not Dick. It's not gonna be Rich either. I'm gonna go by Munsch. Or maybe 'The Munsch.' Now, *you*: Denny, El Denno, Deño, Den-Den . . . What's your middle name? James, right? DJ. *Eh.* Cooverman . . . *Coove*!"

Denis grimaced. "Sounds . . . vagina-ish."

Rich waggled his eyebrows and opened his arms to welcome:

"The Coove . . . *master*!"

Denis looked at his watch. "What time do parties start?"

"Now. Let's open the champagne."

"We can't open it until she gets here."

Rich grabbed the champagne bag. Denis grabbed back, directly above Rich's hand. Rich wedged his left hand above Denis's right. Denis clawed the top of the bag. Rich released the bottle, conceding defeat.

Rich moved on: "So your parents use *condoms.*" He took three seconds to say the last word.

"Not a topic for discussion."

"That means they still—"

"Stop talking if you wish to live."

"Do you think they're lubed or—"

Denis bounced a Ruffles off his friend's face. Rich picked up the chip and ate it. Chewing thoughtfully, he asked, "You ever jerk off with a condom on?"

"*No,*" Denis replied.

"Just asking."

Rich popped a couple of M&Ms.

"Probably not that great," he speculated.

And then the doorbell rang.

DENIS HOPPED UP SO FAST he banged his knees on the table. He hobbled excitedly to the front door.

"I *told* you."

Rich loped behind him. "It's probably just the police telling us to keep it down in here."

Denis pressed himself against the door, peeking out through the sidelight. The waterglass produced an ethereal image, luminous, gossamer, a dream. On Denis Cooverman's porch floated the celestial figures of Beth Cooper, Cammy Alcott and Treece Kilmer.

Denis could not talk, leaving it to Rich to speak for them both.

"Dude. It's the Trinity."

6.

A YOUNG MAN'S PRAYER

SHE'S GOING TO SHOW HER BOOBS!
THANK YOU JESUS!

ROLAND FAYE

I believe in the Trinity (One in Three, Three in One) Beth the first, Cammy the Second and Treece the Third.

I believe that Beth Cooper is an Angel and that She was made human by the power of God. God chose Mary, the wife of Randy, to be the mother of his most Awesome Creation.

I believe that Beth Cooper is the one True Angel, and that Cammy Alcott and Treece Kilmer are merely Sidekicks, who through their chosenness by Beth have attained social oneness with Her.

I believe that Beth Cooper is a gift of God that proves that He loves us without condition.

I believe that Beth Cooper is the One and Only Savior of my Wretched Adolescence and it is through Her that I may achieve Salvation.

7.

LIVE NEW GIRLS

MAYBE IT WAS A DREAM, YOU KNOW, A VERY WEIRD, BIZARRE, VIVID, EROTIC, WET, DETAILED DREAM. MAYBE WE HAVE MALARIA.

GARRY WALLACE

"HOLY CRAP!"

Denis couldn't believe he just said "Holy crap." Or that he was twittering his hands and pivoting indiscriminately as he yammered.

"Holy mother of crap!"

For all his posturing about plausible scenarios, Denis hadn't truly expected Beth Cooper to show up at his house, and had no real plan beyond continuing to hope that Beth would show up at his house. Now that she had, he had nothing. And the prospect that she might enter his home, and see how he lived and what kind of person he was, scared the holy crap out of him.

"What are we going to do?"

Rich leaned in close to Denis's face.

"RUN AWAY!!!!" he whisper-screamed.

Denis staggered, startled, but also thinking *good plan,* and was already dithering about which way to run when Rich started laughing.

The doorbell rang again.

Denis looked through the sidelight. Luminous Beth checked her watch, while ethereal Cammy made exasperated gestures and watery Treece fidgeted.

"They're discussing leaving!" Denis said, as if watching a horrific car accident and being powerless to stop it.

Rich flung open the door.

"Ladies!" he proclaimed.

THIS WAS THE DIFFERENCE between Denis and Rich.

To outsiders, meaning everybody else, they seemed very much the same, and were often mistaken for one another even though they shared about as much DNA as either one shared with a chimpanzee. One was short and slim and the other was tall and skinny, one was topped with a thick pelage of dark curls and the other with fine reddish tufts that looked temporary, one had had braces and the other should have had braces but his father wanted to give it a few more years to see if it would work itself out. Yet the main and signature difference between the two was not physical but metaphysical; they lived in alternate realities.

Denis lived on Planet Fear and Rich resided in Hollywoodland.

Denis was afraid of many things. A very long list of them could be found in a manila folder in the office of Dr. Maple, the phobophilic lady psychiatrist Denis had seen from the age of five until twelve as a result of his parents having too much disposable income (Denis's therapy was completed successfully at age thirteen, a typical outcome for Dr. Maple, who suffered from ephebiphobia, a fear of teenagers). But of the myriad things Denis feared—which included, briefly, a fear of misusing the word *myriad*—the thing he feared most often and most enthusiastically was the future.

Based on a close reading of current events and a misapplication of the third law of thermodynamics, Denis believed that the universe tended toward tragedy. Since his own life had been free of anything genuinely tragic, Denis figured he was due. He feared that if he did anything that was "adventurous" or "unscheduled" or "fun," it would end tragically. Statistically, it almost had to.

Rich had had a much less tragedy-free life. We needn't go into the details, since it's a long, sad and ultimately unoriginal story, but as a result Rich had developed a coping mechanism by which all of the terrible things that happened to him were merely wacky complications that would, before the movie of his life was over, be resolved in an audience-pleasing happy ending. He occasionally worried his life might be an independent film, or worse, a Swedish flick, but he chose to behave as if the movie he lived was a raucous teen comedy and he was somebody like Ferris Bueller or Otter from *Animal House*, or, worst-case scenario, that guy who fucked a pie.

And so Rich threw open the door and proclaimed "Ladies!" knowing that no matter what happened next, or after that, or subsequently, eventually he would be loved and vindicated and everybody would be dancing to a classic song from the seventies.

Denis, meanwhile, thought he had finally met his doom.

BETH COOPER SAUNTERED through the door, swinging the tartan pleats of her Luella Bartley strapless plaid dress, $39.99 at *Targét*. She wore her party face, not unlike her real face, but with the hue and contrast dialed up. Her hair, too, was subtly tarted, with spontaneous ringlets happening strategically around her head. She still smelled like Beth Cooper, only more so.

"Hey," she tossed off, entering Denis's house with such cool authority he wondered if he was the one who lived there. So this was Afterschool Beth. Denis couldn't tell how much he liked this version. At least a lot, he decided.

Cammy catwalked in behind Beth, working a white vintage-wash Abercrombie skirt and black Fitch Premium beaded racerback top, $119 retail, bought on super sale for $71. Nearly six feet and bone blond, she had the gait and mien of a fashion model, to go with the legs and teeth, yet there was something in her slate green eyes, something disturbingly out of place: thought.

"Nice place," Cammy said, her flat contralto displaying no affect while projecting disdain.

Last and slightly least, Treece bounced over the threshold in a red leather bustier that displayed top, side and bottom cleavage and a black nano mini that might have been a rubber band. The semi-ensemble, with the Choo boots, easily cost more than $1,000, though she clearly neither knew that nor cared. She was wide in ways boys and men don't seem to mind, with overdone hair that encircled her face like a toilet seat, and plump brown eyes and pillowy lips that brought to mind a cute cartoon cow. Very cute, but cartoon, and cow.

"I've never been in this house before," Treece chirped with a baby lisp she was unlikely to outgrow.

DENIS WAS PARALYZED. Adrenaline, epinephrine, seratonin, corticosterone, testosterone and several more exotic hormones squirted from various glands or were being synthesized like crazy throughout his body, in far beyond prescription strengths, and so all nonessential functions such as thinking had been shut down.

Rich stepped into the hosting breach.

"So," he inquired cordially, "where's our boy in uniform?"

Denis's testes began climbing their vas deferens again, until Beth uttered those three beautiful words:

"We're hating him right now."

(Denis could count; he just stopped listening after the first three.)

Beth explained, "One of his army buds was getting all date-rapey with Treece."

Treece was clearly annoyed by this. "It wasn't like he wasn't going to get a blow job at the end," she said, making a *duh* face. "I mean, if he was nice."

Cammy rolled her eyes without moving them at all. "And so thanks to Miss Manners here, Graduation Night's crapped."

Treece's mouth popped open. "You're *blaming the victim!*"

"Guys"—Beth stepped in—"it'll be okay. They'll go looking for us at Valli Woolly's, and when they don't find us they'll go to that strip club they tried to drag us to, and then we'll go to Valli Woolly's, just later."

Rich whispered to Denis out of the side of his mouth. "Which scenario was that?"

"Variation on Four," Denis side-whispered back.

Cammy took in her surroundings, looking for a reason to go on living. "So? Until just later?" she asked. "We sit around sucking each other's Suzy Qs?"

If Denis's eyes could have fallen out, they would have. They would have bounced around crazily on the floor, made *yipe yipe yipe* sounds, skedaddled up the stairs and hid under Denis's pillow.

"Thank you, Cammy," Beth said. "Like I'm going to get that image out of my head."

(Like anyone was. Denis's brain had fast-tracked that image into permanent storage, accidentally overwriting some early flying-car sketches.)

Beth made a sudden movement in Denis's direction; he flinched.

"So?" She had a bright and shining smile. "Where's the party?"

Denis almost said *What party?* Even that would have been preferable to what he did, which was blink several times.

"Here," he eventually said, in the dazed, detached manner of a crime victim. "This is"—he gestured to his general vicinity—"it."

"You're a little early," Rich transitioned smoothly. "We weren't expecting anyone until . . . eleven. Right, Coove?"

"Oh, right," Denis blinked. "That's when my paren—"

"*La fiesta es* this way, *chicas* . . ."

Rich pinched Denis's upper arm and led him toward the kitchen, whisper-singing,

Dreams really do come true,

and whisper-citing: "Judy Garland in *The Wizard of Oz,* 1939, Victor Fleming, director, additional scenes by King Vidor.

"You're not in Kansas anymore, dude." Rich placed his hands on Denis's cheeks, signaling he was about to say something of profound importance.

"Follow the Yellow Brick Road," he said, adding slowly, emphatically, deep meaningfully, "Follow. The. *Yellow Brick Road.*"

Denis was dumbfounded. "Is that like . . . *treasure trail?*"

"What? No, God, *no,*" Rich revulsed, "It's a metaphor for *life,* not Dorothy's . . . *yick!*"

BACK WHERE WE LEFT THEM, Cammy was glaring at Beth. The glare said, *Why are we in this strange-smelling house alone with Your Itty-Bitty Stalker and his Gay-And-Not-Even-Fun-Gay Friend, no doubt about to be drugged and undressed and violated in uninteresting ways when we could be getting drugged and undressed and truly violated by members of the United States military?* That's a rough translation.

"Be nice," Beth admonished the glare. "He's the *valvictorian.*"

"And he *loooovs* you," Cammy added in a geek voice that sounded nothing like Denis but sufficed.

"From behind!" Treece blurted, then began whinnying, because anal sex was hilarious, in the abstract.

Beth Cooper was a benevolent cliquetator. She allowed her subjects free rein and even the illusion of equality. Occasionally, though, she needed to reassert her absolute authority, and this was one of those occasions. She did so in the traditional teen-girl manner, through superior attitude and psychological terror.

"It's nice to be loved," Beth said. "You two should try it sometime."

Beth walked away. Cammy achieved a smirk, but her heartless wasn't in it. Treece pouted.

"I try it all the time," she said.

IN THE KITCHEN, Denis stood at attention, like a waiter in an unfun restaurant, as the girls entered. Rich was acting like a waiter, too, but from a José O'Foodle's, the unbearably fun restaurant he had been fired from for exactly this behavior.

"Hi, I'm Rich," he said with high theatrical cheer, "I'll be your cohost this evening. On the central table you will find assorted snackables, sweet 'n' salty *comidas* for your comesting . . ."

The girls considered the crap on the table.

"The pretzels are fat-free," Denis suggested. "A healthful alternative."

Beth scowled. "Are you saying I'm fat?"

"Oh," Denis said. *Goddammit*, he thought.

Denis had not yet learned to preload appropriate responses to fat-related queries (i.e. unequivocal denials) so they could be automatically delivered without hesitation. Instead, he appeared to be processing the question, which can be fatal.

"You, *fat*?" Rich intervened. "Why would he say that? Come on. He's not *retarded*."

Beth frowned more definitively. "My brother is retarded."

Rich froze. There was no appropriate response when somebody played the retard card. Now both he and Denis stood at attention, condemned dorks, without blindfolds.

Cammy snickered, causing Treece to unleash a single whinny and Beth to finally release her smile.

Denis exhaled; he would not, after all, have to move to Europe. Rich let out the laugh he had been choking on.

"That's cold," Rich said. "Damn cold. You probably don't even have a brother."

"No," Beth said. "He died."

Rich guffawed.

Beth did not.

"I'm so sorry," Denis said.

This was a nervy move on Denis's part. If Beth didn't have a dead brother, he would be a double dork. Fortunately for him, she did.

"It was a long time ago." Beth looked directly at Denis. "But thank you."

The raw emotion of the moment unnerved Rich, sending him into a fit of impression. He stretched his face lengthwise and fluttered his fingers over his chest.

Well, shut my mouth,

he enunciated in a British-ish accent. "Stan Laurel in *Way Out West,* 1937, directed by James W. Horne."

"What was *that*?" Cammy asked.

"It's something he does," said Denis, as if it were an unalterable fact of life, like the wind or tragedy.

"*I'm* fat." Treece joined the conversation from earlier. She threw a potato chip in her mouth. "But it's all good fat." She did a quick shimmy, and her good fat shook like bowls full of jelly.

THE FIRST THREE BARS of "Here She Comes" by Very Sad Boy played in a tinny synthesis. Beth pulled a cell phone from her purse. She was displeased by the caller ID, but answered anyway. "What do you *want*, Kevin?"

She walked out of the room. She didn't seem very happy to talk to him, Denis thought. Maybe she'll just tell him to go blank himself, she's having such a wonderful time over at Denis Cooverman's house, 706 Hackberry Dr—

Denis got that old testicular feeling again.

"I NEED BEER," Treece announced.

"Yes, you do," Rich agreed. "*¿Dónde está la* beer, Coovemaster?"

"Um," answered Denis, distracted. "My dad doesn't drink beer."

"How is that possible?" Treece asked.

Rich remembered:

"We have *champagne*!"

He whisked the gift bag off the table, where it had been sitting unrefrigerated for the past ninety minutes, and pressed it into Denis's chest.

"*¡Tienes le champag-nah!*"

"Could you please mangle one language at a time?" Cammy requested.

Treece wrinkled her nose. *"Champagne."* She uncurled the word as if it were French for *excessive and frequent evacuation of watery feces.*

"Same alcohol as beer," pitched Rich, selling hard.

"More," Denis said. "Two-point . . ." He quickly calculated:

$$A_{(beer)} = Avg[.04 \rightarrow .06] = .05$$

$$A_{(champagne)} = Avg[.08 \rightarrow .14] = .11$$

$$\Delta_{(alcohol)} = \frac{A_{(champagne)}}{A_{(beer)}} = 2.2$$

". . . two times as much alcohol, on average."

Rich could only shake his head in admiration at his friend's determination to be true to himself, no matter what the cost. Rich himself was willing to be anybody anyone wanted and would keep trying on personalities until one of them became popular. For some reason, his most recent persona spoke a lot of half-assed Spanish.

"Let's pop this *pupito, rápido!*" habla Rich with insouciance, belied a bit by the way he was clawing at the gift bag Denis was clutching.

Denis removed the bottle from its bag.

It was Freixenet, one of the finer sparkling wines in the under-$10 category.

"Cristal," Rich said. "Black Label."

"Cristal seems to have changed its logo," Cammy said. "And spelling."

Treece bit her pinkie. "Champagne," she said, "makes me do . . . *things*."

Denis would never hear the word *things* the same way again.

Cammy snorted. "*Water* makes you do things."

"Not regular water."

If Rich were a paper-and-ink cartoon rather than a flesh-and-blood one, a lightbulb would have appeared above his head.

"Uno momento." He raced out of the room and romped up the stairs.

"Un momento," Cammy said.

THE SPECIFIC MECHANICS of the champagne bottle were alien to Denis. "Seems self-explanatory," he mumbled as he propped the bottle on his thigh and began peeling the foil back slowly, sweat speckling his forehead, as if dismantling a party bomb.

Beth reappeared in the kitchen, pissed.

"Yeah, well, *Kevin*, maybe, *Kevin*, maybe I have *better* things to do!"

She looked up and pointed at Denis's lap.

"I want some of that."

She meant the champagne, but neither Denis nor his lap immediately figured that out.

Beth started out of the room, her voice rising.

"I'm not going to tell you where I am! *Or* who I'm with! But I will tell you *this,* Kevin: I'm having *champagne*!"

She wants champagne. Denis flailed away the foil and furiously twisted the wire, ten or fifteen times, stopped, then started to untwist it.

"Champagne coming right . . . *Yi.*"

His fingertip was bleeding. He pressed on with no concern for his own safety. Cammy and Treece watched with morbid fascination.

Denis placed both thumbs under the cork and applied steady pressure, suavely at first, desperately thereafter. He leaned against a wall for leverage, clasping the sweaty, slippery bottle between his forearms and applying insufficient force accompanied by girlish exertions. Blood dripped over his knuckles.

"This is . . . odd," he she-grunted. "The internal pressure is 90 psi. It should just—"

In walked Beth, screaming into the phone.

"Don't you *dare* GPS me!"

Denis couldn't even begin to analyze the health ramifications of that, because at that exact moment, Rich appeared behind Beth. He raised his arm and opened his hand. A ribbon of condoms cascaded behind Beth's head.

Ribbed, Rich mouthed lubriciously.

Denis's eyes widened just in time for the cork to pop and ricochet off his cornea.

HE OPENED HIS MOUTH TO SCREAM. A foaming column of lukewarm champagne geysered into the back of his throat. He gasped, gulped, and gurgled in various combinations. That it was not school milk but champagne that came out his nose did not make Denis feel any more sophisticated.

This, as it turned out, was exactly the kind of thing

Cammy found amusing: the pain and suffering of others. Her laugh was surprisingly husky, somewhere between a chortle and a guffaw. Treece was too nice to laugh, but not nice enough to offer help.

Beth snapped her phone shut and rushed to Denis's side.

"You all right?"

"Yeah, I'm great," Denis claimed. "Oh, *ow.*"

He cupped his bloody hand over his bludgeoned eye, and without even realizing he was doing it, slid down the wall to the floor.

"Yee," he said.

"We need ice." Beth turned to Rich, who was tucking the last of the prophylaxis into his shirt pocket. *"Ice?"*

Rich hurried to the kitchen island "bar area" and stuck his hand in the plastic bowl of ice. It came out wet.

"Frozen peas," Beth ordered, snapping her fingers at Rich and directing him toward the refrigerator.

Rich resented being snapped at. This dickhead from Stevenson High School did that at José O'Foodle's once, and Rich spat in his O'Salsa, nearly killing him. Apparently the guy had a peanut allergy and Rich had been eating only Snickers bars that month. No one ever found out how peanut and cocoa traces made it into a salsa made only from fresh tomatoes, chiles and beer, but it cost the Dining Thematics Corporation nearly $2 million.

"What are you *doing*?" Beth yelled at Rich, who had been reminiscing the above paragraph. "This is *your* friend down here!"

Rich abandoned his reverie and went to the refrigerator. He opened the freezer door and began picking through the contents.

"Frozen peas . . . Frozen *peas* . . . Fro-*oh*-zen pa-puh *peas* . . ."

"*Anything* cold!"

Rich hurled a box across the room.

"Stat!"

Beth snatched it out of the air.

"Frozen waffles?"

Rich peered in the freezer. "Either that or Lean Cuisine."

"Whatever," Beth said, meaning *whatever.*

His mission completed, Rich took out a pint of ice cream and went looking for a spoon. He singsang to himself:

> *I scream*, you *scream* . . .

WITH PARAMEDIC SPEED, Beth ripped open the box and extracted two frozen waffles. She dropped to her knees, straddling Denis's thighs, a bodily juxtaposition Denis had only experienced with Greg Saloga prior to a belly-pinking.

Beth took his hand and lifted it off his injured eye. She tenderly pressed the waffles against it.

"Agh," Denis said.

"It's okay," Beth soothed. "This will help."

Why was Beth being so nice to him? Was it because she was so nice, or because it was to him? Either way, she sure was nice. Denis gazed at her through his surviving eye.

"I'm sorry I'm so pathetic," he thought, and then realized he had also said it.

Beth laughed, so lightly and so kindly that Denis felt it in his chest, not his stomach.

"Can I tell you a secret?"

Yes, tell me all your secrets, Denis kept to himself.

Beth leaned in, whispered: "All boys are pathetic."

THIS WAS NEWS TO DENIS, perhaps the best news he had ever heard. If Beth thought all guys sucked, he didn't need to not suck, only to suck *less*. This was doable. Possibly.

Denis relaxed for the first time since the previous Sunday. He became the smart, sweet, moderately clever and only medium pathetic boy he usually was.

"On behalf of all boys, then," Denis said, "I apologize."

Beth made a serious face. "Accepted."

"It's 150,000 years late, but it needed to be said. Also, I'd like to apologize for all that war and stuff."

"You're funny."

"Sometimes even when I'm trying to be."

Beth took Denis's hand and led it back to his eye, transferring responsibility for the waffles.

"Gentle pressure."

Denis twisted a flinch into a grin. "Thanks, Lisbee."

The moment vanished.

"Don't call me that," Beth said. "I hate that."

"But Kevin—"

"That is one of the privileges that Kevin enjoys," Beth explained coldly.

Cammy concurred. "Kevin has many privileges."

"Front door privileges—" Treece began, working into another sodomy whinny.

Beth raised her hand, silencing them.

On the opposite side of the kitchen island, Rich was upside-down spooning ice cream onto his tongue, waiting for such a conversational opening. "So, Beth," he said, "you think your Army Man has triangulated your signal and is on his way over? Because we might need more waffles."

"Never mind him." Beth waved dismissively. "He thinks just because he's killed some guys, he can kill anybody he wants."

That didn't help.

"Let's see under there," Beth said. Denis whimpered as softly as he could as Beth removed the waffles. The blast area was already purple en route to black and beyond.

"Open."

The eyelid stuttered as it retracted.

"Pee-yuke," Treece noted.

"Dude." Rich grossed out. "That's NC-17."

It looked worse than it was, since it looked like Denis was at least blind, perhaps dying, and possibly a brain-eating zombie.

From the inside, it looked: bloody. Denis tried to focus on Beth's face, which he knew was only inches away. What he saw, swirling in a red sea, was a blurry pink mass with two darker circular areas in the upper half and a small horizontal smear in the middle of the lower half. If that was a face, then:

"MY CONTACT!" Denis gasped.

Beth snapped her fingers again.

"Contact down!"

Treece and Cammy initiated contact-retrieval maneuvers, dropping to squats and sweeping the floor with their fingertips in long, overlapping arcs.

"Don't worry," Beth told Denis. "We'll find it. We always do."

"You wear contacts?" Denis asked, enthralled by this defect they apparently shared. "What's your prescription?"

Before either could comprehend the deep geekitude of the question, and before Denis could compound it with whatever he might say next:

"Found it!" Treece said.

She held up the champagne cork. A gelatinous dollop clung to the metallic cap. Quite proud of herself, she marched over and presented it to Beth.

"What do I win?"

"The thanks of a grateful nation," Rich said, presenting her with the half-eaten pint of ice cream.

Treece held the container like an acting award.

"Chubby Monkey!"

Beth peeled the sticky contact off the cork, rolling it around on her fingertip.

"Gucky."

She stuck her finger in her mouth and sucked the lens off.

As she swished it around, salivating, her luscious lips pursed, pulsating. Her pretty pink tongue unfurled and there on the wet tip, bathed in Beth Cooper's juices, was Denis's sense of sight.

Beth Cooper had invented a whole new sex act: the eyejob.

She tilted Denis's head back and gently pried open his swollen eyelids.

"Ohhhhhh." He moaned with pain and pleasure, which is how all the weird fetishes start.

"There."

Denis blinked. His contact was back in. Beth came into focus, framed by a velvety crimson swirl.

"How's that feel?"

Denis didn't have to answer. Beth could see for herself.

Denis grinned shit-eatingly.

"Pretty good, I guess," Beth said.

Beth bounced from her knees to her feet in a single cheerleading move. Denis's ascent was graceless by comparison, hindered by the need to keep a forearm wedged between his legs. He clutched the counter and hauled himself up. Leaning against the kitchen island, hips inward, he twisted his upper torso in the direction of the girls, and smiled. He was fooling almost no one.

"You hurt your back?" Treece asked.

Cammy pointed at the ice cream.

"Chubby Monkey."

Treece looked at the ice cream, then at Denis's crotchal contortions and back at the ice cream. The creamy banana taste in her mouth helped her put it all together.

"Oh," it dawned on her. "The monkey is *chubby.*"

During the polite silence all around, Denis scooted the perimeter of the kitchen island, placing it between his erection and judgment. Rich slid the frozen waffles across the counter. Denis lowered them out of sight.

"You might've scratched your cornea," Beth said. "Maybe you should go to the hospital."

"Oh," said Denis, who had been thinking the same thing, "Let's not spoil the party."

"What party?" Cammy wanted to know.

Denis's tendency to answer sarcastic questions sincerely was short-circuited when he realized he was still gripping the bottle of:

"Champagne!"

"*La bebida de los* gods!" Rich yelled in support. He grabbed a stack of the Krazy Kritter Dixie cups and attempted to set up five in a row. This took a few tries.

"Delicious champagne," Denis said, buying Rich time.

"Delicioso," Rich agreed. He finally accomplished five upright cups, and stepped back with a hand flourish, as if he had just done a magic trick.

Denis filled the first cup. The second cup started strong but quickly faded to a dribble. Denis considered filling the remaining three cups with squeezings from his rugby shirt, but took the high road.

"Even things up a little . . ."

Denis poured from the first cup into the final three,

then some from the fourth cup into the second cup, and then a little bit more from the first into the third, producing five Dixie cups with approximately no champagne in them.

He distributed the cups, making sure to give Beth the one with Ally, the pretty giraffe, on it.

Treece squinted suspiciously. "Why'd I get the hippo?"

"It's all *good* fat," Cammy said.

"That's racist," Treece jabbed at Cammy.

"It's not *race*-ist," Cammy mocked.

"It's fattist."

"*You* said you were fat. Two minutes ago. And every two minutes before that."

"I was *owning* it."

Beth sighed. "You're not fat, Treece."

"I *have* fat," Treece said.

"Everybody has fat."

"Not everybody," Cammy said.

"A toast!" Denis yelled.

Usually when one proposes a toast, one has a toast to propose. This was one of the details Denis had neglected based on its infinitesimal probability of coming up. And yet, here he was, toasting Beth Cooper with a paper cup of champagne. He improvised.

"To the future!"

Rich had his friend's back. "To the future—and beyond!"

"Go future!" Cammy exclaimed with a tiny swing of her fist, suggesting less than complete sincerity.

"*Go*, future!" Treece exclaimed with the same tiny swing, signaling true enthusiasm.

"The future," Beth simply said.

The girls micro-chugged their champagne splashes. Rich sipped his urbanely. Denis, who had left his own cup empty, made a show of guzzling it.

Treece crushed her cup and looked for someplace to

shove it. She noticed something sticking out of Rich's shirt pocket.

"Party balloons!" she squealed, extracting the unfolding ribbon of ignominy.

"Um." Rich raised a finger. "Those aren't—"

"I *know* what they are," Treece said, tearing a foil pouch open with her teeth. She popped the condom into her mouth, breathed in deeply, and blew out a ribbed rubber bubble.

Beth turned to Denis, amused but also a little disappointed.

"What exactly," she wondered, "did you have planned for this evening?"

"Oh," Denis said, sort of maybe pointing toward the contraceptive Treece was inflating. "Those are my dad's."

Treece stopped blowing. "Your dad's not hiding in a closet or something? I hate that."

Beth then said with polite finality:

"Well, this was fun."

Treece tied off the party balloon and flicked it at Rich.

HIS LIFE HAD CHANGED, in some potentially tragic but no doubt important way, and Denis didn't want it to end.

"Not yet," he said. "You can't go . . . yet."

He needed a reason for them to stay. He had a hundred-dollar bill in his wallet, a graduation present from Aunt Brenda, but it might be awkward trying to split it three ways. Also, potentially insulting. His Diamond Series Extra-Extended Special Edition *Lord of the Rings* Trilogy Blue-Ray HD Box Set? If they started watching it now . . .

"We haven't drunk the wine!" Rich declared.

Of course! The forbidden wine!

"Twenty-three bottles!" Denis added, parallel-processing how much time it would take them to drink that much wine and how much trouble each successive bottle would get him into.

"I don't like wine," Treece said. "Unless it's in a cooler-type situation."

Denis hoisted a two-liter bottle of Diet Blackberry Sprite above his head. "We got coolers!" he said triumphantly, as the sweaty bottle slid out of his sweaty hands and exploded on the kitchen floor.

Goddammit.

Rich jumped into the social abyss. "And music!" He handed the iCube to Denis. "Wine, women, and 5,000 songs!"

"Well, I haven't loaded that many yet," said Denis, shaking soda off his shoes. "But I did put together a special playlist for the occasion. A 'Commencement Mix'—"

"DJ C's Slammin' Graduation," Rich quickly saved.

"Or that." Denis pushed ▶. From the iCube came 53Hz to 16kHz of seventies mellowness:

Life, so they say, is but a game
and we let it slip away

"Slammin'," Cammy said.

"That's more for chilling," Rich said. "Ironic chilling."

Denis pressed advance. Out came languid fifties harmonies:

There's a time for joy, a time for tears . . .

"My mom helped me put this together," Denis explained.

A time we'll treasure through the years . . .

Denis ripped the iPod out of the cube and started scrolling through the list. "There's real music on here," he said, spinning. "That Einstein's Brain song, Happy Talk, the Licks . . . you like Very Sad Boy, right?"

Beth touched his elbow. He looked up. She gazed into his good eye.

They really could have kissed ergonomically.

"We do kind of have to go," she said. "Thanks. It was a great party."

She moved in to kiss him, hesitating.

Was it the smell? The smell of fear and pathos?

No, it was she didn't want to hurt him. She kissed the other, uninjured cheek.

"Bye."

The simultaneous bursting and breaking of Denis's heart was drowned out by a tremendous roar. Blinding lights engulfed the front of the house. Denis's first thought was it had to be the Apocalypse, but it was something much, much worse.

8.

MORE WAFFLES

BIFF WILCOX IS LOOKING FOR YOU, RUSTY JAMES. HE'S GONNA KILL YOU, RUSTY JAMES.

MIDGET

"SHIT," Beth said. "Kevin."

9.

PARTY MONSTERS

NUNCHUCK SKILLS, BOWHUNTING SKILLS, COMPUTER HACKING SKILLS . . . GIRLS ONLY WANT BOYFRIENDS WHO HAVE GREAT SKILLS.

NAPOLEON DYNAMITE

DENIS WAS DEAD. This much was certain. The only real question was whether, as he was dying, would Denis cry, or beg, or scream like a girl, or lose control of his bowels, or in some other way abase himself, robbing his demise of the tragic gravitas he felt it deserved. Denis considered hitting the bathroom as a precaution, but Rich and the girls had already rushed to the front of the house, leaving him standing there alone, looking silly without even the simple dignity of being dead.

And his face hurt.

Reflexively, Denis reached up to touch his battered eye and poked it with the iPod he was holding.

"*Yiye!*" he said in response to this relatively minor amount of pain. He was not going to do well, being stabbed, or stomped, or whatever cause of death his killer had chosen.

Denis looked down at his iGouger.

Goodbye to You
Michelle Branch
The Spirit Room

So now his possessions were mocking him too. *Goddammit,* Denis muttered as he dropped the iPod in a pocket, *goddammit,* and joined the party to his execution.

THEY WERE GATHERED in the living room, in violation of house rules, gawking out the front window at the tremendous roar. Denis slunk up and peeked out around Treece.

The source of the roar was a five-ton H1 Alpha Hummer, with 300 horsepower, 520 pound-feet of torque, a MSRP of $140,796 and seating for five assholes. The earth-killing machine was painted *black diamond*, murkier than pure black and slightly more frightening, named for the insane ski slopes and not, as Denis might have guessed, for the moon gem Eclipso used to possess Superman in Action Comics #826 (Denis no longer collected comic books, and hardly ever went through his sixteen boxes of meticulously Mylared back issues, arranged by publisher and title, but AC #826—who wouldn't know that?).

The Hummer was currently off-road, in the middle of the Cooverman lawn, on top of a Beauty of Bath apple tree Denis and his father had planted together that Arbor Day.

The monstrous vehicle snarled a final time and fell silent. Three doors snapped open and corresponding military figures disembarked synchronously. They wore civilian clothes, but identical civvies, a habit that was apparently hard to break. The uniform of the night was black khakis, black polos and black loafers, making the trio look like an elite unit sent into a downtown club to terminate a rogue DJ. None of them had enough hair to gel, but their heads glistened menacingly nonetheless.

Treece waved happily at her date-rapist. "Sean!"

Denis had hoped to go out with some class.

"Shaw-on!" Treece yelled much louder, waving in wide semaphoric arcs, signaling *I'm here! I'm here! Oh, and here's that guy you promised a penilectomy!*

The lights went out on the upper floors of Denis's brain, leaving the lizard in charge.

"Get down!"

Denis hugged Treece and threw them both to the floor. Treece's body recognized this as foreplay and her lips parted in Pavlovian response.

"*Everybody* down!" Denis screamed in a barely audible squeak.

The three left standing regarded him with odd curiosity.

"Why?" Beth asked.

"He's going to kill me!"

"So?" asked Cammy.

"He's not really going to *kill* you." Beth sighed. "He just likes to be scary."

"He's scary," Denis confirmed.

"The *most* he's going to do is maybe beat you up a little."

Denis had been beaten up a little, thrice by Greg Saloga and once by Dawn Delvecchio, whose premature chest he had momentarily ogled in the fifth grade. Being beaten up a little meant bruising but no breaking, twisting but no tearing, and loss of less than a tablespoon of blood. Denis suspected Kevin would not adhere to these guidelines, or even, based on news reports, the Geneva Convention. Given what the military did not even consider *abuse,* Denis shuddered at what might constitute a *little beating* under the U.S. Army Code of Conduct:

27–3. Procedures applicable to 'Beating, Light'

a. Splatter zone limited to 10 feet (3.048 meters)

b. No detachment or removal of extremities or organs;

c. Extremities or organs inadvertently detached or removed must be left with original owner for possible reattachment or implantation;

d. Extremities or organs inadvertently detached or removed and not returned to owner cannot be

(1) Fashioned into a necklace, or

(2) Devoured to gain the owner's power, unless approved in writing by commanding officer;

e. Derisive pointing at genitals prohibited, except to aid owner in locating of same.

As usual, Denis was letting his imagination run wild, shriek and knock things off shelves. Also as usual, he was allowing this to distract him from more immediate practical concerns.

"The door!" Denis eventually realized. "Secure the door!"

Denis scurried across the floor, frantic commando crawling, looking less like a Navy SEAL than an actual seal.

"Is he always like this?" Cammy asked.

"This is new behavior," Rich observed. "But not surprising."

"I think it's kinda cute."

Cammy looked at Beth as if she had just insisted that *Zuma* was still a decent show.

"It is. He is," Beth said. "Kinda."

"Yeah," Treece agreed, squeaking her nano mini back into place. "Like when a puppy gets so excited he pees all over everything. It's cute and funny, but then there's pee over everything."

BY THE TIME HE REACHED THE DOOR, Denis had two severely lacerated forearms (the sisal carpeting was environmentally friendly but otherwise vicious) and something wrong with his pubis, a hairline fracture perhaps or a hip dislocation. He pushed aside his everyday hypochondria in deference to the greater goal of surviving to obsess another day. He lunged upward, grasping the deadbolt and turning it with what could only have been a moment to spare.

Denis fell against the door, dry heaving with relief. He sat there, eyes closed, still breathing.

He opened his eyes.

He had a perfect view of the back patio door, which was presently sliding open.

Kevin did not look very happy.

A hand appeared in front of Denis's face. It was small and downy with sea-mint-lacquered nails; it wasn't holding a knife. It still gave Denis a heart cramp.

"Hey," Beth said.

She was reaching down for him. Her hair fell over

her face in two silky sheets, swaying; it was lightly brushing against Denis's face. This was the most intimate he had ever gotten with a girl, if you didn't count Patty Keck, his secret shame, and Denis didn't. It was obviously the worst time to be thinking about sex, but Denis hadn't been given the choice.

"Don't be afraid," Beth said, correctly reading his expression but not its cause. "I'll handle this."

Oh, yes, this, Denis was reminded. *My assassination.*

Denis took Beth's hand and she pulled him to his feet—with ease, he noticed.

"I wasn't afraid," Denis wanted to explain. "I was . . ." All the words his brain offered up were rough synonyms for fear, from *pusillanimous* to *shitting bricks,* and including *epistaxiophobia,* fear of nosebleeds, and *rhabdophobia,* fear of being beaten with sticks, two of Denis's more reasonable phobias, and ones he was soon to have the opportunity to face (along with his agliophobia, gymnophobia, athazagoraphobia, and a few others).

"Prudent" finally popped out. "I was just being prudent."

"Well, c'mon, Prudence," Beth said, pulling him toward the kitchen.

KEVIN WAS A MAN IN A HURRY. He needed to get this killing done and not let it eat up his whole evening. He was flanked, in the strategic sense, by Sean, who had a bigger body but a much smaller head, and the other one.

Beth entered leading Denis by the hand.

Kevin snarled. A real snarl, like the kind a dog might make, right before biting your eyes.

Beth let go of Denis's hand. He didn't mind. It freed him to tremble on both sides of his body.

"Congratulations, you found me," Beth said, asserting control of the situation with sarcasm. "Now let's just—"

"Shut up, Lisbee."

"Kevin," scolded Beth. "Have you been doing coke?"

"Shut your goddamn mouth!" he responded, louder than necessary.

In a high, tiny voice, Denis said: "He's coked up!"

Treece shook her head sagely. "That is *not* one of the good drugs."

Kevin was not only coked up. He had also been drinking: vodka, bourbon, rum and a red liquid from Cambodia that came in a handblown bottle with a human tooth on the bottom. Since cocaine is a stimulant and alcohol is a depressant, the twin intoxicants should theoretically cancel each other out, but it never seems to work out that way.

The only sound in the room was Kevin's breathing. It probably could've been heard even if everyone hadn't shut his or her goddamn mouth. As it was, the seething hiss of a known killer, inhaling fear and exhaling hate, proved to be an effective mood setter.

Kevin picked up the champagne bottle on the counter and slowly upended it, tilting his head as he did so. He grunted. Denis half expected him to use a stick to try to extract ants from it. Concluding that the champagne had been consumed, and that this was an attempt to lubricate his mate, Kevin became 25 percent more furious. His cobalt eyes swept the kitchen for more anger boosters, and found one on the person of Rich, who was holding a large milky balloon with a reservoir tip. Kevin stopped breathing altogether.

Later, in Denis's dreams, Kevin's hair bristled like the hackles of a demonic dog, and venomous saliva streamed from his canines, burning a hole in the kitchen floor. In reality, Kevin pointed a disconcertingly muscular finger at Denis and shouted:

"PREPARE TO DIE!"

Rich lived for openings like this. "Mandy Patinkin in *The Princess Bride,* Rob Reiner, 1987," he rattled off. "Also, the same line was used by Emperor Zurg in *Toy Story 2,* 1999, John Lasseter, and by Marshall Teague in *Roadhouse,* 19—"

A heavy black object grazed Rich's skull and embedded in the wall behind him. (For an affordable sparkling wine, Freixenet sure made strong bottles.)

"*Kevin Patrick,*" gasped Beth, ratcheting up to the first-and-middle maternal reprimand. "Just *stop.*"

Denis stepped in to aggravate matters. "This is *completely* inappropriate," he said. "We just had this kitchen painted."

Ba-GOOSH Ba-GOOSH Ba-GOOSH went two-liter bottles of Ocean Spray Cranberry Fizz, Blood Orange Faygo and Salted Mountain Dew as they burst around Denis, vividly staining the linen white walls cranberry, blood orange and morning urine.

"I need to warn you," Denis continued in defiance of common sense, "this is willful damage to property; that's a legal term."

Having exhausted his supply of hurlable beverages, Kevin picked up the next available object.

Denis finally shut up when he noticed a midsize microwave oven coming at his head. He felt something hook the back of his neck and pull him to the floor. The microwave, a week out of warranty, crashed through the plasterboard above him. A dry rain of gypsum dust fell upon Denis, followed by the microwave itself, which bounced nonfatally off his head.

"Ow," Denis said. (He did not make a sound like "ow"; he said the word *ow.*)

Denis was crouched, lightly powdered, facing a lightly powdered Rich, who three seconds earlier had yanked him from the path of a speeding appliance. Rich offered some advice.

"This time, truly: *RUN AWAY!*"

Denis ran away. Rich stayed behind momentarily, covering his friend's retreat by heaving the inflated condom at his attacker. Kevin caught the balloon with one hand and began squeezing it slowly. Presumably he thought it would pop at some point, adding to his cool menace. When it did not, he took the thing in both hands and crushed, contorted and clawed it with diminishing menace.

Cammy to Treece, sarcastic casual: "What brand was that?"

Kevin's jaw rippled. He backhanded the condom away and marched forward.

DENIS REACHED THE FRONT DOOR only to discover some moron had locked it. He stood for several seconds, blinking rapidly, formulating how he might pick the lock, or failing that, combine common household products into a plastique. Rich arrived at his side. "Dude, just—" he said, and reached for the deadbolt.

"Too late," Denis mumbled, and ran up the stairs.

"You don't run up the stairs!" Rich yelled up at him. "Have you never seen a movie? You run up the stairs, you *die!*"

Rich was about to cite specifics when he saw Kevin marching toward him. Kevin growled, smashed an overhead light fixture with his bare fist, then kept coming in the ensuing darkness.

Rich ran up the stairs.

"*¡Arribame!*"

RICH BURST INTO DENIS'S ROOM and crashed into a squadron of X-Wing Starfighters, not for the first time. He thrashed in the tangle of suspended *Star Wars* collectibles and, for the very first time, did not hear Denis pissing and moaning that this or that one was made specifically for the Chinese market, making it extremely rare except for the 37 million other ones in China.

Denis was preoccupied. He was rifling through his closet, tossing out *Journals* of *the American Medical Association* and *Juvenile Oncology*, his snorkel, copies of *Famous CGI Monsters* and *Celebrity Sleuth: Women of Fantasy 15*, an old diving mask, Hobbit Monopoly and 3-D Stratego, and a pair of big, floppy, noncombat swim fins.

Wielding the impotent fins, he whined, "Why didn't I play baseball?"

Kevin arrived at the doorway. Sean and the other one fell in behind him.

Denis thrust his hands back into the closet, praying they would reappear holding anything resembling a weapon. A loaded revolver would be ideal, though unlikely (his mother felt hunters should be tried for war crimes and his father drove a Prius); a stick with a nail in it would be acceptable. What Denis retrieved certainly resembled a weapon; it was a 1:1-scale replica of the original Skywalker light saber with electroluminescent polycarbonate blade and ten motion-controlled digital sound effects.

Kevin barked with amusement. His troops barked exactly the same amount. A martial grin spread across his face as he reconnoitered the room: a medical school skeleton wearing a "BGHS Debate Team" T-shirt; the original *Star Wars* poster of Luke, light saber aloft; further charts of human muscular and circulatory systems; a poster of Professor Stephen Hawking posing with a poster of Marilyn Monroe; *Futurama* figurines . . . (In Denis's defense, a girl hadn't been in his room for more than ten years.)

"What a Eugene." Kevin chortled. The laughter triggered an endorphin rush that broke his fragile concentration, and he lost his homicidal focus. Why, he wondered, did he even consider this easily snappable geek a threat, instead of an amusing nuisance to be swatted away, or lightly stepped on?

And then he saw it.

On the wall above Denis's bed: Beth Cooper beaming down, kneeling in her cheerleading uniform. Denis had scanned the yearbook squad photo, Photoshopped the others out (digitally re-creating the portion of Beth's skirt obscured by Treece's knee), enlarged the image 7,000 percent, printed it in tiles, joined the tiles with an X-Acto blade and rubber cement, affixed the assemblage above his bed with wallpaper paste, and moved his bed three inches to the right to center the image. It had taken him five hours, not counting buying and setting up the scanner.

Kevin didn't appreciate all the effort. He grabbed the pelvis of the medical skeleton and tore it off the spine.

"Dr. McCoy!" Denis gasped.

Kevin took a femur in each hand and ripped them free of the pelvis.

"Now," Denis admonished, "that used to be a person."

Fiendish glee best described Kevin's expression as he approached Denis, slowly spinning the skeleton's lower legs around the knee joints.

"That is very disrespect *foo*—"

Twenty-six foot bones kicked him in the ear.

Denis lifted his light saber to fend off the human nunchucks, but Kevin's bone-fu was unstoppable. Flying phalanges of fury booted him about the face and neck.

"Dude!"

Denis turned to see that Rich was at the open window, on the other side of it, beckoning him.

"Don't just—"

Denis took a calcaneus to the temple. He staggered backward into a corner, trapped. So this was it: boned to death in his own room. Not exactly the tragedy he had always dreamed about. He thought of his mother finding his bloody pulped remains, and then he thought of that copy of *Celebrity Sleuth: Women of Fantasy 15* on the floor, lying open to topless shots of Kristanna Løken, the Terminatrix. Embarrassing. If he had time, he would try to eat the magazine before he died.

KEVIN SEEMED TO BE DECIDING. To kill or not to kill? Or how slowly? How excruciatingly? Whichever, he was relishing the decision-making process.

Something splintered against his skull. As it turned out, it was another skull. Beth stood behind Kevin, holding the jawbone of Dr. McCoy. "*Now* will you calm down?" she asked, grabbing his shirt.

Beth was allowed to touch Kevin in places he didn't even allow the army doctors to touch, but his shirt was not one of those places.

"You want some of this?" He raised a femur to her.

"Kevin." Beth backed away, releasing the shirt. "Let's just—"

"*Do* you?" Kevin asked again, in a dead, calm voice.

Beth said "No" very quietly.

She glanced past Kevin, who wheeled around to see the last of Denis going out the window. He turned back with a look of confused revulsion.

"You *like* this dork?"

Beth's failure to vomit at the suggestion was taken as a yes.

"I *am* going to kill him," Kevin said, dropping the bones and heading for the window. His compatriots followed.

Beth looked around Denis's room, shaking her head. When she saw her poster, she smiled so hard she almost cried.

10.

DUMB MONKEYS

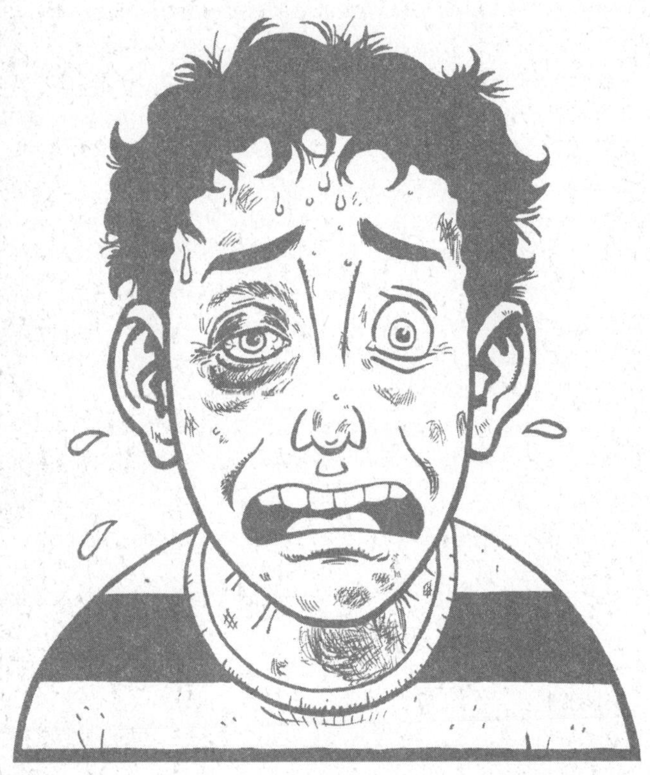

HE'S JUST DOING IT TO GET A RISE OUT OF YOU. JUST IGNORE HIM.

CLAIRE STANDISH

AS HE WAS DEFENESTRATING HIMSELF, Denis observed that the eaves outside his window were only eighteen inches wide and sloped down at a 45-degree angle. This was the sort of detail he had surely noticed before, saw every day, but didn't attach any real importance to until it turned out to be really important. Like, for example, now.

His trajectory was going to take him past the eaves and another dozen feet straight down onto some lawn furniture that wasn't comfortable even when you sat on it properly. Denis would have to take death-evading measures. Using his sophisticated knowledge of physics and aerodynamics, he spazzed about and managed to save himself by wedging his face into the gutter.

"Hey!"

Denis coughed up the leaves he had promised to clean out the previous fall. Rich was twenty feet away, humping the far corner of the house.

"What are you *doing?*"

"Drainpipe," Rich grunted. "Shimmying."

Rich gave Denis a thumbs-up. The drainpipe *jinked* as it disengaged from the gutter, and Rich held his increasingly ridiculous pose as the pipe fell away, slowly at first and progressively faster in accordance with the laws of gravity, and into the darkness.

Denis squirreled it down the eaves and peered over the edge.

"Rich!"

Ca-chunk.

A rivet popped on the section of the gutter he was leaning on.

The gutter *ca-chunked* again, and then *ca-CHANKed.*

Denis plummeted. Just below were bushes planted to commemorate Denis's First Holy Communion, since the jujube was the source of the thorns in Jesus's crown. (Denis's parents treated their Catholicism not so much as a religion as an anthropological teaching opportunity.)

Denis fought his way through the thorns of Christ, his clothes pierced and skin scratched where it wasn't already contused (there too, but harder to make out). He ran over to Rich, who was lying on his back clutching the drainpipe between his legs.

"I'm paralyzed," Rich said with remarkable calm. "I'm a paralyzed virgin."

"Sorry," Denis said.

Above them, the gutter rattled.

Denis watched in shock and awe as three studly silhouettes leapt from the roof in unison and landed on the grass, tumbled together, and seamlessly rose to perfect commando formation.

Denis looked down at Rich. He was gone.

"Yo!"

Rich was standing in the next yard.

"Run, you dumb monkey!"

A very large dog appeared out of the shadows and swallowed Rich.

THE BEAST WAS ALL OVER HIM when Denis arrived. Rich was thrashing his arms and legs wildly, tossing his head from side to side and squeaking and squawking, suggesting the dog was up to no good.

"Kimberly, down!" Denis commanded, yanking the dog's collar. Kimberly backed off Rich and sat, panting happily.

"And now I'm partially eaten." Rich sighed. "The *chicas* don't go for half-eaten guys."

Kimberly was a big dog, a rottweiler-Lab-and-possibly-black-bear mix, but she was no man-eater. She was merely playing with Rich, and maybe tasting him a little.

"Kimberly?" Denis scoffed. "She's just a puppy

d-*ahgoo!*" Denis sneezed, and remembered why he didn't play more often with this big fluffy sack of dander and mites.

He sneezed again, and felt his open eye start to swell closed.

He sneezed again, and there was Kevin.

"Listen, Kevin," Denis began diplomatically, and then, where the abject apology should have gone, he sneezed in Kevin's face.

Kevin wiped off the snot particulates and, looking for a place to dry his hand, settled on Denis's face. He reached out and very nearly got his fingers bitten off.

Puppy Kimberly's large and sharp teeth glinted in the moonlight as she snapped and snarled, lunging at Kevin's body parts. He backed into his backup, feeling, what was it—*fear?* Roadside bombs and sniper fire barely got Kevin's attention anymore, but there was just something about fangs.

"Good dog!" Denis said. He reached down to help Rich up and discovered his friend had once again run off without him. *"Good doggie,"* Denis reinforced, and fled.

DENIS RAN LIKE A DUMB MONKEY through the backyards of Hackberry Drive:

through the Deters', whose son Lawrence went to Notre Dame on a football scholarship but decided to become a priest instead, breaking his father's heart;

through the Lemleys', whose daughter Lucia had once sold Denis fudge and lemonade made from recipes contained in the rhyme *milk, milk, lemonade, around the corner fudge is made;*

through the Cobes', who always gave out full-size candy bars on Halloween;

through the Schmidts', whose twenty-two-year-old daughter Shauna got undressed every night at nine, and took her time about it;

through the Snelsons', who always went out of town on Halloween, leaving a bag of cheap peanut butter kisses hanging off their doorknob, until that one Halloween;

and into the Confers' yard, under which nine cats were buried, and where Denis finally caught up with Rich, who was doubled over and breathing hard.

"Coach Raupp was right," Rich winced. "We are total pussies."

Denis tapped Rich on the back. They both saw:

Kevin and his troops marching at them double time, in a cadenced trot. They hurdled a four-foot chain-link fence without breaking stride.

Rich mulled this. "We may be dealing with cyborgs."

Denis took off toward the front yard.

"Hey!" Rich yelled, betrayed.

ACROSS THE STREET there once was a playground equipped with the monkey bars that Justin Cherry was briefly the king of, before tumbling off and becoming stupid. The Park District had taken the unpopular legal position that Justin was already stupid; as part of the ensuing massive settlement, the playground had been torn down and replaced by "Justin's Jungle," a rain-forest-themed Safeplay™ space, built on a TinyTurf™ seamless safety surface and constructed from EnviromenPal™ recycled plastic play components. Children seemed to enjoy it, despite its safety.

Denis ran up a monkey tongue and into its manic head.

"Have you learned *nothing?*" Rich complained, climbing the structure after him.

The boys clattered across the SynTeak™ Suspension Bridge and through the Eco-Go™ KnowFun™ Pagoda.

"Is there a point to this?" Rich asked. "Is there a plan here?"

Denis dove into a crawl tunnel that was mercifully free of theme, except for being banana yellow.

"Oh," Rich said. *"Hiding."*

Denis curled up near the midpoint of the tunnel, positioning himself between two of the Comfortholes™ that dotted the structure, allowing children to smile and wave at their parents and allowing parents to never ever lose sight of their precious, precious children. Rich didn't fit quite as nicely as Denis; his head and neck pressed against the top of the tube and knees jammed into the opposite wall.

Moonlight filtered in the ends and holes of the tunnel. A warm wind whistled through almost imperceptibly. The boys' panting slowed to heavy breathing. If Rich and Denis were ever going to make out, this was the time.

Rich grinned.

"Beth Cooper was *straddling* you," he said, vastly expanding the meaning of *to straddle. "Excellente."* Rich chortled lasciviously and may have winked; it was too dark to tell.

Denis was raising a finger to shush Rich when a massive limb shot through the hole next to his head. He first mistook it for a leg; the toes grabbed his nose and he realized it was a heavy-duty arm.

About the same time another arm sprang from an opposing hole, took hold of Rich's collar and began whipping him back and forth, slamming his head into the tunnel wall.

Denis freed his nose from its attacker and scooted away, and into a third arm, which wrapped around his neck and began choking him with a definite purpose.

Rich made all the expected sounds as his head spanged off the hard yellow plastic. Denis made no sound at all because there was no air getting in or out of his lungs. Instead he steadily turned the color surrounding his injured eye, which had passed indigo and was entering aubergine.

Based on the rate of his progression to unconsciousness, Denis concluded that he was being *both* suffocated and strangled, in effect overkilled, and that his death would arrive shortly. He wondered where the requisite premortem flashing-before-his-eyes of his life was.

Ah, here it came:

The back of Beth Cooper's head, and then the right side of her perfect face, as she turns to talk to Kate Persky . . .

Neon parrot fish swarming around him, wanting his wet bread, as he scuba-dived in the Great Blue Hole off Belize with his parents . . .

Beth cheerleading on the gym floor, from high in the bleachers, glimpsed around somebody's fatty tattooed head . . .

In his room, reading The Man Who Mistook His Wife for a Hat, *lying on his bed next to Rich, watching* The Valachi Papers *on a portable DVD player . . .*

The back of Beth's head again, turning slightly as she reaches over her shoulder to return a pencil she had borrowed from him.

That about summed it up.

Denis heard celestial trumpets. The tunnel filled with a brilliant light.

White light, Denis thought, *that's a bad sign.*

I'm dead.

In a plastic yellow tube.

Just as quickly, Denis wasn't dead anymore. The arm released him. Air streamed into his lungs and blood flowed to his brain. The sound of celestial trumpets resolved into a high-pitched car horn, and the beckoning light bobbed and veered away from the mouth of the tunnel.

Denis was confused, and then flabbergasted, when a happy face appeared in one of the Comfortholes™.

"Hi!" Treece said.

OUTSIDE THE TUNNEL, a white 1996 Cabriolet convertible had Kevin pinned against a giant laughing giraffe. Beth was leaning on the horn. Under the circumstances, Kevin was conciliatory. "Lisbee?" he said, like a boyfriend who had done something awfully wrong and was so sorry even though he wasn't certain what it was he had done.

And then: "Lisbee!" he screamed, slamming both fists on the car hood, like a guy who was too coked up to wait three seconds to see if the first strategy worked.

Beth responded by easing the brake and tapping the gas, causing the vehicle to gently lurch into her boyfriend.

INSIDE THE TUNNEL, Denis crawled over to Rich. After being yanked to and fro and having his head slammed into a durable plastic enclosure a few dozen times, Rich was a bit discombobulated.

"I'm a shaken baby," he said.

A hairy hand continued to grip Rich's shirt, but was only halfheartedly whipping him back and forth in a distracted manner. Denis got the hand's attention by biting it, hard.

Sean yanked his arm out of the tunnel, yowling.

Denis nudged and shoved and finally shoveled his semi-conscious friend out the tunnel. With Treece's help, he folded Rich into the backseat of the Cabriolet. Beth threw the car in reverse, and Denis hurled his torso over the front door as it backed away.

The Cabriolet was doing minus 40 mph when Beth spun it 180 degrees and Denis's lower body did an impressive demonstration of centrifugal force as he clung to the interior door handle. The car tore forward down a grassy incline with Denis struggling to remain attached, and then hit the curb, throwing the boy aboard.

BETH SWUNG on to Arlington Heights Road without stopping or signaling in accordance with the Illinois Rules of the Road, or without yielding the right of way to the Volvo XC-90 that was already on Arlington Heights Road. This resulted in some sudden brakeage on the Volvo's part.

Rich bounced around in the backseat, more than dazed.

"You okay?" Treece asked. "Is your brain dead?"

"Is blood coming out of my ears?"

"Not a lot."

Denis was up front, in a position that might unfortunately be described as fetal, on top of Cammy, who did not appreciate it. She shoved the boy mass off her lap and down into the passenger legroom space that the Cabriolet wasn't known for.

Denis rocked from side to side on the floorboards as Beth swerved around any object doing less than twice the speed limit.

"We got away," Denis pointed out from his cubby. "You can stop escaping."

Cammy shrugged at him. "She always drives like this."

In the back, Rich stared into infinity.

"I was in driver's ed with her."

DRIVER'S ED WAS TAUGHT by Coach Raupp, who resented having to do it and was incensed that physical education class time was wasted on such an *ass-spreading activity*. This was reflected in his teaching style, which was screaming. He screamed on the test course, *If that cone was a BABY GIRL, you would have KILLED it!* He screamed on the road, *Pull over NOW so I can SLAP you!* The only time he wasn't screaming was when he was showing *Wheels of Tragedy* (1963), and its sequel *Highways of Agony* (1969), two films that had been dropped from most driver's ed curricula because their incorporation of real accident footage of dead, mangled and dismembered teens led to more crying than learning. But every time that imprudent hippie was scooped off the roadway and his stoned brain casually slid out onto the pavement, Coach Raupp could be heard cackling in the back.

He only screamed at Beth Cooper once.

Rich was in the backseat then, too, with Victoria Smeltzer, when she still weighed over a hundred pounds. Coach Raupp was in his typical instruction pose, one fist balled in his lap and the other rhythmically pounding on the dashboard. Beth was driving with blissful confidence, as she always did, unaware she was about to kill them all.

"Yo, Munsch," Coach Raupp snapped, "what is the speed limit on Illinois highways?"

"Sixty-five," Rich answered, for once almost certain he was right.

"Then can you tell me *why the hell* Mizz Cooper is doing over *seventy*?"

Rich's hopes of ever answering two consecutive questions correctly were dashed.

"I'm not doing seventy," Beth responded. "I'm only doing—" She stared down at the speedometer: 71. "The flow of traffic." The vehicle meanwhile drifted off the highway and onto the loose gravel shoulder; Beth tugged the wheel and popped the car back into its lane, more or less.

"Pull over!" Coach Raupp screamed. *"Now!"*

Beth pulled over, now. She neglected to signal or to decelerate. Coach Raupp overcompensated for this by slamming on the instructor brake, sending the car into an uncontrolled skid. Beth tried to steer back onto the highway. The car slid sideways and began to roll, tumbling side over side several times before erupting into an enormous fireball.

"It did not," Denis said at lunch that day, as Rich related the story. "You'd be covered in third-degree burns. Your nerve endings would be exposed. You'd look like this." Denis held up his slice of school pizza. "Only more sauce."

Rich took the slice, folded it lengthwise and funneled the grease unto his tongue. "I was thrown clear. Everybody else got crispy creamed."

"Victoria is right over there." Denis nodded furtively, so as to not attract her attention. Victoria was sitting with Patty Keck, his secret shame, eating her Diet Coke while Patty finished both of their lunches.

"Half of Beth's face is . . . just gone," Rich said. "Like Mel Gibson as the eponymous *Man Without a Face.*"

He held the pizza over one eye.

"Is it this? Is this what you see? I assure you it is human. But if that's all you see, then you don't see me."

Would Denis still love Beth if she were *The Girl Without a Face?*

"Which half?" he asked.

"The good half."

Denis decided he did not have to decide. "And this has been another Richard Munsch dramatic presentation."

Rich swallowed the last of Denis's pizza. "Car did almost tip over."

RICH WAS IMAGINING he was in the scariest, goriest, least educational driver's ed film ever made:

In it, Rich played himself. Treece was played by Shanley Harmer, the actress who starred in *Bitches* on the CW, and then went on to movie fame in *Holy Mallory* and that Internet mp4 with Licks' front man Brent Koz. He was mentally casting Denis—that kid from *Geek Camp*?—when he suddenly flew forward, bounced his face against the front seat and slammed back next to Treece. She buckled him into his seat.

Beth had overshot the red light by a couple of car lengths. Black SUVs coming in opposite directions very nearly crashed into the front passenger and rear driver's sides, tearing the little Cabriolet in half like two wolves fighting over a plump bunny. Beth gave a cursory *my bad* wave and rapidly backed out of the intersection, coming within five-eighths of an inch of hitting a third black SUV behind her.

Denis crawled out of his hole. The last few seconds had brought back Rich's Driver's Ed Tales (there were several) and so he was currently struggling with the conflicting emotions of:

1) intense joy that Beth had just saved his life, choosing him over a former boyfriend;

2) fear.

"That was . . . with the car back there, but—"

"That wasn't for you," Beth cut him off. "I don't want you to get the wrong idea. Kevin can't have another incident. One more, and it's court-martial for sure."

Joy left and fear reigned.

"One more *what*?"

THE LIGHT TURNED GREEN and Beth floored it. Denis, perched between the two front seats, was thrown into the back.

"So," Treece said when he landed next to her. "That was fun."

"Some fun," added Rich, partially recombobulated. His head lolled in Denis's direction. "Your dad would be so proud."

Denis thought of the champagne bottle lodged in the wall, the Technicolor gooshes, the dead microwave and mutilated lawn. He leaned back through the front seats.

"Can I borrow your cell phone? I—"

"Good catch," Beth said. She pulled her cell phone from her purse and tossed it out of the car. "GPS that, asshole."

The phone flew through the window of a passing Honda Civic and hit Harold Angell, a thirty-four-year-old nurse practitioner who had no ironic connection to anyone in the car.

Denis sank back into his seat. He bounced off Treece and then Rich as Beth swerved along her merry way.

"Her driving's gotten a lot better," Rich commented.

Denis felt around behind him for the middle seat belt, finally pulling out something that appeared to have been chewed on by several packs of dogs. The buckle fell off.

"You can use my phone," Treece said, reaching into a pouch that cost more than Denis's entire wardrobe. "Not this one." She dropped a silver flip-phone back in. "My mom has it tapped"—meaning only that her mother scoured the bill for calls to men her mother dated. "Here."

Treece handed Denis a hot pink phone encrusted with jewels and dangled charms that looked as if it had been decorated by a three-year-old but which had been custom junked up in Japan at considerable cost.

"Tell your parents I said hi," Cammy remarked from the front seat.

"What makes you think I'm calling my parents?"

"Because you're you," Treece said, much nicer.

DENIS'S FATHER WAS DRY-HUMPING Denis's mother in the back of the Prius when his phone began buzzing.

"You're vibrating," Mrs. C said.

"That's because I'm about to *explode*," Mr. C moaned, grinding into her.

Mrs. C did not grind back. "It might be Denis."

Mr. C sighed. Yes, it might be Denis. Their son could be calling to ask permission to download a movie off iTunes. Or perhaps to tell them to pick up some milk or a *Scientific American* on the way home. Some emergency of that sort.

Mr. C pulled a cell phone out of his shirt pocket. The screen read CALLER ID BLOCKED.

"Telemarketer," he said. Mr. C slipped the vibrating phone down the front of Mrs. C's slacks.

"Mr. C!" Mrs. C growled.

ON HIS END, Denis, thankfully, only heard the usual leave-a-message-at-the-beep and then the beep.

"It's me," he told the phone. "Rich and I . . . went

out. But we're okay. I can explain the kitchen. You can call me at . . ."

He looked to Treece. She grabbed the phone away.

"That's my *stealth* phone!"

Up front, Beth turned on the radio. In a quavering depressissimo, a future lesbian sang:

I learned the truth at seventeen . . .

Beth frowned. She pushed SEEK. Synthetic drumbeats and electro-boops accompanied a future cartoon composer:

Makin' dreams come true
Living tissue, warm flesh—

Beth turned the music off.

"Radio sucks," she pronounced.

Denis remembered. He pulled the iPod from his pocket.

"Tune to 87.1."

There was much groaning. Undeterred, Denis leaned between the front seats and turned the radio back on. "No, seriously, you'll like this," he promised, tuning and hoping.

Music equally ancient but not the least bit objectionable began blasting out the speakers, a man named Alice repeating the words of a playground chant:

No more pencils,
No more books,
No more teacher's dirty looks.

Beth's head banged to the olden beat. Denis was hugely relieved. Ordinarily, the declaration that school was out for summer made him anxious. But this summer, he thought, might be all right.

School's out forEVER!

Beth sang along, with heavy emphasis on the last

two syllables. Here, Denis begged to differ. School was not out *forever*, just until—

School's been BLOWN TO PIECES!

screamed Beth, taking both hands off the steering wheel and waving devil horns above her head.

"I *love* this song," yelled Treece. "Who doesn't want to blow up their school?"

Denis was happy his song selection was a success, but he'd have been much happier if Beth was steering her vehicle. The car drifted toward the center line, toward oncoming traffic, toward a banner headline in the *Daily Herald:*

Grad Night Tragedy

Valedictorian, 4 others killed on joy ride

Denis decided that if Beth didn't feel like steering she wouldn't mind if he did. He reached for the wheel, planning on nudging it just enough to prevent death. He got two fingers on the rim.

With one hand, Beth matter-of-factly executed a nearly perpendicular right turn at full speed.

Denis toppled forward and fell face first between Beth's legs.

11.

ESTRANGED BREW

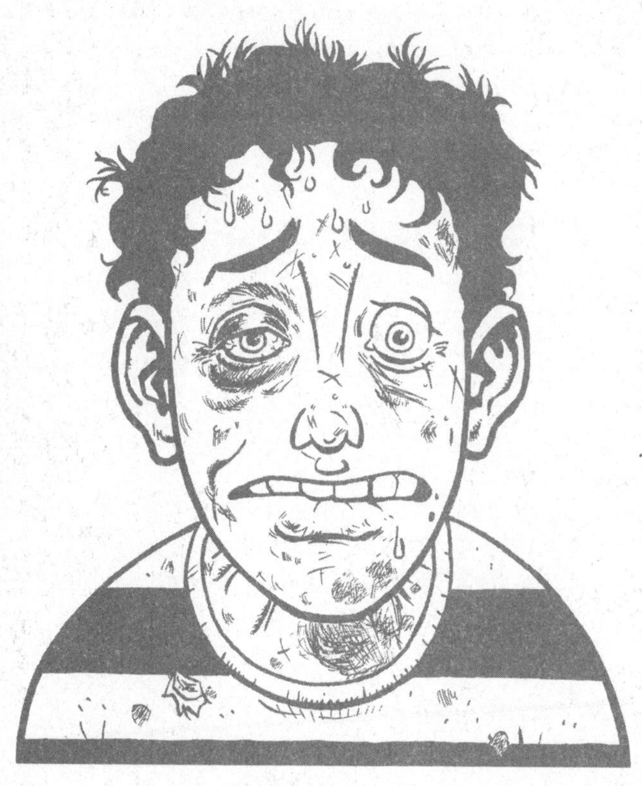

I BET YOU'RE SMART ENOUGH
TO GET US SOME BREW.

DEBBIE DUNHAM

THE CABRIOLET CAREENED into the White Hen Pantry parking lot and skidded into the only available space, bouncing off the concrete wheel stop.

Denis's face remained lodged in Beth's thighs. The moment when he could have withdrawn his head without incident had passed. He couldn't get out now without a good exit line, and he was without one. He imagined Beth was appalled, hurt, violated, furious, fed up and, *oh, no, was she sobbing?*

Beth was chuckling.

It was dark down there, Denis guessed. He took no chances and kept his eyes shut. He couldn't close his nose, however. It smelled musky, a little like butt, less pungent, more floral, and—was *spicier* the right word?

It took Denis a surprisingly long time to realize he was sniffing Beth Cooper's vagina.

His eyes opened involuntarily. It wasn't nearly dark enough down there. Beth's panties were white. They spoke to Denis. They said,

Hello.

The lettering was hot pink. It clashed with the blue-green plaid of the skirt, yet somehow it worked.

Denis felt a hand tugging his hair. He wanted to stay.

I love you, he whispered as Beth lifted his head out of her welcoming center.

"I'm sorry," Denis said.

"Let's get some beer," Beth said.

Beth hopped out of the car and Denis crawled after her. "Two minutes," she called back to the others, reaching the door before Denis and opening it for him.

"Snacks," Treece yelled. "Everybody wants snacks!"

"Everybody," Cammy said flatly.

Treece acknowledged the insult with a grotesque smirk. "And a bucket for Cammy!" She mimed bulimic fingers and then turned to Rich, palm up, awaiting her high five.

Whoa, Rich thought, *catfight!*

"LISTEN," BETH SAID, once they were inside.

Denis had not yet formulated a plausible explanation for the amount of time he had spent in her genital environs.

He went with implausible.

"I think I was knocked unconscious back there, for a minute."

Beth had no idea what he was talking about. "I don't want you to think I'm a bitch or anything. What I said. I mean, I didn't want to see you get hurt, obviously. But I just wanted to be clear, you know, about my motivations."

"Oh, sure," Denis said. "I figured as much."

They reached the beer display. Beth turned toward Denis, brightly, and then not.

"God."

The convenience store fluorescence brought out the colors of everything that had befallen Denis's face so far that evening:

ruby-rimmed right eye tucked in a billowing of black, violet and yellow flesh;

newer plummy bruises on his ears, forehead, cheeks and chin;

across the whole face a delicate lattice of crimson scrapes.

"Maybe you *should* go to the hospital," Beth said.

"Your eyes aren't blue," Denis responded. He had been staring at her as she gaped at him, and seeing things.

"What?"

"There's green in there," he said. "And around the pupil, there's a hazel"—the scientific term came first—“corona . . .” He sprung open his hand: “Starburst.”

“Yeah,” Beth acknowledged. “My grandmother said they were a real ‘dog’s breakfast.’ ”

“Lucky dog,” Denis said, and on purpose.

Beth’s lips twitched upward even as her eyes cast downward. She tilted her face away, and came back with a huge, sanitary smile.

“What kind of beer do you like?”

THE CATFIGHT WAS DISAPPOINTING. Treece and Cammy traded a couple of cryptic remarks, references to previous and ongoing grievances, and fell into an uneasy détente. Rich figured that if it was not for Beth, these two wouldn’t be friends at all.

“So,” Rich said, seeing if he could get them going again, “how long have you two been going out with Sean and—what was the other one?”

“That’s weird.” Treece screwed up her face. “Something.”

“Fuck a duckling,” Cammy said, changing the subject.

Approaching the car were Henry Giroux and his buddy Damien, the only two guys from BGHS that Cammy wanted to hang out with less than Denis and Rich. Henry was the local purveyor of aftermarket pharmaceuticals, not quite a drug dealer though he played the part, replete with an embroidered urban dialect spoken only in the suburbs. What made Henry’s lily-white gangsta act all the more sad was that he was African-American. He was a black whigger.

“Yo, yo, beautiful ladies!”

DENIS DID NOT KNOW what kind of beer he liked. As far as he knew, he did not like beer.

“Microbrew,” he answered.

"What kind?"

"Any kind."

Beth reached into the cooler and pulled out a six of Molson Dark, followed by a twelve of PBR tallboys. She dumped both in Denis's arms.

"Snacks!" Beth said.

Denis followed Beth through the salty snack aisle as she piled on, with seeming indiscrimination, bag upon bag of sodium and partially hydrogenated oils. He thought about what he would do when Beth had her inevitable heart attack. He would have to perform CPR.

Her chest: fifteen compressions.

Her mouth: two breaths.

Her chest, her mouth, her chest, his mouth.

His mouth on her mouth, her lips quivering, returning to life.

"Hey, Spaceboy!"

Beth was at the end of the aisle. She pointed to the left and went that way. Denis shook off his erection and waddled after her, the eighteen beers and eight bags exceeding his carrying capacity. In the next aisle, ten packages of sweet snacks awaited Denis's abiding arms. Beth had a preference for chocolatey coating, he noted.

"I love these!"

Beth held up a package of Suzy Qs, the Hostess snackcake that would be forever dendritically entwined in Denis's brain with the verb phrase *sucking each others'.* Seeing the labial cakes oozing creme only strengthened the connection, as did the way Beth flicked her tongue when she overpronounced the word *yum*. This freely associated with his mother's *yumming* earlier in the day, creating a gooey endocrinal mess.

Was Beth consciously trying to pop his pituitary gland, or was this kind of sexual sabotage purely instinctual, or was it all a figment of his anterior hypothalamus? One thing was certain: Denis knew too much about biology and not enough about women.

"How much money you got?" Beth asked.

"Oh," Denis said, blinking back into the real world. "I, my wallet . . ." He nodded over his shoulder, to suggest he could not presently reach his back pocket, not that Beth should stick her hand in there.

Denis barely felt it, unfortunately.

"Money, money, money," Beth said as she flipped open his billfold. Denis's mind flashed on its terrible contents:

his school ID, taken during a severe acne storm;

a Photobooth picture of Rich and him that could easily be misconstrued;

a video-game token;

his official identification card for the Starfleet Academy, *goddammit*, which he kept meaning to archive.

Beth plucked out the hundred-dollar bill.

"Thank you, Denis Cooverman!" she sang, and then noticing the lavender glitter pen inscription, "And thank *you*, Auntie Brenda!"

Or that.

"GO AWAY, HENRY."

Rich was pleased with the cold shoulder Cammy was giving Henry Giroux. There was a limited niche for "characters" in the high school ecosphere, and Rich felt his Smooth-Talking Film Aficionado was going underappreciated due to unfair competition from Henry's Retro Ghetto Jivist. Rich chalked this up to the fact that Henry possessed drugs, albeit lame ones, and that he was nominally black. (The only other black person in their class, Lisa Welch, was in band and therefore invisible.)

Henry did not go away. He leaned a hip against the car and stylishly tipped the porkpie off his head and sent it rolling down his arm. The hat bounced off the crook and tumbled to the pavement. Henry turned to Cammy with the same cocky expression he would have used had the hat rolled effortlessly into his hand.

"What do you *want*, Henry?" she asked.

"*Bumboklaat*, girl," Henry shucked. "Jes' seeing if you wants to partay."

"No."

"Whaddya got?" Treece asked.

"We got the Ritz," Henry said, using his own slang for Ritalin. "The 'D' [Claritin-D] and some sweet Mercedez."

"You don't have any Benzedrine," Cammy said.

"*Adderall*, beeyatch!"

Treece was disappointed with the selection. "Don't you have any real drugs?"

"Fo shizzle my pizzle!" Henry said.

"Why do you talk like that, Henry?" Cammy asked.

"Jes' representin'."

"Your parents are doctors and you live in Terramere. Why don't you represent that?"

"Salty!" interjected Damien, who looked like a pig with hair.

Henry was not about to let some ho dis him like that. "Why are *you*"—pointing ten fingers at Cammy—"rollin' with Dick Muncher and The Penis?"

"I can't answer that."

Rich did not like the direction this conversation was taking.

"You too fine for candy cracker ass scrubs."

"You'll get no argument from me."

"Why don't you ice the bustas and kick it with a brutha?"

Rich stood. "I'm going to go check on the *cervezas*."

"*Adios, muchacha*," Henry dismissed Rich, and returned to Cammy and Treece. "Come on over to the Dark Meat Side."

"I don't believe that's gangsta, Henry," Cammy said. "I believe that's geeksta."

Treece giggled, but Henry was unbowed. "Once you go black," he Courvoisiered them, "you never-fo'ever go back."

"That's not true," Treece said with some authority.

RICH WAS MAD AT HIMSELF for not going mano a mano, mouth to mouth, with Henry Giroux back there. At first, he had seen no need; he was enjoying, admiring, the way Cammy dismantled that little minstrel showoff. But then she turned and sided with Henry against him. Rich prided himself on not caring what the popular kids thought, feeling that their very popularity demonstrated their inferiority, somehow, but it hurt him that Cammy agreed he was a *candy cracker ass scrub,* whatever that meant, exactly.

And *Dick Muncher and The Penis?* Was that common usage? Rich had been called *Dick Munch* since the seventh grade and he himself had called Denis *Penis* earlier in the evening, but it never occurred to him that people would put the two together, turning them into the gaynamic duo or something. *Dick Muncher and The Penis.* More like supervillains.

Well, at least he got first billing.

Beth was at the candy rack, standing next to a giant pile of junk food with legs. Beth spotted Rich's approach and shooed him away. He kept coming.

"Back to the car," she said as he arrived.

"Why?" he asked.

Beth was unaccustomed to having her orders countermanded. It became very cold in there.

"Just go back to the car, Rich," the junk food said.

On his way out, Rich stopped to look at a magazine, mostly for spite. He picked up a copy of *American*

Man, the Magazine for American Men. On the cover was a lustrous male chest with impossible pectorals and a brightly feathered fishing lure dangling from one nipple.

read the coverline. "Cocktail Music: Which Tequila Goes Best with Beck?" was also promised inside, along with "Have You Forgotten Your Glutes?" As a matter of fact, Rich had forgotten his glutes, along with his abs, pecs, lats, and all three types of ceps.

"Hola, Ricardo."

Standing next to Rich, perusing that month's *Details*, was a middle-aged man in a white jogging outfit. He was in decent shape for his age, but not for terry-cloth shorts.

"Oh, hi, Mr. Weidner," Rich said, shoving his *American Man* back in the rack. "I mean, *hola, Señor Weidner.*"

Sr. Weidner closed his magazine, leaving a finger inside to mark his place. He smiled. "You can call me Cal, now."

"Okay. *Muy bien. Hola, Cal.*"

"You're keeping up your Spanish."

"Todo las veces."

"Todo el tiempo."

"Right," Rich said, pointing to his head. *"Soy retardo."*

Sr. Weidner smiled again, a little pained. "So, listen, *cenemos alguna vez. Si te gusta. ¿Comeremos tapas y hablaremos Español?"*

Rich had no idea what Sr. Weidner was saying. Guessing it was a question, and reading hopefulness in his former teacher's expression, he replied, "Yeah. *Sí.*"

"*¡Maravilloso!*"

"*Excellente,*" Rich agreed. "But I should probably go. I've got two *chicas calientes* waiting for me in the *autobus.*"

"*Bien,*" Sr. Weidner said. "*Llámame,*" he added as Rich walked away. "I'm in the book."

BETH LED DENIS to the checkout counter. As she unpacked him, she whispered, "Follow me." Denis nodded. He would follow her.

The clerk behind the counter was a loser, and a pretty sizable one. His hair looked as if it had been washed far too often but not for the last month or so. He had a skinny head and narrow shoulders and spindly arms and a truly humongous ass. He looked to be anywhere between twenty-eight and forty-three, as is often the case with losers.

Beth plunked the beer on the counter with a bored look.

The loser started scanning the snacks, staring at Denis. He sneered more than usual. "What's with your boyfriend?"

"My little brother," Beth corrected.

Denis winced. He understood the exigencies of the situation, and knew he did not look twenty-one (ticket takers would occasionally ask if his parents knew he was seeing this movie, which was rated PG-13 and contained scenes of intense action that might give him nightmares). And yet, the only thing worse than a girl thinking of you as a brother was her thinking of you as a little brother. Brothers, at least, got long hugs. Little brothers got head pats and lollipops.

"What happened to his face?" the loser asked.

My injuries, Denis thought, *must add a certain weathered maturity.*

"Dad beats him," Beth said.

The loser picked up the Molson and swung it toward the scanning plate, only to jerk it back at the last second, returning it to the counter.

"I need to see some ID."

Beth looked surprised. She shrugged, a tad much, and produced a small coin purse. It was stuffed with bills, Denis noticed. She fished out her driver's license with two fingers and flicked it at the clerk.

"You've lost weight, Cheryl," the loser said, examining the ID. "And you certainly don't look thirty-seven."

"Thank you."

The loser handed back the ID, slid the beer away from the snacks, and hit the total button. "That'll be $56.72."

Beth dropped the pretense. "C'mon," she pleaded. "It's graduation night."

"Con-*grad*-ulations."

"You're a cool guy," Beth cajoled. "Be cool."

"I could lose my shitty job."

Denis began working on a Plan B. Appeal to reason. *Rejected.* Smash loser over head with beer, grind jagged bottle neck into his throat. *Rejected.* Grab beer and run. *Analyze.*

Beth already had a Plan B. She smiled shyly at the loser.

"I'll touch your dick."

"AND THEN SHE TOUCHED HIS DICK."

Denis sat in the back of the Cabriolet, a six-pack of Molson Dark in his lap.

"Ew," Treece opined. "Even I wouldn't do that. Unless the beer was free."

Up front, Beth and Cammy were sipping tallboys,

heads shagging to DJ C's unexpectedly slammin' graduation mix:

You're my one, baby, yes you are
My sweet hot secret cherry tart
We've been playing in a minor key
But you've finally reached majority

"She touched his dick," Denis repeated.

"So there's hope for you," Rich said.

Treece qualified, "*If* you've got beer."

You're legal
Oh my oh my oh my
You're legal now
Oh my oh my oh my

"Inside or outside?"

Denis pretended not to understand.

"The pants. Inside or outside?"

Treece did a little clap. "Good question!"

INSIDE, FOR LESS THAN A SECOND, and then out.

Inside, a moment's grope, and then out, her fingers splayed apart.

Denis's brain rewound again.

Inside, her sea-mint fingers curled around his un-washed

grease pole,
cheese stick,
night crawler,
chancre factory,
Jergened gerkin,
rancid flaccid fetid flesh appendage,
dick, dong, dingle,
peter, pecker, pork-sword, pud,
wiener.

Inside, a swift kick to Denis's gut, and then out.

"That's no good," the loser said when Beth withdrew before the party could start.

"I touched it," Beth responded. "That was the deal."

The loser began walking the beer back to the cooler. Beth followed him, and Denis followed Beth.

"You can't. I did what I said."

"What are you gonna do, sue me?"

"Call the police."

"A consensual act." The loser sounded like a man who knew his way around the sexual assault laws. "Your little brother saw it."

Yes, he had. If he had died right then, which he was considering, the coroner would've found the exculpatory evidence burned into his retina.

"Completely," the loser licked his skinny purple lips, relishing "con-*sensual*."

"That doesn't matter," Denis heard himself say, "when she's only fifteen."

On their way out with the beer, Beth grinned at Denis and patted him on the head. "Good job, little brother!"

"I DON'T WANT TO TALK ABOUT IT," Denis said, back in the car.

Treece took him at his word, and spoke over him to Rich. "I saw you chatting with Señor Weidner."

"Yes, and?"

"I always thought he was a handbag."

"So why are you telling me?"

" 'Cuz you're right there."

"And anyway, why would you think Weidner's gay? He dresses terribly."

"He's always lisping." Treece demonstrated, substituting interdental fricatives for her usual sibilance: "*¿Donde estha la cothina?*"

"That's Castilian. That's the way they talk in . . . some place in Spain."

"Castile," said Denis, on automatic.

"Cathstile."

"I guess that's why you don't see many *Cathstillians.*" Treece thought this was tremendously funny.

"You know," Rich spoke over the loud whinnying, "it's not right to assume someone's gay just because of the way they talk, or look, or act."

Treece stopped with a snort. She regarded Rich with fond pity. "Nobody cares if you're gay."

"I'm not."

"No one cares." She threw up her hands festively. "So be gay already."

Rich thought, *No one?*

You're legal
Oh my oh my oh my
You're legal so
Bye-bye bye-bye bye-bye

The Licks song went into an endless fade, perfectly soundtracking the swirling collapse of Denis's mental universe.

Beth Cooper was a nice, pretty girl who always returned the pencils she borrowed. She did not touch dicks for beer.

Bye-bye bye-bye bye-bye

"She's not Beth Cooper," Denis said quietly.

Treece furrowed one brow then the other.

"I'm pretty sure she is."

12.

NIGHT MOOS

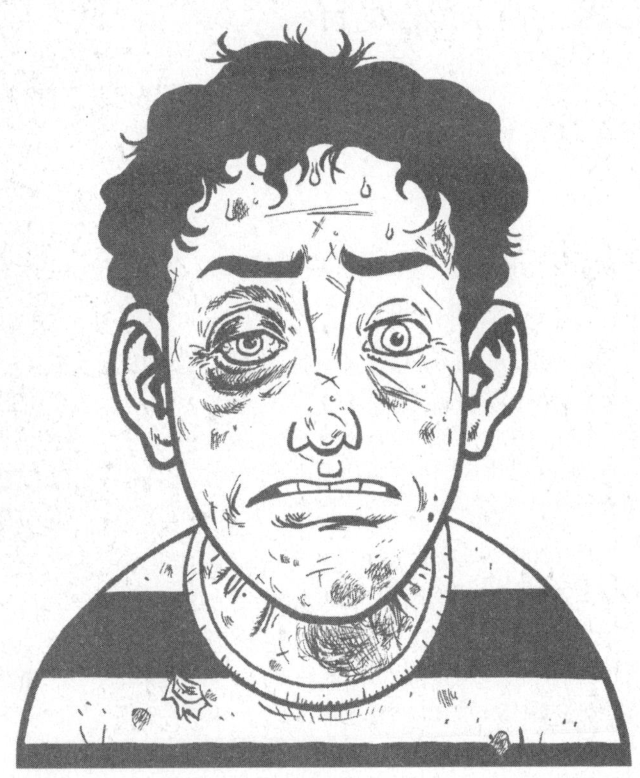

MARTY, DON'T BE SUCH A SQUARE.
EVERYBODY WHO'S ANYBODY DRINKS.

LORRAINE BAINES

FIVE TEENAGERS DRANK BEER on a dark country road covered with a pale green mist. It was midnight.

"Ever been out here before?" Beth asked.

"Who hasn't?" Denis evaded. "I mean, *Old Tobacco Road . . .*"

Old Tobacco Road wasn't called that anymore. In the eighties, antismoking advocates insisted on changing it, but split between the heart-disease faction, which wanted Camino Corazon, and the cancer crowd, which wanted the more on-message Smoking Causes Cancer Road. In the end, the village board discovered the road was in an unincorporated area and that they had no authority to change it. Some time during the nineties, the county quietly changed the name to Gwendolyn Way, after somebody's mother. But all the teenagers who hung out there still called it Tobacco Road, or Old Tobacco Road, or recently, the OT.

"This place creeps me out," Beth said. She finished her tallboy and crumpled it in her fist. "I don't know why I keep coming out here."

"It's peaceful." Denis baby-sipped his Molson Dark.

"Except for the ghosts," Beth said.

DENIS HAD NEVER HUNG OUT on Old Tobacco Road, and had never been there after dark. He had only seen it once, one Saturday afternoon when he was ten, on a Tales of My Youth drive with his father. Denis's father had grown up in Buffalo Grove and never tired of showing his son his personal historical landmarks (the house on St. Mary's Parkway, the baseball field where he hit a grand slam, the water treatment plant where he saw a dead kid). Many of the elder Cooverman touchstones were not there anymore, or ruined somehow. Tobacco Road was exactly the same.

The narrow, barely paved road ran fairly straight but swooped up and down wildly, over hill and dale and steeper hill and deeper dale. Running along the eastern edge of the road was the Old Maguire Farm, the only major parcel of land in the area that had not been converted into a subdivision named for the English countryside. This was because Old Man Maguire had killed dozens of teenagers and fed them to his pigs, burying their bones in the corn, and therefore was reluctant to sell. Either that or he had killed his wife and nine kids one night by burning down his farmhouse, which reappeared every full moon, disappearing in the morning along with anybody foolhardy enough to have gone inside.

On the other side of the road was a three-story turn-of-the-century building that had once been a home for the criminally insane, or an orphanage, or a home for children who killed their parents, or a whorehouse, or an insane asylum-cum-whorehouse. Next to it was a small cemetery, haunted by the restless souls of insane whores, and next to that was a bog, which had monsters.

Denis's father had told Denis these tales (minus the whores) that afternoon, emphasizing they were just "silly stories" teenagers liked to tell each other. Denis's mother slept in the boy's room for the next three months, mostly to punish his father.

THE MOON WAS FULL. Beth's convertible was parked at the highest point of Old Tobacco Road, overlooking a soupy pea fog that was either slightly radioactive or ghost children at play. This was the ideal vantage point to see the reappearance of Old Maguire's farmhouse. It was behind schedule.

"How's that microbrew treating you?" Beth asked Denis.

The brew was treating him very well. His fifteen sips, approximately half a bottle, was six ounces more beer than Denis had ever consumed, and the dose was having the psychopharmacological effects he anticipated: slight euphoria, tension reduction, loss of concentration. As a result, while Denis still knew Beth Cooper was no longer Beth Cooper, he was having difficulty maintaining his distress, his mind wandering over to Rich's point of view, that Beth Cooper's sexual generosity with the physically less gifted could work in the favor of a Denis Cooverman.

"It's good." Denis said. "Very . . . brewed."

He sat in the front passenger seat next to Beth, at her invitation. Rich and Treece sat atop the backseats and Cammy was out of the car, sulking over being made to surrender shotgun to Denis. Why did she even cede authority to Beth Cooper? Cammy was smarter and had better technicals in all the beauty categories. Was it simply that Beth was head cheerleader? Was Cammy that much of a sheep?

"Nik-nik-nik-f-f-f-Indians!" Rich hollered as he drained his first Molson Dark.

Cammy eyed him with appalled disinterest.

"Jack Nicholson in *Easy Rider*, 1969, Dennis Hopper."

"There's something wrong with you," Cammy said.

Beth popped open her second PBR, sucking off the foam. For a moment she had a thick, gorgeous beer mustache.

"You do know," Denis advised, "open liquor in the car, you could lose your license?"

"Too late!" Beth tipped her can in toast, and then chugged.

Denis had no idea that a woman guzzling cheap beer could be so sexy, the way she kissed the rim and her throat undulated as the golden domestic nectar flowed through it. The *gulugulugugug* was less sexy but could be filtered out.

Denis bit a swig off his Molson. That went so well he took another, and another. Soon enough his lips ceased parsing and the beer freely drained down his gullet.

Beth crushed her beer can and tossed it. Denis reflexively squeezed his beer bottle and it slipped out of his hand, spilling in his lap. He waved off nonexistent help, pinched the bottle by the lip and flung it into the dark. He immediately reconsidered. "We should probably pick those up," he said, leaning out of the car.

Beth prodded him with another Molson. Denis forgot everything his mother had ever taught him about caretaking this delicate planet and took the bottle from Beth. He twisted the top effortlessly, producing no effect. He applied more pressure and his hand slid off the cap. His palm was sweaty. Of course it was. Everything was. He could hear the sweat beading inside his ears. *Goddammit.* Before long he would need to explain he had not wet his pants, or, *oh, god, she wouldn't think that, would she?*

"You're having bottle trouble tonight." Beth took the bottle, gave it a quick twist, and to Denis's everlasting relief did not open it. Undeterred, she brought the bottle to her mouth, wedged it between her back molars and

she bit the fucking cap off!

"I know." She took a quick slug before returning the bottle. "I'm going to *ruin my beautiful teeth*."

Denis's whole mouth throbbed.

Beth popped her third PBR, sucked it off. "So," she grinned, "ever come up here with Patty Keck?"

Denis glared at Rich.

"Girls talk," Beth corrected him.

Denis gulped his beer and winced. Beth Cooper talked to Patty Keck, his secret shame? This could not lead anywhere good. He searched his brain for a change of subject. What a mess it was in there. It was as if somebody had broken into his cerebrum and dumped all the neurons on the floor. They flopped around unhelpfully.

And then Denis heard, coming over the radio, driving eighties synthpop and a topic:

Will you recognize me
Call my name or walk on by . . .

"This song." Denis directed everybody's attention to the radio. "What if," he said, "our parents, on their graduation night, what if . . . ?" His ex tempore skills were below his tournament best. "They could have been sitting right here, on Old Tobacco Road, in their vehicles, cars that were available at the time, and they could have been parked in this exact spot, listening to this *exact same song.*

"Which *means,*" Denis built to what seemed a profound cosmological observation, "we were here, too . . . *in cell form.*"

There was a silence, which Denis took to signify amazement.

"I don't remember getting high," Cammy deadpanned.

"We're high?" Treece asked.

"I just thought it was interesting." Denis backpedaled from profundity. "How we all go through this. The same songs. The same rituals . . ."

"Intriguing, professor," Cammy said.

"I mean, we all . . ." Denis struggled for a common and yet precisely right word. ". . . *graduate.*"

"My parent's didn't graduate to this song," Treece said. "They're, like, forty-plus."

"This song is at least twenty years old," Denis said.

"Uh, no," Treece argued. "They didn't have cool music back then."

" 'Don't You (Forget About Me),' Simple Minds," cited

Rich, "from the sound track of *Breakfast Club*, 1984, John Hughes."

"Are you going to do that all night?" Beth asked.

"I can't help it. I'm like Dustin Hoffman in *Rain Man*." He did a slightly more nasal version of his Pacino.

I'm an excellent driver. Qantas.

The girls all turned away from him. He finished, involuntarily, "1988, Barry Levinson."

"If we want to get high, I could get us some," Treece offered, adding for the boys' benefit, "My dad's a lawyer."

Denis, incredulous: "Your *dad* gives you pot?"

"Uh. *No.*" Treece huffed. "His *clients*."

The prehistoric but cool song faded as a pretty pianissimo crossfaded up. *That* pretty pianissimo. All of the blood that hadn't coagulated in Denis's face drained out.

"I don't know how that song got in there," Denis dissembled. "Into that mix. I don't even know how I got it, must have been a compilation or something."

Beth was merciful. She signaled to Cammy, making walking fingers. Cammy shook off the sign. Beth gave a more adamant thumb jerk. Cammy sheepishly grabbed Treece's wrist and pulled her from the car. Rich joined them, glad to not be around when the first line of the song struck.

Beth, I hear you calling . . .

In the distance, Denis heard a chortle and a whinny.

THREE TEENAGERS WALKED after midnight down an isolated road known for its dungareed maniacs and zombie hookers. Rich, recognizing the sudden genre switch from raucous teen comedy to teen slasher pic, was a little jumpy. He reassured himself that either Cammy or Treece, probably Treece, would go first, and that as the comic relief he had a better than fifty percent chance of ending up being the killer, who might die, but only temporarily.

"Why are we walking?" Treece complained. "When I get my own car I'm never walking anywhere again. My dad was going to give me his old car but then that stupid cunt Cheryl crashed hers."

"That's what you get for splitting up your parents."

"Mean, *mean.*" Treece turned to Rich. "Never admit your innermost fears to Cammy."

Rich didn't respond. He was preoccupied, toeing the middle of the road, eyes darting right to watch for plunging bloody pitchforks, darting left for oncoming bosomy corpses.

"I don't see what's so spooky," he said, affecting an air of unspookedness.

"They say the succubus Gwendolyn wanders in a white teddy," Cammy related a recent addition to the Tobacco Road canon, "looking for virgins to deflower and devour."

"Not *my* problemo," Rich lied. "Anyway, it's not like we're trapped in a house or on a boat or in the woods miles from civilization. There's all sorts of ways to run."

"Oh my god!" Treece gasped. *"Look!"*

Rich's feet left the ground. They made a jerky paddling motion as if trying to tread air. He landed offkilter, and his "What?" came off less curious than craven.

Cammy indicated: "Cow."

Through the mist Rich could make out the silhouette of some creature, possibly a cow or a Hellbeast. It was about fifty feet off the road, standing in a meadow, increasing its cow chances.

"Let's tip it!" Treece was delighted with her own suggestion.

Rich tried to think if succubi could take cow form. Not in *Flesh for the Beast* (2003), or *Sorority Succubus Sisters* (1987), or *Necronomicon* (1968). There really weren't very many great succubus movies, Rich decided. He felt a sharp pain in his side.

It was Treece's elbow. "*Tip* it!" She pointed emphatically at the cow.

"Me? It was *your* idea."

"You're the guy."

"More or less," said Cammy.

"You know, these challenges to my sexuality are just *wrong*," Rich said, marching toward the cow.

DENIS WAS GETTING A GOOD LOOK at his lap.

Oh, Beth what can I do?

"Here," he told his crotch, "let me change it."

He fumbled in his pocket for his iPod. A hand pressed against his chest. He looked up. Beth was smiling at him.

"I was named after this song."

"You were named after a *Kiss* song?"

Beth fell back in her seat. "My parents were, you know, headbangers." She half-laughed. "Still are, kinda."

Denis's parents were normal kids who became normal adults with normal jobs. His father was an information systems analyst and his mother did freelance graphic design for progressive causes and products. So normal Denis had never given them much thought. But now Denis wondered what his life would be like with head-banging parents, being named for a song by a band who dressed in black-and-white face, spat blood, and whose other hits included "Lick It Up" and "Love Gun."

Beth was gazing through the windshield.

"I'm sorry," Denis said.

Beth sipped her beer. "Why?"

RICH HAD NOT NOTICED the barbed wire fence at first and this had caused a slight delay. He was now in the field, approaching the west face of the cow, not nearly fast enough.

"Go, go," Treece insisted. "Go!"

Rich turned around, tamping his hands as he stepped backward, "Don't . . . wake . . . the . . ."

PLORP.

Rich felt his shoe sinking into a thick mud that was not mud. It made a wet sucking sound, pulling his foot in deeper. He had stepped in quickshit.

He jerked his leg up. Balancing on one foot, he inspected the befouled area. It was bright yellow, the exact color of his socks. In horror, he looked down. The cow plop had swallowed the toe of his shoe and was methodically oozing up the tongue, threatening to breach the rim. He reached down to rescue it, lost footing, hopped and

SQUITT.

THERE SHE WAS, feet on the seat, arms around her knees, rocking back and forth, not at all in time to the music. Denis had something to say but decided to wait until the song was over in about twenty seconds.

"Beth," he jumped in anyway. "I lied before. About this song. I mean, I wasn't expecting to be listening to it with anyone, you especially . . ."

Beth opened another beer. "Life's full of surprises."

"Not mine," Denis said. "Usually."

Beth turned off the car; the radio went silent. She swiveled toward Denis. She swigged her beer and perched the can on a kneecap.

She was staring into Denis's eyes, not saying

anything, but asking something. Denis didn't know what, and didn't care. He couldn't get enough of this eye-to-eye stuff.

And yet, just below Beth's eyes, her knees were ten inches apart.

It took all the willpower Denis possessed to not look up her skirt. *You've seen everything there is to see down there*, he told his visual cortex, *there's no need to—*

Hello.

spoke the panties.

Beth closed her knees without calling attention to Denis's pubic snooping. She smiled at him in a tentative way.

"So . . . why me?"

Denis had never considered this question, putting it on a very short list of unquestioned aspects of his universe. Beth Cooper was an axiom, an irreducible truth, like the sky being blue (though the latter is a more complex phenomenon, involving the differential scattering of electromagnetic radiation by particles with dimensions smaller than the wavelength of the radiation, as Denis exhaustively lectured Mrs. Anclade in the third grade). The choice of Beth Cooper was simple, and pure, and for Denis's purposes here, completely inexplicable.

"You?" he said after much too long a pause.

"Why not Claudia Confer? She's prettier than me, and a *lot* nicer."

"I don't think she's . . ." Denis began compiling a Beth Cooper vs. Claudia Confer Benchmark Comparison, but lacking sufficient data, he said the only thing that came to mind.

"I didn't sit behind Claudia Confer."

Beth laughed, dribbling beer onto her chin. She

wiped it off and licked her fingers. Denis decided that if reincarnation was real, through some heretofore undiscovered nonquantum mechanism, he would like to come back as one or more of Beth Cooper's fingers.

"You never even *talked* to me," Beth said.

"You didn't seem too interested." He stated a truth he had successfully repressed until now. "I'm surprised you even know who I am."

"I know who you are!"

Beth had two distinct memories of Denis Cooverman:

Denis, at a blackboard, finishing an equation. He turns around, his fly open, stars on his underpants;

and

looking up Denis's nose as he says, "I love you, Beth Cooper."

Beth took a long slurp of beer. "How could I *not* know Denis Cooverman?"

RICH SCRAPED THE SIDES OF HIS SHOES along the grass as he approached the cow in anger. Earlier he had no beef with this specific cow, was merely going through the motions of tipping it. But now it had attacked him, indirectly, and it was going down.

The cow stood there, eyes closed, legs locked. This was the secret to tipping cows: they were fast asleep yet completely rigid. One push and they were sideways cows.

Rich positioned himself at mid-cow and placed his hands on its side about two feet apart. He pushed. The cow's belly gave slightly but its hooves remained firmly in the meadow. He shoved. The cow remained upright.

"Use your physics!" Treece advised from the sideline.

Rich repositioned his hands closer together, bent his head down, and put his back into it. He switched his feet back and forth, marching in place to gain a hold, and then running, his shoes spinning on the shit-slick grass.

He went down.

"Little help, ladies?"

CAMMY AND TREECE WERE LAUGHING at Denis again; he could hear their merriment in the wind. It was quiet in the car. Beth had stopped talking, the music wasn't playing, and Denis didn't know what to do. Before tonight, he had never spoken to Beth without her speaking to him first. He had had plenty to say, much of it well-rehearsed, but when the opportunity arose to say it, he had always *pussed out,* in Rich's helpful analysis. The lone exception had been graduation, and even then he had been careful not to look in her eyes, knowing that if she had seemed the slightest bit upset or saddened or repulsed by his declaration, his heart would have arrested and his face would have bounced off the lectern as he crumpled to the podium, dead. Or thrown up at the very least.

There were her eyes now, two delicious dog's breakfasts, watching him from behind a sixteen-ounce can of Pabst Blue Ribbon.

What was she thinking?

"What are you thinking?" Denis asked, cheating.

"Nothing."

Goddammit. That was all he had.

How could that be? Denis spoke nine languages, three of them real, had countless debate trophies (16), had won the Optimist Club's Oratorical Contest with a speech the judges had called the most pessimistic they had ever heard. Was there no romantic line, no conversation starter, no charming anecdote, no bon mot, no riddle or limerick he could pull out of his ass right now?

He swallowed some beer. And it came to him. Alcohol was amazing.

"We *did* talk," Denis said, arguing with something Beth had said nearly seven minutes earlier. "You borrowed a pencil once. You signed my yearbook."

Beth allowed the pencil, but "When did I sign your yearbook?"

Alcohol was a bastard, Denis realized. "Seventh grade."

"What'd I write?"

"I don't—"

"You remember."

He remembered:

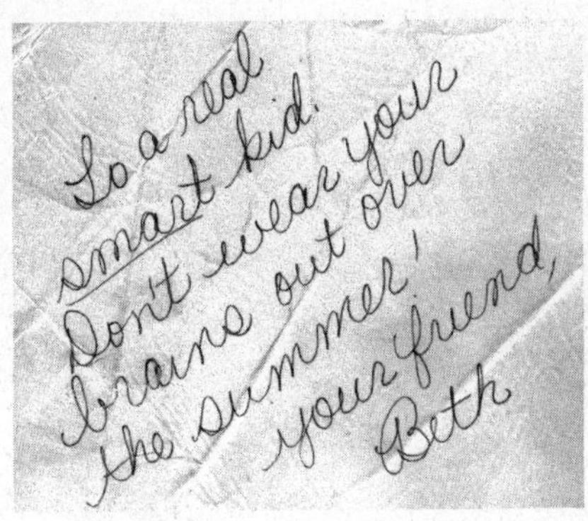

Denis cringed as he recited it, and left off *your friend, Beth*, because it was already sufficiently pathetic.

Beth put down her beer. She reached out and touched Denis's shoulder. "I'm sorry I led you on."

Denis almost thanked her for the apology, but read her eyes, and laughed. So did she.

This was going incredibly well. Denis was determined to keep it going until he figured out a way to destroy it.

"So, we can talk *now*. Here, how about: what are you doing after graduation? I'm going to, it's this six-year combined pre-med/med-school thing. After that I'm not sure if I want to practice or maybe do research . . ."

Beth retrieved her beer. "Hey, good luck with that."

"So, where are *you* going?"

"I dunno." She finished the can. "Maybe Harper's."

Offering credit courses in:

Applied Porcelain Sanitation;

Certified Dining Assistance;

Apparel Folding Science . . .

"Oh," Denis said. And: *"Yeah?"*

"Maybe. If I can afford it."

There, that wasn't so hard. It only took him thirty seconds. Not a record, but a solid effort. Denis couldn't determine what was worst, his dweebish braggadocio, Beth's disturbing educational plans, or that his condescending horror at them was so obvious.

"I have to pee." Beth got out, walked behind the car and squatted out of view.

Denis sat in the car, not sure of anything, only that he hated himself, and listened to her pee.

TWO GIRLS AND A BOY lined up along the cow.

Treece sniffed. "Don't these things ever take a shower?"

"Sh," Rich hushed. "Okay, on four."

"Four?"

"You want to supervise this project?"

Cammy demurred.

"Then, on *four*."

Cammy was almost as bad as Denis, Rich thought. Almost. Denis was a real killjoy. He could construct a timeline between any idea and fatality. This had prevented Rich from pursuing many intriguing notions, such as sticking Alka-Seltzer up his butt (at seven, Rich had never heard of an embolism, but Denis made a convincing case against wanting one). Rich chafed at Denis's brain ruining all their fun, and by mutual agreement went to amusement parks without him, but the doom-modeling had saved Rich's life on at least five occasions:

the "Super Juice" made from Orange Powerade, *Batman Returns* cereal, crushed Superman vitamins and topped with Mr. Muscle oven cleaner (age 5);

the reenactment of the mining car chase from *Indiana Jones and the Temple of Doom* (age 9);

the *Harold and Maude* fake suicide reenactment and sympathy ploy (age 14);

the bulk-up and get-revenge plan predicated on taking "steroids" supplied by Henry Giroux (age 16);

the April Fool's Day Columbine "gag" reenactment (age 17).

Tipping a cow was less potentially deadly than any of the above, but Denis's joy-killing might have proven useful here.

"Uno, dos, tres, catorce!"

On *catorce*, they all began pushing and Cammy muttered *quatro*. Had Denis been there, he would have pointed out it was nearly impossible to tip a cow, for the same reason Treece could not sleep on her stomach: ballast.

"This is stupid," Cammy grunted.

Denis would have agreed. Because, in addition to the mechanical difficulties of overturning an underslung half-ton object, cows can't lock their legs and they don't sleep standing up. This cow was just resting her eyes, and though she was laid-back, even for a cow, she had come to the conclusion that these people weren't going to go away by themselves. Her head turned with remarkable swiftness, her muzzle close enough to Rich's face that her whiskers tickled his lips when she screamed, *"Moo!"*

A HIDEOUS SOUND followed by a shriek disrupted absolutely nothing in the Cabriolet.

"What was *that?!*"

"Sounded like a cow," Beth said.

"A *cow?* That was no . . . ordinary cow."

Beth was deep into her fourth beer. "You're not afraid of cows, are you, Denis Cooverman?"

"Vaccaphobic?" Denis shook his head. "Of course not."

"Jesus fuck!" Rich sprinted out of the mist and hurdled into the backseat, winded. Cammy and Treece, falling over each other with throaty and nasal laughters, staggered up a few seconds later. Treece had to lean against the trunk with both hands to keep from passing out with amusement.

"What's wrong?" Denis asked.

"What's so funny?" Beth asked.

"Nothing's funny," Rich wailed. "A cow bit me!"

"Cows can't bite," Denis said. "They lack upper incisors."

Rich jabbed viciously at a fantastically large hickey on his neck. "Well, *this one fucking could,* Tiny Einstein!" He had never called Denis that in front of anyone else before.

Cammy traced a nail along Rich's throat. "It's just a love bite." She puckered her lips next to Rich's ear. *"Moo moo moo moo moo,"* she cooed.

"Hey," Rich said, "what if it was a mad cow?"

"She was pretty mad," Treece agreed.

Cammy gasped dramatically. "You're going to turn into a werecow." She glanced up, saw the full moon, and gasped again.

Rich turned to Denis, with need and regret.

"*Now* you want my expertise?"

"Yes. Please."

"There hasn't been a confirmed case of bovine spongiform encephalopathy in the United States for four years," Denis uploaded. "And even if this one did have mad cow disease, it can't be transmitted by biting, which cows can't do."

Beth's cute nostrils flared in an unpretty way. "What's that smell?"

Rich said nothing.

Cammy directed Beth's attention to the backseat. "He pooped his shoes."

Beth did not allow poop in her car. "Lose the shoes."

"These are my best shoes!"

"Well, now they're shit."

"I *paid* for these shoes!"

"They go," Beth said, "with *you* in them, or not."

Rich got out of the car. He shuffled to the side of the road, slipped off his shoes, and got back in the car. Treece and Cammy settled in around him.

"So!" bubbled Cammy, rubbing her palms together with camp perkiness. "And what have our head cheerleader and Tiny Einstein been up to?"

That didn't take her long, Denis noted. He didn't know she was saving *Dick Muncher and The Penis* for later. *What had they been up to?*

Were they connecting, opening up, sharing, in preparation for making out, or were they merely dancing around one another with Denis doing the herky-jerkoff?

"We were just—"

"Storytime!" Beth announced.

13.

SUBURBAN LEGENDS

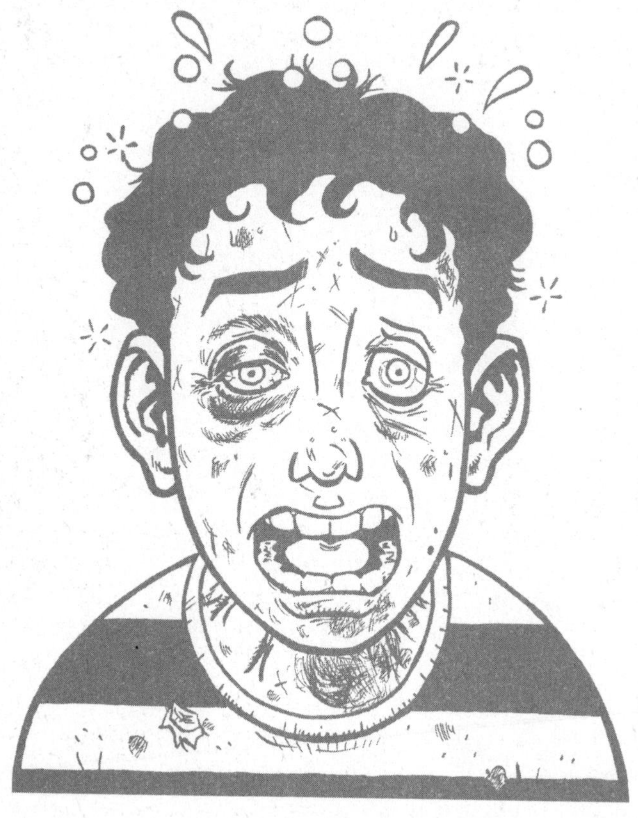

HOW COME YOU DON'T HAVE ANY STORIES?
I'VE GOT LOTS OF THEM,
AND YOU DON'T HAVE ANY.

MICHELLE FLAHERTY

TREECE CLAPPED. She loved Storytime. Cammy smiled, too, in a slightly sinister way, Denis thought. Beth nestled her beer between crossed legs. She raised her hands, a call for silence. Her eyes widened. Her voice was soft but urgent.

"It was thirty-three years ago tonight . . ."

Treece began to sing,

Sweeeeeeet emohhhhhhtion

Cammy backed her on drums,

Dit-dit dah-dah dit-dit dah-dah

This was quite a production. Denis felt privileged they would go through all this trouble for him.

". . . on this very road," Beth continued. "A VW bus was parked in this exact spot."

Denis could see the bus. It bore a remarkable resemblance to the *Scooby Doo* Mystery Machine.

"It's a moonless night."

Denis killed the moon.

"Inside, this hippie and his chick . . ."

Denis had always identified with Velma, but took on the Shaggy role. He cast Beth as the hippie chick who stuck flowers in rifles in his Anti-American History class (its official name was "The History of Patriotic Dissent: Boston Tea Party to Kent State" and was taught by Ms. Calumet-Hobey, who probably should have worn a brassiere in the seventies).

". . . were smoking this humongous bong."

His seventies bong knowledge being limited, Denis improvised something psychedelic with a bright yellow smiley face on the bowl.

"The chick starts to tell this story . . ."

Hippie Beth spoke but Treece's voice came out.

"So, it was, like, the fifties, man."

Treece was the perfect hippie chick, but Denis was disconcerted at the sudden change in narrator.

Cammy and Beth sang,

One o'clock, two o'clock,
three o'clock rock . . .

This wasn't the first time the girls had told this story. Denis felt a little less special.

"And like, this, '57 T-Bird comes to a stop in this exact spot, dig?"

Denis questioned the use of *dig* but re-dressed his mental set. Big-finned coupe, sock-hop rock, and for some reason, the fifties were in black and white.

"And this dude, like, tells his lady he's out of gas . . ."

The biker jacket and ducktail looked good on Denis. Beth wore Chantilly lace and a ponytail all hanging down, with a light pink sweater and magenta poodle skirt. An ice cream soda with two straws sat between them in a historically inaccurate cup holder.

". . . and then he tries to get groovy."

Groovy was entirely the wrong word; at any rate, Denis was way ahead of her. His greaser doppelgänger took bobbysoxer Beth into his distressed leather arms and—

"She's not copacetic with that, and, like, bags him and tells him to go get gas . . ."

"Wait," Denis protested, "is this 'Hook Man' or 'Trippin' Hippies'? You're mixing up your urban legends."

"Shut up," Beth said sweetly.

Denis shut up. In the backseat, Cammy and Treece quietly secured their seat belts. Rich didn't notice; he was mesmerized. It was like drama club, only the girls were popular and didn't cry all the time.

"So the chick is totally alone in the car . . ."

Totally an anachronism.

". . . and she, like, turns on the radio to keep her company."

Out of the radio came Cammy. "Hey all you cats and kitties," she growled in a truly remarkable impression that large-print readers will recognize as Wolfman Jack. "News flash, baby: a deranged killer with a hook for a hand has escaped from the local mental hospital!"

This was awfully elaborate, Denis thought; it must be a skit they did at cheerleading camp or something. Rich, meanwhile, was upgrading his opinion of Cammy.

"Now here's the Surfaris, y'all!"

Treece mimicked the deranged falsetto perfectly:

Yihahahaha hahahaha . . . Wipeout!

Okay, now it was just weird. Never mind the Surfaris didn't come along until the sixties . . .

Denis looked over at Beth. She was sitting forward, her hands on the wheel; the engine idled quietly.

"Just then," Beth picked up the narration, breaking the story-within-a-story structure, "there's a scratching at the door!"

Cammy did the scratching, quite effectively.

Didn't Beth turn off the car a few minutes before?

"The girl is so freaked out, she . . ."

Beth stepped on the gas.

THE CABRIOLET HAD EXCELLENT PICKUP. It helped that they were going downhill at a fifty-degree angle. The car plunged into the toxic haunted fog.

And then Beth shut off the headlights.

Denis heard himself scream. His teeth were clenched so tightly the scream was reverberating in his sinus cavity and coming out his nostrils, he hypothesized, and then realized the scream was coming from the radio.

We don't need no education . . .

There had been a family argument over whether to include this song in Denis's Commencement Mix. His mother felt it was bleak and arbitrarily antiauthoritarian; his father argued that Pink Floyd kicked major ass. A stupid dispute, Denis thought; this was the perfect song to die to.

We don't need no thought control . . .

The girls all shrieked as the convertible swooped through the dale of the hill and began rocketing up the next one. Rich shrieked, too, but clutched the broken seat-belt strap to his chest as if, well, his life did depend on it.

Denis had automatically fastened his seat belt when he climbed into the front seat and had never unfastened it. He was now trying to remember whether this Cabriolet came equipped with passenger-side airbags.

"BETH!" Denis shouted. "WHAT . . . *MODEL YEAR* . . . IS *THIS CAR*?"

She turned, hair in her face, lashing her eyes and nose.

"TO THE FUTURE!" she screamed.

Denis looked to the immediate future. Fog crashed against the windshield, scrambling in skittish rivulets to the corners. Visibility was zero. They were going to crash into whatever might be in front of them; for example, another car full of idiots. They were on a Highway to Hell, or Heaven, or the Endless Abyss that Denis's head and heart kept arguing about.

As if in answer to his ambivalent prayer, the mist swept away as the car climbed out of the ground cloud, and Denis saw they were headed straight for the moon. It loomed huge and yellow at the top of the hill, casting a cold shadowless light on the road before them. It was a small comfort that he would now be able to see what killed him.

All in all, it's just
another brick in the wall

Unlike most people his age, Denis did not feel the least bit immortal, and so did not enjoy impending death as much as the average teenager. Nor could he understand the appeal. He looked over at Beth. She had stopped singing. Her hair floated behind her. Her expression was neither happy nor sad. She blinked. A tear streamed sideways across her cheek. It was just the wind, Denis thought. After all, there were tears in his eyes, too.

All in all, you're just
another brick in the wall

BETH SWITCHED the headlights back on as the Cabriolet crested the hill, conveniently illuminating the car parked directly in their path.

She swerved.

The front of the convertible sailed clear but the end fishtailed. It careered into the parked car, screeching along its side. Beth slammed the wheel right and the Cabriolet whipsawed completely around. It skidded backward for about a hundred feet before coming to a stop.

We don't need no—

Beth killed the ignition. A high-pitched sound permeated the car. Denis's mouth was open slightly. He swallowed.

"Sorry. I was unaware I was . . . emitting that."

Beth pressed a finger into her eyebrow. "Denis Cooverman, please stop apologizing for being you." She turned to the backseat. "Anyone dead?"

Cammy was straightening her clothes and Treece was reapplying her lipstick. "Not yet," Cammy reported.

Rich clung to the belt. "Never been more alive." He tried to let go of the strap but could not.

Denis was palpating his abdomen for signs of internal bleeding when it occurred to him, "The airbags didn't go off."

"I sold those years ago."

"Isn't that illegal?"

"If it isn't, I got ripped off."

A metallic groan redirected Denis's attention through the windshield. It came from the car they had just hit, a late-model black Prius.

"Oh . . . crap."

The crumpled rear door of the Prius whined open and Denis's father backed out. He staggered, not because he was injured, but because his pants were around his ankles. Denis's mother emerged after him, scooting into her slacks.

"Hey," Rich pointed out. "*Meet the Parents!*"

Denis exhaled deeply. "I had a lovely time this evening," he addressed his friends, old and new. "But now I must die."

He started to unbuckle his seat belt.

"You do not," Beth said, restarting the car, "want to talk to your dad when he's not wearing pants." She shifted into reverse and peeled out. The car's headlights disappeared into the mist as a thousand English schoolboys sang,

Hey, Teacher! Leave those kids alone!

"KIDS!"

Mr. C zipped his pants. "Goddamn kids!"

Mrs. C rubbed the back of his neck. "Still wish our son was more 'normal'?"

"Not if *that's* normal."

Mr. C got in the driver's seat and pressed the POWER button. The car made a long unfriendly beep.

"How could we be *out of gas?*"

14.

WHO'S SOIREE NOW?

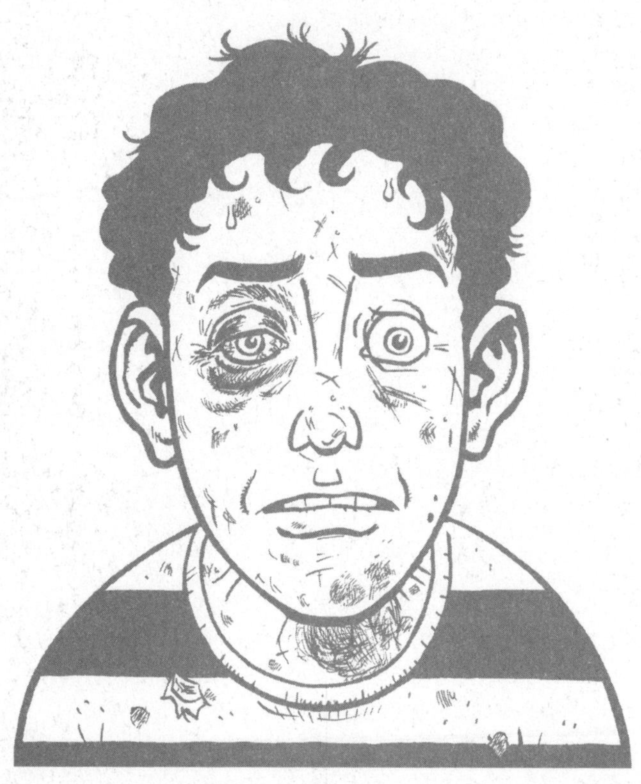

MONEY REALLY MEANS NOTHING TO ME. DO YOU THINK I'D TREAT MY PARENTS' HOUSE THIS WAY IF IT DID?

STEFF MCKEE

VALLI WOOLLY LIVED in Duxbury Woods, an unwooded area that used to be part of Berkley Square before a developer tore down a bunch of $300,000 homes and put up a bunch of $1.4 million mini-estates in their place. Duxbury Woods out-fauxed all the other local English countrysides—Devonshire, Amberleigh, Manchester Green and even Canterbury Fields—with an authentic British duck pond that had to be constantly restocked with rare Aylesburys, on account of their being quite loud and delicious. The "private community" also adopted somebody's idea of Her Majesty's address system; Valli Woolly's house was located on Croydon-on-Duxbury, with no number, just a name: Heathbriar. Thus, a letter addressed to:

Valerie Woolly
"Heathbriar" at Croydon-on-Duxbury
Arlington Heights, IL 60004

got thrown in the undeliverable bin with the rest of the irritating mail.

Beth circumnavigated the main Duxbury loop three times, prompting two 911 calls, before locating the Croydon tributary, marked only by a hand-painted rock. Heathbriar was easy to find from there, being the only tract mansion with all its lights on at 1 a.m. and a valet parking kiosk in front.

Heathbriar was neo-Georgian, meaning it had red brick on the front. It was otherwise a 6,000-square-foot conglomeration of awful architectural ideas throughout history executed in twenty-first-century Vulgarian; chief among the offenses was a wall-to-wall, floor-to-ceiling bay window that cantilevered out like a body-builder who spent way too much time on his abs. The steroidal terrarium was presently overpopulated with high school students.

"Shit my panties," said Beth, dropping her keys close to the hand of a valet. She had never been to Valli's house, nor had anyone else in the car, nor had pretty much everybody already at the party. Valli was not much liked. This party wasn't designed to change that. It was designed to make all those people feel like poor morons.

"Weird," Rich said. "In the movies, the rich bitch is always the popular one."

"We're not in the movies," Cammy informed him.

"*I'm* popular, and *my* dad's rich," Treece said. "I mean, he has to hide it. From my mom. And that stupid cunt Cheryl. But he *has* to be rich. Some of his clients are *kingpins*. And *I'm* popular."

No one said anything, making Treece suspicious. "What are you trying to say, Cammy?"

"I didn't say anything."

"What are you trying to *not* say? That I'm not popular, or I'm not rich?"

DENIS STARED at Valli Woolly's house with a Denis look on his face.

"Maybe I should just wait out here," he said.

Cammy patted his head. "If she attacks, go for her throat. She'll be protecting the nose."

"Cammy," Beth reprimanded. Her expression was hard to read. Her brow knitted and her lips curled up on one side and down of the other. "Denis Cooverman."

Denis figured out what it was: *affectionate frustration*. The kind a girl might have for a piddling puppy or a goofy boyfriend, annoying but still lovable.

Beth's head drifted in and out; she placed the heel of her palm against Denis's shoulder blade and put some weight on it. "Would you like me to take you home, Denis Cooverman?"

Oh, Denis refigured it out, *she's drunk*.

"I can walk. It's only a mile."

Beth jerked her hand away with a *whatever* flip. She pointed at Cammy and Treece, then pointed at Valli Woolly's house. "You know," she said over her shoulder, "she's probably pulling a train by now. She won't even know you're there." With that, she strutted up the walk, Cammy and Treece beside but also behind her. Her hips swayed in a wide irregular pattern. She stumbled, and Cammy caught her by the elbow. "Fucking bricks," Beth said, and went inside.

Denis watched through the bay window as the crowd greeted the appearance of the Trinity with cowering and hushed exchanges. A pack of guys swarmed over the girls, absorbed them into the partying mass, and they were gone.

Rich put an arm around Denis's shoulder. "We walking?"

"As long as we're here. What the F—"

They approached the party.

"So," Denis said, "Valli Woolly pulls trains."

"Dude," Rich said, "we went to the wrong high school."

IT WAS LOUD. The entertainment for the evening was a black MacBook operated by Zooey Bananafish, an exotic-looking sophomore who claimed to be half Thai and half Cherokee (She was half Thai and half something, at any rate). Zooey charged $300 to bring her laptop to parties and press ▶. She was charging Valli an additional $300 because she didn't like her, and because Valli was insisting on a playlist that perversely only included songs with *friend* in the title. Right now Mr. Woolly's $45,000 MAXX Series 2 speakers wept as they faithfully reproduced the microdynamics of a wirelessly streamed crappy pirated mp3 of every twelve-year-old girl's favorite Queen song,

You're my best friend.

This would be followed by Mariah Carey's "Anytime You Need a Friend," the Kelly Clarkson and Justin Guarini version of "That's What Friends Are For," the Rembrandts' "I'll Be There for You (Theme from *Friends*)," that Vitamin C song that wouldn't go away, several other dollops of sugar pop, and then finally, before she kicked everybody out, Fall Out Boy's "Champagne for My Real Friends, Real Pain for My Sham Friends."

Zooey wore softball-sized headphones, through which she was listening to Thelonious Monk.

IT WAS CROWDED. Of the 513 graduates in the class of 2007, 509 of them were in this house. (Luke and Matthew Andreesen were both in prison, on unrelated charges; Heather Lally was in labor; and Josh Bernstein thought he was at Valli Woolly's but was still at home, toasted.) In addition, there were a hundred or so graduating seniors from Adlai Stevenson and John Hersey High Schools, a few dozen BGHS juniors and underclassmen, and a handful of female eighth-graders who, unfortunately for Mike Bogar, did not look like eighth-graders. All of them were yelling to be heard over the music, which Zooey had started at 90 dBs and was increasing by one decibel every ten minutes. In about an hour, the people nearest the MAXX 2s would start falling down.

AND EVERYBODY WAS TOUCHING. Denis traced an epidemiological path from the foyer where he was, up the double-curved staircase teeming with intertwined limbs, and across the mammoth, two-story front room that held a writhing, sweaty beast with two hundred heads.

"This is a good way to get impetigo," Denis yelled to Rich.

"She invited *band* people," Rich shouted back. "She invited *mathletes—but not us!*"

Valli Woolly invited no one. She had disinvited just enough people ("I have to keep it small") for word to get around. She wanted everybody to be crashing, so that they would all feel unworthy and she could eject anyone at any time. She was that much of a bitch.

"Look," Rich yelled, "an ice bison."

From his disadvantage point, Denis could see only backs, shoulders and the occasional female head. He toed his way up the crowded staircase to get a better view. He wasn't interested in the ice bison.

The Woollys had spared no expense in lording their wealth over a bunch of teenagers. In front of the bay window was laid out a gratuitous buffet, offering top-dollar antipasti and crudités, chip, crackers and ethnic breads, along with dips, salsas and rémoulades that disconcertingly only came in BGHS school colors, orange and blue. Next to it was that ice bison, decorating a champagne fountain that had been spiked with green-apple-flavored vodka earlier in the evening by Scott Nigh. And adjacent to that was a pony keg, which was getting all the traffic.

"Your party was better," Rich yelled, and disappeared into the crowd.

BETH WAS EASY TO SPOT. Everybody in the room was oriented toward her, sort of orbiting her, radiating out in circles of diminishing popularity. Denis estimated he was in the Kuiper Belt, out there with Pluto, not even a planet anymore.

The innermost circle consisted of Treece and Cammy

and seven guys Denis recognized from various locker-room towel-snappings. In most direct competition for Beth appeared to be Dave Bastable, all-state tight end and nerd tripper, and Seth Johansson, soccer star and deer killer. Beth had apparently forgiven Seth his vehicular Bambicide, judging from the way she was laughing at every goddamn stupid face he made. Dave would not be so easily cockblocked, however; as Beth finished one glass of fortified champagne, Dave was ready with another. Seth said something pithy or at least short, punctuating it with a simian grin, and Beth laughed and laughed. Dave left to get more alcohol.

Reality had returned to its usual programming.

DENIS SIGHED slowly and continuously until he was completely deflated. He felt not defeat, but release. He was philosophical: he had gotten more than he expected and, frankly, deserved. He had been straddled by Beth Cooper. He had spoken to her panties. He had been kissed on the cheek, patted on the head, talked to and laughed with. He had also been beaten with human bones, choked to near death, and crashed into his parents.

Denis had had two hours with Beth Cooper, and he should be simply grateful he had survived it.

With that epiphany all of Denis's systems went off high alert, his adrenals dropped to normal, and he at once felt exhausted, hungry and with a tremendous need to urinate.

He would pee, eat and sleep, in that order.

"Whup," a body said as it fell on him from above, escorting him through the air the four feet to the floor.

Denis was on his back, probably broken, and the body was on top of him. It was a big body and it smelled like beer, but also cherry and flowers and wintergreen. "Sor-ree," the body said and reared its head, redistributing its significant weight to Denis's bloated groin. "You 'kay?"

The body belonged to a big girl who Denis recognized as someone from the murky middle of his class, not smart or dumb, popular or pariah, or any category he could use to recall her name. He had seen her in the library. *Jane? Emily? Charlotte?*

"Hey," the Big Girl said, "you're that dork who gave that creepy speech!"

"I'd like you to get off of me."

"Please."

"Please."

"Woof!" the Big Girl barked and licked Denis's nose with a thick yeasty tongue, twirling the tip in one of his nostrils. She lumbered off him, pushing one hand, and the other, into his bladder to steady herself. By the time she was upright she had forgotten he was there and kicked him slightly in the kidney as she stumbled over him on her way to the pony keg.

Denis decided not to wait until the ambulance came and got up himself.

THE LAST BIG PARTY Denis attended had a bouncy house, in which Debbie Bauman had given him a bloody nose that lasted for three days. He stopped going to parties after that, around the same time he stopped being invited to them.

And yet, as he poked and prodded his way through this party, he felt oddly at home. More precisely, he felt like he was back in the halls of BGHS during passing period; he was in a hurry and nobody else was going anywhere. Life after high school was identical to high school, evidently; the people were the same, if slightly better dressed, arranged in the identical dyads, triads and quartets, all holding red cups. That was different. Yet for all their legendary powers, the red cups had done nothing to loosen the brackets of the teen taxonomy they had all lived inside since the sixth grade. No jock had his arm around any stoner, sharing a heretofore unknown common appreciation of *Hong Kong Fooey;* no hot chick was making over any mousy fat girl; no brainy nerd was heavily petting any popular cheerleader who had been won over by the depth and everlastingness of his love.

Denis chuckled at how naive he had been, up until three minutes ago, and was keenly reminded that laughter was not recommended on a full bladder. Feeling greater urinary urgency than he thought biologically possible, Denis squeezed past Eric Gallagan and Brett Pister, two future business administrators arguing over whether Valli's father made his money in commodities or derivatives (he owned fourteen KFCs), sidestepped Eric's twin sister Julia, who was talking to Alicia Mitchell about the relative merits of Alicia's ninety-two-year-old Nana just dying already, and frantically wriggled around an intransigent Goth brood, all of whom were mutely glowering and mentally dismembering every body at the party including each others'.

Denis finally saw an open door and, knowing he would pee in there whether it was a bathroom or not, dashed inside.

There was a toilet, which was nice if not strictly necessary. There was also, staring right at him, Valli Woolly.

SHE WAS EVERYWHERE. There were photos of Valli Woolly on the walls, small cameos of her cluttering the sink, and, above the toilet tank, a large oil painting done by Nelson Shanks, who did Princess Diana's official portrait, according to the *Philadelphia* magazine article that was framed just below it.

Denis stood before the painting and tried to urinate.

He couldn't. Valli Woolly's eyes seemed to be following his penis. The pain, slightly past excruciating, only exacerbated the problem. His entire urogenital system was experiencing a fatal error; he would have to reboot. He closed his eyes and wiped away the image of Valli Woolly watching him pee. It was replaced by the image of Lady Di watching him pee. *This is just like that "Don't think about Pink Elephants" paradox,* Denis thought. And soon enough he was thinking of pink elephants and whizzing like one. It felt tremendous. It didn't sound right, though.

Denis opened his eyes and redirected the stream into the bowl. Fortunately, he hadn't hit any of the Valli Woollys. He would mop up later. He looked around the room, musing on whether turning your downstairs guest bathroom into a shrine to your daughter was an act of love or depraved parenting. Maybe both. The photodocumentation was unpleasantly complete:

Infant Valli sitting on a cloud dressed as an angel, nothing being cuter than a dead baby;

Toddler Valli, plump and happy right before being put on her first diet;

six-year-old Valli faking her first smile, commemorating her tooth-losing debut, the missing chiclet entombed in a separate mat;

assorted girl Vallis seemingly photographed to accentuate her childhood nose, which mysteriously fell off at summer camp when she was fourteen;

Sweet-and-Sour Sixteen Valli, shortly after breasts miraculously appeared on her over Christmas break;

Malibu Valli, Paxil Valli, Hair-Extensions Valli, Celexa Valli, Liposucked Valli, Stairmaster-Abusing Valli, Ears-Pinned Valli;

Equestrian Valli, standing next to Spencer, her personal horse, his gigantic black schlong snaking up the back of her jodhpurs . . .

That couldn't be right. Denis finished his business and took the photograph down. The schlong was anatomically incorrect and a recent addition, judging from the **stuK** carefully inked into the corner of the frame. Denis tried to rub the offending appendage off with his thumb. Stuart Kramer only worked in permanent marker, it seemed. Denis spat on Valli Woolly and pressed harder. Imagining he was getting somewhere, he placed the frame on the counter, spat twice, and rubbed as hard as he could with the heel of his palm. The glass cracked.

"Fine," Denis said aloud, "if that's the way you want it." He wrapped a towel around his hand and smashed the glass. He picked out the schlong shards and tinkled them into the toilet. He then placed the frame on the ground, as if it had fallen off the wall.

Denis found it supremely ironic that he was doing all this to protect Valli Woolly, after that vicious whispering campaign she financed against him when they both ran for student council vice president. He uncovered the dirty trick when one of the hired lips came up to him in the hall and said, "You know that Cooverman kid? My uncle's his doctor. Says he's got that disease where you don't have any pubes. That's why he doesn't go to gym." That her own henchmen didn't know who Denis was suggested Valli was wasting her money. Nevertheless, Denis assured his own defeat, over Rich's strenuous and colorful objections, by writing a letter to the *BG Charger* denying he had Kallmann's syndrome but arguing it shouldn't matter if he did as the presence or absence of pubic hair had no bearing on the duties of student council vice president, and that his gym attendance was not significantly below average. *Charger* editor Dana Musgrave illustrated Denis's impassioned defense with a photograph of a hairless micropenis she had found on the Internet. Dr. Henneman confiscated all copies of the paper, except for a dozen or so, which were enough. Denis and Valli subsequently lost by spectacular margins to Steph Wu, who handed out fortune cookies reading VOTE WU VP FOR STUDENT PROSPERITY.

DENIS WAS ON HIS KNEES, carefully arranging unmarked shards in a statistically likely scatter pattern on the floor, when he heard the door open behind him, then shut.

The smell of lunch meat and salad dressing permeated the bathroom.

"Good evening, Greg," Denis said without looking. He rose to his feet, his back still to the door. He sighed, and turned.

Greg Saloga's face was as large and red as it had ever been.

"Go ahead," Denis said. "If somebody's going to kill me tonight, it should be you. You've earned it."

Greg Saloga's lip spasmed with rage. His hands reached for Denis's throat. They went past it. He dropped his big tomato head on Denis's shoulder and began to cry.

Denis's relationship with Greg Saloga was complicated. It had begun in the fifth grade, with threats and extortions, and had gotten physical in middle school. The usual bully-pantywaist dynamic. Then came high school. While other young thugs left behind the childish pleasures of brute violence and graduated to the more sophisticated sociopathologies of torment, terror and pain as theater (wedgies, swirlies, et al.), Greg Saloga did not have the mental toolbox for psychological abuse and could not understand the appeal of physical assaults designed to deliver more humiliation than pain. So he kept doing what he had been doing to Denis, figuring it was either him or small animals, and that led someplace bad. Denis wasn't happy with the stunted arrangement, but convinced himself that being Greg Saloga's punching bitch protected him from the state-of-the-art degradations that were visited upon Rich nearly every day. It didn't, but that's enabling for you.

And now Greg Saloga was bawling all over him, taking their relationship in a whole new sick direction.

"How did you know?" Greg Saloga wailed.

Denis reviewed the inner monologue he had attributed to this sorry mess on his shoulder:

"I am cruel and violent because I was unloved as a baby, or I was sexually abused or something."

Denis hoped it was the *something.* He wasn't prepared for either of the other conversations. What he didn't know was that Greg had already had those conversations with Becky Reese, his very special date for the evening. Over the past eleven hours Becky and Greg had shared ice cream and tears; Greg had admitted dark terrible things and Becky had assured him that he was still a good person and that he was loved. She would spring Jesus on him tomorrow.

And so, Greg Saloga was not looking to Denis for answers. He wanted forgiveness.

The blubbering went on for some time. Denis stood still, soaking up Greg Saloga's pain, a little afraid of what might happen if he tried to wrap it up. In the meantime, he concluded that Valli Woolly looked better with her old nose. It was very British royal family, a shame she lopped it off. Her new nose was too small for the available space, floating like a tiny sailboat in a sea of cheek.

After what in real time was less than two minutes, Greg Saloga lifted his head. He looked stricken. "Did *I* do that?" He reached tentatively for Denis's face, and pulled back, repulsed.

"No," Denis said. "An accident. Series of."

"Sometimes I don't remember doing it," Greg Saloga said.

"I'd have that looked at," Denis advised.

"Yeah," nodded Greg Saloga. "Can I call you? To talk about it?"

"Sure. Or maybe a trained professional would be better."

"Hug," Greg Saloga said. He hugged. "Hugging's good," he snuffled. Then he blew his nose on Denis's shirt.

Outside the bathroom, Greg Saloga checked to see if anyone had noticed them exit together. Satisfied no one had, he viciously twisted Denis's tit.

"Ahgg!" responded Denis.

"You're lucky I'm in a generous mood!" Greg Saloga yelled for the benefit of everyone, swaggering away.

Denis was ready to go home now. He would leave through the back, so as not to disturb the gang bacchanal Beth was no doubt hosting in the front room. *Wow,* Denis thought, he had gone from smitten to bitter in less than an hour; he was healing remarkably well.

THE KITCHEN was unnecessarily immense, as no one in the Woolly family ate anything with the exception of Mr. Woolly, and all he ate was scotch. It was done in Country Quaint, with lots of milk green and white cream slopped onto fresh-cut wood cabinets and floors that had been given "a story" by a guy named Tommy with a motorcycle chain. The endless counter space was covered with the asses of thirty party girls, dangling their legs like bait for the school of party boys who were rotating through the selection counter-clockwise. It was less deafening back there, meaning the girls could understand the inane things the boys were saying to them. They didn't seem to care.

Denis wandered into a sales pitch Henry Giroux was giving two sophomore boys who were not yet onto Henry Giroux.

"You got any X?"

"What you wants is *f*-X," Henry Giroux said. "The *Effexor* be inhibitin' the reuptake *fo'real.*"

"How about acid? You got any acid?"

"The Ritz been known to cause some serious hallucinatin'."

"If you're into imagining insects and snakes crawling on you," Denis kibitzed.

"Whoa," the first sophomore said.

"How much?" inquired the second one.

GLANCING AROUND THE KITCHEN, not looking for Beth at all, Denis's eyes stumbled upon huge brown boob tops that to his amazement belonged to Divya Gupta, his debating partner. She was across the room, wearing a party sari that was missing some essential drapings, accentuating her zaftigitty in a way that wool pants and white Oxford shirts never did. Her black hair was unbound from her skull and fell nearly to her waist. She was attended by two males, neither of them dweebs, who were obviously from another school and did not know her alter ego as Denis's studious but loose-lipped sidekick. So *this* was what those leibfraumilching New Trier guys wanted, and not her negative constructive. Denis considered the proposition that while he had been off chasing an angel, the real woman for him was right in his own intermural backyard.

Their eyes met from across the room.

She gave him the finger.

"Let us vow to never again choose indulgence over excellence, whether it be getting sloppy drunk, revealing secrets and betraying our partner, or something else."

The wounds were still too fresh. He would try her again at Mr. Peterson's Declaration of Independence and Rebuttal barbecue in July.

DENIS WAS ALMOST TO THE DOOR when he noticed the phone. He should call, he thought, to spare his parents the additional twenty minutes of anguish it would take him to walk home, or better yet, get them to come pick him up.

It went straight to message. (There were already several messages from neighbors wanting to know what the hell was going on over there; and three from Denis's mother, saying they were stranded on some old road on account of his father always having to relive his glory days, and where was her son, at which hospital?) "I guess you're asleep," Denis said, *or still publicly fornicating,* he shuddered, "but I just wanted you to know I'm on my way home, and . . . I have an explanation and . . . I love you. See you soon, or in the morning. Love you."

"Le Coove!"

Rich ambled across the kitchen, carrying two plates heaped with nosh.

"Check it out," Rich yelled. "Pedophilia!"

Denis was still holding the phone. "There's no pedophilia here," he said quickly into the receiver and hung up. "Where?"

In the pantry a compact balding man in pink polo shirt and black warm-up pants had cornered Annabelle Leigh, technically now a sophomore. He was acting sophisticated and older-mannish, tossing a five-pound bag of sugar from hand to hand.

"I always thought he was gay," Rich said.

"Coach Raupp?"

"The way he always watched to make sure we took showers. Which just goes to show, my gaydar sucks donkey dick."

Rich handed Denis one of his plates. It was filled with all of Denis's favorite party foods, carefully arrayed in the approximate order Denis would eat them. It was like they were married.

"Thanks."

"Hey, did you know they call us 'Dick Muncher and The Penis'?"

"I can't say I'm surprised."

"So, hey, *¿Dónde está Elizabeta?*"

"Wherever." Denis folded some blue hummus into his mouth to underline his ennui.

Rich swirled a bluish chicken wing in some orangey honey mustard. "Told you that speech was a good idea."

"What are you talking about? What that's happened tonight could possibly be construed as 'good'?"

"Closure, dude. If you hadn't given that speech, you would've never found out what a scary whackjob Beth Cooper was, so no other girl would ever measure up to her mythic proportions, and the one you ended up marrying because she got pregnant or your mom was dying, she'd be haunted and tormented until she had such low self-esteem she'd be willing to put on a cheerleading outfit and a Beth Cooper mask just to get some conjugal pipe."

"Do you write these things out or do they just *flow* out of your ass?"

"Improvisation *is* writing."

"Well. She's not a scary whackjob." Then: "She's not a whackjob."

"Don't backpedal, dude. Onward. *¡Vamanos!* In fact, your new unrequited obsession might be at this very party. And speaking of, did you see Gupta?"

"She has lady parts, evidently."

"Talk about your hot and spicy curry coconuts!"

"Coconut curry is Thai, Rich, not Indian."

"I'll remember that the next time I have to write a term paper about international boobs."

"Oh, no," Denis said.

Rich saw it, too, but his reaction was less dread than uncontainable glee.

"Your secret shame!"

PATTY KECK just happened to wander up, unconvincingly. She was with Victoria Smeltzer, or as she was known in the girls' locker room, Skeletori. Patty was wearing hip huggers and a belly shirt, neither of which was a good idea. Victoria had on a black shift and so much foundation it was disconcerting to see her upright.

"I didn't expect to find *you* here."

"Patty."

"I *loved* your speech, Denis," Victoria said. "You said some *very perceptive things*."

Patty redirected her friend at Rich. "Richard, you know Victoria?"

"*Certanamente*," Rich said. "You've lost weight, Vick."

Victoria bared her see-through teeth. She bowed her head shyly, and noticed Rich's stocking feet. "You're not wearing shoes."

"Nobody wears shoes anymore," Rich said.

Victoria swooned, though it may have been her blood sugar.

"Denny," Patty said, using the special name Denis hated. "What happened to your poor face?"

Denis did not immediately answer. Patty, he knew from experience, did not require responses in order to keep a conversation going. Instead, he was thinking, *This is my rung.* This was where he was going to spend the rest of his life, in regrettable grapplings with women he was ashamed to be seen with, women who were his social and physical equals. Denis had dared to court the sun, and for this hubris he was hurtled back into the muck. He was the Icarus of love.

"—all purply and icky yellow," Patty was yammering. "Greg Saloga beat you up, I'll bet. Did you see him here with that wheelchair girl? What disease does she have again?"

Denis had a horrible thought: What if Patty Keck was it? What if hers was the only tongue ever to enter his mouth, rooting around like a dog with his head in a bucket of chicken? Or, what if Patty got that stomach stapling she always talked about, and it turned out she really would be cute if she lost forty pounds? That would be the end of him, most likely. Patty would move up to average-looking guys, and with Rich spending all his time with Skeletori over there, Denis would be alone.

"Valli Woolly *paid* someone to beat you up! Is that what happened?"

Patty paused, meaning Denis could speak now.

"Uh, no," Denis said, mentally sorting his accumulated wounds in correct chronological order. "First—"

"The Coove had a little dustup with Beth Cooper's boyfriend," Rich interjected.

Patty Keck's eyes slat. *"Beth Cooper."*

"Yeah," Rich casually falsified, "her ex-boyfriend, army, dark ops, couldn't stand the idea of Beth and the Coove together. So it came to blows. You think this is bad, you should see him."

Denis liked this scenario much better than the truth. "I feel terrible about it," he went along, shaking his head sadly. "He's at the hospital. I hope he makes it."

"Actually," Victoria said, "he's upstairs."

15.

THE DEAD KID

I THOUGHT THIS WAS
A PARTY! LET'S DANCE!

REN MCCORMICK

"WHOA, THE TIME!" Rich said, glancing at his bare wrist. "My female fiancée is getting off her shift, at Hooters, and we promised to meet her."

Denis was struggling with the back door. It was locked, dead-bolted, to prevent any of Valli's so-called friends from messing in her father's authentic English garden with its valuable antique gnomes.

Rich grabbed the back of Denis's shirt and yanked him in the other direction. Denis waved noncommittally as he was dragged away. "Nice seeing you."

"Me, too," Patty called after him.

THE FRONT DOOR TANTALIZED DENIS, three cliques ahead. He just needed to get past the French Clubettes, slurring the best French of their lives, some gearheads, not so surreptitiously casing the alarm system, and the mathletes who had made it just inside the door and stayed there. Denis could almost smell the safety of his home, of his bed, where he intended to spend the next ten weeks before leaving for Northwestern, where even the football players were his size.

Two large hands clamped his shoulders from behind, and spun him around.

"Will you remember me?"

It was the Big Girl, only she seemed bigger.

"I will remember *you*," she said, and then sang it,

> *I will remember you . . .*

Then she remembered him, "Hey, you're that creepy dork who gave that creepy dork speech!"

Despite or perhaps because of this, the Big Girl cupped the back of Denis's head and mashed his face into hers, prying his mouth open with her strong, sinewy tongue. She pillaged his teeth and tonsils with a voracity that made Patty Keck's frenching seem coy.

Plus, there was suction. Denis once had a dream like this, involving Gardulla the Hutt, which did not end well. He tried to tear himself loose, but found that every move sucked him deeper inside her.

"Hwuwuw," Denis said.

Rich interceded, wedging a forearm between their necks and jimmying them apart. The Big Girl undocked with a wet pop, shook it off, and then fastened onto Rich. Rich grabbed her by the ears, and through a series of tugs and twists dislodged her. He steered her groping maw away and tossed it into the French Clubettes, where it lip-locked onto Elizabeth Nagle, who protested only momentarily.

ALL THAT STOOD between Denis and reaching adulthood was Ian Packer. Packer still had a wild hair up his butt about Denis's refusal to join in the mathletics program, which he felt had deprived him of a divisional championship. Denis declined participation because Packer made team members wear YEAH, I'M A MATHLETE T-shirts and even Denis had some status consciousness (named Rich). Packer contended the real reason was that Denis didn't have the r^3s to see who was the true Euclid of the class, Denis's barely more perfect SATs notwithstanding. So whenever the occasion arose, as it did now, he liked to hurl a fiery equation Denis's way.

"Riddle me this, Cooverman," Ian Packer said, blocking the front door. "If x is an integer—"

"Not now, Packer."

"Oh, come on, this should be easy, for the *valedictorian*."

"*Seven*, okay?"

Tragically for Ian Packer, the answer *was* seven. He stood aside.

Through the open door, Denis saw the rest of life. It

was dark, and getting chilly, but there was Rich, waiting for him on the porch.

A SCREAMING CAME ACROSS THE ROOM. It sounded inhuman, a car alarm or air raid siren, but very clear in its meaning.

"Asshole!"

The shriek was piercing enough to be heard throughout the house, even within the killzone of the MAXX 2s, even under the ear cups of Zooey Bananafish, who, sensing this party was finally happening, pushed ⏸. The sudden loss of sound pressure popped ears across the room and created an aural vacuum; all anyone could hear was the persistent ringing they would be hearing for the next two or three weeks, if they were lucky.

Everybody looked to the staircase, the source of the scream. Valli Woolly stood about halfway down, in a stylish but easily accessible black tube dress. Lined up behind her on the steps were Kevin, Sean and the third Army Man.

Across the room, Cammy said what Beth was thinking.

"Choo choo."

DENIS COULD HAVE RUN AWAY. He could have crazy-legged it out of there, escaping under cover of ducks, humiliating himself in front of his entire class and for many classes to come. He could have done that. And he would have been happy to, but that bastard Ian Packer slammed the door on him.

Rich reopened the door just as Kevin's cavalry arrived, placing both him and Denis in elaborate and internationally unacceptable chokeholds.

Kevin took his time coming down the stairs. His fury had dissipated, having unleashed a good portion of it on a thirty-four-year-old male nurse who would not tell him where Beth was or explain why he had her cell phone. Nurse Angell had also begrudgingly supplied Kevin and his troops with a deluxe assortment of pills he'd been skimming off invalids and the elderly. Accordingly, Kevin moseyed up to Denis with his pain killed, mood elevated, and erectile function greatly enhanced.

"So . . ." Kevin grinned, his vocal molasses thickened into a treacly drawl, "we meet again."

Rich could not have been more delighted. "Blofeld in just about every Bond movie! Lon Chaney Jr. to Bela Lugosi in *Abbott and Costello meet Fr—*"

With a minor adjustment of his left index finger, Sean paralyzed Rich's windpipe. As if to further punish him, Kevin's next line was:

"Shall we dance?"

Using the reserve air left in his upper throat, Rich got out, "Jack Nicholson to Michael Keaton in—" before passing out. Annoyed, Sean disengaged his kill finger and shook the boy back into consciousness. Rich mumbled something incoherent, something like *urton.*

Denis had just thought of the perfect thing to say to Kevin, the thing that would keep everybody out of jail and the hospital, when Beth stepped between them. She had the saucy smirk and sloppy swagger of a person who thinks she has total command of a situation but really, really does not.

"Kevin. Stop this now." She raised a finger, but couldn't keep it stationary. "Let's just get you out of here"—she eyed Valli—"and get you tested for gonorrhea—"

Kevin took Beth's whole face in his hand. "Lisbee," he said, still quite friendly sounding, his thumb and forefinger digging into her temporomandibular joints. *"This isn't about you anymore."*

"Do you speak in *nothing* but clichés?" Denis blurted. (This wasn't the perfect thing he had been thinking of saying earlier.)

Kevin chuckled and roundhoused Denis in the abdomen, never letting go of Beth's face. Denis's arms were pinned back, preventing him from doubling over in pain but not the pain part, a sucking, searing, intensely special feeling that made Denis realize that he had never truly been punched in the stomach before, and that all the emotional setbacks he had previously compared to being-punched-in-the-stomach weren't all that bad.

"Oh, Denis," Beth said. This was the first time she had not used the affectionate yet trivializing *Denis Cooverman* construction, which Denis noted but did not dwell on, given more pressing matters.

"Promise," he said, "if he kills me, you'll break up with him."

Kevin placed a valet ticket in Beth's palm and squeezed her fingers around it. "Now why don't you get that pretty little drunken butt of yours in my vehicle," he gallantly ordered her. "And *sit* there."

Kevin moseyed off, signaling his soldiers to follow. They frog-marched Denis and Rich with them. Beth hung her head as Valli Woolly wiggled past.

"Gonorrhea?" Valli sniffed. "You *wish*."

ACTING ON PRIMAL INSTINCT, the partygoers pulled back to open a killing floor. Denis was dragged to the far end; Kevin assumed the lion position on the opposite side. Everyone politely awaited the bloodletting.

"Are you just gonna let this guy murder me?" Denis asked his classmates.

They were.

"Wait."

Valli Woolly wiggled over to Denis. She pushed into him, her breasts poking his chest, her nose stabbing at his face. Adenoids quivering, she hissy-whispered, "I am *not* worthless. Look at this party. Look at all my friends."

She smelled like masturbation.

Wiggling away, she waved regally and decreed, "Now you can kill him."

It was official. Denis was to be executed and no one would save him. Beth was gone, doing what she was told. Rich was seriously indisposed, and would be lucky to survive himself. Cammy and Treece were off to his right, Cammy with an expression that said, *This certainly is an awkward social situation,* and Treece mouthing, *Good luck.* Across the room, Patty Keck watched with worry and potato chips. Skeletori, beside her, snacked on no-fat fingernails. The Big Girl was holding hands with Elizabeth Nagle, wondering who the dead kid was. Ian Packer and his fellow mathletes lined the staircase, at a safe distance should the proceedings devolve into a wider geek beatdown. To Denis's left, a few rows back, Divya Gupta sat on the shoulders of two Stevenson gymnasts. Denis had never seen her smile before.

Valli Woolly's party had accomplished something. She wasn't the least popular person in the class anymore. Her parents would be so prou—

Valli Woolly's parents! Surely Mrs. Woolly wouldn't want Denis's common blood all over her Ethan Allen furnishings; Mr. Woolly wouldn't want Denis's skull smashed repeatedly into his thirteen-inch woofers and titanium dome tweeters.

"Help!" Denis yelled. *"Adults!"*

He'd have to yell louder than that. Mr. and Mrs. Woolly were at their condo in Cabo. Adult supervision had been left to Valli's twenty-three-year-old brother, Willie, who had taken his heroin for the evening and was in his bed passively participating in a threesome with Ryan Petrovic and Lucy Amo, who only discovered Willie after they were already deep into the proceedings, and were using him mostly for leverage.

Denis's call for adult help broke the tension. Everybody had a good laugh, especially Kevin, who kept laughing as he started toward Denis.

Denis's military escort shoved him into the killing zone.

"YO!"

DENIS KNEW THAT *YO!* He hated that *Yo!* He was so happy to hear that *Yo!*

Coach Raupp muscled his way onto the killing floor, man-walked up between the predator and his prey and placed a smallish hand on each of their chests.

"Okay, ladies, some ground rules . . ."

"Wait," Denis said. "You're not going to *stop* it?"

"All I want is a fair fight."

"Fair? He's a *trained killer!*"

"You should've thought of that before you raided his cabbage patch." Coach Raupp pistol-pointed as he said it. "Don't worry, Cooverman. Just remember what I taught you in boxing."

"I opted out of that unit!" Denis protested. *"I had a note!"*

Coach Raupp addressed to the crowd: "Let that be a lesson to you juniors." Then to the combatants: "No biting, scratching, hair-pulling, any other sissy business . . ."

"Head butting?" inquired Kevin.

"Go crazy. But once your opponent loses consciousness, the beating is over."

Coach Raupp stepped back, raising a hand.

"Aaaannnnd . . . *fight!*"

Kevin presented his fists, knuckles out. He hopped up and down, scissoring his legs back and forth, thrusting out his lower lip.

"Shall we dance?" he repeated for the benefit of those who had not heard him the first time.

The crowd loved it, at Denis's expense, as usual.

Kevin didn't seem very serious about killing Denis, not as much as he wanted to make the slaying fun to watch. Denis, unaware of the change in Kevin's pharmaceutical status, found this chipper villainy oddly disturbing, though not nearly as disconcerting as his opponent's rather noticeable hard-on.

"Yo!" Coach Raupp snapped his fingers in Denis's agog eyes. "Dukes up, Cooverman!"

Denis kept his dukes down.

"I'm not going to fight."

"Aw, Cooverman!" Coach Raupp screamed. "Don't be a pussy, you *pussy!*"

Denis was going to be a pussy. A pussy with a *plan.*

"Look, Kevin," he began, with the studied reasonability that had won him many worthless debate trophies. "You've won. You got the girl. I've been humiliated in front of all of my peers. I apologize and surrender unconditionally. Is that satisfactory?"

Kevin punched Denis in the mouth.

HE DIDN'T RECALL FALLING, but warm liquid had collected in the back of his throat, leading Denis to conclude he was supine. He swallowed and was slightly surprised to taste blood. He ran his tongue along the inner rims of his teeth. None was outright missing but two incisors on the upper left were loose. That side of his face burned and stung and ached and felt wet and sticky.

Denis opened his eyes. Zooey Bananafish was staring upside down at him.

"Any last requests?"

" 'Here She Comes' by Very Sad Boy."

Zooey's head exited and was replaced with a right-side-up Kevin face.

"Upsie," Kevin's face said.

"I'm bleeding. Happy *now?*"

In answer, Kevin reached down, took Denis by the shirt, and lifted him to his feet and two inches farther, dangling him on tiptoes. Adding insult to impending injury, Zooey Bananafish had overruled his last song request, replacing the downbeat dirge with some uptempo sino-blaxploitation. Kevin seemed to approve, pursing his lips with white-boy negritude and bopping Denis up and down to the beat.

" 'Battle Without Honor or Humanity,' Tomoyasu Hotei," Rich explained to Sean, "originally used in *Shin Jingi Naki Tatakai,* 2000, Junji Sakamoto, recycled in the chop-socky pastiche *Kill Bill, Volume One,* 2003, Mister Quentin Tarantino."

"Fuckin' A," Sean agreed.

Kevin continued to shake Denis like a maraca, apparently waiting to pummel him at the upcoming horn break. This was beyond embarrassing. It was sorry enough to be beaten to the delight of your peers; to be made to perform meat puppetry as your own premurder entertainment was at the very least unsporting.

"I am not your plaything!" Denis said, all pissy insistence. "Hit me or put me down!"

"Glad to oblige." Kevin cocked his fist.

Then, as is often the case with carefully planned military operations, something huge jumped on Kevin's back.

"Leave my friend alone!" Greg Saloga yelled, latching on to Kevin's eyebrow ridges and yanking hard. Kevin let go of Denis and staggered backward, spinning and stumbling as the big red boy clawed his face and throat. The third Army Man stepped in, and in a flurry of expert hand combat mixed liberally with playground flailing, disengaged Greg Saloga and secured his arms. This annoyed Greg Saloga. He screamed and threw his head back, butting his captor's eyes. The soldier fell to the carpet.

Sean released Rich and grabbed a crystal ladle from the champagne fountain. He swung it at Greg Saloga, who allowed the leaded glass cudgel to shatter harmlessly on his temple. Greg Saloga then harmfully kicked Sean in the testicles. Sean went down.

Coach Raupp stormed over to Greg Saloga.

"Yo, *time out,* Saloga—"

Greg Saloga punched Coach Raupp in the throat. He went down.

Kevin, in villain tradition, had stood back and watched his henchmen vanquished like henchmice. With the seething hulk of Greg Saloga now facing him directly, Kevin had the option of fighting this obviously less skilled and now exhausted boy, or honoring the other villain tradition and running away. Kevin began to edge back toward the door. There was no need. Greg Saloga glanced at the inert and writhing bodies around him and fell to his knees, letting out the most primal wail anyone had heard in a couple hundred thousand years. He covered his face and screamed into his hands, "Why must I . . . *hurt?*"

An electric whirr preceded Becky Reese as she maneuvered her wheelchair through the crowd and motored over to Greg Saloga. He grasped both wheels and dropped his terrible head into her withered lap. He sobbed, and she stroked his greasy hair, for wasn't he also one of God's creatures after all? And the only boy in the entire class who had ever voluntarily talked to her?

Everyone had forgotten about the execution of Denis Cooverman, and were caught up in the heartrending saga of borderline retarded Greg Saloga and his repulsive love for the genetically defective Becky Something, until Greg Saloga looked up and screamed, *"Stop looking at us!"*

Everybody stopped looking at them, and turned back to . . . *Denis?*

Kevin himself was surveilling the perimeter for his missing plaything:

Rich was at the champagne fountain, rubbing his raw neck on the ice bison . . .

some kid . . .

Cammy staring back with light contempt . . .

Treece with vacant evasiveness . . .

another kid . . .

nice tits . . .

Valli with a needy grin . . .

"*Yeeuh!* Stop breathing up my skirt!"

Kevin ratcheted back to Treece. She stepped sideways, swatting behind her, revealing Denis crouched there, breathing up her skirt.

Denis reflexively went back into debate mode. "Kevin, let's assess." The swollen lower lip and blood dripping off his chin undermined his rhetorical authority to some extent. "It appears as if I'm gonna require major dental work, which I think we can agree was your *ultimate* goal . . ."

Kevin did not agree. He started coming for Denis, and he wasn't laughing anymore.

Another huge something jumped on his back. This time it was the Big Girl. She was not trying to save Denis. She just thought it was a party game.

"Wooo!" she whooped, riding Kevin. "Wooooooo!"

From there it degenerated quickly. Assorted skirmishes, some four years coming, broke out. Eric Gallagan and Brett Pister mixed it up over their junior year Young Trump project, which failed because Gallagan used too much peanut butter or because Pister couldn't market fresh assholes at a homo convention. Jon Eggert had always wanted to punch someone and thought this the ideal cover; unfortunately he chose Aaron Farrington, who had just completed his black belt in Kuen-Do and had been looking for an ethically acceptable situation in which to use it. The gearheads started peeling the Mathletes off the stairs, one at a time.

"Yeeee-*ha!*" the Big Girl yelled in response to Kevin hurling himself backward into a wall in an attempt to dislodge her.

Stuart Kramer tried to get a food fight going, first by chanting "Food fight! Food fight!" and then by flinging a couple of fistfuls of corn relish around, but nobody took up the challenge, perhaps because once a class clown graduates, he loses all his power to amuse. Valli Woolly emerged from the bathroom, shrieking, "Which one of you degenerates pissed all over the floor in there?!"

In the midst of all this, Denis made his escape. He skirted along the buffet table toward the door, dodging assorted scuffles and avoiding anybody he might have referenced in his valediction. He had gone as far as antipasti, just flatbreads from the door, when he heard a monstrous bellow that seemed to be directed at him.

It was Kevin, of course. He lumbered under the Big Girl, lurching toward Denis, lunging with arms outstretched in the manner of classic monsters and zombies. Denis responded with a classic silent scream.

And that's when the front of Valli Woolly's house exploded.

THE INITIAL BLAST CAME from behind the buffet table, which upended in rather dramatic fashion, sending chip shrapnel across the room and spraying dips and salsas in less dynamic but more devastating arcs. Denis took a platter in the chest. The two-story bay window blew out at ground level, with the upper panes raining down in a cascading shatter of glass. All this was accompanied by the requisite screaming, shrieking, and religious conversion.

Everyone thought: terrorists. Because, really, what else was there to worry about? Valli Woolly immediately suspected those animal rights losers who wore bloody chicken suits in front of her father's restaurants, and, being Valli Woolly, was annoyed they would firebomb her party and not one of her father's boring business dinners.

It was a few moments before anyone noticed the large repurposed military vehicle sitting halfway in the living room.

"Go go *go go go*," Beth Cooper called urgently from the Hummer.

Kevin stopped bucking the Big Girl and simply gaped. The Big Girl swayed. "I wanna get down," she said, and threw up on Kevin's head.

Denis couldn't see what was going on, because his face had been blown off. Cold chunks of cheek or forehead flaps hung over his eyes, assuming there were still eyes under there. Denis thought about changing his specialization from neurosurgery to facial reconstruction, though it just occurred to him that the wet stuff on his hair might be brains. Denis heard Beth calling him, using his full name again. As he turned in the direction of her voice, the pieces of his face fell away and into his hands: roasted red pepper and hot *sopressata.* That would explain the smell.

"Denis Cooverman!" Beth called again.

Denis shook off his imagined injuries and started toward the Hummer, picking his way through the party carnage.

Something grabbed his ankle.

It was Coach Raupp, lying on the floor, holding his throat.

"Don't get in the car with her," he rasped.

This was excellent advice. However, Denis noticed some movement at his back, which he correctly suspected was Kevin. He yanked his ankle away and ran to the vehicle, its front wheels already spinning in reverse, spitting orange and blue hummus on everyone and everything. Denis only had one foot inside when the Hummer lurched out of the living room and onto the lawn with Denis suspended between the front seat and the swinging door. Treece and Rich pulled him inside as the Hummer crashed through the valet stand, killing no valets, and then roared through Duxbury Woods, upsetting the expensive ducks.

CELL PHONES FLIPPED OPEN throughout Valli Woolly's house. "Can you come get me?" a sophomore asked her mother. "Party ended early."

Kevin, covered in puke and defeat, couldn't believe it: that little shit had his girl *and* his car. Until that moment Kevin had been just playing, in his fashion. He was merely pretending to kill Denis, and was only going to continue killing him until Denis became convinced he was genuinely being killed, and then stop. This was Kevin's idea of a funny joke.

He wasn't in a joking mood anymore.

Kevin didn't even feel Valli Woolly beating him on the back, and he couldn't hear her screaming, "You ruined it! You ruined everything! I can't believe I gave you a blumpkin!"

Jacob Beber, bystanding, looked confused.

"Oh," Valli Woolly shrieked at him, "go Google it!"

16.

HOT NOSTALGIA

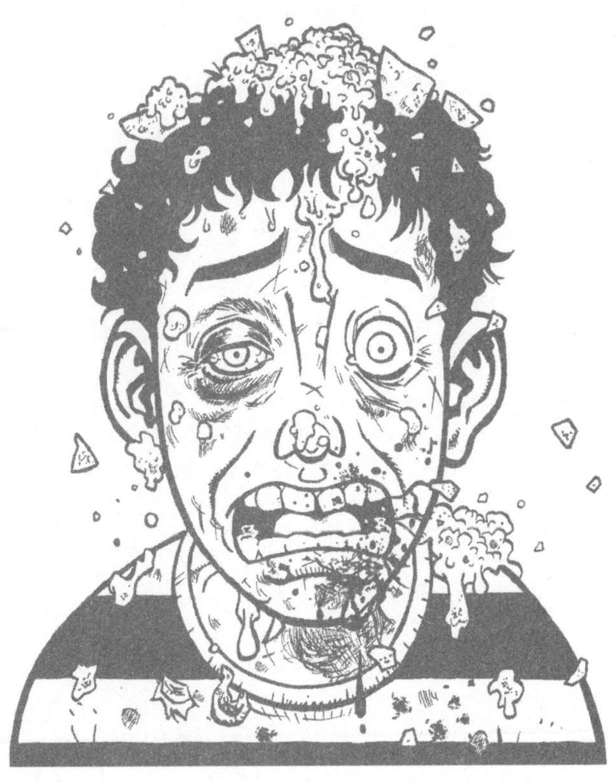

ALL I'M SAYING IS THAT IF I EVER START REFERRING TO THESE AS THE BEST YEARS OF MY LIFE—REMIND ME TO KILL MYSELF.

RANDALL "PINK" FLOYD

THE MOOD INSIDE THE HUMMER was mixed.

Beth was pumped up, drumming the steering wheel to some song playing only in her head. *"Wow!"* she kept repeating, with increasing insistence. *"WOW!"*

"Yeah," Cammy said flatly. "Wow."

"Was that not the coolest thing you ever saw?"

"It was very realistic," Treece said.

Rich was ambivalent. While the practical side of him recognized that driving a car into somebody's living room was going to attract a bunch of negative attention, his artistic side felt the movie of his life finally had the kind of action sequence that would make for a kick-ass trailer. "Great production value," he said.

Denis was pumped, too, but not up. *"Do you know how many laws you just broke?"*

By Denis's count:

Grand Theft Auto;

Criminal Destruction of Property;

Assault with a Deadly Weapon;

Aggravated Battery;

Leaving the Scene of an Accident;

Speeding; and, just now,

Failure to Signal.

"Seven—*at least!*"

"A new record!" Beth declared.

"I don't think that's a record," Treece said.

Denis took a closer look at Beth. Her eyes were bloodshot, rheumy. The tip of her nose was cute, and pink.

"Are you too drunk to drive?"

"Eight!"

Beth took her hands off the steering wheel.

"What are you doing?"

Beth crossed her arms. "I'm too drunk to drive."

The Hummer went through a red light.

"Nine!"

Denis took the wheel and successfully kept them from crashing into oncoming traffic, had there been any at two a.m., but in his zeal to survive he pulled too far to the right and started riding the curb. Beth grabbed the wheel back, swung the Hummer off the curb and into the relative safety of the left side of the road. "Where did *you* learn to drive?" she mocked.

"You're on the wrong side of the road."

"How do you know we're not in Europe?"

"*Please* drive on the other side," Denis pleaded.

"Beth, stop being a dick," Cammy added from the back.

Beth harrumphed and swerved the Hummer back into its lane, where it *baWHUMP*ed over something large.

"*Good call,* Denis Cooverman."

Treece glanced out the rear window, and delivered the good news: "It wasn't wearing clothing."

"Beth." Denis tried to sound calm and authoritative. "I think it would best if you pulled over."

"Fuck you." Beth didn't respond well to calm authority figures. "How about, *Thank you, Beth. For saving my life . . . again*?"

Denis had imagined that he and Beth would be one of those couples who never quarreled, that when they weren't kissing they would be laughing or lying in each other's arms, serenely, deliriously happy. He could never have imagined that she would make him so crazy angry he would scream at her in front of their friends. But in that instant, he learned a little about love.

"Saving my life?!" Denis screamed at Beth in front of their friends. "*Saving my*—? You almost ran me over with a military vehicle, owned by that homicidal rage ape you call a boyfriend who has thus far this evening attempted my murder with: 1) a hurtled microwave, 2) playground strangulation and 3) well, a beating . . . a *to-the-death* beating!"

Denis's cathartic breakthrough left Beth miffed. "You're spitting blood on me."

"You're supposed to keep your bodily fluids to yourself!" Treece admonished.

Denis covered his mouth. "Sorry," he said, reverting to Denis Cooverman.

"You forgot the skeleton attack," Rich pointed out.

"We missed that," Cammy said.

"It was pretty cool. Like *Karate Kid* meets *Pirates of the Caribbean.*"

"So," Treece addressed Rich, "you were making out with E. J."

"Who?"

"E. J. Charlotte? The best girls' basketball player in the country maybe? Big girl?"

"Her," Rich said. "I wasn't making out with her."

"It sure looked like you were making out. Denis, too."

"What are you, like a blogger now?"

"I just thought it was interesting. I mean, it was like, *almost* heterosexual."

"Yeah, that's right," Rich said, overdoing the sarcasm. "I'm trying to work my way back. When I'm ready for a real woman, I'll let you know."

"Okay," Treece said.

"MUSIC!" BETH DECIDED.

She turned on the radio, predictably tuned to US 99.5, America's Country Station, this month heavily rotating Sgt. Dirk Dugan's post-*Idol* debut:

Can't come home
Until we're done
'Cuz, baby, you know me
I don't cut and run

Beth fiddled with the dial. "87.1, yeah?"

"Yeah," Denis mumbled, resenting Beth for ignoring his outburst and rebuking himself for not following through on it, and for outbursting in the first place.

Beth caught the tail end of Cheyenne Kimball's cover of Chrissie Hynde's version of an old Rod Stewart hit, based on a song by Jakob Dylan's dad:

May you stay
forever young . . .

Beth liked the first three chords of the next song, or felt the need for noise, and cranked the Hummer with the petulant guitars and angsty beat of Happy Talk and their hot new power bummer, "Passing Through."

All these years and I'm alive
This town does her killing slow

Amid the emo cacophony, it got very quiet. They were driving down Dundee Road, which for the want of an actual downtown served as the main drag, a strip of malls, of chains and franchises, that collectively constituted what they conceptualized as their *town*, or to be municipally correct, *village.**

Takes you to her drying breast,
suckle sucks and won't let go,

Everything was closed but all the lights were on. The music and the hour and the drink made for a melancholy parade through their adolescence.

There was the Jewel-Osco where checker Cammy staved off workplace rage by mentally totaling the items she swiped endlessly across useless scanners, where Beth bought the family groceries, where Rich shoplifted his first *Premiere* magazine.

*Incorporated 1958.

There was the José O'Foodle's Rich got fired from, where Beth, Cammy and Treece went after basketball games and thirty-year-old guys with mustaches bought them ice-cream drinks, where Denis begged his mother not to picket the Szechuan Veal Stickers.

There was the AMC Loews Six where Denis and Rich saw *Star Wars I, II* and *III* at crowded midnight previews, where they saw *The League of Extraordinary Gentlemen* by themselves, where Cammy saw *Bring It On* in the sixth grade and inexplicably decided to become a cheerleader, where Treece was caught sharing a seat with a patron and got fired.

There was the old Starbucks, where they all acquired their first addiction.

That Curves used to be Comics & Comix, where Denis bought his comics and everybody else bought their paraphernalia. Next to Curves was a Baskin-Robbins where Mrs. Rama fired you if you gained more than ten pounds and where Rich worked the summer between eighth grade and high school after Mrs. Rama ran out of thirteen-year-old girls.

I was born here,
I won't die here too

On the left was the PJ Fingerlings Rich got fired from, and where Treece lost her virginity, out back. Next to it was the Blockbuster where Rich still worked, at least until the next time he talked a divorced father into watching *Sin City* with his twelve-year-old son. In the same strip was Payless Shoes, where Beth worked thirty-five hours a week, where Rich had bought his best shoes, currently composting at the side of Old Tobacco Road, and where Denis went shoe shopping more than necessary.

And just up the road was the White Hen Pantry where only three BGHS students were allowed in at a time, supposedly, and where Beth Cooper touched that guy's dick.

> *I'm not stayin',*
> *I'm just passin' through*

Denis had included this song based on its popularity and adherence to theme, but he didn't like it—*drying breast? suckle sucks?*—and moreover didn't understand it, couldn't grasp the desperate desire to escape your upbringing, to kick off the dust of crummy towns that rip the bones off your back.

Why would you want to leave, and if you did, what's stopping you?

Beth turned off the music.

"WE ARE THE BISON!"

They were passing the high school, and Beth was cheering, and clapping, and not holding the steering wheel again.

> *Mighty, Mighty Bison*
> *Say hey-hey, hey-hey . . .*

Maybe she really is a scary psychobitch, Denis thought, as he found himself screaming again.

"Put your hands on the steering wheel!"

Beth stopped cheering. She stared ahead sullenly and put her hands in her lap.

"Never take your hands off the steering wheel!" Denis screamed. "You *never* take your hands off the steering wheel! You keep your hands at ten and two! *Ten and two!*"

Denis took Beth's hands from her lap and applied them to the wheel in the proper configuration.

"*Ten* . . . and *two,*" he said in a tone that even he recognized as patronizing.

Beth gripped the wheel tightly, elevating her dainty wrists, and turned to Denis with a wide, iced smile.

"Better?"

"Eyes on the road."

Still looking at Denis, Beth executed an acute left, using proper hand-over-hand technique, at a speed that would have rolled over anything short of a tank, which was more or less what she was driving. As fortune would further have it, where she turned there was also an exit.

The Hummer pulled into Buffalo Grove High School's parking lot. Beth accelerated straight toward the school, all the while maintaining approved driving form. A few seconds before they would vault the curb and crash into the gymnasium, making the national news, Beth applied the brake aggressively, stopping with a satisfying skid, an inch from the sidewalk.

Denis was gripping the door handle with one hand and the chest strap of his seat belt with the other, a fairly typical pose for someone riding shotgun with Beth Cooper.

Beth, cordial: "You requested that I pull over?"

"Thank you," Denis said.

Beth opened her door and dismounted the vehicle. She began running toward the back entrance to the school. Cammy and Treece got out on their respective sides, and ran after her.

"What are they doing?"

"Something," Rich said, and jumped out to join them.

Denis did not like not knowing what he was doing, which he had already had quite enough of this evening. But, the alternative was staying in a stolen vehicle owned by a drug-addled maniac who had thrice attempted his murder. He arrived at the door just as Beth reached into her purse and produced a large brass master, the kind usually only found on janitors.

"You have a key?"

Treece answered for Beth. "Head cheerleader is a position of trust and responsibility."

"Fools," Cammy added.

DENIS WAS IN THAT DREAM, the one he would continue to have for the next thirty years: wandering through Buffalo Grove High School at night, everything the same and oddly off, comforting and disconcerting, a feeling that he needed to be here and didn't belong, that he had forgotten to prepare for *something*. At least, in the present version, he was wearing pants.

"Could I ask what we're doing here?" he asked Beth.

"Homecoming."

"At the risk of repeating myself and continuing to aggravate you, which is not my intention at all, you do know this is illegal."

Perhaps it was his tone, polite and petrified, that softened her, or perhaps she had slipped into a more mellow state of inebriation, but Beth gave him those *poor puppy* eyes again. "Denis Cooverman. This is the *least* illegal thing we've done all night. Relax. You're going to enjoy it."

She winked at him.

While he processed that massive emotional data dump, Beth and the others disappeared into the gymnasium.

THE GYM WAS HALF LIT, dusky and cool. The chairs from graduation were stacked on rolling carts, a few orange tassels scattered on the floor. The podium was still up. Denis wondered, if he had it all to do over again, knowing all the injuries and indignities that would befall him, would he still give that speech?

"Ready?"

Beth stood at center court, legs apart, arms akimbo.

Yes, he would, *yes.*

"Hit it!"

Beth, Cammy and Treece began to cheer.

Are you ready?
Ready for the best?
B-G Number One!
Oh yeah, nothing less!

Rich joined the girls. His moves were suspiciously perfect.

Going to the top
We can't be stopped
Let's go girls,
Yell orange . . .

They all stopped and looked to Denis. He was the crowd, apparently. He played along: "Orange."

Yell blue!

He yelled: "Blue!"

Mighty Bisons (oh yeah)
Let's fight!

Denis wasn't especially spirited or overly true to his school, but he choked up, a little. He would miss those basketball games, with those players whoever they were, winning or losing or whatever they did, and with Beth, there on the court and on the sidelines, smiling and jumping and, yes, bouncing. And he would never forget tonight, when she cheered one last time, just for him. That last part wasn't true, and he sort of knew it, but if you can't lie to yourself, who can you lie to?

The cheer, for whoever it was, wasn't finished.

"And now," Beth said, *"real slow."*

Cammy and Treece decelerated sensuously. It was as if the imaginary marching band accompanying them had vanished and been replaced by a seedy jazz quartet.

"Can you feel it?" Beth cooed.

"What?" co-cooed Cammy and Treece.

"Feel the *heat.*"

The girls bumped and ground in a not-for-game-day version of the cheer, the one they did at camp, or sometimes for a small audience of generous dates. Rich was thrown at first, but quickly got with the saucy program.

"Orange and Blue," Beth moaned.

"How sweet," Cammy and Treece and Rich rejoined.

Together they throatily chanted,

With spirit and spark
We steal the show
We're Mighty Bison

"Kiss Kiss," Beth meowed.

"Gotta go," the girls and Rich purred.

Treece, Cammy and Rich hopped up and down, clapping gleefully. Beth just stopped. Her shoulders dropped and her hands fell to her sides. She caught Denis noticing this and curtseyed.

Rich puffed out his chest in a halfway decent impression of Coach Raupp. "Good game, ladies!" With two crisp claps, he woofed, "Hit the showers!"

To Rich's surprise and Denis's astonishment, Beth shouted "Showers!" and trotted off the court. Treece giggled and pranced behind her; Cammy cocked her head in a *what-the-hell* and joined them.

Rich double, triple and quadruple took, mugging between the girls and Denis. "They're *hitting the showers!*"

Rich ran all the way out of the gym before having to run back in to get Denis.

17.

SKINNY DRIP

SAY "WHAT THE FUCK" . . .
IF YOU CAN'T SAY IT, YOU CAN'T DO IT.

MILES DALBY

"COME ON."

"What are you doing?"

"Come on."

"What are you *doing!?*"

"Come *on!*"

Rich was dragging Denis down the double staircase that led to the girls' locker room. From inside could be heard the giggly echo of girls taking off their clothes.

"We weren't invited."

"I'm pretty sure we were." Rich tugged.

"Rich, you don't have to prove anything."

Rich released Denis's wrist and went into the locker room by himself.

Denis watched the door close. He rubbed his wrist, contemplating the three-dimensional nude model of Beth Cooper he had rigorously constructed in his brain. Many data points were mere speculation, placeholders lifted from magazines and the Web, and it would be interesting to compare his hypothetically nude Beth Cooper with live field observations. It was what any true scientist would do.

"Muy chiquitas!" Denis heard through the door, followed by assorted girlish sounds.

DENIS STUCK HIS HEAD IN. Spinning blades did not decapitate him. He stepped all the way inside.

The girls' locker room smelled different than the boys', but less different than he thought it would; it was the same sour milk and lemon bleach mélange, overlaid with stale perfumes playing on a dozen piquancies simultaneously. The place smelled exactly like his Great-Aunt Peg.

Denis moved toward the giggling. The locker room was laid out, as he suspected, as a mirror image of the boys'. That meant, he calculated as he crept, the showers were just off the very next row of lock—

Beth Cooper's butt.

He saw it for only a moment.

At 2:32 a.m. on June 4th, in the two-thousand-and-seventh year of Christ (Our Lord).

A Monday.

It was more than perfection: more round, more buoyant, more everything you could want in an ass. It had a single, perfect flaw: a birthmark, on the right cheek, exactly where it would be if Cindy Crawford's face were a butt.

And then it was gone, with the rest of her, into the showers.

Denis had been so enraptured he only now noticed Treece at the end of the aisle, facing him stark naked as well as totally nude in addition to fully, frontally, *au naturel.*

"Come get wet," Treece said, and ran to join her two nakedly nude female friends.

Denis momentarily considered the possibility that he had fallen asleep watching Showtime Extreme.

"That invitation good enough for you?"

Denis also hadn't noticed Rich, on the floor at his feet, struggling to get his pants off without taking the time to undo his belt and unzip his fly.

"I don't know about this, Rich."

Rich was up, trying to undo all the buttons of his shirt at once.

"What's to know? Stop thinking with your brain, dude!"

The girls were laughing, shrieking and, apparently, slapping wet parts of one another.

"They're drunk."

"I know! We are *so lucky!*"

"I just don't want to ruin anything."

Rich was down to a pair of slightly irregular Tommy Hilfiger boxer briefs.

"Dude, first of all, there's nothing left to ruin, I regret to inform you. Except *this.* And this, my friend, is a rare occasion. Chances like this don't come along every day! In fact, they *never* come along! *This does not happen.*"

From the showers Treece singsang, "You guys *coming?*"

Rich pointed emphatically in the direction of the moist female pulchritude. "*Carpe diem! Seize the day, boys; make your lives extraordinary!* —Robin Williams, *The Dead Poets Society. Eat, drink and be merry, for tomorrow we die* —William Powell, *The Thin Man. You only go around once in life!* —Some beer commercial!"

"Tonight I'd be happy just to stay alive," Denis said.

Rich shook his head as he shoveled off his underwear. "You're not alive unless you're living."

"Who said that?"

Rich looked up, surprised.

"I think I did."

He ran to the showers, where he whipped out his Nicholson:

Heeeeeeeeeere's Johnny!

The girls whooped.

Denis stared down the aisle. Draped across the bench that ran lengthwise between the locker banks was a predictable progression of shoes, blouses, brassieres and skirts. And there, at the end, was a swath of white cotton with tiny pink lettering.

Hello.

it called to him from afar, welcoming him to the party.

The panties talked him into it. Yes, he was going to go for the gusto, *carpe* the *diem.* He was going to shower naked with three beautiful girls and his best friend. He was going to live. He certainly was!

Denis sat on the bench and unlaced his shoes. He removed his right shoe, then his left, and placed them next to one another on the bench next to him. He removed his right sock, then the left, and stuffed them into his right and left shoes, respectively. He stood up, unhooked his belt, and began carefully snaking it out of his pants.

"Hey," he heard Rich giggle. "I can do that myself!"

Denis whipped the belt from his pants like a ripcord. He dropped his trousers, quickly folded them over his arm, and opened the locker, looking for a hanger. A hand reached over and took the pants from his arm. Denis closed the locker door and there was Kevin, holding Denis's pants with one hand and punching him with the other.

Denis stumbled into the bench and fell onto it, landing on his back with his legs on either side. Blood poured from both nostrils in symmetric streams down his cheeks. Kevin swung one foot over the bench and stood astride Denis, looming above him.

Denis was confused. "How did you find us?"

"LoJack, dipshit."

"But *I'm* the geek," said Denis, truly aggrieved. "*I'm* supposed to use technology against *you!*"

Kevin wound up to deliver a face-changing blow, targeting the strike with cruel precision.

"Stop punching me!" Denis insisted.

Denis scooted on his back, in modified crab walk, sliding twenty feet until there wasn't any more bench. He launched off the end and *oofed* onto the concrete.

Still straddling the bench, Kevin speed-waddled down the aisle until he was once again on top of Denis. He reached down and

SWHACK!

"Jah!" Kevin fell back, grabbing his eye.

SEVENTY-FIVE INCHES of dripping freckles, packing two twisted white gym towels, thrust out a sunken chest.

"Taste my wet blade!" Rich cried.

Kevin came at him. Rich coolly snapped once, striking Adam's apple; he advanced, snapping both wet towels with synchronous precision, driving Kevin back down the aisle.

The girls rushed in behind him, gathering up clothing.

"Doyle, Klepacki!" Kevin screamed.

"Klepacki?" Treece vaguely recalled. "Oh, right. *Dustin.*"

Sean Doyle and Dustin Klepacki stormed in, hoping to see the female flesh Kevin had forbidden them (he was an abusive lout of a boyfriend, but a gentleman). To their disappointment, the only flesh on display was pale, red and male. The girls were wrapped in tiny towels that nevertheless left far too much to their meager imaginations.

Kevin pointed angrily at Rich.

"Aren't you going to say, '*Get them!*'?" cracked Denis, back on his feet. "Or, '*Bring them to me!*'?"

Kevin chose, "Kill them both!"

"Oh, boy!" Rich said. "Gollum in *LOTR: The Two Towers*—"

Sean and Dustin advanced. Rich sidearmed them both, snapping their outermost nipples.

". . . 2002, Peter Jackson."

They came again. Rich overhanded them in the mouth and ear, respectively.

"Also Vladislaus Dracula in *Van Helsing*, 2004, Stephen Sommers." Rich tossed a wet towel back to Denis, who caught it with unexpected élan. As Rich tactically retreated, Denis moved forward until they presented a united defense. "Go," Denis called over his shoulder.

"We can handle these three. We've been preparing for this all our lives."

Without even looking, Denis snapped Kevin in the belly button, which he knew from experience was exquisitely vulnerable.

THEIR FRESHMAN YEAR, Rich was on the receiving end of a mass towel-snapping that briefly landed him in the hospital. He feigned unconsciousness to halt the assault; the school nurse, who once sent a headachy kid back to class with meningitis, called an ambulance. The MRI, which his father was certainly not going to pay for, showed nothing, and Rich was sent home with a doctor's note that kept him out of gym for the rest of the year.

Rich vowed he would never again be the victim of this specific sort of attack, and dragooned Denis as his sparring partner. Together they developed the perfect *rat tail*, experimenting with rolling patterns and moisture levels; they discovered the most devastating towel was rolled wet, so tightly as to wring it nearly dry, and then resoaked just before use. They practiced on each other, first using Indiana Jones, the Skywalkers and the Bride Who Killed Bill as battle models, moving on to bullwhip fetish videos that weren't terribly useful, eventually graduating to enthusiast Web sites and barely legal books such as *Filipino Fighting Whip* (Tom Meadows, Paladin Press, $20), which taught Advanced Training Methods and Combat Applications based on the ancient martial art of Kali.

They got quite good.

Denis was not the towel master Rich was, but could hold his own, as evidenced by the double snap he had just applied to both of Kevin's cheeks, very nearly simultaneously. They were backing up the staircase, casting long shadows on the wall like some black-and-white guy from some old movie, with Rich supplying the matinee sound track.

"Dah dah *dah*-dah, dah dah-*dah*," he *Indiana* a cappellaed. "Dah dah-dah, dah dah dah-dah-*dah!*"

The army men, despite their combat experience, couldn't seem to outflank these two boys and their John Williams score.

"Dah *dah*-dah! dah *dah*-dah! Dah *dah*-dah! Dah dah-dah dah dah!"

Near the top, Kevin perceived an advantage and led a charge.

"Yaaaaaaaa—*ach!*"

Rich tagged him right on the tongue.

Kevin recoiled onto his compatriots and they all tumbled down the stairs together, landing in a hopefully broken heap.

"Classic!" Rich yelled.

"Great. Let's get out of here."

"You go." Rich assumed the heroic persona. "I can hold them off."

"They'll kill you."

"They don't want me. They want you. And I can run twice as fast as you can."

That was debatable, but with the forces below rapidly regrouping, Denis decided to accept the gesture as best as one teenage boy could accept the love of another.

He handed Rich his towel.

"I'd hug you, but you're naked."

"Understood."

18.

THE PUNCHLINE

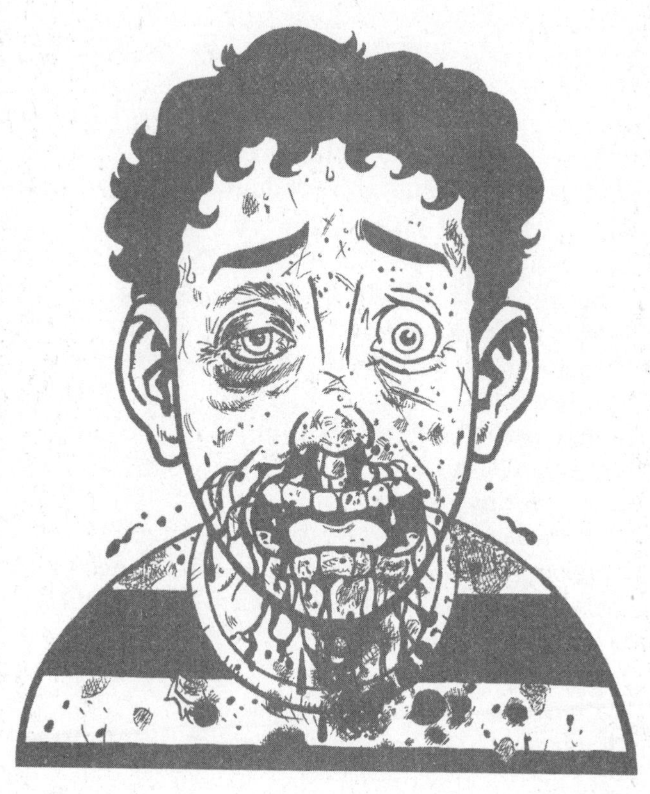

THAT WAS WAY HARSH, TAI.

CHER HOROWITZ

THE GIRLS WERE AT THE BACK ENTRANCE, discussing something, when Denis arrived. He was pinching his ruptured nose, to little stanching effect.

"What's ub?"

"We're fucked," Cammy said, summing it up nicely.

Flashing lights directed Denis's attention outside, where a police car was parked next to the Hummer. A Buffalo Grove peace officer had a clipboard wedged against her belly and was writing down license plate information.

Denis was about to be arrested. He was trespassing in his high school, and he wasn't wearing pants.

"It's like that dream," Denis said.

"Shush," Beth said. She pointed. Fifty feet from the Hummer, its wheels half up on the curb, was her Cabriolet. Kevin had taken it from the party, after Sean and Dustin had persuaded a valet that he didn't need a ticket. Denis had never seen it with the top up; it was a crummy little car.

"Come on."

"Come *what* on?" Denis asked.

Beth and the girls had slipped out the door and were darting between clumps of bushes en route to the convertible. Denis briefly balanced the positives and negatives of eluding the police with the positives and negatives of surrendering to the police multiplied by the exclusively negatives of the infantry men behind him, and followed.

BETH CRAWLED to the passenger side, the one facing away from the crime scene. She discreetly opened the door and climbed in. The others bunny-hopped and monkey-walked into the car. The stealth was unnecessary; the police officer was on the phone with her husband, telling him where the goddamn diaper wipes were for the five-hundredth goddamn time.

"Fuck," Beth whispered, finding no key in the ignition. She reached into the sun visor. "*Fuckety* fuck," she said, "fucker took the fucking *spare*."

Denis had never heard a complete sentence that was more than fifty percent *fuck* before.

"Listen," Denis suggested. "Maybe we should just—"

"Shut the fuck up, Denis!"

Beth reached under the steering column and popped a panel out of the dashboard. She fiddled with some wires. Nothing could surprise Denis at this point, and yet this did.

"You also hotwire cars?"

"Just this one. Sometimes my parents take away the keys."

The car started. Still hunched below windshield level, Beth put the Cabriolet into drive.

"Wait," Denis said, "Rich!"

"Forget him," said Cammy. "He's already dead."

"I can't leave without my friend." Denis reached for the door.

Beth grabbed his thigh in such a way as to not cause an erection. This was remarkable; Denis sometimes got erections from grabbing his own thigh. Beth was gritting her teeth and Denis saw something in her face he had never, ever seen before. She was desperate.

"Denis," she said. "I could go to jail."

You're going to jail anyway, Denis thought, *and you'll probably go to less jail if you turn yourself in.* But he knew a little about Beth now, and a lot about desperation, and so he determined this advice would likely not be received in the spirit it was given. He also knew he wasn't leaving Rich behind, which meant letting Beth go. Rich wouldn't approve.

Nevertheless.

Denis tried to think of an appropriate exit line, something romantic and yet manly, like *See ya in the funny papers, Funny Face*, except it would have to make some sense in this context and not use the same adjective twice. Ironically, if Rich were here he'd have the perfect line, only then it wouldn't be necessary. That was ironic, wasn't it? It was so hard to tell anymore.

Beth's desperation was beginning to take on exasperated and peevish undertones.

"I won't give you up," Denis said finally, too late to have any iconic impact, even if it hadn't come out as *I woe gib oo ub.*

Denis reached for the door again but the handle fell away. A long speckled creature clamored across his lap and into the backseat.

"We should probably go," Rich said.

HAD THE POLICE OFFICER been paying attention, she would have noticed the driverless convertible drop off the curb and slowly roll away. She was, however, dealing with a domestic disturbance. "Oh, well, *here's* an idea: you get a job that pays for more than your *goddamn beer* and then I'd be goddamn *delighted* to stay home and take care of *our child!*"

Through the rearview mirror, Beth could see the officer waving her arms and screaming into her cell.

"What's she doing?"

"She's calling for backup," stated Denis.

"HEY!"

The yell came not from the police officer but from the entrance to the building, where Kevin, Sean and the one called Dustin had just emerged.

"Shit," Beth said, and floored it. The police officer noticed this, sighed, "I gotta go, sweetie," and hung up the phone. She did not leap into her patrol car, light the cherries and peel out while shouting into the radio about being in pursuit of suspects traveling west on Dundee Road, because this was Buffalo Grove.

There were no high speed chases in Buffalo Grove, especially of teenagers, because in Buffalo Grove, the teenagers, no matter what they had done, eventually went home.

She pulled out her clipboard and added a line to her report.

BETH HAD THE REMARKABLE ABILITY to dress herself under a towel without revealing anything, while at the same time driving recklessly at high speed.

Clothing flurried about the backseat as two girls and a guy sorted out their wardrobes.

"That's my top," Cammy accused Treece.

"I'm borrowing it."

"You're going to boob it all out."

Treece threw the top, hitting Rich on the face. He caught it in his teeth, and offered it up to Cammy, doggy-style.

"Drop it," Cammy commanded.

Denis wasn't getting dressed. He was squeezing his nose and estimating his rate of blood loss.

"Where's your pants?" Beth asked.

"Your boyfriend has them."

"Well, they're not going to fit *him*." She glanced at Denis, frowned, reached behind him, and extracted something from inside his collar.

"Oh, those," Denis explained. "They must've gotten there when I slid—"

"I don't care, Denis," Beth said, pulling on her panties as she cut off an eighteen-wheeler and veered onto the on-ramp for I-53 North.

"Where are we going?"

"We broke at least nine, *ten*, laws. We've got to get out of town."

"Let's go to my dad's cabin!" Treece suggested. "He lets me go there any time I want, as long as I don't tell Mom where it is."

Denis shook his head vigorously, reopening the nasal bloodgates. "I can't 'get out of town'!"

Beth angrily shook the splatter off her hand.

"Enough, Denis. *Enough,* okay?! *You* started this!"

"Me?"

"Yeah, *you.* You're the geek who stood up in front of our entire school, and all our family and friends, and declared your 'love' for someone you don't know a *thing* about!"

"He knows a *lot* about you," Rich defended Denis. "Quiz him!"

"He didn't know about Kevin," Treece pointed out.

"There were lapses in the intelligence," Rich acknowledged, then remembered: "He can do your signature!"

"You said it was sweet," Denis murmured.

Beth snorted. It wasn't a nice snort.

"*And* you came to my house!" he countered her snort. "If you didn't think it was sweet, why'd you come to my house?!"

Beth didn't answer.

Cammy answered.

"What do you think, super genius? We thought it would be *funny.*"

"Oh," Denis said.

Rich went for the face save: "Us, too. I mean, the head cheerleader and captain of the debate team? That's *always* hilarious . . ."

DENIS'S BRAIN PLAYED IT ALL BACK FOR HIM, another hilarious episode of:

LEAVE IT TO PENIS
"THE GRAND DELUSION"

FADE IN:

INT. BUFFALO GROVE HIGH SCHOOL -- CAFETERIA

STANDING AGAINST THE CINDER BLOCK IS DENIS "THE PENIS" COOVERMAN. HIS GRADUATION GOWN DRAGS ON THE

GROUND AND HIS MORTAR IS TOO SMALL FOR HIS HUMONGOUS HEAD. HE FIDGETS AND TWITCHES AS HE TRIES TO ASSUME A "COOL" POSE AGAINST THE WALL. HE DOES A DOUBLETAKE AS HE NOTICES...

BETH COOPER, HEAD CHEERLEADER AND PROM QUEEN, IS WALKING TOWARD HIM.

DENIS GYRATES AND CONTORTS IN AN EFFORT TO LOOK LIKE HE DOESN'T NOTICE. HE LOOKS LIKE A SPAZ.

SFX: LAUGHTER

BETH STOPS A FEW FEET FROM DENIS. SHE IS SLIGHTLY TALLER THAN HE IS.

BETH

You embarrassed me.

DENIS'S MOUTH HANGS OPEN. A BEAT. ANOTHER BEAT.

SFX: LAUGHTER

BETH (CONT'D)

(BEGRUDGING) But it was so "sweet",
I'll have to let you live.

DENIS

(VOICE SQUEAKING) Great. That's great.

SFX: LAUGHTER

BETH, UNCOMFORTABLE, LOOKS BEHIND HER. HER TWO FRIENDS, CAMMY AND TREECE, ARE LAUGHING. THEY URGE HER TO CONTINUE.

BETH

So... Henneman must've given you major junk.

DENIS

(ACTING "COOL") Some junk. Little junk.
A modicum of debris.

BETH ROLLS HER EYES.

SFX: LAUGHTER

BETH

(CHANGING SUBJECT) Was it like 800
degrees in there? Like boiling?

DENIS SNORTS POMPOUSLY.

DENIS
("PROFESSOR KNOW-IT-ALL") Actually, the boiling point -- of water -- is 212 degrees. Fahrenheit.

HE SWITCHES TO HIS "COOL" GUY.

DENIS (CONT'D)
(COCKS FINGER) One-hundred Celcius.

SFX: LAUGHTER, CONTINUING, AT HIS EXPENSE

DENIS FELT LIKE he had been punched in the heart.

He let go of his nose. The blood poured forth like tears, only red and disgusting.

Beth expressed some concern.

"Are you going to keep bleeding?"

"For about three days."

"Tip your head back."

Denis tipped his head back. He made a face.

"Now it's running down my throat."

Treece's hand appeared next to his head, holding two tiny white cylindrical objects.

"Here, stick these up there. They're super absorbent."

"Gah!" Denis said.

"They'll fit," Treece assured him. "They're comfort minis."

Denis batted her kind offer away. She dropped them in his lap.

"Fine," she said. "Bleed to death."

Denis quietly bled to death.

It was all a joke.

Or, more accurately, *he* was all a joke. A beaten, bleeding, pantless joke.

Denis picked up the tampons.

Perfect, he chuckled, choked on some blood, and cacked it onto his lap.

19.

LOVE MEANS

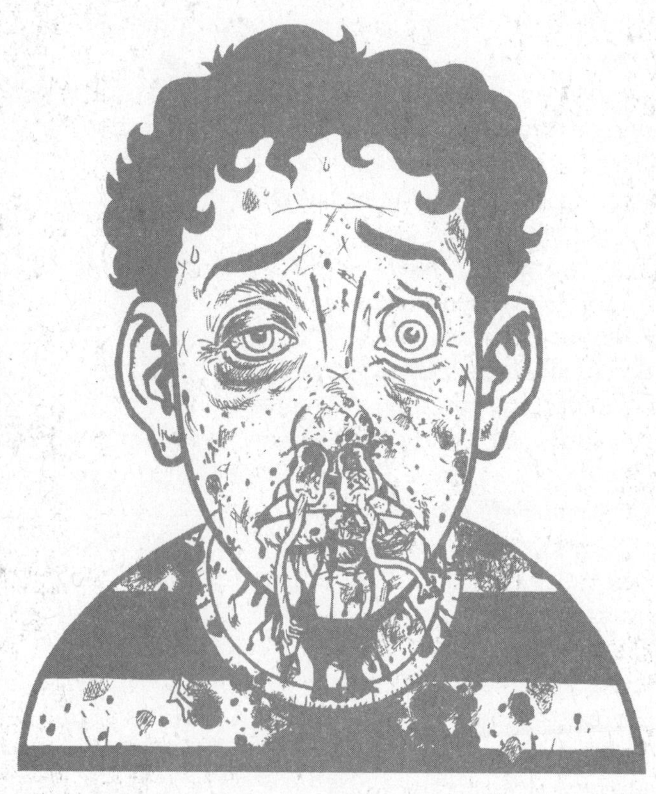

LOVE MAKES ROOM FOR FAULT.

GIDGET LAWRENCE

THE ROAD WAS DARK, lit only by fireflies.

They were headed north through Lake County, which was known for its lakes. Fox, Griswold, Nipersink and Pistakee Lakes. Lakes Catherine, Louise and Marie. There were a few hundred thousand others, according to the brochures.

Denis had never been to any of them, though he had snorkled in three oceans and four seas. His parents had wanted him to be cosmopolitan, rather than a child.

It was almost 4 a.m. In the backseat, Treece was asleep on Rich's shoulder, her mouth wide open. Rich, in turn, was leaning on Cammy, dreaming in widescreen. Cammy considered shoving him off her. Instead she closed her eyes.

The radio kept playing DJ C's Slamming Graduation Mix. They had been through:

"Graduation," by Third Eye Blind, "The Graduation Song" by Dave Matthews, and that Vitamin C song that wouldn't go away;

"Graduation Day"s by Head Automatica, Kanye West, Chris Isaak and Gym Class Heroes;

The Goo Goo Dolls' "Better Days" and 10,000 Maniacs' "These are Days";

"Bittersweet Symphony" by the Verve or Semisonic or one of those;

"Blackbird" by the Beatles and "Free Bird" by Lynyrd Skynyrd and "Fly Like an Eagle" by Steve Miller and "I Believe I Can Fly" by R. Kelly and "Fly Away" by Lenny Kravitz, and Dropline's "Fly Away from Here (Graduation Day)".

Now playing was the Calling's "Our Lives," or the Ataris's "In This Diary"; Denis had trouble telling them apart.

These are the days worth living . . .

DENIS AND BETH HAD NOT SPOKEN to each other through any of it. It was possible that they would never speak again. Denis would never figure out if Beth was nice, crazy, sad or mean, or some combination and in what proportions. Beth would never learn that beneath Denis's geek exterior there was a far more complicated Denis, roiling with neurosis, obsession and fear, and if that wasn't enticing enough, beneath that lay a sea of undifferentiated rage, the kind women like. Beth and Denis would be like two ships, two ships that sideswiped, causing ugly but not irreparable hull damage, and then passed in the night.

What kind of fool was Denis to ever imagine it could have been any different? There was no fool like a high-IQ fool. He could calculate π two different ways, the Wallis method and the Leibniz Series, but he could not see what any idiot could see, what everyone saw, many of them idiots: Beth was beautiful, popular and had a peerless derriere, and he was just another dweeb with two bloody tampons hanging out of his nostrils.

Let's make the best out of our lives

"HEY," BETH SAID. She turned down the radio. She did not look at him, which was for the best.

"I wanted to say," Beth said, "about what Cammy said. *She* thought it would be funny. I mean, we all thought it would be like a fun thing, and . . . I guess I did think it would be kind of funny. I'm sorry."

Denis said nothing.

"But I—" Beth went silent for several seconds.

Then she said:

"Guys tell me they love me all the time. But that's usually when . . . they want something."

Denis had not wanted *that,* not specifically, not right away.

"So I just . . . I don't know."

She seemed finished.

"Well," Denis said, "it was *kind* of funny."

He took the ends of the tampons and strung them out, making a superabsorbent handlebar mustache.

Beth laughed, and gagged. "Is it possible that you could please take those out now?"

"Let's see." Denis comically yanked the strings.

It hurt so much.

His nostrils had stopped bleeding, but now they burned like he had snorted fluorine. Denis dangled the assailants in front of his face. There were tiny hairs stuck on the end. Denis blinked back tears so as not to undercut the humor of his amusing mutilation.

"Voilà," he said with brave insouciance. "Do you have, one of those, um . . . bags?"

Beth reached down next to her seat and pulled out a McDonald's bag. She looked away as she handed it to him.

"Thank you," Denis said, debonairly dropping the bloodied wads into the bag. "You know, it's funny. Or interesting. *Tampon* is the actual medical term for the cotton plug they use to treat epistaxis, or nosebleeds . . ."

"Fucking Kevin," Beth said, slamming the steering wheel with her palm.

Denis sensed the subject had changed. He didn't have a lot more on tampons anyway. "Yeah," he said in support of Beth's statement. "Fuck that Kevin."

"Have you ever been in love?" Beth asked Denis.

Denis didn't know how to answer that. He knew the answer, or thought he knew the answer, but this didn't seem like the appropriate time to bring it up.

"I mean, truly in love," Beth continued, as if responding to what he thought. "In *true love.*"

A couple of weeks before, Denis had gotten an e-mail from Rich.

> **From:** RichMunsch@yahoo.com
> **Subject: True Love**
> **Date:** May 19, 2007 11:25:39 PM EDT
> **To:** *DenisCooverman@yahoo.com*
>
> "There's her poop. It just came out of her butt. I can feel it. I can feel the poop. It's warm. It just came from her butt. This was just inside of her. My girl. I'm touching it. It's her poop. It's Wendy's poop. I know it may seem weird that I touched her poop, but it was inside of her."
>
> *—Timothy Treadwell*

It was a quote from a movie, like most of Rich's e-mails were, and while Denis never figured out which movie, he found himself agreeing with it. That was true love. By that definition, he had not quite made it to true love.

Beth had a different definition.

"You know, where you love someone, with your whole heart, you just *love* them, and they can be mean to you, and hurt you, not physically, but hurt you, you know, make you feel like shit or worthless, but you still love him? You know what I mean?"

"I'm beginning to," Denis said.

Beth smiled.

"It can really suck, huh?"

Denis could see what was happening here, what he was being repurposed as, but it was better than nothing, he figured.

"How long have you two been going out?" Beth's new friend who was a boy asked.

"Since Christmas. We met right after. And, you know, he's been away since then, but we kept in touch, and the whole thing sort of happened through e-mail."

"That's great."

"He's a really sweet guy," Beth said. "Online."

"Sweet," Denis repeated. So both he and an abusive whoremongering, child-killing cokehead were *sweet.*

"You don't want to talk about him," Beth said. "Let's talk about something else."

Too tired, perhaps, Denis spoke without even overthinking.

"Can I ask you a personal question?"

"Is it about my boobs?"

"No, but I do have several queries in the arena, which I'll get to."

"They're Cs. Bs during basketball season. Ms. Levitt doesn't like us flopping all over the place. Except Treece. She can't help it. I'm sorry. What was your question?"

"Oh, I was just wondering about your brother."

"What about him?"

"I don't know. Like, what was his name?"

Denis had speculated that his name was Dennis.

"David."

"What was he like?"

"I have no idea," Beth said. "He was already sick when I was born. He died when I was two. He was twelve. I don't remember him at all. There's this picture of me visiting him in the hospital, but it's like he's just some sick kid."

WHEN DENIS WAS TEN, he told his parents he wanted a baby brother. Since he had never expressed any interest in a sibling, they asked him why. He said that he thought he might be coming down with leukemia, and that he would need a close blood relative for bone marrow transplants. He had read about the bioethics of parents having a second child to provide marrow for an ill sibling in an issue of the *Journal of Juvenile Oncology* that he had been secretly subscribing to. He theorized there would be no ethical issue if his parents had the child *before* he was diagnosed, as a preventative measure. Only he used the word *prophylactic.* That's when they knew he was going to be a doctor.

Denis's parents said they would see what they could do, but they didn't, not really.

"LEUKEMIA," DENIS SAID.

Beth was spooked. "How'd you know that?"

"What else do little kids die of?" Denis said.

"Oh, right," said Beth. "You're the doctor."

"I'm sorry. About David."

"It's kind of stupid. My big sad story. It's like the dramatic tragedy of my life, and I wasn't even there. And it's not even an interesting story. Excuse me."

Beth stopped the car, opened her door, and threw up. She closed the door, and continued driving.

"You okay?"

"That was shitty champagne." She turned to Denis, smiling through watery eyes and lips glazed with vomitus. "Yours was much nicer."

The radio was now playing Ataris's "In This Diary," or the Calling's "Our Lives," whichever the other one was.

These are the best days of our lives

"Um," Beth said, "Can *I* say something personal?"

Please do. "Uh. Yeah. Sure."

"You kind of . . . reek."

Denis sighed heavily. "It's the fear."

"I think it's your shirt."

Denis looked down. His rugby shirt was a goulash

of putrefying meats, molding cheeses, salmonelling creams and ptomaining tapenades.

"I kind of spilled some dip on it."

"Take it off."

Denis's pupils constricted involuntarily.

"I'm not going to *molest* you."

"I wasn't terribly concerned about that."

Denis removed his shirt in the manner of a girl at a strip poker game, maintaining maximum coverage until the last possible moment.

"Personally," Beth said. "I hate hairy chests." She put out her hand and snapped her fingers. "Hand it over." Denis handed it over.

"Let's give it a little air . . ."

Beth held the shirt out of the window and shook it. Smelly bits and rancid ooze took to the wind and the whole operation went swimmingly until the shirt flew out of her hand.

"Oh, shit!" Beth laughed.

She slammed on the brakes.

In the backseat, Cammy woke up to discover she was cradling Rich like a baby. She flung him off like he was a severed head that had landed on her in a horror movie.

Treece, who lay in Rich's lap, jostled half awake. "Okay," she mumbled. "Okey-dokey . . ." She started to unbuckle Rich's belt. Rich reached down and eased her automated mouth away from his fly. She happily went back to sleep.

Beth threw the vehicle into reverse and spun the wheel to execute a three-point turn in only two points.

"THERE IT IS." Denis spotted the shirt crumpled at the side of the road. Beth stopped.

Nobody said anything for a moment.

"I'll get it," Denis said.

The cold gravel on his feet and cool breeze on most of his skin reminded Denis: he was a man in underpants. He crouched as he entered the high-beamed proscenium, reflexively covering his ass, and was further reminded: he was a man in *lucky underpants.*

These were the briefs his mother had begged him to burn: inelastic and threadbare with three or more holes conspiring in the rear. At least they were white(ish) and not star-spangled or Spider-Manned, styles he retired sophomore year after the Geometry Incident. He had worn this lucky pair to every debate tournament except State, when he let his mother pack, and look what happened there. He had worn them for his graduation speech, washed them, and put them on again with his party attire, feeling they would boost his confidence and possibly perform miracles.

His mother suspected as much.

"You're not wearing those awful underpants," she asked.

"Mom," he answered.

"What if you *do* get lucky?" his father argued. "Then you're wearing ratty underpants."

His mother rejected both sides of the proposition. "He is not wearing those things. And he is not getting lucky, not like that. Not on my watch."

Denis swiveled to remove his rear from direct view, sidling away from the headlights in nondominant primate fashion. He reached down for his shirt, intending to tie it around his waist like a big-assed girl, and discovered he was not alone.

He saw their eyes first. Four red circles, vibrating. Then he heard the high chittering sound. Two raccoons were inspecting his shirt, and finding it delicious. From inside the car, where Beth and the others were watching, they must have looked awfully cute. But from Denis's perspective, low to the ground and close enough to see their rabid little teeth and razor yellow claws, they appeared as what they were: fierce competitors for a valuable resource.

"No," Denis said. "That's not food, it's a polyblend."

The raccoons switched from nervous trill to robust snarl with stunning alacrity. Denis was back in the car almost as quickly.

They all watched as the raccoons clutched the shirt, nibbling, and then scampered with their catch into the woods.

Cammy and Rich found this rip-snorting.

"Oh, Denis," Beth said, utterly contrite. "I am *so* sorry." And then she cracked up.

Denis smiled, and smirked, and chuckled, and began to laugh, for the first time in a very long time. It possessed all of the therapeutic effects he had read about.

Beth was laughing, and gazing at Denis with amusement and what seemed genuine affection. "Look at you. You're naked. Cam, throw me my poncho."

A bright purple knit poncho flew into the front seat.

"It's okay. Really. I'm kind of hot, right now, actually."

"Put it on."

"I don't see any need, at the moment, to wear a purple poncho."

"It's fuchsia," Beth said, spreading it in front of her coquettishly. "And it's my favorite."

20.

FOOL MOON

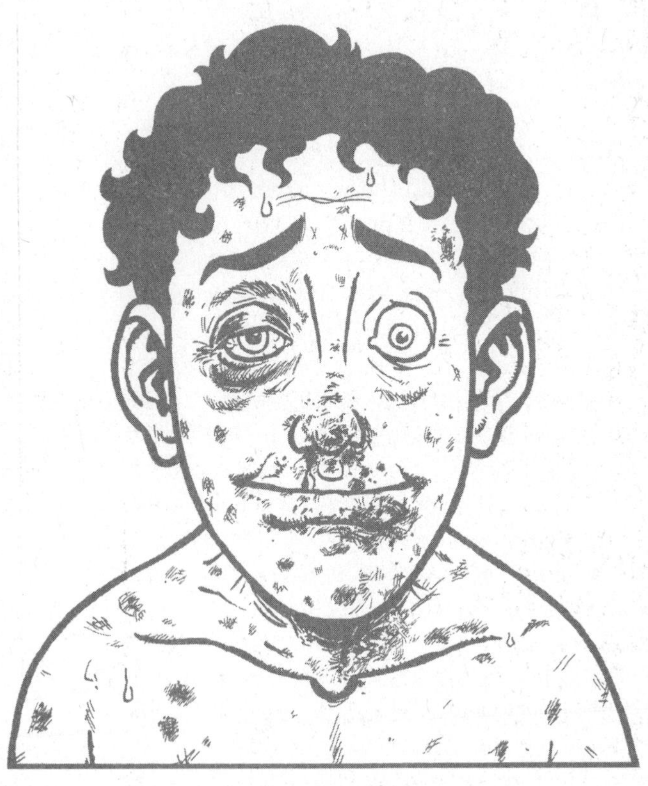

IT'S REALLY HUMAN OF YOU
TO LISTEN TO ALL MY BULLSHIT.

SAMANTHA BAKER

TREECE'S FATHER'S CABIN sat on Lake Hakaka, named by the Ho-Chunk after their word meaning "dead male bear," for reasons that were not immediately apparent. It was one of Lake County's lesser lakes, usually left off tourism materials and occasionally official maps; once the county argued, unsuccessfully, that it was in Wisconsin. The lake had water, though, and was private, being unpopular, and only smelled like a dead male bear from late July through early September.

Three girls, a boy, and a ponchoed figure of indeterminate sex approached the cabin by the light of the setting moon.

"Originally it was Al Capone's," Treece inaccurately related the cabin's history. "He used it as a hideout, because if the police raided, he could just run into Wisconsin. And then the guy who played Bozo the Clown, not the main guy but some local Bozo, had it for a bunch of years, and threw these really sick clown parties up here. There's supposedly a couple dead clowns buried in the woods over there. And then Sammy the Seal or Snake or some other S animal owned it, and that's how my dad got it."

Treece turned on the light. She yawned. Everybody else gasped.

Fowl and fauna lunged from the walls and coffee tables; animal skins draped all the woodsy furniture; the outside of a grizzly bear lay on the floor.

Rich dropped the bag of snacks.

"Feel the death," Cammy said.

Several of the animal cadavers came paired in death-throe tableaus: a glass-eyed owl with a flexiformed snake "writhing" in its talons; a former fox tearing apart an ex-squirrel; and, *holy crap,* a tanned hunting dog retrieving a stuffed pheasant. Denis was by no means an animal lover; he consumed animals, he dissected them, but he didn't *hate* them. This cabin felt like an act of revenge.

"I think maybe animals killed his parents," he said.

"Oh, my dad just bought all this stuff," Treece responded blithely, adding with a rare note of disdain, "He's never killed *anything*." She pointed to the fireplace, below a hunting rifle mounted between the heads of a mother deer and its fawn. "If anybody wants to make a fire . . ."

She opened the refrigerator, pulled out a bottle and frowned. "Weird beer." She opened the freezer, and brightened. *"Yodka!"* she bellowed in what she supposed was a Russian accent.

AN OLD BOOM BOX channeled Denis's iPod:

Here's to the nights we felt alive

The Eve 6 song, regarded as a graduation classic, was in reality from another venerable rock genre, the "Let's Spend the Night Together and Then I Must Be Ramblin' On" song.

Are you cool with just tonight

Nobody cared. The mood of the music combined with the crackling fire and the wilderness milieu to create an irresistibly maudlin setting. The five stood around a wicker Tiki bar, drunk and/or punch-drunk, as Treece poured generous *yodkas* into the only five available vessels:

a ceramic pineapple;
a pink coffee mug shaped like a breast;
a monkey head carved out of a coconut;
a *Playboy* toothbrush tumbler;
and a World's Greatest Dad Trophy.

"There," Treece said, and "*Yikes.*"

She was looking at Denis's face. And then everyone

was looking at Denis's face, in the light for the first time in a couple of beatings.

"Pretty bad?" Denis asked.

The eye had coagulated into bold concentric circles of red, yellow and black. The bruises from the boning and scrapes from the bushes provided a muted backdrop for other dramatically battered facial features: the nose a magenta bloom with rusty crust around the nostrils; the lower lip a fat purple sausage split open on the right.

"Not that bad," Beth said.

"Better than dead," said Rich.

"Your lip looks great," Treece said. "That stupid cunt Cheryl paid like two grand to have that done to her lips."

"Yes," said Cammy, softening her usual deadpan. "You look totally hot."

"A toast!" Treece said, lifting the World's Greatest Dad Trophy. "You know what's weird? I didn't give him this."

Everybody grabbed a drinking container; Denis, not fast enough, got the Titty Mug.

"To . . . ," Treece said, thinking. "I know: Here's to the nights we felt alive!"

Beth touched her pineapple to Denis's ceramic nipple.

"Ching."

She chugged her shot.

"I'm going out for a smoke."

With a tilt of her head, she bid Denis to follow. Denis, as always, followed, adding one last brushstroke to his chiaroscuro portrait of *Beth Cooper, Girl in My Head.*

"She smokes."

BETH DANGLED HER LEGS off the end of the dock, lighting a cigarette. Denis sat down next to her.

"No cancer statistics, please."

Every eight seconds, someone in the world dies from tobacco use.

Every minute, ten million cigarettes are sold.

There are 599 government-approved additives for tobacco, including chocolate, vanilla, prune juice, dimethyltetrahydrobenzofuranone and "smoke flavor."

Tobacco companies have also been adding ammonia, arsenic, formaldehyde and mercury to their cigarettes to help achieve that great taste.

A 1998 study showed that smoking significantly reduces the size of the smoker's erect penis.

Smokers fart more than nonsmokers.

"Oh," Denis said. "I don't really know any . . ." He slapped a mosquito on his forearm.

Beth blew out a stream of carbon monoxide, hydrogen cyanide and forty-three known carcinogens.

"I always think the full moon is so pretty."

The moon, hanging just above the water, was waning gibbous with 93 percent of its visible disk illuminated. The technical full moon had been Friday. But it was, Denis agreed, pretty: golden.

"It's the Honey Moon," he said. "The first moon of June is called that. It's where *honeymoon* comes from, because people used to get married at the summer solstice, which is June twenty-first this year."

"It's huge," Beth said.

"That's an optical illusion. It only looks larger when it's close to the horizon. The prevailing theory, used to be, was that it's a Ponzo illusion, that we see it as bigger in context to the objects around it, but that's been discredited. There's a couple intriguing alternatives, but nothing proven."

"You know everything, Denis Cooverman."

Denis Cooverman was back.

"Not everything. No, no. There's things I don't know. Multiple things."

"Here's something you don't know," Beth said, sucking in some early menopause. "If a girl tells you the moon is beautiful, or that it seems really big, you know what you say?"

"Not what I said, I assume."

She blew out secondhand smoke rings.

"You don't say anything. You put your arm around her."

Was Beth suggesting—

"Just something for future reference."

"Thanks," Denis said. "I'll remember that." He slapped his thigh. "For future reference."

"SAY ALLO TO MY LEETLE FREN . . ."

Rich was using the rifle from the mantel as a prop for his one-night-only one-man show.

"Pacino, *Scarface*, '82, DePalma . . ." The attribution was hurried and sloppy, an indication that he did not chug vodka often. He repositioned the gun, switched the accent.

"*Hasta la vista, baby*—Schwarzenegro, *T2*, '91, Cameron Crowe."

Treece and Cammy sat on the leopard, calf and sheepskin couch, passing the bottle back and forth. Treece giggled maniacally; Cammy chortled unironically.

Rich held the gun straight up, bowed his legs and thrust back his shoulders. He placed a hand over one eye and swaggered his shoulders.

"*Fill your hands, you son of a bitch!* —John Wayne, *True Grit*, '69, directed by some guy."

Cammy guffawed.

Treece fell off the couch. "Uh-oh," she squealed, "I'm *peeing!*"

"It's not *that* funny," said Rich, clearly rattled by this level of positive feedback.

"It's funny," said Treece, presumably no longer peeing, "because you . . . *you*—"

"What?" Rich snapped. "Because I'm gay, or so you think? You think incorrectly."

Cammy smiled, almost kindly. "The lady doth protest too much, *me*thinks."

"Oh, like *you* know Shakespeare."

"Queen Gertrude to Hamlet, act three, scene two." Then, in perfect mimicry: "1602, William Shakespeare, or possibly Edward de Vere."

Rich fell a tiny bit in love.

"Just because we're beautiful, it doesn't mean we're stupid," Cammy said.

"Yeah," Treece added.

THE HONEY MOON MELTED into the lake. Beth smoked, and Denis swatted.

"Careful what you wish for, huh?"

"Huh?" Denis scratched his neck.

"So . . . still love me?"

"What?"

"Now that you know me. Am I everything you ever masturbated to?"

"No. I never . . . not to *you*."

That was such a lie.

Beth took a long drag, leaving a silence for Denis to fill with a truthful answer to her question.

"You're different than I expected," he answered accurately. "I mean, you're not—"

"Perfect."

Beth Cooper was like a Persian rug, her imperfections proof that God exists. Unfortunately, that last vodka shot had knocked out Denis's metaphor center, and he was on his own.

"Not perfect, but better. You're not . . ." He smacked

his forehead. "You're still great, and it's . . . real. You're real. A real kind of real." Denis stared down at his knees, and the five mosquitoes feasting there. "I'm not good at talking . . . about things."

"*Denis Cooverman!* You're a debate state finalist!"

"How'd you know *that?*"

"We were going to go cheer for you. Well, we joked about it. But anyway, you were talking about how real I am."

"Well, one example: you're pretty, but not like a picture. And you have a . . . personality."

"*There's* a compliment."

"You're sweet."

"I don't get accused of that very often."

"You are. And you're interesting, and you're smart—"

Beth put her fist to her throat. "I am *not* smart, Denis," she hacked. "I'm kind of an idiot." She laughed, and coughed.

Denis was prepared to argue but had no contradictory facts at his disposal. Instead he itched. Beth puffed her cigarette, coughed a couple more times, and puffed again.

A few seconds passed like nothing.

"You're a lot of fun."

Beth laughed. "*This* is your idea of fun?"

Denis looked at her, the unswollen parts of his face forming an expression of excruciating sincerity.

"All my memories from high school are from tonight."

Beth looked away.

"You need to get out more."

21.

THE SEX PART

FUCK ME GENTLY WITH A CHAINSAW.

HEATHER CHANDLER

INSIDE THE CABIN, something was happening, and Rich suspected the worst. As if through telepathy or subtle hand signals, Cammy and Treece had agreed to play some game, and not only were they not telling him what it was, Rich sensed the game they were playing was him.

Cammy sashayed up, revealing for the first time that she had hips, took a long suck on the vodka bottle, and handed it to him.

"So, hetero-boy," she said with, if this is possible, sultry sarcasm, "if you're so not gay, why so unchubby in the shower?"

"I was just being cool." He took a big swig of vodka to underline this. "And it was uncool of *you* to notice."

"*And* you pushed Treece away when she tried to service you in the car . . ."

"I did?" Treece asked, simply curious. "That sounds like me." And then realizing the grievous insult to her reputation, "Yeah, what is *wrong* with you? I'm really good at that! I'm *known* for that!"

"You were *asleep*. So that was me being cool, once again."

"No seventeen-year-old boy is that cool," Cammy said.

"*I* am that cool," Rich disagreed, and then lost interest in that subject. He picked up the bag he had dropped earlier.

"¿Quien quieres las snaquitas?"

"You know, Rich," Cammy said. "The movie quotes, the bad Spanish. Not working. Too many shticks."

"It is kind of not ideal," Treece agreed, "from a branding point of view. Unless you only quoted movies in Spanish. And there's like, what, five of those."

Rich unwrapped a Suzy Q, considering the criticism. He sat between the girls on the couch.

"Which shtick do you like better?"

"Ooh, that's tough," Cammy said.

Rich shoved the Suzy Q in his mouth and bit it in half.

Cammy chuckled.

"You, Richard Munsch, have never been with a woman."

"Whuh?" Rich said, creamy lipped.

"I NEVER BOUGHT BEER BEFORE. I never went on a joyride, I mean, a reckless one; was never in a car accident; never, well, I've been beaten up, but never with that many spectators; never broke in anywhere; never skinny-dipped, and I almost did, I was going to; never eluded the authorities before . . ."

"Never sniffed a girl's panties before?"

"I *did not.*"

"You were down there a long time."

"I closed my eyes and held my breath. That's how I lost consciousness." He scratched his cheek.

"Well," Beth said, lighting another cigarette, "sounds like I really popped your cherry tonight."

Denis did not want to talk about his cherry.

"You know, even if your grades and SATs aren't amazing, you could still go to a good college. You could get a cheerleading scholarship."

"A cheerleading scholarship?"

"They have cheerleading scholarships. Not at Northwestern. But there isn't anything to cheer at Northwestern anyway."

Beth exhaled. She sounded a little tired.

"Denis, it's nice you're watching out for me, but look: I'm not even that good of a cheerleader. You, you're going to go on and become a doctor and cure cancer or whatever new diseases there are, but this, this is about it for me."

Beth seemed so matter-of-fact, so resigned.

"I know high school wasn't that great for you."

"No," Denis said. "It was, some of it was . . . The last eight hours: pretty fantastic."

"I know about all the swirlies, and wedgies and all the nicknames . . ."

"What nicknames?" Denis asked. "I know about Penis."

Beth chewed her cigarette. "Here's the thing. High school was *really* great for me. I had a great, great time. But now that's over. Everything from here on out is going to be . . . ordinary."

Denis couldn't believe that, wouldn't accept that. "You're not ordinary. You're *beautiful*."

"I may be pretty, but not enough to make a living at it. Except maybe in porn."

The mere thought of this gave Denis the creeps, and wood.

"I'm not doing porn, Denis."

"Oh. Good. It's a limited field."

"Besides, I'm going to get fat."

"You won't get fat."

"I'll have to introduce you to my mom."

Denis knew enough about obesity and genetics to argue against, and for, Beth's proposition. Instead, he sat there, slapping and scratching, and thinking about what she had said. He had never looked at his life the way Beth described it, as *promising*. It was obvious and true, but Denis had always been too caught up in immediate terrors and humiliations to look forward to anything; even his obsessive long-term planning was mired in worry over whether it was currently on schedule. And Denis had never given much thought to Beth's life—her real life as opposed to the one he had constructed for the two of them (and even this life was more a matter of moments and scenes than a fully articulated existence). What Beth said about her own life was pessimistic but not inaccurate. Her family, her finances—she was always at that shoe store—her academic credentials, none of it augured well for the kind of future that guidance counselors talk about. Beth would do fine, Denis had no doubt, but her life was unlikely to get *better* than it was right now. That Beth knew and accepted this broke Denis's heart, and impressed the hell out of him.

It occurred to him: *I'm the idiot.*

"You know, Beth," he said, "for someone who claims to not be smart—"

Beth tossed her cigarette in the lake. "You wanna mess around?"

"You and me?"

"I'm not gonna ask twice."

Denis was an idiot, but not that much of an idiot.

He kissed her.

She kissed him, right on his swollen, ruptured lip.

"Ow," Denis said.

"Ooh," Beth said, kissing an unbruised patch of his cheek. "Sorry."

"It's okay," Denis said. "It's a good *ow.*"

And it was.

Sweetest memory
Sweetest memory

QAJE, THE GORGEOUS QUADRA-RACIAL SINGER who had once been or still was a man, filled the cabin with the kind of sensuous jazz-inflected pop that grown-ups like to pork to.

Rich sat in the middle of the couch, gripping vodka and snack cake, with the quick rigidity of a rabbit surrounded by animals that eat rabbits.

Treece was curled up on one side of him, and Cammy was stretching her long legs, resting her toes on his knees. They were both holding up freshly peeled Suzy Qs, spokesmodel style.

"Watch," said Cammy.

"And learn," said Treece.

The two girls oriented their pastries vertically, and proceeded to lick the creme from their crevices in alternating short and long strokes.

Rich wondered what the MPAA Ratings Board would make of this.

Cammy pulled her face out of her Suzy Q; she had a white dollop on her nose. She put a foot in Rich's lap.

"You cool?"

"Long as everyone else is cool."

Treece leaned in and ran a creme-filled tongue up his cheek.

"See?" Rich said. "I'm liking that. I'm"—he pointed to his crotch—"*reacting* to that."

"How about *this?*" Treece gave Rich what he had previously known as a Wet Willie. Something about it being a girl's tongue in his ear and not some guy's licked finger altered the tenor.

"Oh, yeah." Rich swallowed. "That works."

Treece continued wet-working the left side of his face, and Cammy began to unbutton his shirt. Rich wondered, *How far do they plan on taking this joke?* Were there people waiting to jump out when he took off his pants? No, they could have done that back in the girls' locker room. Maybe this was a game of sex chicken. If that was the case, Rich thought, then *cluck cluck cluck cluck cluck.*

"Hey, this is all great and all, but, unfortunately, I left my latex sheaths back at the house—"

"Don't worry," Cammy said, twirling Rich out of his shirt. "Treece has got some. Don't you, Treece?"

Treece reached behind her back and her top sprang off. "Gobs."

DENIS COOVERMAN WAS MAKING OUT with Beth Cooper.

CAPTAIN OF DEBATE MAKES OUT WITH CHEERLEADER HEAD

SIGN OF 'END OF TIMES'

Perversion of Caste System
Cited as Dogs Mate with Cats,
Cities Plunge into Boiling Seas

The corporeal reality of making out with Beth Cooper was different than all the hypothetical times he had made out with her. It felt better, and hurt more. Also, even in his wildest dream scenarios, it was always just him and Beth, and not a carnal blood orgy of the two of them and nineteen thousand six-legged females with wings.

More troubling were the stylistic differences. Where Denis was a (mostly theoretical) adherent of soft kisses and slow caresses, Beth was apparently more of a rutter. She had pulled him on top of her within moments and had her hands under the poncho, grabbing and scratching his back. That was much appreciated. Yet Denis did not know what to make of it when she wrapped her thighs around one of his legs and started humping him dryly and, he couldn't help but notice, fiercely.

She was making a lot of noise. Louder and more guttural than was warranted, Denis felt, but something else as well. Intermingled with sexual growls and bucking grunts was a high keening moan, one Denis knew from his reading could signify pleasure but which he sensed did not.

Denis sat up.

"Listen . . . I'm sorry." And he was truly, profoundly sorry, and would be much sorrier later, he suspected, and for a long time after that. But he had to ask: "Why me?"

Beth remained on her back on the deck. Her eyes glistened, too much.

"Because it's graduation night," she said. "And to not be with someone would just be too sad."

Don't be sad. I can't stand you sad.

"Good answer," Denis said, and climbed back on.

I don't want to be
just your sweetest memory

CAMMY, TREECE AND RICH HUDDLED NAKED under leopard, calf and sheep skins, respectively. They all had the glazed expressions of people who had just shared a terribly intimate horrific mistake.

"That was," Cammy said, "expeditious."

Treece found the silver lining. "At least we know you're not gay."

"Tell that to my dad," Rich said.

"What's his number?"

Rich's father wouldn't have answered. Rich's mother was sitting by the phone, waiting to hear back from the Coovermans and the police. But Mr. Munsch was fast asleep, as he had been for much of Rich's life, because, as he liked to explain at parties or anytime his BAL went over .08, "After three daughters, I really wanted a boy."

What wasn't being discussed in the cabin was what had happened *after* Rich had proved he was not gay. That took only a few seconds, but then things . . . continued. Rich had originally thought no one had noticed his startling emission and continued to play along, but it gradually dawned on him that his participation was not strictly necessary. He was not having sex with two girls. They were having sex with each other on top of him. Rich withdrew to a neutral corner and watched, with distressing disinterest, as matters reached mutually agreed-upon ends.

"And you two can't be gay," Rich pointed out, "because my penis was in the mix."

"Right," Cammy said.

Treece frowned. "I just realized. My dad's juices are probably all over this couch!"

Even worse: "And *Cheryl's*."

Treece shuddered, then seemed absolutely fine. "This is why I'm so screwed up," she said matter-of-factly.

DENIS WAS TRYING to get into the spirit of things, servicing Beth while ignoring the sorrowful surroundings. As Beth bucked into him, he bucked back, until they had a satisfying rhythm going. On his own volition, he had put his hand into Beth's blouse and had managed, with some difficulty, to roll and fold her brassiere up around her neck.

He fondled her breasts, stroking and pinching and randomly manipulating them, not thinking the whole time, *Holy crap, I'm fondling Beth Cooper's breasts*, but praying, *Please, God, make this feel good.*

His other hand rested on her hip bone, occasionally squeezing it. Beth took the hand by surprise and slapped it on her panties. Denis's fingers twitched, then settled into the fabric. He felt a raised stitching, and giggled into Beth's mouth.

"What's so funny?"

"Hello."

"You *did* look!" She slapped him on the ass. Once there, her index finger found the second largest breach in his underpants.

"Woo," she said, wiggling her finger inside.

Denis reacted much like those foxes in that video Ariel Kaminer always played in the cafeteria during lunch, in other words, as if 240 volts of electricity had been pumped up his anus. It really fluffed out his fur.

To say he flew off her would be an exaggeration, but he was off before either of them knew it was happening. He sat up on the dock, trying to catch his breath. This was where he would ordinarily spiral into abject mortification, wishing he were dead or invisible, or vaporized, accomplishing both. Instead he found that between gasps he was laughing, at himself, and happily.

"That was . . . *ha,* I was taken by surprise there," he said. "It wasn't you. I'm sure you did it perfectly. I'm just . . . unaccustomed . . . Let's try that again, shall we?"

Beth was already sitting up, lighting a cigarette.

"It's okay." She left her brassiere dangling around her neck.

"No, really," Denis said. "I would very much like to."

"Maybe later."

Goddammit goddammit goddammit goddammit goddammit goddammit goddammit goddammit goddammit goddammit goddammit goddammit goddammit goddammit goddammit goddammit goddammit goddammit goddammit goddammit.

Denis tried to quickly retrace the steps that had taken him to this point, not *this* point but the one immediately preceding it, the one with him on top of Beth. He couldn't find a way back on top. Events and actions stretched into the past in an unbreakable chain of cause and effect, to the talk they just had, to all the talking, back through each of his injuries, each a new intimacy between them, to Rich answering the door when she arrived, to the moment in his speech in which he said *I love you, Beth Cooper*, to the week before, when Rich talked him into saying it, to the first time he sat behind her and smelled her hair. There were so many things he would do differently, but any of them done differently would have arrived at a different moment, and the odds of any of those other moments involving Denis Cooverman on top of Beth Cooper were incomprehensibly high.

And so, he decided to take another tack. It was a time-honored one, and one that showed our Little Denis was becoming a man, unfortunately.

"Beth," he said, putting his arm around her. "I really do lo—"

"Oh, *fuck me!*"

Only she didn't mean that. She meant that Denis's face frightened and repulsed her. Given that only a few minutes before she had found it kissable, that was saying something. Now, by the light of the submerging moon, Beth could see that Denis's face, in addition to its previously catalogued irregularities, was a swarming mass of mosquito bites. So much blood coagulated and contused up there it was rather remarkable that he had been able to maintain an erection all this time.

Beth reached out and touched Denis's cheek gently. "That must itch."

"I was distracted before, but now it does, yeah." Denis scratched, leaving four red streaks down his cheek.

"Don't do that," Beth said.

Bloody mosquito bites were a turnoff with no turn back on, Denis realized. "So," he asked for posterity, "am I the most hideous creature you ever kissed?"

"God no," Beth said without hesitation, making Denis feel both good and bad.

Beth stood.

Yes, Denis realized, it was time to go.

He turned to get up and that's when he saw the two headlights, very far apart, coming very fast.

THE HUMMER RUMBLED ONTO THE DOCK at a speed inadvisably high for a rotting, waterlogged structure built by a drunk handyman. The vehicle didn't indicate any intention of stopping. When it did finally do so, five inches from the end, Denis was in Lake Hakaka. Beth stood at the edge of the dock, her knees touching the bumper.

22.

DEATH IN DENIS

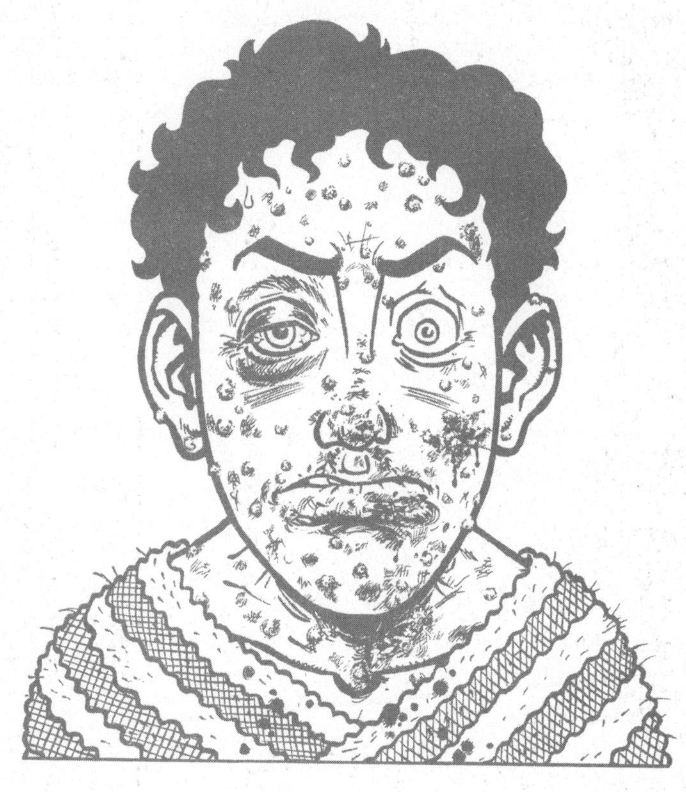

MAKE UP YOUR MIND, DUDE, IS HE GONNA SHIT OR IS HE GONNA KILL US?

JEFF SPICOLI

SEX WAS A TERRIFIC ICEBREAKER.

"Really?" Rich asked Cammy. "You're studying acting at U of I? *¡Yo tambien!* I mean: Me, too. And directing. I'm in business but I'm transferring as soon as my dad's not paying attention."

"Your dad sounds like a real prize."

"Oh, you know, he doesn't hit me."

They were all huddled together under the bearskin rug, nude but aggressively oblivious to their recent sexual interactivity.

"Wait, if you want to be an actress, why weren't you in drama club?"

"Survival."

"Good call."

"Hey," Treece said. "What dorm are you in?"

"Florida Avenue."

"Us, too!"

When Treece and Cammy decided to room together, they hadn't given it much thought. Not like they were now.

The silence was awkward for only a moment, because of all the screaming.

THREE NAKED TEENAGERS shuffled to the window under cover of bear.

"What the Christ?" Rich said.

Sean was dragging Denis out from under the dock as the one called Dustin struggled to maintain control of Beth, whose kicking and shrieking showed a lot of stamina after the night she had had. Kevin was in the Hummer, trying to back up off the narrow dock and swearing quite a bit.

"How'd they find us?"

"Oopsie," Treece said.

Cammy's right eyebrow requested elaboration.

"I kind of invited Sean up here before," Treece explained, before getting defensive. "Well, he should've known he wasn't invited anymore!"

Rich had a strange feeling, a sort of déjà vu, that he had been here before, only he had been Kevin Bacon. And then he remembered where he had seen this: *"Come on, I love you." —Kevin Bacon to Jeannine Taylor, shortly before they fornicated on a bunk bed and he was impaled by an arrow through the throat, in* Friday the 13th, *1980, Sean Cunningham.* And then he remembered the countless other times he had seen the same setup, always ending the same basic way, with sometimes clever variations.

It fairly freaked him out.

"Don't you *get* it?" He rattled the bearskin to get their attention. "We're stupid teenagers who just had sex in a cabin by a lake! We're dead! We are *so very dead.*"

Cammy was unfazed. "I'd hardly call that sex."

Treece, meanwhile, was getting excited. She grabbed them both by the shoulders and momentously announced, "I have an idea!"

She was disappointed in their reaction.

"I have ideas!" she pouted.

"SEE THAT?" Kevin jabbed at the front grille of the Hummer, which looked remarkably intact, considering. "My dad is gonna shit," he whined, mostly to himself.

"That's your *father's* car?" Denis was bewildered. "I thought you were from Texas, or a swamp."

"He's from Glenview," Beth spat, still flailing against her restraint. "He went to Maine North. He only talks that way to be cool."

"Talking like a hillbilly is cool?"

Kevin sauntered over to Denis. "We'll see how cool you talk when I'm through with y'all."

"I'm pretty sure that's a misuse of *y'all*."

Kevin whispered in Denis's ear: "By the time I am through with *y'all*, y'all will be *begging* me to kill *y'all*."

Denis smiled.

Kevin took umbrage.

"Is that a *cliché?*" He pronounced it with excessive southern elongation. "Is *this* a cliché?"

Kevin punched Denis in the left eye, the only unaltered portion of his facial topology.

"Stop punching me!" Kevin's Denis was a fluttery, effeminate clown. "Talk about your clichés."

As he passed Beth, Kevin noticed her brassiere necklace. He registered this with feigned disinterest. He flicked her hard on the nipple.

"Dick," she said.

"Whore," he replied, both syllables.

"As matter of fact, it is," mumbled Denis, returning to full consciousness a few beats behind the conversation. With his less recently pummeled eye, Denis watched Kevin return from the back of the Hummer with jumper cables.

"Gentlemen," Kevin addressed his military colleagues, "remember all those excellent techniques the CIA taught us, which we were subsequently forbidden to employ?"

The troops nodded approvingly.

SUDDENLY, A FEROCIOUS WILDCAT *leapt out of the bushes!*

"Ya!" Sean said, throwing Beth at it.

Further suddenly, a huge owl flew at the Dustin guy! He dropped Denis and batted about his head frantically.

"Run!" Treece yelled, holding the owl.

Cammy thrust the wildcat at Sean again, and he reflexively cowered.

Denis and Beth ran past Kevin, who, though

disappointed in the performance of his troops, was amused by the outcome and not terribly concerned.

"Now just *what* did y'all hope to accomplish with that?" Kevin mused, as he pivoted into the barrel of a gun.

"Create a temporary distraction," said Rich, "so they could escape and I could get the drop on you." He wore the bear as a cowl and cape, its claws draped across his chest. Unlike the girls, he had remained otherwise naked, excepting the condom, which added a certain tribal quality. "Treece's idea."

Treece curtseyed with her owl.

"You don't know how to shoot that thing." Kevin took a step toward Rich.

Rich had never held a gun before, but had mimed one a million times. It was a showy, movie move, but the gun cocked just the same.

Kevin stopped. "It isn't even loaded."

This was Rich's best impression.

"You gotta ask yourself one question: Do I feel lucky? Well, do ya, punk?"

"Oh," Treece exclaimed, "I know that one!"

Kevin put up his hands. "Let's cool it, okay, guy?" He dropped the army accent, sounding much more like the teenager he still was. "We were just goofing on you. Maybe we went a little too far. But if you shoot us, what's that going to look like?"

"Self-defense," Cammy said.

"Enough." Denis shook his head. "Kevin, just get in your dad's car and drive away. Don't come back. Never bother Beth again . . ."

"Denis," Beth chided.

"Okay," Denis revised. "Never bother *me* again."

Rich gestured toward the Hummer with the rifle. "You heard the Coove."

Denis rolled his eyes.

Kevin, Sean and Dustin marched with Rich at their

backs. Rich, imitating a move he had seen in *Cool Hand Luke, Deliverance, et al.*, stuck the rifle butt in the crook of his arm and let the gun swing down at his side, casual-like.

The barrel fell off.

"Yee," Rich said in a tiny voice. He dropped to the ground, scrambling to stick the barrel back into the stock. He was quickly surrounded by three sets of black khakis.

RICH WAS ON HIS STOMACH, his wrists and ankles bound together with jumper cables, the ends of which were clamped to his ears. He rocked back and forth on the dock.

"Could someone turn me around, so I could see?"

Sean kicked Rich in the head, spinning him toward the lake, where the action was.

"Thanks, dude."

"Any time."

Beth, Cammy and Treece watched forlornly as the canoe paddled further into the lake.

"Cheer up, ladies," Sean said. "Once Michaels teaches mini-Romeo a lesson, we're going to party."

"I'm kind of partied out," Treece said.

"No," Dustin said, "you're not."

EARLY TWILIGHT gloomily illuminated the small canoe as it slid across the dead lake. Denis was paddling. Kevin played coxswain, smacking Denis every few seconds to keep him on task. It was more humiliating than painful at this point.

"Your error was not striking when you had tactical advantage back there."

Denis kept his head lowered and continued paddling.

"How long can you swim, Cooverman?"

Water was the only thing that had ever come close to

killing Denis. His mother had left the bathroom for only a moment, to get a cleaner towel. The toddler was facedown in the tub when she returned. He wasn't moving.

"I don't know."

Baby Denis's eyes were open, watching. He was fascinated by the no-slip fish and was unaware he was drowning.

"Well then," Kevin said, "let's you and me find out."

Denis could swim forever. His father had made sure of that. The boy had been snorkeling since he was five, diving since he was ten. He had a half dozen international scuba certificates, including one for diving in caves. Water had tried to kill Denis, and he had made water his bitch.

So Denis was certainly not afraid of getting thrown in some smelly puddle. He could sink to the bottom of the lake and swim underwater all the way to the shore without being seen. He could hide in the woods until morning, or until the authorities arrived to dredge the lake.

The only problem with that plan was that it once again required Denis to run away.

"I hope you fucked her," Kevin said, making conversation.

He wasn't afraid of Kevin anymore, Denis realized. These constant attempts on his life were getting annoying, as a matter of fact.

"It would be a shame for you to die without the privilege of fucking Beth Cooper," Kevin said. "No, *privilege* isn't right. More like, without getting *your turn*."

That inchoate rage deep inside Denis was beginning to differentiate itself.

"You did fuck her, didn't you?"

The rage had a face.

"Won't say? You're a *gentleman*? Well, that would be a first for her." Kevin peered into the water. "This is deep enough."

Kevin saw the paddle but wouldn't remember it.

FROM THE SHORE, it was difficult to tell who had gone into the water. Then Denis stood up in the canoe, legs apart, and thrust the paddle into the air. The poncho helped immeasurably in completing the cinematic silhouette.

Rich grinned. "*Star Wars* one-sheet, 1977."

Sean kicked him in the head again.

HIS MOMENT OF GLORY savored, Denis turned his attention to his victim. He scanned the water around him.

"Kevin?"

Kevin's face floated a few inches below the surface. The eyes were closed and a thin red ribbon wafted off the temple. The face grew darker as it sank.

A vision of Dr. Henneman, uncharacteristically dressed as Obi Wan Kenobi, appeared to Denis.

*Denis, with your SAT scores, you'd practically have to kill someone to not get into Northwestern.**

"Oh no," Denis whispered. "I've practically killed someone!"

Denis threw off the poncho and dove into the lake.

NO ONE ON SHORE wanted Kevin completely dead, and there was a general sense of relief when Denis resurfaced and started back with the soldier in tow.

Treece nudged Sean.

"Go! Get in there and help!"

Sean, insulted: "Do I look like a *fucking marine?*"

Denis did not need the help. Among his assorted international diving certificates was one for lifesaving; he had even worked a couple of summers lifeguarding at the Cambridge on the Lake condominium complex,

*His brain filled in the *Northwestern.*

where his main duty was finding out whose kid was pooping in the pool.

As he reached chest-high water, Denis shifted Kevin onto his shoulders in a fireman's carry. He emerged from the lake, clad only in wet tighty whiteys, and it became apparent to all assembled he was no 98-pound weakling. He was 105 pounds of sleek swimmer's physique, previously hidden by shy hunching and frightened cowering. His hair was wildly tousled and his wet hairless body shimmered in the first morning light.

Treece was awed. "It's like when Clark Kent turns into Batman."

"Check out the underpants," Cammy said approvingly.

"I have," said Beth.

DENIS DUMPED KEVIN onto the grass. "I'm going to need some help," he said, rolling the body over. He looked to Sean and Dustin. They looked back.

"Don't they teach you guys CPR in the army?"

"Yeah," Dustin shrugged. "I wasn't really paying attention."

"The job's not really about *saving* people," Sean said.

"I know CPR." Beth crouched next to Kevin.

"Okay," Denis said, "you do breaths and I'll do compressions."

"I'm not putting my mouth on his! We're broken up."

"You are?" Denis asked a little too transparently.

Beth was annoyed. "Why would I mess around with you if I was still with him? *What kind of person do you think I am?*"

The tiff would have to wait.

Kevin rolled to his side and vomited some water. After several seconds, he opened his eyes. He smiled.

"There you go, Cooverman," he said with a wet rattle, "giving up your tactical advantage again."

Kevin shoved Denis to the ground as he staggered to his feet. He cleared his throat and clasped his hands. "Okay!"

"It's getting real late," Dustin complained. "Can't we just beat the shit out of him and go?"

"Fine," Kevin said. He lifted his foot to stomp on Denis's kidneys. He was in this pose when the spotlight hit him.

"Step away from the boy," a loudspeaking voice said.

The squad car flashed its cherries and gave a short burst of siren for emphasis. The other Lake Hakaka police car pulled up behind it.

The army men seemed perplexed by this turn of events.

"*Duh,*" Rich informed them. "We called the police."

"We're not like stupid teenagers," Treece added.

23.

THE MOST EXCELLENT AND LAMENTABLE TRAGEDY OF DENIS AND ELIZABETH

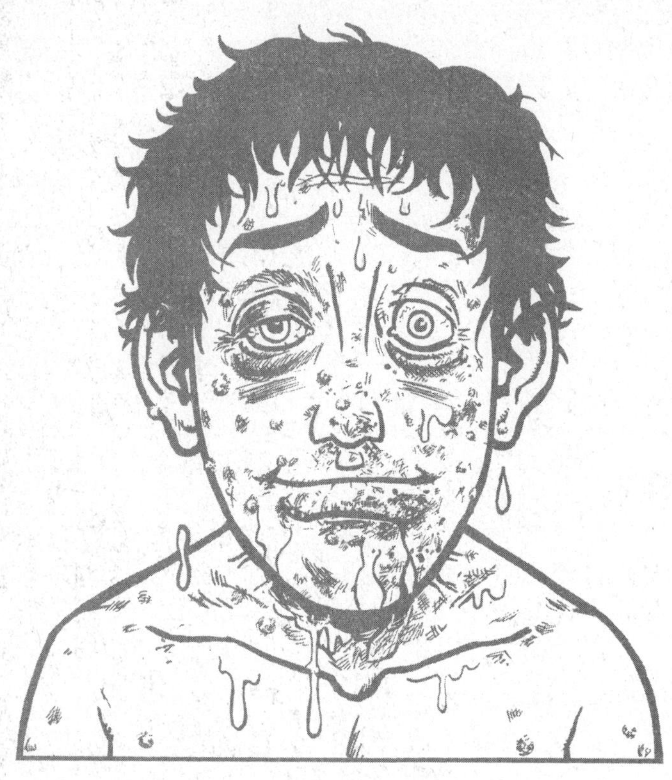

I'VE JUST HAD THE BEST SUMMER
OF MY LIFE, AND NOW I HAVE TO GO AWAY.
IT ISN'T FAIR.

SANDY OLSSON

IT WAS MORNING when the squad car pulled up to 22 Mary Lu Lane, a tiny ranch house only a block from where Denis's father grew up. This was what was known as Old Buffalo Grove, which local Realtors touted for its large selection of *starter homes*.

Denis, Rich and Beth were in the backseat, being delivered home by a Lake Hakaka police officer who, in all honesty, had nothing better to do. Cammy and Treece were escorted in the other patrol car, after sitting on Sean and Dustin's laps for the ride to the station.

Denis's anxious predictions to the contrary, it did not appear as if Beth was going to be charged with ten crimes. Kevin's father had quickly agreed to forgo larceny charges in exchange for Denis's statement that he didn't feel as if he was being murdered at any point in the evening. Treece's father dealt with the Woolly family, persuading them that seeking justice for the front of their house was not worth a class-action lawsuit over knowingly serving alcohol to minors at a party supervised by their drug-addicted son. Later it would turn out that none of the kids at the party had seen anything anyway.

On the ride home, Rich had entertained Officer Peasley with Pacino cops from *Serpico, Sea of Love, Heat* and *Cruising*, as well as Pacino robbers from *Dog Day Afternoon, Scarface, Donnie Brasco* and *Dick Tracy*. He threw in a little *Scent of a Woman*, even though it was off-topic.

Denis and Beth fell asleep on each other, briefly, and at different times.

BETH GOT OUT OF THE CAR. She left the door open to say good-bye.

"Thank you for a *very* memorable evening."

"We'll have to do it again sometime."

"Sure," Beth said.

Denis said, "Sure."

"Good luck. With Northwestern, and everything."

"You too. With everything."

She extended her hand. Denis took it. Beth grinned, and bent down and kissed him.

On the forehead.

She walked away.

Denis got out of the car. "Wait."

Beth turned around.

"See you at the reunion," Denis said.

"Yeah."

"If you're not too fat, I'll marry you."

"Thanks," Beth said. "That'll give me some incentive."

She fluttered her fingers in farewell, and started back toward the house. None of the lights were on. She took out her keys and let herself in.

Denis got back in the squad car.

"YOU'LL SEE HER AGAIN," Rich said as the car pulled away. "She's had a taste of the Coove."

"Please stop calling me that."

"You know, I think we might have more traction with 'The Penis' anyway. We just need to spin it, give it a legendary angle—"

"You said it would be better if I got over her."

Rich didn't answer right away.

"I just want what you want."

Denis gazed out the window. He got what he wanted. Didn't he?

A minute or so later, Rich spoke again.

"Hey, guess what? I think I'm gay."

Denis's reaction was more pronounced than he thought it would be.

"Dude," Rich said. "I'm not gay *for you*."

"That's great." Denis recovered. "I mean, the first part."

"I may be bi. Cary Grant was bi."

Denis spoke next, but not for another couple of minutes.

"So," he said, "what're you doing later?"

"I gotta go get my shoes."

"After that, want to come over?"

"What for?"

"I don't know."

"Sure."

THE PATROL CAR TURNED onto Hackberry Drive. Rich spoke again.

"The DVD for *Go, Mutants!* just came out. On the unrated disc, Shanley Harmer is 30 percent more nude."

"I thought you were gay."

"Celebrity nudity transcends sexual orientation. You want me to bring it over?"

"By all means."

Denis's parents were waiting for him on the front lawn. His mother hugged him, started to cry, and ran into the house. Denis and his father walked to the door.

"I hope you had fun," he said.

"I did. I had fun."

They stepped over the apple tree.

"You know we're going to have to punish you . . . somehow."

"I know."

"What do they do these days? Do they still ground you? I don't even know."

"Whatever it is, it was worth it."

Mr. C put his arm around his son.

"Let's not tell your mother that."

24.

THE CRAWL

ALL MY MEMORIES FROM HIGH SCHOOL ARE FROM TONIGHT.

DENIS COOVERMAN

Denis grew seven inches that summer, and gained nearly forty pounds. Growing pains kept him in bed for most of July, but he didn't mind.

Rich gave homosexuality a shot, didn't like that either, and was holding out to see what the other alternatives were.

Cammy and Treece decided they were just good friends, who should not drink so much around each other anymore.

Denis didn't see Beth Cooper again until late August, a week before he had intended to leave for school . . .

OBLIGATIONS

I've always thought that endless acknowledgments have no place in a novel, but then I wrote one, and found a place.

And so I must thank my book agent, Sarah Burnes, without whose hounding this book would never have been written. And all my other agents—Gregory McKnight, Matthew Snyder and Jeff Jacobs—who keep my children fed. And my old agent, Cara Stein, because I adore her.

I must also thank my editor, Lee Boudreaux, who I signed with because she was the only one to offer me a goddam Diet Coke, but then it turned out she is also magnificently underhanded and makes your book good without you even noticing it.

Thank you to my parents, whose loving upbringing meant I had to write a novel, rather than a much better-selling memoir. And thank you to my foxy wife, Becky, and I'm sorry for the long summer of not showering and acting more like a writer than usual.

For lending their real names to this book when I got tired of making up new ones, I thank: Jill Rosenbaum, Ariel Kaminer, Claudia Confer (who really was the nicest and prettiest cheerleader at BGHS) and my brother, Kevin, and his sons Sean and Dustin (who really aren't that villainous.)

Future obligations to Kurt Andersen, Dave Barry, David Schickler, and Tom Perrotta for reading the thing and risking their reputations by endorsing it.

And thank you, Beth Cooper, all of you.

The Novels of Wright Morris

Books by Wright Morris in Bison Book Editions
Date of first publication at the left

1942 My Uncle Dudley (BB 589)
1945 The Man Who Was There (BB 598)
1948 The Home Place (BB 386)
1949 The World in the Attic (BB 528)
1951 Man and Boy (BB 575)
1952 The Works of Love (BB 558)
1953 The Deep Sleep (BB 586)
1954 The Huge Season (BB 590)
1956 The Field of Vision (BB 577)
1957 Love Among the Cannibals (BB 620)
1958 The Territory Ahead (BB 666)
1960 Ceremony in Lone Tree (BB 560)
1963 Cause for Wonder (BB 656)
1965 One Day (BB 619)
1967 In Orbit (BB 612)

In Preparation

1962 What a Way to Go (BB 636)
1972 War Games (BB 657)

Also available from the University of Nebraska Press

Wright Morris: Structures and Artifacts
Photographs 1933–1954

Conversations with Wright Morris (BB 630)
Edited with an introduction by Robert E. Knoll

THE NOVELS OF Wright Morris

A Critical Interpretation

BY G. B. Crump

UNIVERSITY OF NEBRASKA PRESS
LINCOLN AND LONDON

The publication of this book was assisted by a grant from The Andrew W. Mellon Foundation.

LIBRARY OF CONGRESS CATALOGING IN PUBLICATION DATA

Crump, Gail Bruce, 1942–
The novels of Wright Morris.
Bibliography: p. 243
Includes index.
1. Morris, Wright, 1910– —Criticism and interpretation. I. Title.
PS3515.07475Z63 813'.5'2 77–15796
ISBN 0–8032–0962–2

Contents

The Novels of Wright Morris

1

Introduction: The Two Sides of Wright Morris's Fiction

GRANVILLE HICKS begins his introduction to *Wright Morris: A Reader* with a familiar lament: "Those of us who strongly admire the work of Wright Morris . . . are always wondering why everybody doesn't see his writings as we see them, as one of the most imposing edifices on the contemporary literary horizon. We, who look forward to each book of his as it is announced, and talk about it with excitement when it appears, cannot understand why so many pulses remain calm."[1] Indeed, the continued public and scholarly indifference to Morris, whose career as a novelist, essayist, and photographer now stretches over more than thirty years and twenty-five volumes,[2] is epitomized by the fact that *Wright Morris: A Reader* (1970) has pointedly not done for him what *The Portable Faulkner* did for Faulkner. If this neglect were deserved, of course, it would not be worth mentioning, but I believe, with Hicks, that Morris is an important writer. In an effort to demonstrate his importance and clarify his contribution to modern fiction, I begin this study by looking at some critical comments made about him which help to isolate significant features of his work. Since I believe that these comments represent an incomplete and sometimes inadequate view of Morris, I offer a new theoretical groundwork for criticizing his fiction. Specifically, I distinguish two broad currents in Morris's art, both of which must be taken into account in order to arrive at a satisfactory picture of it. When both are considered, I believe one can see that Morris's fiction encompasses a wider range of human experience than has generally been thought.

In a brief judgment, Alfred Kazin goes to the heart of what many readers must feel on opening a Morris novel for the first time:

> I confess that I have never been able to get very much from Wright Morris, though he is admired by influential judges. In reading Morris's *The Field of Vision*, I thought of George Santayana's complaint that contemporary poets often give the reader the mere suggestion of a poem and expect him to finish the poem for them. Morris's many symbols, his showy intentions, his pointed and hinted significances, seem to me a distinct example of the literary novel which professors like to teach and would like to write: solemnly meaningful in every intention, but without the breath and extension of life.[3]

Presented without illustration, this one-paragraph assessment (of a book which won the National Book Award) would effectively quench any reader's desire to look at the novel itself. The core of Kazin's indictment, the sense of incompleteness related to the presence of "significances" both "hinted" and "pointed," is unquestionably discernable in *The Field of Vision* (1956). In the following passage, depicting the failed artist Boyd's memory of a scene in a children's playground, the narrative voice is distinctively Morris's:

> A small child leaned against the heavy wire fence, her eyes to one of the holes. So absorbed with what she saw, or what she thought she saw, she gazed into Boyd's face as if he were blind. As if she could see into his eyes, but he could not see out of them. He felt himself—some self—in the midst of a wakeful dream. Had he dozed off with his own eyes wide open, seeing nothing? Had this child stood there for some time, gazing in? This child—for that was all she was, a soiled-faced, staring little monkey—seemed to have seen in him what Boyd could not see himself. What she saw moved her to pity. Pity seemed to be all she felt. But what *Boyd* saw, and what *he* felt, was something else. He could not seem to

> close the eyes that she stood gazing in. He could not speak to her, smile or wink, or indicate to her that *he* was now present. He could do nothing. If the child had run up the blind on his true *self*, he could not run it down. He seemed to be fixed, with his eyes wide open, a freshly mounted trophy with the pupils of the eyes frozen open so the passer-by could look in.
>
> Had he been mad? For the length of that moment he might have been. Or had he been—as he had come to think—for once in his life sane. Able to see, at that moment, from the other side. Behind appearances, such as the one he made himself. Eagle Scout Boyd, the pocket snatcher, turned inside out like a stocking, so that the underside of the stitching showed. [p. 198]

There is definitely a quality of Joycean epiphany here, an intimation that something very important to and about the character is being revealed. Superficially Morris's method is more direct and explicit than Joyce's often is in *Dubliners*; unlike many of Joyce's characters, Boyd is a sensitive artist of whom we get a candid inside view. The passage contains relatively little of the dramatic irony and few of the external dramatic details Joyce frequently relies on to establish character and situation. The images in the passage are Boyd's own, deliberately chosen from his own experience, and if he knows to choose them, he should also know what they mean. Yet the full significance of his epiphany constantly eludes us, always escaping into the next sentence and the next, and the passage never seems to come to any resolution. Readers might very well feel that Morris expects them to finish the paragraph for him.

Nevertheless, I would suggest that while Kazin perceives an effect that is certainly present, he misses its purpose and its true character. The real quality of this passage is not incompleteness, but tentativeness. The rhetorical questions substituted for statements, the qualifying adverbial clauses beginning with *if* and *as if*, and the complete thoughts broken into two or more sentences—all capture the mind in the process of thinking, an effect readily recognized in more conventional stream of consciousness ("direct quotation" of the flow of thought using free association, a high concentration of figurative language, materials from prespeech levels of consciousness, and syntactic distortion), but often missed in the works of writers like Morris or D. H. Lawrence, where the narration is third-person limited omniscient and the syntactic distortion is slight.

It is especially important to recognize the tentativeness implied in Morris's style for what it is because the style reflects his deeper conviction that the truth of the passage remains relative, tentative, and a product of process, rather than an absolute. This explains why the prominent verbs are *seemed* and *might*, and it also explains why the novel as a whole is narrated through the eyes of several characters who perceive reality differently from one another. This feeling that truth is tentative is tied to Morris's belief that life, experience, and the universe itself exist in a state of constant becoming, a belief fundamental to an understanding of his work.

A second critical judgment illustrates that the nature and scope of Morris's fiction is not completely understood. In a recent book surveying contemporary American literature, Ihab Hassan lists Morris among several "prominent" novelists and yet seems uneasy with a sizable portion of his work:

> Satire and nostalgia mingle in Morris's work. However, in such later fictions as *What a Way to Go* (1962), a kind of lightness, an amusing triviality, begins to show. Hoping to catch the new mood of erotic comedy, he shifts his focus; his locale ranges from Italy to Mexico. But his lasting contribution lies elsewhere. Trained initially as a photographer, Morris composes in his best novels a montage of static scenes through which the lost life of Americans may be glimpsed.[4]

Since Hassan's book is a broad introduction, we cannot expect him to be an expert on every writer he mentions. Thus, he can be excused for repeating the common misconception that Morris turned to fiction after first being interested in photography,[5] and probably Hassan ought not to be held too accountable for the overall gist of his remarks. However, this comment does reflect a view, widely held even among Morris specialists, that only his American novels (often only his midwestern novels) and those with "static scenes" are of any account. "Nostalgia" is the war cry of this group. Their predilections are evident in a recent, more extended and specialized treatment, which occasionally sounds as if only the midwestern novels exist: "In *The Field of Vision* Morris finally hit upon the technique of developing several centers of consciousness within a novel, each representing a particular 'field of vision.' "[6] Actually, the technique first appears in mature form in *The Deep Sleep* (1953), one of Morris's best novels, although it is set in Pennsylvania.

The problem with this attitude is not the judgment it leads to on the relative worth of the midwestern novels; the judgment may even be correct. Rather it is that the work of a writer is no more divisible than his sensibility. What T. S. Eliot once wrote in an essay on Yeats is true of Morris: "You cannot divide the work of a great poet. . . . When there is the continuity of such a sensitive personality and such a single work, the later work cannot be understood, or properly enjoyed, without a study and appreciation of the earlier; and the later work again reflects light upon the earlier, and shows us beauty and significance not before perceived."[7] To see Morris steadily, we must see him whole, and the real challenge facing his critics is not to decide which books he should have written and which not, but rather to arrive at a perception of his career which can accommodate them all—good and bad, those set in Nebraska and those set in Europe, those that are nostalgic and those that are farcical.

One critic to accept this challenge has been Wayne Booth. In an important article entitled "The Two Worlds in the Fiction of Wright Morris," Booth argues that Morris's fiction is structured around a cardinal distinction between the "phony" and the "real," between the everyday, time-bound world of "reality" in the ordinary sense and the timeless world of a deeper, more perfect platonic reality.[8] In Booth's words, Morris believes that "the real world, gruesome as it is, is not as real as it looks. To endure it, indeed to live at all, a man must . . . find a more genuine reality by getting 'out of this world' " (p. 377). There are three "bridges" available to him: "Imagination: the moment of truth" (p. 380), "Heroism: the moment of real action" (p. 377), and "Love: the moment of compassion" (p. 387). Thus, "whatever has been 'really' *done*, *imagined*, or *felt* has been, in fact, recreated, transformed from one world into another" (p. 395). Morris, then, is "attempting the fictional voyage of discovery into the nature of reality itself, and . . . he discovers the real in whatever is permanent in a world of change. The permanent is permanent by virtue of being outside of time and yet as human beings we discover it only in time, only in the world of impermanent things" (p. 394).

Booth's two worlds have special meaning for Morris's theory of art, but of more immediate interest is their relevance to his conception of time and, through that, to the theme of nostalgia mentioned by Hassan. For Morris, proof that an act transcends the real world is its power over the imagination, and the proof of that power is the vividness of its impression on the memory. Thus, the central tension between time and timelessness often resolves itself into a tension between the perceived present and the imperishable memories of the past.

The force of Booth's observations is best seen by applying them to a particular work. The first manuscript of *Cause for Wonder*, a relatively late novel (1963), dates from 1935,[9] making it one of Morris's earliest works in conception. The prolonged gestation demonstrates the power the book had over his imagination, and perhaps as a result of this power, it is Morris's most explicit and schematic examination of time and memory and is especially useful for purposes of illustration. Read in the light of Booth's observations, *Cause for Wonder* becomes a testament to the power of the imagination to rescue life from the depredations of time. The protagonist

Warren Howe had spent an unforgettable winter at Schloss Riva in Austria, thirty years before the present time of the novel. He associates this stay with an artifact from his childhood, a castle in a snow-filled glass ball, which becomes a symbol of the past. Howe characterizes the castle in this paperweight as being "both in and out of this world" (p. 9), a concrete existent in the "phony" world of becoming which, by virtue of its power over the imagination, is preserved from time in a platonic realm of ideal reality (the ice-snow image applied to that which has escaped life as process is one of Morris's favorites).

In *Cause for Wonder* and several other Morris novels, movement in space is equated with movement in time. The novel's two-part structure follows Howe from California and "Time Present" to Schloss Riva and "Time Past." The trip to Riva, actually made in the present time of the novel, symbolizes the power of memory to recapture the past and produce a sense of time similar to that in the opening lines of Eliot's *Burnt Norton*: "Time present and time past / Are both present in time future, / And time future contained in time past." In *Cause for Wonder*, time, as experienced in the consciousness, amounts to "skull-time. . . . A form of daylight time salvage, a deep-freeze where time was stored like the mammoth in the Siberian cakes of ice" (pp. 268–69).

For Howe, the past is in one sense not unredeemable, not already behind him where the dark fields of the republic rolled on under the night. Nevertheless, both Morris and his critics have been concerned with Jay Gatsby's problem, the typically American nostalgia for a mythicized personal and historical past which no longer exists in fact. Nostalgia becomes a problem when, as for Gatsby and to a certain extent Howe, it interferes with man's functioning in the present.

Before attempting a critique of Booth's view, I think it would be useful to look at some of its further ramifications, as worked out in the four articles and one book by David

Madden.[10] These constitute the most sizable body of criticism on Morris. Drawing on the theories of Booth and of Joseph Campbell in his study of myth, *The Hero with a Thousand Faces*, Madden argues that Morris's novels center around a "hero," who generally has transcended Booth's real world through "audacity," "improvisation," and "transformation." The terms are taken from Morris's own criticism. Audacity denotes the brazenness to try anything; improvisation, the talent for implementing one's audacious impulses with the materials of the moment; and transformation, the conversion of reality into fiction or ideal reality. The first two are tools, the last the product. But "the uncommon men exist for the edification of the common" (p. 28). Every hero has his witnesses, and it is sometimes they who achieve transcendence as their imaginations transform the heroics they have observed. For Madden, the interaction of hero and witness is at the heart of Morris's fiction: "A central, recurring theme in Morris' novels, around which many other themes revolve and through which his vision is often focused—is the relationship between the hero and his witnesses. . . . who become in some way transformed as a result of their relationship with the hero" (p. 34). The Nebraska plains along the ninety-eighth meridian become Campbell's world navel, the source of mystic life to which the hero penetrates and whose power of transformation, traditionally represented as the elixir of life, he imparts to his witnesses. In these plains Madden also perceives opposite poles of the American culture and character; they mark the meeting point of East and West, realism and idealism, agrarian novel and western romance (p. 28).

Again *Cause for Wonder* is useful for illustration: Castle Riva receives its imaginative charge from its resident heroes—the mad caretaker George and his no less mad employer Dulac. During Howe's first stay, George played practical jokes, like sweeping snow from the roofs onto unsuspecting guests below. During the second visit, George paints everything within reach white, symbolically recreating the snow of thirty years before. In this way, he preserves the past in the present. Dulac ensures that he too will remain both in and out of this world, like his ugly wife with the face of a frog and the voice of an angel, by inviting the latter-day guests to Riva for his funeral, even though he is alive when they arrive. Dulac's remaining alive after his death is announced is emblematic of his ability to cheat death through his immortal impression on his witnesses, and when he later throws himself down a hill, he deliberately courts death to cast his lurid charm over the boy Brian: "He had . . . taken the plunge. In what way could he leave a more memorable impression on the boy. . . . Senility had not deprived him of the wisdom of his folly. A dead man, he returned to life in the boy" (p. 189). Like nostalgia, the hero-witness relationship can become a problem since the hero, if the spell he weaves is too strong, can imprison his witnesses in a single heroic moment. Booth acknowledges this problem (p. 180), and it is central to Madden's work.

The criticism of Booth and Madden is so fundamental to a study of Morris that no subsequent criticism can afford to leave them out of account, and the debts I owe to them in this book are frankly ubiquitous. Nevertheless, I would like to suggest some qualifications of their views. Booth admits that transcendence as a response to the unpleasantness of reality is "full of the paradoxes that plague any mystical solution in 'real' life. Achieving timeless triumphs does not really deal with the world, 'the world of men here below.' Attempts to deal with 'this temporal kingdom, this bloody cockpit,' inevitably involve a man in evil. . . . Yet attempts to escape the 'battleground' leave the victory to 'the Prince of Darkness' " (pp. 395–96). In spite of this admission, Booth's choice of the label *platonic* inevitably implies a preference for the timeless. It suggests that reaching for the transcendent world is somehow a higher and better course than trying to live in this world, and both Booth and Madden tend to treat transcendence in itself as an unalloyed good. The main reason for this admiration for the transcendent, aside from whatever internal evidence is available in the fiction, is that they equate all kinds of transcendence with the transcendence of art, which Morris discusses in his critical writings and seeks to accomplish in his own art. Yet to assume, as Booth and Madden do, that Morris is setting up the artist's creation of a transcendental fiction as a model for his characters to emulate is a mistake. Although art is essential in character, realistic art, like Morris's, labors to give a representation of existential life, a sense of how life really is. Yeats perhaps best expressed the dominant sense of modern life when he wrote, "Man can embody truth but he cannot know it."[11] A man or a character does not set out to live with imagination; he sets out to live—to write, to make love, to build friendships, to hate some things and embrace others, to plant crops where there is no rain, in Morris's words, to "face the battle of daily life" (*The Huge Season*, p. 169)—and if in the end he lives with imagination, if his life has a style, it is because of the way he does the other things. No matter how similar the result, Morris and his characters really set out from two different directions. By approaching the novels as if they are primarily intended to illustrate Morris's critical dicta, Booth and Madden inject an unnecessary degree of abstraction into their studies.

Moreover, the Morris who emerges from Booth's essay and from Madden's two early essays is Morris near the middle of his career. He is one Hassan would feel at home with, for this is largely the nostalgic Morris of the midwestern novels.[12] A more comprehensive view of his work, especially one which includes novels like *What a Way to Go* and the novels since *Cause for Wonder*, suggests that, while he recognizes the value of transcendence in art, Morris's feelings about it as a goal for people and characters are ambivalent and subject to change.

I suggest Morris's fiction should be examined using a somewhat different conceptual framework from Booth's. It is one which can be supported in the novels as a whole, which places books like *What a Way to Go* in relation to Morris's overall work, and which also throws new light on the quality of tentativeness observed earlier in the passage from *The Field of Vision*.

Morris's most comprehensive statement about the relation of life to art is in *The Territory Ahead* (1958): "In the novel it is conceptual power . . . that indicates genius, since only conception responds to the organic pressures of life. The conceptual act is the most organic act of man. It is this that unites him with the processes of nature, with the nature of life. If man is nature self-conscious . . . art is his expanding consciousness, and the creative act, in the deepest sense, is his expanding universe" (p. 229). Anyone prepared to find an emphasis on the transcendental character of the creative act will be surprised to find it tied so closely to a nature very much in this world. The stress on conception, consciousness, and the preeminence of the creative act is characteristic, but no more so than the emphasis on nature and process. Art is man's expanding consciousness. Since expansion implies process, it can occur only in time, only in a world which is in a state of becoming. Art represents the evolving consciousness of the artist, unfolding to the eyes of the beholders an ever widening moral horizon, and consciousness, the faculty whereby nature knows itself, is the most advanced product of evolution. Physical and imaginative conception are related acts. Morris's career reflects this world view. The gradual maturing of his craft and the evolution of his attitudes toward his material are instrumental to the tentativeness in the Boyd passage and have helped to make his fiction the best example of sustained creative growth in modern American literature.

The emphasis on the dynamic and organic is so intrinsic to Romanticism and is still of such great importance today that there is no reason to attribute Morris's ideas to any particular source. The philosophy of Henri Bergson, however, is especially helpful and appropriate to use in studying Morris, first, because Bergson's view of time resembles Morris's so closely, even employing some of the same images, and second, because Bergson's theories demonstrate particularly well the shortcomings of Booth's emphasis on a platonic dualism. To Bergson, there is a reality independent of man's perception of it and readily apprehensible by him. Existing in time-space, this reality is in a constant state of becoming: "There do not exist *things* made, but only things in the making, not *states* that remain fixed, but only states in the process of change."[13] In all living things including man, change is driven by what Bergson calls in one essay "the vital impetus," or the Life Force, which impels living things to evolve into higher and higher forms:

> All organized beings, from the humblest to the highest, from the first origins of life to the time in which we are, and in all places as in all times, do but evidence a single impulsion, the inverse of the movement of matter, and in itself indivisible. All the living hold together, and all yield to the same tremendous push. The animal takes its stand on the plant, man bestrides animality, and the whole of humanity, in space and in time, is one immense army galloping beside and before and behind each of us in an overwhelming charge.[14]

One aspect of the Life Force is consciousness, which the evolution of life requires in order to have some conception of its own needs and direction. Consciousness develops into instinct, in lower organisms, or intellect, in man, according to the differing needs of the various species. But the intellect developed in man is of such a kind that it does more than fulfill narrow and immediate needs. It is like an invention from which "we derive an immediate advantage," but of which it can be said that the advantage "is a slight matter compared with the new ideas and new feelings that the invention may give rise to in every direction" (*Creative Evolution*, p. 201). Indeed, the chief difference between man and the animals is that the intellect is "set free" from consideration of immediate ends and can turn to more philosophical self-contemplation (ibid., p. 203).

The similarity is obvious between these ideas and those in the passage from *The Territory Ahead* quoted earlier. Bergson's view of human awareness and human perception of time also resembles Morris's. Man perceives life as Bergson's "duration," which is the consciousness of time's motion made possible by memory: "There is no consciousness without memory, no continuation of a state without the addition, to the present feeling, of the memory of past moments. That is what duration consists of. Inner duration is the continuous life of a memory which prolongs the past into the present" (*Creative Mind*, p. 211). Man's apprehension of self is an apprehension of his own indivisible duration, which constantly grows as he moves forward in time and accrues more and more memories; the self is "a succession of states each one of which announces what follows and contains what precedes." Further, "it is just as much a continual winding, like that of a thread into a ball, for our past follows us, becoming larger and larger with the present it picks up on its way; and consciousness means memory" (ibid., p. 193). Thus, though time moves in one direction, man's memory makes his perception of it multidirectional, and time is experienced as a subjective state, as in Morris's "skull-time."

The emphasis on memory as defining the individual self and the problems it raises for the consciousness in keeping the past and present in their proper relationship are major themes in Morris's work, as my remarks on *Cause for Wonder* have partly illustrated. "Time might well be my subject. But how does one begin with time?" asks Howe at the opening of the novel. How does one begin with what has no beginning since it has always been? The similarity between Morris's "skull-time" and Bergson's duration is demonstrated by the fact that Howe uses an image very like Bergson's to describe his accumulating impressions as he moves through time and space: "We put everything on tape today, even time. The tape I have in mind is the line that runs down the center of a blacktop highway. . . . At sixty miles an hour time and space seem to wind on the spool beneath me. Or within me, which is more accurate. . . . At the wheel of the car, at sunrise, with the dawn light behind me, the road opening out before me, I sense a dimension of time that otherwise escapes me, the spool of tape being myself" (p. 50).[15]

The paradox of a timeless work of fiction about the subject of time is a central one in *Cause for Wonder*. Bergson's treatment of the same paradox leads me to my major point. The sense of duration, Bergson believed, could not be captured by rational analysis, which "generalizes at the same time that it abstracts" (*Creative Mind*, p. 196), that is, which reduces duration to uniform, discrete, and disembodied concepts. It could only be apprehended through "intuition," a sympathetic identification with the flow of time, which is experienced as "an uninterrupted continuity of unforseeable novelty" (ibid., p. 39). Although words partake of the abstraction of concepts, intuition can be verbally evoked by a "convergence of images" that "direct" the consciousness to a "precise point where there is a certain intuition to seize on" (ibid., p. 195). The value of a verbal structure like a novel is that it constitutes a highly organized pattern of images which stands above the flow of life and time and yet evokes an intuition of it. The novelty of art, made possible by the expanding consciousness of the artist and the accretion of past imaginative triumphs, keeps pace with and makes comprehensible the inexhaustible novelty of life.

I can now make a more formal statement of an earlier observation: Unlike art, life must remain in the flow, and novels, though verbal constructs, function to provide some intuition of the nonverbal, mobile reality. Booth's characterization of Morris as seeking a platonic reality is finally misleading because for Plato the mobile real was only an imperfect reflection of the static ideal, whereas for Bergson the static concept is only a relatively crude approximation of the mobile real. Although art may be transcendent, it is too strong to argue, as Booth seems to, that Morris always prefers stasis over mobility and heroic transcendence over imaginative engagement with the finite world of concrete existents for his characters. He is a novelist dealing with the world of experience, after all, not a philosopher dealing with the world of concepts, and he is especially a novelist whose developing consciousness of his material has led him to a constantly shifting sense of what constitutes the successful life.

Many of Morris's conceptions about man and his relation to the universe are presented in expository form by his friend the naturalist-essayist Loren Eiseley in *The Immense Journey*. In the course of his evolution, man became "something the world had never seen before—a dream animal—living at least partially within a secret universe of his own creation," which he created in his imagination and through which he "has escaped out of the eternal present of the animal world into a knowledge of past and future."[16] The point of my remarks about Bergson is implied in Eiseley's speculations on man's ability to imagine himself in other people's shoes, a special form of which is the novelist's dramatic identification with his characters. Eiseley sees imagination as the most remarkable testimony to nature's powers of expansion: "This is the most enormous extension of vision of which life is capable: the projection of itself into other lives. This is the lonely, magnificent power of humanity. It is, far more than any spatial adventure, the supreme epitome of the reaching out" (p. 33). As this observation implies, the powers of nature to evolve and man to imagine, though analogous in creative impetus, occupy very different realms, for nature evolves in time and space, while imagination, expressed in the immobile, conceptual images Bergson describes, transcends "any spatial adventure."

In other words, there are indeed two worlds in the fiction of Wright Morris, and any adequate conception of his work must make room for both. The first has an absolute reality; it is a playground of natural forces which do the work of time, destroying each moment in order to create the next. The second is the habitat of a supernatural force, imagination, which nevertheless grows out of the natural process of evolution.

The real-ideal dualism points to an emerging pattern of contrasts, or opposites, which can be found in Morris's work. They include physical conception and imaginative conception, life and art, flow and arrest, process and culmination, text (outside of space but experienced in time) and photo (outside of time but experienced in space), man and nature, hero and witness—all but the last three pairs subsumed under Booth's two worlds. The relative weight Morris assigns to one side of the dualism or another varies from book to book depending upon the specific situation depicted, the side which other themes happen to give the greater stress, and the point to which his developing consciousness of the world has brought him. His reservation of absolute judgment grows first from an ambivalence toward his subject, an ambivalence which is the only legitimate and truthful reaction to a profoundly ambiguous world, and from his basic premise that life is process. His tendency to think in patterns of opposites on whose relative worth conclusive judgment is withheld is further evidence of his deliberate tentativeness; respect for the unfinished character of the world prevents him from emphasizing once and for all one side of a dualism when tomorrow he may find the other more cogent.

Morris has always been a strong spokesman for the importance of tradition in shaping the individual talent, and his own talent has been partially formed by two very different writers—D. H. Lawrence and Henry James—who are both singled out for praise in *The Territory Ahead.* Morris himself has said that his admiration for other writers is "remote from imitation";[17] it is rather an awareness of literary tradition as part of the total culture out of which any writer must write. Because, as he says, echoing James's judgment, "It is the fiction that shapes the fact,"[18] Morris was "influenced" by

Lawrence and James before he ever knew their work.[19] Like any good artist, he was attuned to his time and place, which owed a part of their sense of themselves to these men. The debt to James has received more attention perhaps because it involves technique, especially in the well-defined matter of point of view. One thing I want to do is at least partially to redress the balance by exploring his debt to Lawrence.

Anyone familiar with Lawrence's expository writings, especially *Apocalypse*, *Psychoanalysis and the Unconscious*, and *Fantasia of the Unconscious*, will recognize the family resemblance between his world and Bergson's.[20] In *Apocalypse* one finds a close cousin of Bergson's organicism: "The cosmos is a vast living body, of which we are still parts. The sun is a great heart whose tremors run through our smallest veins. The moon is a great gleaming nerve-centre from which we quiver forever."[21] In *Psychoanalysis and the Unconscious* one finds Bergsonian "consciousness" called the "unconscious," made the measure of individual identity, and equated with physiological life processes: "Where the individual begins, life begins. . . . And also, where the individual begins, the unconscious, which is the specific life-motive, also begins. . . . this source [of the unconscious] . . . is the first ovule cell from which an individual organism arises. At the moment of conception . . . does a new unit of life, of consciousness, arise in the universe."[22] Such consciousness, for Lawrence, was truly "blood consciousness," the pulse in the heart and sinews of the total man. It resembles what Morris calls in *What a Way to Go* "the wisdom of the body," just as the sexual ethic in that novel and *Love Among the Cannibals* resembles the sexual ethic in Lawrence's fiction.

But these explicit resemblances, striking as they are, are less profound than some subtle affinities between the personalities of the authors. Morris spells out what Lawrence means to him in an interview: "Temperamentally, I now [1958] lean very strongly to such an imaginative figure as D. H. Lawrence, who in his later years defined to me the serious predicament of a man coming to terms with the present and using the past, not abusing it; in an effort to make this imaginative act possible" (Bleufarb, p. 35). To "come to terms with the present" is to recognize creation as an unending process of becoming, to accept what Lawrence called "the immediate present"[23] as the one point at which man, through his choices, can determine the shape of the uncreated future, and to exercise the responsibility thereby incurred. A man's use of the past is to let evolution work through him; he recognizes that in choosing he chooses not only for himself but also for the strange and strangely wise life processes that have devoted a billion years of evolution to producing him. This is his tie to the past; his tie to the future is the imaginative act in life and art which helps to determine what form that future will have. As Morris writes in *The Territory Ahead*, "the man who lives in the present—in his own present—lives to that extent in both the past and the future: the man who seeks to live elsewhere, both as an artist and as a man, has deceived himself" (p. 230).

In Morris's work, the treatment of choice more nearly resembles that of such doctrinaire existentialists as Sartre than that of Lawrence: characters are often confronted with very difficult dilemmas resulting from the nature of the contingent world in which they find themselves. Nevertheless, like Lawrence, Morris senses a creative presence in the universe that comes close to being God and that debars him from the radical states of anxiety, fear and trembling, and sickness unto death usually associated with existentialism. Impersonal forces are working their obscure ends in man, but there are ends, however obscure. Moreover, existentialism is an extremely self-oriented philosophy, while Morris's most sensitive characters, like those of Lawrence, have an instinctive sense of belonging among the larger forces of life in the cosmos and recognize that the universe is not a mere backdrop for their own self-absorbed little dramas.

To Morris, in *The Territory Ahead*, Lawrence is "indispensable" to writers in the immediate American present because he is the modern author whose work most fully expresses the dynamic and organic character of life. While Eliot cultivated familiar gods "to make the modern world possible in art," Lawrence quested after strange gods to make "life possible in the modern world" (p. 225). Eliot required familiar gods to evoke an order and an absolute from the past which would make artistic sense of the chaos of the present. For Lawrence this chaos represented, not disintegration of past order, but unlimited possibilities for choosing a new order. Each man, each day, could become the resurrected Christ of *The Man Who Died*, dead to the old world yet newly awake and alive to a new world. Old gods must be replaced with new, for only eternally changing gods can satisfy the eternally changing nature of life. A strange god, which nevertheless "will bear an astonishing resemblance to the one it displaced" (p. 230), is the visible sign of the new cosmos which Lawrence, with his ever expanding consciousness, perceived and, in perceiving, created.

When Morris takes as his subject "blood consciousness" and its habitat, the life of the present, he has D. H. Lawrence looking over one shoulder. When he turns his own consciousness, in the sense of his shaping imagination, upon moral and psychological nuances in the American present, he has James looking over the other, for the real protagonist in his novels is often the sensitive observer whose consciousness, in the Jamesian sense, expands in perceiving subtler and subtler ramifications of the observed experience. Lawrence speaks for the life in art, its "raw material," its humanly meaningful "object," but, as Morris writes in *The Territory Ahead*, James refined the "object" in art almost out of existence. For him, life, embodied in the author's "experience," and consciousness were one: "Experience is never limited, and it is never complete; it is an immense sensibility, a kind of huge spider-web of the finest silken threads suspended in the chamber of consciousness, and catching every air-borne particle in its tissue."[24] Thus the object is replaced by the subject, raw material by the author's consciousness of his material, or in Morris's metaphor, the sock by the unraveled yarn (*The Territory Ahead*, p. 100): "One thing always leads to another, that in turn to another, and this play of nuances, like ripples lapping on a pond, is the dramatis personae of James, the novelist. His subject was his own ceaselessly expanding consciousness" (ibid., p. 97). It is also, in a very real sense, his technique. In narrating his stories from the point of view of his "lucid reflectors," James placed his readers behind the artist's all-seeing eye and all-comprehending vision and gave the very act of vision a local habitation and a name. If "the material seems missing," Morris says, we find instead "the *im*material . . . in his books" (ibid., p. 95), a result predictable and fitting from a writer who found experience in the artist's "power to guess the unseen from the seen, to trace the implications of things, to judge the whole piece by the pattern" ("The Art of Fiction," p. 35). For Lawrence, his artistic consciousness was in the service of moral perceptions which could renew the world if accepted by all. For James, on the other hand, consciousness was a sufficient end in itself: "It is in the Jamesian moment of experience that one is most alive, most real; for . . . the Jamesian moment leads to full consciousness, through which one's inner, personal reality is achieved."[25]

Morris is deeply indebted to James in countless ways: for his emphasis on the importance of art, for his use of limited narrators rather than an omniscient narrator, for his insistence on the need for technique generally, and, not the least, for his clear-eyed criticism of America in *The American Scene*, which Morris still finds valid fifty years later. Like James, Morris believes that "Life *is* consciousness. Therefore . . . art *makes* life—by extending consciousness" (Cornwell, p. 136). Like James, Morris seems at times to be writing novels in which little happens, in which external action is subordinated to the intense drama of consciousness in the process of perceiving a moral revelation. This effect is best seen in what James thought was the finest moment in *The Portrait of a Lady*, "my young woman's extraordinary vigil on the occasion that was to become to her such a landmark. . . . it is but a vigil of searching criticism; but it throws the action further forward than twenty 'incidents' might have done. . . . It is a representation simply of her motionlessly *seeing*, and an attempt withal to make the mere still lucidity of her act as 'interesting' as the surprise of a caravan or the identification of a pirate. . . . but it all goes on without her being approached by another person and without her leaving her chair."[26] In *The Territory Ahead*, Morris describes the precise stylistic effect of such a scene: "The mind of James . . . gives off and and receives a series of vibrations that find their resolution in parenthesis. Nothing is closed. Closure means a loss of consciousness" (pp. 96–97). This is a reasonable description of the Boyd passage cited earlier, just as James's comment aptly characterizes *The Field of Vision* as a whole.

Morris associates the organizing power of man's consciousness with metaphors of sight, as James does in the passage quoted above and in one of his most famous statements about fiction:

> The house of fiction has . . . not one window, but a million—a number of possible windows not to be reckoned, rather; everyone of which has been pierced . . . by the need of the individual vision and by the pressure of the individual will. These apertures, of dissimilar shape and size, hang so, all together, over the human scene that we might have expected of them a greater sameness of report than we find. They are but windows at the best, mere holes in a dead wall, disconnected, perched aloft; they are not hinged doors opening straight on life. . . . at each of them stands a figure with a pair of eyes, or at least with a field-glass, which forms, again and again, for observation, a unique instrument,

> insuring to the person making use of it an impression distinct from every other. [*Art of the Novel*, p. 46]

In places the metaphor suggests paintings on a wall as well as windows, reminding us that both James and Morris use works of visual art in their fiction as devices to suggest the quality of vision in various artist-characters. However, thinking of fiction in terms of an essentially spatial art form has results in Morris it does not have in James.

Lawrence and James serve to isolate and illuminate two distinguishable, though finally inseparable, modes in Morris's fiction. The first mode, built around what can be called "the still-point structure," exhibits qualities which especially show Morris's affinities with James, though occasionally with un-Jamesian results. The best example is also one of Morris's best books, *The Field of Vision*. In novels using the still-point structure, Morris expands a moment of consciousness like that experienced by Isabel Archer to encompass his entire novel. To do so successfully, he must subordinate external action to the inner drama of consciousness; this, in turn, causes the setting to be static and the time which elapses in the work to be drastically shortened (it is about three hours in *The Field of Vision*). The combined result is much more of a sense of a timeless, spatial aesthetic experience than is ever found in James, for all his visual metaphors; like Morris's photos, these novels seem to freeze reality by removing it from time, an effect sharpened by frequent flashbacks suggesting the timeless skull-time of *Cause for Wonder*. Multiple centers of consciousness are used to tell the story in the third person. The ongoing "action" of this mode is not so much movement in time, as a movement from narrator to narrator, with each seeing the action according to his own peculiar psychological angle of vision. As the author returns to the same character a second and third time, he creates the effect of circling the observed action, each time broadening its implications and deepening the reader's understanding. As a stimulant to consciousness, the action becomes a still point, like a mystic world axis, around which consciousness circles. The true still point rests, not in the action itself, but in the locus it provides for a moment of full consciousness in the beholders, an almost mystical moment of intuiting the truth at the heart of reality. One critic has described a similar effect in James: "The development or extension of consciousness was to be achieved by what James termed the 'process of vision': the gradual accumulation of separate moments of experience, 'the happy moments of our consciousness'. . . . a succession of lesser moments leading to the moment of vision . . . of full consciousness—a moment of acute, mental and emotional awareness similar to Eliot's timeless moment of illumination" (Cornwell, p. 128). The mystical implications of the phrase *the still point*, used by Morris himself in *The Field of Vision* (p. 111), need to be further explored, but it can best be done later in discussing the kinds of heroes in Morris's fiction.

Although these similarities between Morris and James exist, Morris does not always manage to dramatize in this mode a "development" of consciousness of the sort found in James, a development which convinces us there is a permanent change in a character's moral makeup. Isabel Archer's character seems truly to grow in wisdom because her moment of consciousness is the culmination of a long, slowly developing dramatic action and because it is then tested in the crucible of subsequent action when she must decide whether or not to return to Osmond. By shortening the elapsed time of his novels and using the circular pattern of narration, Morris creates the effect of character not truly developing but serially revealed in a static moment that fills the whole book and approaches the effect of a painting.

Morris's fondness for almost Dickensian caricatures drawn with one or two grotesque traits and his overreliance on symbolic rather than dramatic resolutions for character conflicts further militate against a true sense of character development. In *The Field of Vision*, the fraudulent psychiatrist Lehmann illustrates the first of these and the resolution of

Boyd's problem, the second. If there is development in his mode, it usually comes in a witness's movement from ignorance to wisdom, though there is sometimes doubt even about this. The bullfight in *The Field of Vision* focuses and intensifies the characters' insights, but because so many of these insights are tied to past memories, the effect is that the characters are reviewing what they have always known rather than learning anything new. The real insight may come to the author in writing his novel or the reader in witnessing this heroic act.

The second mode in Morris's fiction, built around the "the open-road structure," tends to show his affinities with Lawrence. Considering that the open-road structure has been used in more books than the still-point structure, from his very first, *My Uncle Dudley* (1942), to one of the most recent, *A Life* (1973), the static structure of *The Field of Vision* would seem a late-developing and secondary offshoot of Morris's career. Nevertheless, as the Hassan comment shows, many critics still see nothing but stasis. The open-road structure appears in its purest form in *Love Among the Cannibals* (1957). To capture a sense of life as dynamic, this mode typically deals with a journey from one place to another, the movement in space rendering visible the movement in time. The locales through which the characters travel have symbolic value; for example, the Midwest usually stands for the American past and all that goes with it in the imagination, while California and Pennsylvania represent the present. Thus, even though Nebraska sets up poetic vibrations for Morris as no other place does, all his settings have meaning and importance in relation to the works in which they appear. In contrast to books with the still-point structure, those with the open-road structure employ one or two narrators, cover a longer span of time, and place greater stress on external dramatic action. Although the hero is sometimes spoken of as getting out of this world, this mode emphasizes not transcendence, but immanence: the hero and sometimes the witnesses are manifestations of the creative force immanent in nature and striving to perfect itself through them. This process is expressed in their obedience to their most organic impulses, impulses which can be realized only in time. In the best novels of this type, the change of place is emblematic of a real, dramatically rendered development of character, usually on the part of the narrator-witness who observes and reports the behavior of a hero. Sometimes, though, the change in the witness is again an enlarged awareness of life's shaping forces as revealed by the hero during the journey.

Often a single novel will contain vestiges of both modes. For instance, "The Roundup" and "The Ceremony" sections of *Ceremony in Lone Tree* (1960) adumbrate the open-road and the still-point structures, respectively. As has already been suggested, these two modes point to another distinction to be made about Morris's heroes, in addition to those offered by Booth and Madden. The hero who more nearly deserves to be called platonic is the one whose transcendence of the real world is complete and permanent, either through death or through a resistance to change which cuts him off from life; such transcendence repudiates the world of flux and contingency. The agency whereby transcendence is achieved varies from book to book. A second kind of hero, who may be termed *immanent*, embodies a Dionysian rather than platonic mysticism. He does not reach beyond nature, but feels for once attuned to her: "Nature which has become alienated, hostile, or subjugated, celebrates once more her reconciliation with her lost son."[27] The timelessness of this hero's state consists in its transpiring in the eternal now, that moment of imaginative stasis within the flux of time. The immanent hero resembles the existential hero in that he accepts the responsibility for selfhood in a contingent world, determining his essence by a continuing series of choices in the realm of existence. In doctrinaire existentialism, and at least sometimes in Morris, the transcendence Booth describes amounts to a cowardly evasion of responsibility, for strictly speaking, only man's essence can be transcendent because only it can exist in the past and therefore be complete. The immanent hero's essence is timeless, but he remains in the existential flow. It is only in this sense that any hero is (and thus only the immanent hero who can be), in one of Morris's favorite phrases, "*both* in and out of this world."

The transcendent hero comes to be symbolized in Morris's fiction by the figure of the Minotaur, an out-of-this-world beast inhabiting the labyrinth of the human psyche and barring the way to continued change and development. He frustrates the ongoing process of life. The converse symbol of the centaur stands for the immanent hero. Man above and beast below, the centaur connotes, first, the unified relationship between man's shaping consciousness above and "the wisdom of the body" below and, second, the course of evolution, beginning in the lower forms and eventuating in man. Both kinds of heroes embody transpersonal forces of the cosmos, and both represent special manifestations of American culture. The former is more common in the early Morris and the latter in the recent Morris.

The question now arises whether the Jamesian moment of full consciousness, achieved by the witnesses who register the hero's imaginative charge, is to be identified with transcendence, as Booth seems to argue when he speaks of imagination as a "bridge" out of this world and as Morris implies with the term *the still point*. As the instant when the "material" becomes "immaterial," this moment certainly smacks of mystical apotheosis, and at least one commentator treats it that way in dealing with James: "James offers full, personal consciousness as his source of life, vision, and experience; it is his means of reconciling beauty and ugliness, good and evil, and of bridging the gap between the individual and his fellow men, the individual and his world" (Cornwell, p. 156). Surely, though, the moment of full consciousness, in both James and Morris, is a state of heightened moral awareness, not a metaphysical experience. Above all, it is a state of being able to make ever finer moral distinctions, not an annihilation of the need to make distinctions. Therefore, it should be distinguished from other kinds of transcendence in Morris's novels. In fact, imagination is sometimes manifested in the witness's heightened consciousness, sometimes in a work of art created by the witness or the hero, and sometimes in the audacious behavior of the hero. If consciousness leads to the production of art or to the performance of a heroic act, the art or the act may be transcendent, but the producer remains immanent so long as he continues to change.

When the distinction between the hero and the witness is regarded as a distinction between the doer and the knower or, in a larger sense, between life as it is and life as it can be understood in the imagination, then one can see that Morris's work is itself a witnessing of his own life and of the American experience. Moreover, as part of the expanding consciousness of nature, Morris's own consciousness of his material remains in process. Consequently, it is a mistake to read as fixed and complete from the first what really constitutes a long process of development. That is, it is a mistake to interpret Morris's early works in terms of his mature pronouncements on fiction. As Morris admits in *The Territory Ahead* (p. 15), these pronouncements grew out of his early failures, which unintentionally display as problems what some critics have treated as consciously dramatized themes. For example, when Morris speaks of nostalgia in connection with *My Uncle Dudley*, he is acknowledging in retrospect his own difficulties in coming to terms with his past, not referring to a conscious theme.

Although an unusually large number of Morris's works are excellent in themselves, they take on greater meaning and power in light of his whole career; his sustained development makes him especially satisfying to read in his entirety, from *My Uncle Dudley* to *Fire Sermon* and *A Life*. For the power and suggestiveness of these last two come in no small measure from the fact that they retell Dudley's story in the light of thirty years of reflection. The difference between the two tellings is a visible lesson in the power of consciousness to transform life and of Wright Morris to process the raw material of his experience into lasting art.

2

Portraits from Life: My Uncle Dudley *and* The Man Who Was There

"IN THE BEGINNING was the word," wrote Morris in "Made in U.S.A.," "and the word was made flesh, American character emerges from the American language."[1] It was a lesson he was not to learn until his first abortive attempts to portray the characters who had made such a deep impression on his own life: it is art which makes the character, not mere fidelity to life that makes art. In the beginning for Morris were Uncle Dudley and Agee Ward, both portraits from life, the former a composite of Morris's father and Uncle Verne,[2] the latter a version of Morris himself. Through them, he discovered that they could not become characters in the true sense, could not become fictions, until he had found the deeper meaning of the facts from which they had sprung. With that meaning would come a firmer control of the two shaping structures in his work, the open road and the still point. Testifying to the profundity with which they reflect aspects of Morris's sensibility, however, is the appearance of these structures in a rudimentary form in *My Uncle Dudley* (1942) and *The Man Who Was There* (1945). At the same time, Dudley and Agee are Morris's first tentative sketches of the immanent and transcendent heroes.

In "Made in U.S.A.," Morris also wrote, "Character . . . is primarily an imaginative act, a fiction, to which the flesh is incurably responsive. It is the fiction that shapes the fact" (p. 483). Man learns where he is by understanding where he has been. Past imaginative insights give form and meaning to the bewilderingly formless present. Morris had the facts when he sat down to write. He did not recognize the fictions which colored his facts until later. Apparent contradictions in Morris's subsequent statements about *My Uncle Dudley* actually reflect the differences between his original, somewhat unsophisticated, perception of the facts and his mature assessment of the power of his fictions. In a 1964 essay, Morris describes *My Uncle Dudley* as having a "close affinity, both in style and substance," with *Love Among the Cannibals*, which marks an "engagement with the present."[3] In 1966, he places *My Uncle Dudley* in "Time Past" and acknowledges a similarity between it and *Huckleberry Finn* ("Origin of a Species," p. 128). The first description indicates his original conception of Dudley as a character who is theoretically committed to the present, while the second records his later recognition that the adventures of Dudley and the Kid resemble Huck's archetypal American flight from repressive civilization.

It is tempting to try to make parallels between *My Uncle Dudley* and *Huckleberry Finn* more explicit, especially since both books are structured around journeys and use juvenile first-person narrators, but Morris's further admission that he had not read *Huck* at the time he wrote his novel (ibid., p. 123) makes it clear that he is acknowledging a kinship with the spirit of Twain's classic, not an imitation of its theme or structure. *My Uncle Dudley* follows the adventures of Dudley, his nephew the Kid (also the narrator), and a band of assorted travelers on an auto trip across the depression Southwest from California to Arkansas, where the remnants of the group are jailed overnight. Writing about the book, David Madden argues for an explicit imitation of *Huckleberry Finn*, and both he and John Hunt see the focus of the novel as the emerging identity of the Kid as he matures under Dudley's heroic influence.[4] But the picture of California and life along the road in *My Uncle Dudley* is very sketchy and not in any way to be compared to the sustained and explicit criticism of life on the shore in *Huckleberry Finn*, and the narrator of *My Uncle Dudley* is not the protagonist of the story he tells. The most fully dramatized character and the one who is center stage is

Dudley, not the Kid, who, unlike Huck, hardly shows any character at all (one critic calls him a "sound-camera which recorded no emotion" and which "enabled the author to appear completely detached from the experiences recorded in the book").[5] As the title indicates, it is the progressive examination of Dudley's character which gives the book whatever unity it possesses. Although the Kid and Red, the sailor who forms a cheering section for Dudley and shares some of his views, serve as witnesses, the other characters function as conventional foils to Dudley.

In a later photo-text book, *The Inhabitants* (1946), Morris tried to capture the varieties of American character through photos of national locales. In a sense he had already done that with Dudley. Hailing, as he says, from "everywhere," (p. 38), Dudley becomes the American Everyman, all the inhabitants rolled into one. Indeed, two of his oracular pronouncements about America—on the need for hardship to forge a hard people and the impossibility of finding one label for all the people (p. 193)—are repeated in *The Inhabitants.*[6] In the words of the epigraph to *My Uncle Dudley*, Dudley's story is "the grass that grows wherever the land is and the water is"; it is the yield which results when the American experience, the American land, is watered by the American imagination.

It is Dudley's native shrewdness and showmanship, the initiative born in the land of the go-getters, which comes through most clearly as he drums up passengers for the trip. With a folksy quip—"If I could lay my own eggs I'd like it here!" (p. 4)—he grabs their attention. With sharp insight into character, he appeals to the weak spots in each—to nostalgia in Hansen, to greed in Natchez, to love of a bargain in Mr. Demetrios. His quick wit has an answer to every question and cavil. Both Detroit and Omaha are "right next door" to Chicago; Natchez thinks Dudley wants too much for the trip only because he has never had to buy gas in New Mexico. Pressed for the location of the Biltmore hotel, where he claims to be staying, Dudley directs the question to the Kid until someone else volunteers the information that it is right down the street. He has counted on the fact that "there's always a Biltmore" in every city (p. 18). He handles the bargaining for the car with the expertise of a Down East horse trader, first offering five dollars less than the Kid estimates the car is worth and finally getting it by dropping the bid even lower to intimidate the salesman. But Dudley's shrewdness is only a part of his role as the spokesman for the profound folk wisdom of the American common man. This wisdom turns his ready-made wisecrack about Natchez into a telling appraisal: "You're trying to be a slick basterd. . . . But you're only wearing off your finish slidin around here" (p. 12). Having stuffed himself with the common man's equivalent of the Harvard classics, the Haldeman-Julius *Little Blue Books*, he qualifies as an instant authority on a hundred subjects from the "big fella you can't keep down and the little guy you can't keep up" (p. 97), to the true meaning of bravery, to the value of a real woman. But in the pragmatic tradition of a Franklin, his knowledge is all of a kind which can be proved on the pulses.

Dudley's wisdom finds its larger expression in what he is—a representative of American individualism and egalitarianism in their purest forms. The individualism resides in the conviction that each person should have the right to become what he most profoundly wants to be, and the egalitarianism consists in the guarantee that he will be judged only by that. In *My Uncle Dudley* Morris introduces the phrase "the real thing" to denote the genuine essence of people and things, but here it has little in common with that "reality" characterized by Booth as being out of this world. It is much more like what a man sees when he finally takes his blinders off, when he stops seeing the lies others believe and lets his common sense show him what is truly there. Dudley's talent for intuiting the real thing lets him believe in what he calls a "piece of the people" when it is really them and not when "it's what someone wants them to be" (p. 104). His talent involves a profound distrust of collective emotions like patriotism and fancy words like *love*. Speaking of Los Angeles, Dudley says that it is "full of white trash lookin for sex trash—whole goddam town a bluff. Trouble is a man never calls it—calls it romance instead. Black man tells you he wants a good woman, white man tells you he wants Love. I like a good woman more than average but I'd never find one lookin for love" (p. 39). If a woman has the real thing, love is only a word; it cannot do justice to the feeling a good woman excites any more than romance, another word, does justice to the tawdry reality of Los Angeles.

Besides being represented by the figure of Huck Finn, this archetypal American egalitarianism is embodied in Whitman's democracy as it is interpreted by D. H. Lawrence in *Studies in Classic American Literature*: Each "soul is known at once in its going. Not by its clothes or appearance. . . . Not by its family name. . . . Not by a progression of piety. . . . Not by works at all. Not by anything but just itself. The soul passing unenhanced, passing on foot and being no more than itself. And recognized, and passed by or greeted according to the soul's dictate."[7] It is a democracy founded upon the soul's instinctive, nonrational attraction or antipathy to the other souls it meets. Dudley consistently measures others against impulses fundamental to himself. He disparages the racism of the salesman Jeeves by gibing that it takes a lot of "niggers" "to make up for all the white basterds I know" (p. 39). When he meets a kindred spirit like Jerry O'Toole, they are quickly "slapping and cuffing each other like . . . old friends" (p. 91). His behavior toward Natchez, who has "something on the ball" but is still a "heel" (p. 99), is appropriately mixed. Dudley's earthy version of Emerson's self-reliance was carried to its furthest extreme when he went to jail rather than fight in the Great War because "this was one country where a man could be choosy 'bout who he'd shoot." If murder was "going to be lawful" Dudley says, he would prefer targets close to home: "There was more foreign basterds right in his own family and why trouble to go so far to kill them off?" (pp. 43–44). A man's race or nation does not determine whether he needs to be shot; what he *is* determines that.

The ability to intuit the real thing depends on a larger condition of the self. The soul's responses are gut responses, and permeating *My Uncle Dudley* is the principle that to heed one's gut responses is to be attuned to the forces of physical nature. Lawrence's essay on Whitman ties the evolving self to an evolving universe and identifies the characteristic metaphor by which their oneness is represented in American culture and in Morris's novels: "Whitman's essential message was the Open Road. The leaving of the soul free unto herself, the leaving of his fate to her and to the loom of the open road" (p. 187). The raft on the river and the car on the open road place their passengers in the ever expanding heart of life itself. Implicit in the freedom conferred by the newness of the continent, this is "the American heroic message" (p. 187). The life of the open road represents an opening of the self to the eternal novelty of the present and an acquiescence of the self to the winds of fate, the flow of time, and the growth of nature. When the travelers are stranded in a blizzard and robbed of their luggage, the Kid says, "At last you begin to feel like you're getting somewhere. . . . For the first time you sort of feel like you're breathing free" (p. 139). Only Liszt, the European, who conceives of the soul as a state of established being rather than a fluid condition of becoming, finds the uncertainty of the open road unbearable.

Although only the bare bones of this vision are close to being worked out in the novel as we have it, the authentic response does govern Dudley's relations not only with people, but also with animals and inanimate nature. He prefers cats to dogs because a cat, like "a good woman," had "her own what," her own selfhood, "and you had to meet her halfway" (p. 140). He is most himself in Carlsbad Caverns, where he is most aware of nature as having a separate reality of its own: "Standing down there . . . was as near to being something as he could stand it . . ." (p. 122). He scoffs at the Kid's scientific explanations for small rock crystals because he will not tolerate the phenomenal thing's being abstracted into a set of geological laws: "He had a reason for everything but his bag of rocks. And he used all of his reason just to keep your reason away. . . . He wanted the Land to know something more than anybody and do something that nobody could figure out" (p. 173).

Dudley's attitude toward sex illustrates the instinctive character of his responses. Whether sizing up women in Los Angeles or eulogizing the faded beauty of a matron in Arizona, Dudley is frank and frankly physical in his appreciation. But he is aware of more than physical beauty: "Uncle Dudley was saying there was them you loved with your eyes and then there was the other kind. The other kind needn't look worth a dam but they had everything" (p. 48). Whatever the inexpressible everything is, it is felt in the blood, not seen in the eye. Sex is so important in the novel that good and evil polarize along an axis of sexual attitudes. Dudley's feeling for women is neither "dirty," in the conventional sense, nor belittling. The physical is to be respected. Only when a woman becomes no more than an object to be exploited is sexuality dirty. Dudley says, "My talkin . . . takes a detour when it's dirt. Whole point of my talkin is to drain off the dirt" (p. 60). In contrast to the healthy sexiness of Dudley and Red, the novel's three most important evil characters are all marked by their sexual perversity as measured against Dudley's standard. The foulmouthed Jeeves talks about sleeping with two women at once, Natchez is a homosexual, and Cupid, the brutal policeman who comes to embody all the negative forces in the novel, is the "kinda man like to 'vestigate lady crappers all the time. When he was a kid he was always wearin dresses and goin in the ladies side" (p. 171).

Other foils are O'Toole and Liszt, who define the quality of Dudley's relation to the cosmos. O'Toole finds the desert peculiarly conducive to introspection: "I don't know . . . why

I like it here. I don't even know if I like it or not. . . . When a man gets along his eyes turn in anyhow. Sittin here I can turn them in or out by myself. Maybe that's what I like about it—if I like it here" (pp. 95–96). When Liszt tries to account for the appeal of such a life by saying that "here a man hass a spirit . . . a soul . . . ," Jerry counters that a spiritualized soul is only an abstraction, not the authentic selfhood which the desert nurtures: "Well . . . what I once thought myself. Now I know it's a lot of sentimental crap. . . . This soul stuff is a lot of gook spread on a man before he's learned to wash himself. Out here there's some chance of being washed clean. Whatever you are at bottom you get to be more everyday" (p. 96). True selfhood requires wholeness and includes the body as well as the soul. To Jerry, it gives a sense of oneness with the organic universe, like that of the Indians: "If a tree could pray he'd ask for sun and rain and fruitful seeds—and that's what an Indian asks for. . . . He's like something that grows out here. . . . give him a soul—and you've got a potted plant" (p. 96). The Kid says that, for Dudley, listening to Jerry "was like hearing himself talking without troubling to" (p. 97).

When the soul gets far enough down the road of life, it becomes character, "whatever you are at bottom." Morris justifies the hero's roguish buffoonery by saying that he is obliged "to be something of a damn fool in order to be himself. Blake plagiarized me here, as he does elsewhere, when he said that a fool who persists in his folly will become wise" ("Letter to a Young Critic," p. 95). The key word is *his*: a fool who persists in his folly, who persists in following the impulsive vagaries of his deepest self, will arrive at a condition of selfhood which is existentially wise. Furman, jailed for spitting in the eyes of policemen, says, "There more than one thing true. . . . spittin in eyes is just what I been called on to do, an what a man really called on for he must" (p. 194). Following one's deepest impulses wins existential freedom from external necessity and asserts the greater reality of the imaginative self. One prisoner observes that Furman only seems to be in jail (p. 193). The Kid's memory of the nightmare Dust Bowl episode makes the same point. This story, retold so frequently in Morris's fiction, suggests Dr. Rieux's stoic endurance before the Oran plague in Albert Camus's *The Plague.* It represents man alone and on his own, heroically confronting a hostile nature and an absurd universe with nothing but his courage and his will to be.

Metaphorically, of course, Rieux's struggle is against fascism, and in *My Uncle Dudley* too, as might be expected in a novel published in 1942, the drive for selfhood ultimately comes to be linked, rather simplistically, with bravery and the commitment to human values and against dehumanizing "fascist" institutions like the jail, which imprison people for feeling deeply. At one point Dudley has admitted, "I've learned how to think being brave isn't so smart" (p. 104). In the imagery of the novel, he is a "horseless knight," lacking what he calls a "horse," an appropriate cause for showing the bravery which consists in "knowing what the hell guts is for" (p. 104). He gets a lesson in "what guts is for" from Furman, who says he has been a "good horse" much of his life but who has turned to spitting on policemen to protest their inhuman repressiveness. Furman, the free man, is no longer a beast of burden; he has become man, then myth. He is the centaur-hero, a horse "that was up front a man" (p. 191), man emerging from horse, from animal nonbeing to sentient being. While the myth-essence is out of this world, the man remains in it, and in the jail where his choice of defiance has landed him. In spitting in Cupid's eye, Dudley joins Furman to become the second of the "Two Men on a Horse," mentioned in the title of the last section. But, as the Kid believes, bravery is the by-product of being oneself: "A really brave man doesn't want to be brave. He just wants to be something else first and brave tags along. He just wants to be *something*" (p. 185).

Furman and Dudley are Morris's first immanent heroes, assuming responsibility for their choices in a contingent world. Morris also stresses the American quality of their heroics by casting Dudley particularly in the mold of a characteristic national archetype—the cowboy. The title of the first subsection, "Roundup," suggests a cattle drive, and Morris's description of the cowboy figure in "Made in U.S.A." fits Dudley: "He is that hero with a thousand faces cut down to our size. He is that archetype, the self-sufficient man, reduced to his wits, his guts and his horse, who takes on single-handed the forces of evil in a world he never made" (pp. 488–89). Although it is treated comically, the stand against Cupid resembles a traditional western shoot-out.

For all his affinity with this figure from the past, Dudley consistently lives for the present moment because it is only in the present that the immanent hero can flourish. This habit allows him to glory in the departure from Los Angeles undisturbed by the Kid's rueful recollection that when they left Kansas City earlier, the car's transmission fell out after only two blocks and to weather each setback with unshakeable aplomb. If a patched tire works today, why worry about tomorrow? And if tomorrow Omaha does not turn out to be "right next door" to Chicago, he will cross that bridge when he comes to it. If it takes more than five minutes to fix a corroded valve, he is having a nice time right this minute anyway. Because he lives in and for the present, Dudley's character is supposed to remain in a state of becoming: "You couldn't wonder long about any one thing" Dudley does, the Kid thinks, "because in no time another wonder was there. After a while you just gave it up." For Liszt, who thinks of the soul as fixed, Dudley remains an enigma and a terror: "You can think of some people and make one soul do. But I have never heard of a soul that Uncle Dudley would fit" (p. 120).

The past enters into the composition of *My Uncle Dudley* through Morris's failure to render his own past, his personal experiences and literary influences, into art. Nostalgia is his problem, not his theme. The charge he levels at American writing generally has special relevance to his portraits from life in his first two novels: "Americans feel that if a thing exists it is important, if it happened to *me* it is important, and all I have to do is to record it."[8] In spite of some fine touches, *My Uncle Dudley* is full of weaknesses traceable to the use of personal experiences Morris expected to speak for themselves. For instance, although Dudley is supposed to grow consistently through his adventures, there is no real sense that he acquires heroic virtues until the final episode in Arkansas (only the last fourth of the book).[9] On the contrary, the pitch he uses to collect passengers for the trip requires the very qualities of shrewdness, presumption, and wit that he shows on the road. As a result, the journey is not so much a quest as a series of convenient opportunities for him to display his heroic credentials, and even the moments that dramatize his heroism—when he fast talks the Tucson police or defies Cupid—are only isolated scenes within a journey too often given over to meaningless and random details having no significant relation to the book's theme or structure. Within the episodic and unfocused journey, promising situations are discarded or never properly developed. Through the first half of the novel, conflict mounts between Dudley and Natchez, one of the most complex and interesting characters, but their eventual confrontation is a disappointingly short and abrupt anticlimax.

Another problem is the Kid, who is not drawn fully enough to justify the claim by Hunt and Madden that the novel traces the growth of his identity and who is thus only a mechanical device for creating objectivity and distance between the author and his material. The style of *My Uncle Dudley*, especially in the opening paragraphs and in the dialogue, bears witness to the strong influence of Hemingway and Steinbeck, and the latter may also have influenced Morris's sentimental treatment of lower-class American types. The reduction of the ethic of selfhood to simple courage in a good cause is also to be expected in a first novel begun when the reputations of Hemingway and Steinbeck were at their heights and the war was impending. With a little more detachment from his past, Morris might have realized that others had mined this lode before him. He might have recognized the limitations of the heroic ideal seen solely as protest and have questioned whether Dudley ever really learns what "guts is for" since his gesture of spitting on Cupid has no practical value. He might have wondered whether the hero does not have the obligation to choose his battles with more discrimination, and he might have looked askance at the element of hardheadedness in Dudley's independence which keeps him from being "the world's greatest Christian" because he did not think of it first (p. 178). And finally, Morris might have been a little suspicious of Dudley's orphic eloquence, which is implausible and often makes him sound like Sandburg at his worst. All of these doubts about Dudley's style of heroism Morris was to show in subsequent books.

An improved understanding of the difficulties and implications of his material makes Morris's *The Man Who Was There* a technical advance over *My Uncle Dudley*. While he still cannot sustain a lengthy dramatic structure, he camouflages its absence by dividing the novel into three discrete stories unified by interwoven themes and images and by a common character, Agee Ward. The style is now definitely Morris's own, using for the first time in a consistent and calculated way the device (later called liberating the truth from the cliché) of punning on hackneyed expressions or placing them in new contexts to give them renewed significance. The very situation of *The Man Who Was There* was a cliché in the art and life of the war years—the effect of a soldier's disappearance in battle on those left at home. But Morris's interest in it is uniquely his, and his treatment is completely original. Although the center of interest is again the hero, he is part of a much more complex set of relationships than in *My Uncle Dudley*, and his portrait is less intuitive, more a logical extension of a carefully reasoned philosophy of life. Morris's unprocessed memories again impinge on the action, but they are now part of the author's conscious journey into his past in an attempt to discover and define its relationship to the present. It is the same journey which, in *The Home Place* and *The World in the Attic*, culminates in his final break with the dead past shrouded in nostalgia.

The kinship of the man who was there, Agee Ward, with Uncle Dudley is clear. Like Dudley, Agee is a local boy—born and bred in Nebraska—who makes good in the highest principles of American idealism. Like him, he treasures the human enough to fight for it against fascism; as one of his friends says, "The reason he's missing . . . is because of the human predicament and the fact that there's places where it isn't human any more" (p. 193). Agee shares Dudley's healthy respect for the real thing in women and his distaste for false sophistication and sham. Thus, the calculated skinniness of fashion models amounts to a worship of inessentials, a skinniness of soul: "A naturally skinny girl had her fat inside her. . . . these women are skinny, inside and out" (p. 210). In contrast, Agee himself radiates a physical presence which is disturbingly sexual. His relations with his spinster landlady, Gussie Newcomb, were disquietingly physical and intimate: "Miss Newcomb's way with men had stopped with the young man who liked to stand, wherever he stood, with his fingers just touching her hips. She had never got over the feeling that something was following her" (p. 152).

In each of its three books, *The Man Who Was There* celebrates the continuity and indestructibility of life in its triumph over death and dissolution. The epigraph, from Job, expounds this theme and introduces the major images of trees and water, symbols of fertility and continuity. Agee Ward, missing in action, is the tree which will not die, putting forth new shoots through his effect on the imaginations of his witnesses and through a physical unity of all things which share the spark of life.

Book 1, "The Vision of Private Reagan," adumbrates the still-point structure in its use of multiple centers of consciousness to explore one central event and the open-road structure in its use of a journey and its focus on the physical perpetuation of life. The funeral of Grandma Herkimer is the setting for the missing hero's resurrection in his boyhood pal Reagan. At the graveside ceremony, Reagan's unblinking stare startles Reverend Horde into an unorthodox sermon which is one of the most important brief passages in Morris's work: "All life is Holy . . . but its desire is to be immortal, and in mortal man this is the divine thing—that he might conceive. In mortal life it is conception that links man through woman to God, and she through God to him, and this is the trinity" (pp. 55–56). Gripped by a power stronger than himself, Horde ends by "listening" rather than truly speaking: "This is the Resurrection . . . that man should die so that he might live, that he should go so that thereby he might come again" (p. 56).

The key word in the sermon is *conception*, and it is used in both its procreative and psychological senses. Establishing for the first time a pattern he generally follows in all his fiction, Morris identifies the creative power of reproduction with the female and the creative power of imagination with the male. Through woman's gift of life, man experiences the physical aspect of God immanent in nature; through her intuitive experience of God's spiritual aspect, woman gets some inkling of the kindred power of imagination in man. Inspired by the sermon, Reagan, in whom Agee is imaginatively reborn, announces the hero's spiritual return. Simultaneously retrieved from the womb of the grave, the child Annie Mae signals the physical rebirth of her grandmother in a subsequent generation. With a saintly smile but "monkey-like" feet, Annie Mae personifies the whole course of biological evolution as well as man's dual physical and spiritual nature. Although she may be feebleminded, her inability to perform abstract thinking frees her for a more instinctive and immediate grasp of elemental life. The tree images (Reagan as "sapling" with "planted" feet, the small tree by the grave) and water images (the name of the undertaker, Mr. Lakeside, her mother's practice of soaking Annie Mae's feet, Reagan's watery stare) have foreshadowed the dual rebirth.

The second book, "The Three Agee Wards," traces the imaginative and physical traits of Agee himself to their sources in preceding generations. "The Ward Line" examines the male side of Agee's heritage as he returns to the farm of his Uncle Harry and Aunt Sarah in Nebraska. Although the beautiful stand of trees which once surrounded the farm has died in a drought, Harry clings to the hope that his dying family might put forth new shoots through the continuation in Agee of the "Ward Line," the moral tradition of pioneer hardihood and austere courage (Harry's son, with his fire-engine-red combine, represents a deterioration of this tradition). Although it is not clear, the pioneer heritage is apparently Agee's imaginative inheritance and his vocations as artist and soldier are its perpetuation in contemporary equivalents.

In "The Osborn Look," Agee visits the garrulous barber of Lone Tree, Eddie Cahow, who postulates a physical continuity between the generations insuring that the entire race is reborn in each of its members: "If Methuselah had a barber shop . . . and lived in a land where nobody moved away, and where the boys and girls got married and had babies, and if I was Methuselah—wouldn't I find myself trimmin' the same head every twenty years? And after two, three hundred years wouldn't I think it was the same man, no matter who it was that walked in with the head?" (p. 130). The physical bonds coupling him to the past and the future, his Osborn look, are Agee's feminine inheritance. On his mother's gravestone, he reads "She died so that he might live" (p. 132). Grace Osborn died in childbirth so that Agee might live and that she might be reborn in him.

Patently autobiographical, this portrait of the artist as a young man is recapitulated with more thoroughgoing analysis of the author's feelings and motives in *The Home Place* (1948) and *The World in the Attic* (1949). The late and retrospective photo-text book *God's Country and My People* (1968) is a spiritual return to Nebraska which finally arrives at a definitive statement of what the state has meant to Morris.

The counterpart of Agee's imaginative rebirth in Reagan is his physical rebirth in his landlady and symbolic "next-of-kin," Gussie Newcomb. The focus of book 3, "The Ordeal of Gussie Newcomb," is her "ordeal," her initiation into life, after she is notified that Agee is missing in action. Her resurrection from a living death of spinsterhood is made possible by a progressively closer identification with Agee. She signs his name to the War Department telegram, moves into his garage apartment, repeats his wisecracks, and meets many of his friends. Concurrently losing her reserve, she gets tight at a meeting of a women's club, plays a pinball machine, and eventually becomes engaged to Mr. Bloom. At the conclusion, she vows to name her first child after Agee. Though missing, Agee is still in action: He "didn't believe . . . that if you were alive you were ever really missing. . . . anything really alive just went on and on" (p. 194). Morris reinforces his theme by filling Gussie's story with suggestions of rebirth, including repetition of his water imagery in the scene in which she wades in a mountain pool, allusions to the survival of both Bloom and Agee's cat after they have been given up for dead, and the names Newcomb (come new) and Bloom.

The Man Who Was There is a divine comedy of life's victory over death, with a mixed mood of exuberant good humor and religious awe. The two emotions reflect complementary sides of the hero. In one of the post cards he mails from Europe, Agee stands on the deck of a steamer with a life preserver circling his neck and framing his face with a telling legend: "On one side of his head can be seen the word *Buda* and on the other side the word *Pest*" (p. 78). As these puns suggest, Agee is a kind of life preserver himself—both something of a Buddha and something of a pest—a vitalistic saint who, as the title of his book "Chain of Being" implies, discovered the immortality of life in the unity of life, and a comical eccentric who combines an irreverence for sham with what Yeats called "Gaiety transfiguring all that dread." As a Buddha, Agee more nearly resembles Hermann Hesse's Siddhartha, who discovers that nature and spirit are one, than Hesse's Gotama, who seeks renunciation of the flesh for an other worldly spirit. By inspiring a greater vitality in others, he justifies the cliché newspaper tribute that he brought life into the community. As a pest, he strolls around Bel Air wearing one brown sock and one blue in a calculated love of disorder and with his infectious laughter causes a staid judge to collapse on his lawn in a fit of uncontrollable merriment. He would agree with Reverend Horde that "All things are Holy," but only in the spirit of his favorite boyhood expressions—"Holy Moses" and "Holy Mackeral."

At the funeral, Agee's first two disciples—Reagan, whose first name is Christian, and Annie Mae, who was once called "Madeline" by a stranger who thought "she belonged over a church doorway" (p. 19)—behave in the tradition of the master. The sterile funeral home, its prissy directors, and the Sunny Slope cemetery, with its fireproof grass and barren view, are supposed to make death easier to accept, but by smothering genuine sorrow in unctuous sentiment, they rob death of its dignity to the point that Sergeant Brace mentally compares the funeral to a burlesque show. Years later Morris speaks in his own voice in *God's Country and My People*: "One paid for the miracle of life with the labor of death. . . . A man should be long suffering, his death long remembered, the funeral a consecrated working party" (n. pag.). Death is part of the life cycle, and to demean its human importance is to demean life. The antics of Reagan, Annie Mae, and Brace, who uses his funeral pass to get roaring drunk, both affirm life and restore the humanity travestied by the mortuary owner. The idea and effect resemble those in Wallace Stevens's "The Emperor of Ice Cream."

Agee the life-bringer, the hero whose power shines through his witnesses, is a fairly successful fiction. But Agee the portrait from life, the persona of his creator, the character who stands apart from the witnesses, evidences many of the same artistic flaws as Uncle Dudley. "The Three Agee Wards" begins and ends with sections entitled "The Album," which describe various photos and newspaper clippings relevant to Agee's development. The first album section shows Agee as vague and undefined in the early photos, then becoming clearer and more vivid as his character matures, until he stands out strong during his European *Wanderjahre* as quintessentially American. In an early Chicago photograph, he contrasts with a blurred line of older boys who are distinguished, not by "who they are," but by "where they have been." By virtue of their greater experience, they stand for more than they are, while Agee "only looks like himself. . . . that is to say—like nothing" (p. 75). In the newspaper photograph described in the second album section, Agee has joined the shadowy line of experienced figures, and the center of attention is usurped by another young man who is no more than himself (p. 138). The second photo illustrates the role Agee plays in the novel: Reagan mistakes the vivid youth for Agee, the missing hero reflected in the faces of others. Between the first and second pictures, Agee has the experiences which mark him by where he has been; the most important of these is the return to Nebraska.

Agee's sketches point to the meaning of the return. Almost all of these drawings of Nebraska scenes and artifacts are incomplete, partly because of a simple failure of memory and partly because of an inability to reconcile the conflicting demands of truth and imagination. In one sketch "either the barn is much too close or the pump is much too far away. . . . The only solution to this was to draw both pumps in, reconsider the matter, and then take one pump out. This he did, but the pump that he left was where no sensible pump would be. And the one he took out was the pump in which he couldn't believe" (p. 82). Here raw material and technique are imperfectly wedded; the deleted pump met realistic demands but not aesthetic ones, while the one left in did the opposite. Agee cannot yet control technique so that it gives a sense of reality to what is actually a highly formalized rendition of reality. In realistic art, the technique has failed when the formal element is too apparent. This failure is the outward sign of Agee's inability to establish his own identity in relationship to the past and the present. By taking *The Journey Back* (the title of his last European painting), he can master the lesson of the past in his imagination and thereby break its spell, to become an artist-hero.

His concluding meditation on Lone Tree is meant to demonstrate such mastery: "Roads that led out in the morning led back when the lights came on" (p. 135). What a man has been, is, and will be are parts of one continuum, an interweaving of acts and their consequences, adventures and their outcomes. Thus, an understanding of the past is necessary for an understanding of one's identity. But "the shadow of a man had to pass from morning to evening by going before him—not by lapping at his back. For when he turned, it turned, and the shadow had foreshortened until he stood upon himself, shadowless, here in the street" (p. 135). You can't go home again, not permanently. As in the case of Peter Spavic's infant son, the shadow of man's psychic development is always on the move—forward into the future, not backward to the nostalgia-locked past. To cling to the past and resist growth is to find the high noon of the timeless now. Agee's painting *Journey's End*, which pictures a mirror image of a rural street with morning on one side and evening on the other, expresses his vision of life as a continuum, and Mrs. Krickbaum's claim that it is unfinished indicates that, though Agee's journey has ended, the larger journey of human experience goes on in his witnesses.

Most of these ideas are far from clear in book 2, a fatal flaw considering that this is the intellectual heart of *The Man Who Was There*. One reason for the failure is that Morris tries to make his point with imagery alone—the descriptions of photographs and the shadow passages—and without resorting to expository commentary. In effect, he expects verbal imagery to speak for itself as photographs do. But photos present only a perceptual experience, and there are limits to the explicitness and complexity of conceptual ideas which can be presented perceptually. A more characteristic effect in fiction is the drama of consciousness, where the mind in the act of discovering its ideas becomes as palpable and real as a photograph without giving up the resources of expository language. Morris discovers this kind of drama in later novels.

Agee's vision in *Journey's End* is an immanent vision, emphasizing the various interconnected stages of life, and Morris himself subsequently placed Agee in the theoretical present, which is the immanent hero's natural province ("Origin of a Species," p. 129). Agee's "shadowless" vision is not so clearly a vision of transcendence. To cast no shadow is to have lost one's finitude: the man who evades psychic growth by clinging to the past transcends time and escapes change, but suffers the disadvantage of being cut off from life. In stressing Agee's continuance in his witnesses, the novel stresses immanence, but because Agee himself is dead and changeless in the story and because he aspires to a timeless vision of art, he is finally more like a transcendent hero. At the same time, the interwoven stories recapitulating a single theme create the effect of Morris circling his subject, going over the same ground again and again. The effect of the book, and especially book 2, is therefore static, and the still-point structure is adumbrated. The reason for the effect of transcendence, which undercuts the book's unmistakable focus on the theme of immanence, is that the problems of transcendence are Agee-Morris's own: he has not yet broken the spell of his own past.

Signs of this are plentiful. The return to Nebraska supposedly accomplishes two things for Agee: he works out his problems as an artist and in some way acquires the power to bring others to a fuller awareness of life. But the awareness which is subsequently aroused in the other characters comes, not through the natural product of the imagination, art, but through personal traits of the artist (sexiness and courage) which have no necessary connection with his ability to paint pictures or with the Nebraska experience. This confusion bears compelling witness to the fuzziness of Morris's thinking in "The Three Agee Wards," and the fact that in his later books he generally separates the active hero and the imaginative observer suggests that he came to recognize the fuzziness himself. In equating Agee's problem with his own, Morris was satisfying an emotional need rather than making a necessary psychological connection. To paraphrase his own observation, because it had happened to *him*, he felt the exile's return to the home place must be important; because his memories of rural life aroused an undefined emotion in him, they would have something to offer Agee; because he sensed that his own artistic problems were somehow dependent on coming to terms with those memories, Agee's would be too. In fact, the connection between the memories and Agee the hero is never made. Moreover, any break with the past Agee the artist is supposed to accomplish remains on the theoretical level, while the actual drama produces a feeling of sentimental indulgence in nostalgia. The evidence of Morris's continued bondage is that his portrayal of Eddie Cahow is like the pump which Agee included in his drawing: it serves his aesthetic purposes but is unrealistic. Cahow makes a convenient mouthpiece for philosophical remarks about the continuity of generations, but he is a very implausible small-town barber because of them. Unlike his hero, Morris does not learn in this book that in real life the pump was behind the barn.

Book 2 leaves Agee, in himself, a vague and shadowy character lacking Dudley's vivid immediacy and color. It may be fine to decide theoretically that he should be seen almost exclusively through his witnesses and come alive only in relationship to them, but in reality the novel calls for more direct and dramatic proof of his heroic authority in order for his impact on the others to be plausible. As it is, the man who was there often seems not to be there after all, and in a much more significant way than his mere physical absence. Nevertheless, *The Man Who Was There* completes the picture of the Morris hero begun in *My Uncle Dudley* and, by contributing to the author's growing awareness of the crippling effects of the personal past on his fiction, prepared him to exorcise that past in the three books which immediately followed.

3

The Return: The Photo-Text Books and The World in the Attic

THE ASPECTS OF Morris's work which have probably been most fully discussed both by Morris himself[1] and by his critics[2] are his experiments with combining prose texts and photographs and his return to the Nebraska "home place" to "repossess," and thereby make sense of, his past. The process of repossession has both personal and artistic benefits for Morris, as it has for Agee Ward. In the very first chapter of *The Territory Ahead*, Morris diagnoses a problem in his own career which is shared by all of American writing: "Raw material, an excess of both material and comparatively raw experience, has been the dominant factor in my own role as a novelist. . . . Too much crude ore. The hopper of my green and untrained imagination was both nourished and handicapped by it" (pp. 14–15). This problem, already amply illustrated by *My Uncle Dudley* and *The Man Who Was There*, could be solved by processing his raw material into art with shaping technique. The solution requires of the author a sense of detachment from his material built upon a fuller understanding of it. To get that understanding, Morris returned to the rural Nebraska of his boyhood, which had a greater impact on his imagination than his later life in Chicago. The problems of the artist and the man come together in what John Hunt, speaking of the early novels and especially the homecoming books, calls a search for "meaning," "coherence," "a connection," and a way of making "available" meaning from the past "for use in the present." Morris's search leads him "to the past where he attempts various strategies for grasping the meaning he knows is there" (Hunt, p. 59).

The Inhabitants (1946) and *The Home Place* (1948), both combining photos and text, represent the culmination of one of those strategies. The act of photographing America constitutes Morris's moral return to his roots; the narrative begun in *The Home Place* and continued in *The World in the Attic* (1949) chronicles his actual return to Nebraska in the forties. Here, in the character of Clyde Muncy, he visits first the Nebraska home place and then the small town of Junction. Although *God's Country and My People* contains photographs taken at the time Morris's early photo-text books were being prepared, it was published much later (1968), and, as the title implies, it ranges back over the real plains and the fictional people with which Morris inhabited them in his major novels. Thus, it differs in purpose and effect from the early books. Morris has related how the recent book of color photographs and text, *Love Affair: A Venetian Journal* (1972), grew accidentally out of photographs of Venice he took for his own enjoyment in 1969 (*Structures and Artifacts*, pp. 116–17). Although the beauty of these color pictures is staggering, Morris is correct about the aesthetic difficulties they pose: "The black and white negative has already been enormously selective, merely by the act of eliminating color." Since the essential challenge of aesthetics is just this—to select what is of particular meaning and importance in the subject—the color photo presents problems because it "not merely says, but too often shouts, that everything is of interest. And it is not" (ibid., p. 117). Perhaps as a result *Love Affair: A Venetian Journal* adds little to the reader's understanding of Morris's career or even to his use of Venice as a setting in *What a Way to Go* and *One Day*. I will, therefore, concentrate on the books of black-and-white photos, particularly those which grew out of Morris's concern with his past in the forties.

With photography, Morris wrote, "I was trying to lay my hands on the object *itself*. The photograph seemed the logical way to achieve such ends" ("Letter to a Young Critic," p. 97).

In all three of the native photo-text books, the objects are chiefly buildings and occasionally implements, clothing, or interiors of farm houses. In *The Home Place*, the locale is rural and small-town Nebraska; in *The Inhabitants* and *God's Country and My People*, it is all of America. Except for five pictures of the real-life counterpart of Morris's Uncle Harry character and one family photograph, the scenes are all deserted and frequently decaying, presenting a portrait of an older and vanishing America. But the photos, though unpeopled, are not empty of humanity. In the epigraph to *The Home Place*, Morris quotes from James's *The American Scene*: "To be at all critically, or . . . analytically, minded . . . is to be subject to the superstition that objects and places, coherently grouped, disposed for human use and addressed to it, must have a sense of their own, a mystic meaning proper to themselves to give out. . . . " The look of artifacts reflects the lives of those who have used and built them, an old man's pair of shoes telling their eternal tale of his industry, hardships, and endurance. Thus, the inhabitants have left their pattern on the objects: "The carpet wears out, but the life of the carpet, the Figure, wears in" (*The Home Place*, p. 176). At the same time, the objects have left their pattern on the inhabitants; as Harry disappears into the barn at the end of *The Home Place*, "the figure on the front of the carpet had worn through to the back" (p. 176). The people inhabit the objects, and Morris the artist-observer, is inhabited by the objects, by the inescapable impressions they have made on his sensibility.

It is tempting to divide photos and text into fact and fiction, raw material and art, "the object *itself*" and the vibrations the object sets up in the imagination. But this is too easy. For Morris, as for Wallace Stevens, even to see nothing that isn't there and the nothing that is implies a particular subjective orientation. There is simply no experience of reality available to man, the dream-animal, which has not been colored in some way by human vision. If a photo seems to give us the thing itself, that is only because the imagination of the photographer has possessed it and then processed it in such a way as to make it appear immediately accessible. "The modalities of reality are inexhaustible," says Morris. "But they have their origin in the eye of the photographer, not the lens of the camera" (*Structures and Artifacts*, p. 119). Thus, Morris asserts, borrowing a phrase from Wittgenstein, even a photo supplies a "model of reality. . . . Until recently it was felt that the photographer was confined to the surface of our illusions. But if we achieve a picture of the facts, we have one of many models of reality" (ibid., p. 118).

Both the photos and the text, then, offer an interpretation of Morris's experience, in perceptual and conceptual terms respectively. Combining them allows him not only to make the best of both media, but also to achieve a unified effect in which the whole is greater than the sum of its parts: "The words must not *soften* the picture, the picture must not merely *illustrate* the words. The fusion I want is organic, rather than applied. . . . Together [language and image] convey, I believe, a larger reality" ("Guest of Honour," p. 15). This, at least, is the theory behind the photo-text books.

To enthusiasts of the nostalgic Morris, the static Morris, the midwestern, great-plains Morris, these works are bound to have a tremendous appeal, thus the copious elucidation. Unfortunately, in going from the elucidation to the books themselves, one often feels that the commentaries supply what is missing in the books. In a statement which incidentally throws some light on Alfred Kazin's criticism examined in chapter 1, Morris has said, "I now seem to believe that the important things are those that remain unsaid; that the problems of art are concerned with how we hint at them. The bold front, the bare-faced statement, give the lie to both the heart and the mind."[3] This may well be the real charm of photography for Morris—that it speaks without speaking. Or does it? The answer is, I think, that it depends on the kinds of meaning one wants to articulate. The bare austerity of Morris's black-and-white compositions, the stark contrasts of light and dark, the rigidly geometrical outlines unrelieved by the presence of human forms—create a subdued impression of abstract expressionism beneath a surface of documentary realism. But this effect can only be described; it does not express meaning that can be stated as a proposition. At the same time, the photos do suggest a kind of journalistic truth, and some give testimony of the lives of the inhabitants. Over a few there may even hang an indescribable aura which may be James's "mystic meaning." Nevertheless, few of the photos convey the kinds of explicit meanings Morris and his critics have verbally expressed in statements about the photo-text experiments. The photos are experienced as concrete percepts; the concepts attributed to the books—for instance, that a given artifact reveals the character of its users, or that the repossessing of artifacts in *The Home Place* is essential to the maturing of Muncy-Morris's feelings about the past—must be included in the text. The fact is that if one intends to get at meanings which can be verbalized about, it is literally impossible to leave things "unsaid."

For the books to yield such meaning, the reader must be able to associate the objects depicted in the photos with some significance gleaned from his own experience or from Morris's text. Although it is indeed to the fusion of picture and text that one must go for meaning beyond the physical beauty of the photos, the minute we look at specific juxtapositions of photos and texts we see that the fusion yields mixed and uncertain results. The differing structures of the American books produce three distinct effects. *The Inhabitants* has two sets of text: one is spoken by a first-person narrator who provides a running commentary on the central theme that the edifices and locales of America have inhabited her people and helped to make them Americans, and the other is a series of vignettes and monologues portraying a variety of American types—the black, the plainsman, the gangster—in a variety of moods—awe, exuberance, despair. The indirect relationship of the two texts and of the pictures and texts allows for a freer play of the imagination than in the other works, but the book's potential strength is vitiated in places by some of the same self-conscious folksiness in the presentation of lower-class types as in *My Uncle Dudley*. *God's Country and My People*, which has a commentary in Morris's own voice, is the most articulate of the three perhaps because it accrues meaning from the books preceding it. Because of the very insight it gives into Morris's works, however, the commentary strongly overshadows the photos, about half of which have been published before and all of which appear to date from the forties. *The Home Place*, a novella concerning Clyde Muncy's Agee-like return to Nebraska, is the weakest of the three because the narrative is weak as fiction and tends to reduce the photos to the status of illustrations.

The kinds of specific effects elicited by juxtaposing photos and text can easily be illustrated. In *The Home Place*, a picture of the safety pins and American Legion poppies listed among the odds and ends Muncy finds in Ed's cigar box (p. 141) appears earlier on a page whose text deals with Ed (p. 55). The objects become a kind of symbol of Ed's presence, with the photo functioning like a cut in a motion-picture montage. Another effect is illustrated on a page of *God's Country and My People* in a paragraph describing the tendency of prairie people to violence. The photograph on the facing page depicts a small, square house surrounded by an immense plain covered with snow. The great, blank expanse of whitness forms an image of the natural obstacles which plains dwellers face and, by extension, of the hopeless metaphysical absurdity of their lot. It is the feeling of impotence bred by these obstacles which moves the people to violence. In *The Inhabitants*, a darker print of the same picture appears, inverted and slightly cropped; it has a less powerful relation to its accompanying text and is less powerful in itself because the smallness of the house in relation to the background is deemphasized. As a final example, *God's Country and My People* couples a picture of a phallic fireplug with a saying of Morris's father about

America: "There's no place that has such a fine erection, so little seminal flow" (n. pag.).

At its best, as in these examples, the photo-text technique succeeds in suggesting oblique but clearly defined meanings. More often, however, the experiment fails. The failure takes several forms. The importance of the artifacts for Morris's career or for the American experience is never made as explicit and unequivocal as one expects from the statements of critics. Often the photos are just photos, mercifully free of picturesque prettiness but not conveying much "mystic meaning" let alone anything specific about the nature of the inhabitants. Often a photo seems a redundant illustration of the text; more often the text seems a superfluous explanation of the photo.

Although Morris's success in fulfilling his stated intentions for the two early photo-text books is debatable, the at least partial failure of the experiment had the practical effect of turning him toward purely fictional means. His growth as a writer of fiction in these crucial years can be measured by comparing *The Home Place* and its sequel *The World in the Attic*, a book originally planned as a photo experiment as well ("Origin of a Species," p. 124). As Morris has said, the return which the books record led to his growing disenchantment with the "conviction that the past was real and desirable, and should be the way life is" (Bleufarb, p. 45) and to his accompanying recognition of nostalgia as a major artistic and personal problem for himself and for Americans generally.

That nostalgia and undigested raw material remain problems in *The Home Place* is evident from Morris's later description of his plan for it: "I used the device of the returning prodigal son. I tried to contrast, in this manner, urban and rural life" ("Privacy as a Subject for Photography," p. 53). No truly meaningful contrast comes across in the book, the actual events being few and commonplace. The scene where Muncy's city-bred children get caught in the flypaper at a country store hardly amounts to a contrast of values. The running debate between Muncy and his wife Peg about the relative merits of city and country life also fails to touch on significant issues. Muncy hints that he prefers old-fashioned methods of child-raising to treating children like grownups in the modern manner, and inveighs, only half seriously, against the "damn tiled privacy" (p. 109) of modern bathrooms which, unlike outdoor privies, provide a place to worry but no place to think. But this hardly qualifies as a profound examination of anything. Both here and in *The World in the Attic*, the portrayal of Peg, ostensibly a critical intelligence whose urban background is to balance Muncy's sentimentality about rural life,[4] makes her seem simply querulous rather than representative of a broader realism about the home place. She nags Muncy for not pressing his claim to Ed's farm and throws a temper tantrum when he reminds her, with some justice, that she had been grumbling about living there earlier. In the end, her only tangible complaint about farm life is that her morning egg was fried too hard. The eventual decision to give up Ed's farm is based, not on any realization by Muncy and Peg that rural life is unsuited to them, but on their recognition that Ed has inhabited the house too thoroughly for them to feel at home there.

The Home Place does demonstrate Morris's increasing insight into his past, but the insight is evidenced only on the conceptual level, not in mastery of his fictional technique. As a piece of dramatically meaningful fiction, *The Home Place* fails just as badly as "The Ward Line," which it closely resembles. The action simply does not have the significance claimed for it, although Morris's maturing insight is reflected in some largely incidental expository meditations on the home place. Muncy decides that the appeal of the frontier past lies not in its beauty, but in a more "Protestant" virtue—character: "All I'm saying is that character can be a form of passion, and that some things, these things, have that kind of character. That kind of Passion has made them holy things. That kind of holiness, I'd say, is abstinence, frugality, and independence—

the home-grown, made-on-the-farm trinity. . . . Independence, not abundance, is the heart of their America" (p. 143). These stringent, protestant virtues have allowed the rural people to endure the hardships of their lot—the drought and consequent loss of their fine orchards, the death of a patriarch in a train wreck, and the defection of college-trained sons to the city—and has raised them to heroic stature. The fate of Ed, doomed to lie paralyzed and helpless for eight days before Harry discovers him, demonstrates the isolation of their lives and its sometimes terrible consequences. In spite of this "epic" power to endure, the protestant ethic has taken its toll of the land and the inhabitants, driving the more gifted young people away and, by instilling a hardheaded adherence to the old ways, helping to create the Dust Bowl. Morris writes of Harry (a portrait of a real uncle) in *God's Country and My People*: "He gave his opinion that no fool gas tractor would replace the horse. . . . he never gave an inkling if he liked or didn't like the woman he married" (n. pag.). Endurance can be impressive, but it comes at the cost of numbing the emotions; Harry's "home-grown virtues were anesthetic: they killed pain by drugging his feelings" (n. pag.). This was to become a major article in Morris's indictment of America's rural past, and he later said that *The Home Place* and *The Man Who Was There* first suggested to him his mature conviction that abstinence and frugality were not enough to make life truly livable ("Origin of a Species," pp. 129–30).

The abandonment of the photo-text format in *The World in the Attic* leads Morris to rely more heavily on his novelistic powers, to good effect. Although this sequel inexplicably repeats Muncy's visit to the same barber as in *The Home Place* (Cahow again, not very well disguised with a different name), the focus is the small town of Junction rather than the farm and the genteel middle class which succeeded the pioneers in Nebraska rather than the pioneers themselves.

Though episodic and unfocused, the first half of the novel, "The World," is unified by Muncy's growing disenchantment with Junction. He sees small-town provincialism when a waitress laughs at his request for iced coffee, its terrible austerity when he remembers how a citizen committed suicide by driving a buggy into a train, the cultural poverty of the Hibbards's Sears, Roebuck furniture, and the intellectual aridity and ignorance which allow a citizen to write a "scientific" book predicting the end of the world. Early in the visit, Muncy feels his nostalgia for the past go sour, to be replaced by the "home-town nausea" of intolerable boredom: "Before you know it . . . you're sick with small-town-Sunday-afternoon. This sickness is in your blood . . . a compound of all those summer afternoons, all those fly-cluttered screens, and all those Sunday papers scattered on the floor. . . . everything is there, in abundance, to make life possible. But very little is there to make it tolerable" (p. 26). In addition, the novel repeats the charge that the pioneer tradition has led to a rejection of feeling and joy, especially the enjoyment of sex. "Out here," Muncy decides, "there was lust enough, there was mind and heart enough, but let there be no delight—no careening of the heart. Somewhere it had been resolved that the clapper be taken from the bell" (p. 78). Peg summarizes Muncy's conclusion when she tells Nellie Hibbard that she lives "in New York because Junction was like this" (p. 107).

"The Attic," for the first time in the homecoming books, effectively dramatizes Muncy's changing attitudes toward his youth, as Morris examines the disparity between the once potent hopes of its founders and what Junction has become. The symbol of these hopes is the lone streetlight next to Clinton Hibbard's palatial home on the west edge of town. The home was Clinton's vote of confidence in the future, but when Junction turned its eyes to the East in the generation after his, its vitality drained away, leaving the light suspended over a garbage dump. Angie, Clinton's mother, and Caddy, his wife, represent the hardihood of the first generation of pioneers and the genteel aspirations of the second. The failures of Junction have grown from the success of the protestant virtues which shaped the pioneer tradition, for "abstinence, frugality, independence were not the seeds of heroes, but the roots of the great soft life. Out of frugality—in this land—what could come but abundance, and out of abundance different notions of a brave new world" (p. 66). Caddy's failure to produce children represents the failure of the "soft" genteel tradition to beget an heir with Angie's pioneer vigor. Together the women personify the abiding dreams of Junction and America, and the lone streetlight, a version of Gatsby's green light, unites a nostalgic myth of the past (Angie, the West as seen from the East) with an optimistic hope for the future (Caddy, the East as seen from the West). As Muncy says, "The Great Gatsby, don't forget, was born and raised out here" (p. 76).

The death of Caddy makes final Muncy's awakening from his mesmerizing dream of the past so that he can be "born again" into the present (p. 147). As he departs, he tips "the rear-view mirror to keep the light [from Caddy's funeral-lit house] out of it" (p. 189). With eyes toward the future, Muncy catches one last glimpse of the past about to follow the dream, to fade and disappear: "Whatever remained at this edge of town did so at a risk, and a bad one, as only the husk of several time-tired buildings remained. They faced to the west—a row of old men with their hands tied behind them, with blindfolded eyes—facing the firing squad, the careening globe, and the impending flood" (p. 179).

Considered as a transitional novel between Morris's early and middle works, *The World in the Attic* is significant in showing his first true disillusionment with the frontier past, his first adaptation of allusions to another author for his own purposes, and his first explicit attempt to understand the meaning *The Great Gatsby* has for his own experience of America. In addition, *The World in the Attic* introduces prototypes of important later symbols (the light, the castle in the snow-filled glass ball) and, in Angie, Purdy, and Scanlon, important later characters (Grandmother Porter, Parsons, and Tom Scanlon). The image of the attic as the storehouse of American dreams suggests the timeless, out-of-this-world character of these dreams and looks forward to the explicit treatment of transcendence in *The Works of Love*. Nevertheless, the many themes beginning to take shape in the early photo-text books and *The World in the Attic* are not fully realized. The real fruit of what Morris learned from the return to Nebraska is harvested in the four remarkable books that followed.

4
The Getaway: The Transcendent Hero in The Works of Love, The Huge Season, *and* Cause for Wonder

It is hard to discuss *Man and Boy* (1951), *The Works of Love* (1952), *The Deep Sleep* (1953), and *The Huge Season* (1954) in order of their publication because they represent parallel and overlapping stages in Morris's developing skill as a novelist and in his evolving attitude toward his material. The first two, composed about the same time,[1] are complementary examinations of love and married life in America, the first centering on their forms in the present and the second on the development of the forms from the frontier past into the present. To oversimplify, *Man and Boy* depicts effects and *The Works of Love* their causes. For that reason, it makes sense to discuss *The Works of Love* first and *Man and Boy* (and *The Deep Sleep*, with its similar themes and situations) later. Although *The Huge Season* looks forward to *The Field of Vision*, it also shows evidence of a maturing in Morris's attitude toward transcendence, which is dealt with explicitly for the first time in *The Works of Love*. Considering these otherwise very different works together clarifies the direction that maturing takes. *Cause for Wonder*, a much later novel, merits a brief look here because its treatment of transcendence resembles that in *The Huge Season*.

Unlike most of Morris's novels, *The Works of Love* is focused, not by unities of time and place, but by the life story of a single character stretching from the frontier past of

Nebraska in the 1880s, to the big-city present of Chicago between the wars.[2] The effect is to sketch America's emotional coming-of-age in the experience of Will Brady, like Willy Loman an archetypal average American. Although the water is muddied by the intrusion of a secondary theme of success, the central strand of the story shows Brady successively attempting various modes of love and failing in each. *God's Country and My People* (1968) indicates that the inspiration for Brady came from Morris's relation to his own father, who could tell his son about his long-dead wife only that "you got her eyes, you know that?" The son grown into the author thinks, "It is the custom of the people to look you in the eye, but not through it. To look you in the face, but not behind it" (n. pag.). Perhaps because he was so emotionally bound to the Brady character, Morris's tone is sometimes out of control in the book; his sympathy for Brady threatens to become sentimental and his commentary, condescending. Moreover, Morris never quite solves the technical problem of sympathetically communicating to his readers the consciousness of a character whose major problem is his inability to communicate. The inarticulate quality of Brady's emotions often makes him seem almost dull-witted, and his story comes across as pathetic rather than tragic.[3]

The pattern of failed love is established in Brady's family before Will himself is ever born. The lies Adam Brady writes to woo his mail-order bride and the snowstorm that keeps her from running away before the marriage can be consummated foreshadow Will's experiences with the duplicity of the human heart and the accidental nature of human connections. The titles of the novel's first and last sections point to the course Will's experiences will take. Adam Brady's fall into the uncertain toils of personal relationships leads to Will Brady's forty years of emotional wandering "In the Wilderness" between the past and the present. At the end he finds the promised land at best insecurely realized in material success and at worst cruelly travestied by the emotional failure evident "In the Wasteland" of modern life.

The troubles in *The Works of Love*, like those in *The Great Gatsby*, arise from the inability of reality to conform to man's romantic expectations. When the real world is a sod hut under a great overturned bowl of a sky, when it offers a man Daisy Fays instead of true golden girls, he takes refuge in dreams made in his own bewildered and bewildering image. Indian Bow "had been God's country to Adam Brady, but to his wife . . . a godforsaken hole. Perhaps only Will Brady could combine these two points of view" (pp. 12–13). Will combines the two in that he first senses the absurd reality and then embraces the dream in order to escape it.

Elaborating on his practice in *The World in the Attic*, Morris borrows light images from *The Great Gatsby* to serve as beacons marking the various dreams that call to Brady. At the start of his lifelong pilgrimage in quest of love, he follows the retreating light of a train toward the big-town East framed in the passenger car windows and stops in Calloway, where a lantern hangs outside the door of Opal Mason, the prostitute. Brady's "love affair" with Opal is not a marriage of true minds. "A lover . . . but not too bright," he "brought nothing along, said nothing loving" (p. 20); Opal cries with loneliness while he sleeps contentedly and laughs when he solemnly proposes marriage. When he tries an aggressive approach and carries off Mickey Ahearn, another prostitute, Mickey responds by mailing him her baby son by a railroad worker. Symbolically, Brady is sterile, a pseudofather with no connection to the offspring he hereafter regards as his son, even though his one forceful moment leads to a connection of sorts.

The mirror image introduced when Brady meets Ethel Bassett, later his wife, is one of several images underscoring the through-the-looking-glass unreality of emotional life within the family. The protestant ethic has led to the cliché distinction Ralph Bassett makes between "suitable" and "unsuitable" women (p. 24). Because Opal, Mickey, and later

Gertrude are depraved prostitutes unsuitable for marriage, they are allowed to feel sexual desire (it works both ways—because they feel desire, they are typed as prostitutes), but Ethel's purity, though it makes her suitable for marriage, also dictates that she be frigid. Her repressed sexuality is vented through her "spiritual" love for her son, "who liked to hug his mother most of the time" (p. 24) and who is allowed to lace her corsets. A counterpart of this relationship is Brady's love affairs with various daughter figures in the novel. Ethel forces the marriage with Brady to preserve her respectability, but the marriage ironically belies his image as the man around the house, previously established when he does odd jobs for her. The only new job her new husband gets is replacing the son in lacing her corsets. At the moment of her proposal, Brady echoes Morris's own judgment quoted earlier from *God's Country and My People*: the "look she gave him, was meant to be an open one. He was meant to look in [into her self], and he tried, but he didn't see anything" (p. 46). On their wedding night, she is already emotionally dead, wrapped in a sheet "from head to foot, as mummies are" (p. 53). Brady's second wife, "the girl," who combines the daughter and prostitute figures, stars in a vaudeville skit which exposes the charade of married sexual relations. On the stage, the men who flee from her bed like moths "afraid of the flame" (p. 196) are objects of ridicule, but their plight in the skit dramatizes the real-life plight of the men in the audience who get their only sexual satisfaction from ogling the girl. Her dubious character and the unreal stage setting provide a sanction for the audience's vicarious enjoyment of a "naughty" situation convention forbids in marriage.

Part of Brady's tragedy, then, is that the protestant ethic prevents him from finding satisfying physical and spiritual love within a single relationship. Throughout the novel he moves alternately from homes to hotels (with their connotations of licit and illicit relations), but he is never any more at home in one than in the other. He is consistently depicted as physically remote from others, speaking from adjoining rooms, on the ground when others are at the tops of buildings, in a tower when they are on the ground.

Brady's responses to the charade of marriage aggravate his problem. His dream of becoming a "man of caliber" by producing eggs is appealing because eggs are easier to understand than people and often have more life in them. In turning to business to fill the void in his personal life, however, Brady merely makes his relations with others worse by giving them less of his time. Moreover, the disease that kills his chickens is one more triumph by the finite world over the world of dreams; the metaphysical character of the event is established by the fact that the "wonder" of the disease makes Brady "a religious man" (p. 122) and makes the prospect of escaping finitude all the more attractive.

After the debacle of marriage, Brady's feelings are given an emotional outlet in the asexual love of a father for his son, but his relations with the boy are no better than those with his wife-daughter, the girl: the boy and the girl "would sit . . . looking at him from a long way off. Very much as if he were an imposter. A father, one who didn't know what being a father was like, and a lover, one who didn't know much about love" (pp. 147–48). Although the boy is obviously hungry for some communication—donning his Boy Scout suit once a week so Brady can look at him—their only real conversation never gets beyond the fact that the boy significantly prefers to be called "kid" rather than "son."

Brady's bungling of the father-son relationship underscores the personal limitations which contribute to his failure as a lover. As the girl says, "Will Brady knew how to give . . . but what he didn't know was how to receive anything" (p. 196). Like so many Morris characters, Brady relates to the world through things. Unable to give love directly, he tries to express it indirectly by giving people things, but he is afraid of reciprocal gifts because he is shy of the love he instinctively feels they express. Even the turtles slipped in his pocket by

Manny Plinski upset him. This is one reason why Brady is so often drawn to the prostitute-client relationship. He buys a ring for Opal, a house for Ethel and the girl, camping and sports equipment for the boy. He buys the affection of street children with pennies, of Manny by acting the fool, of the department store children with balloons, but all these material gifts are finally as unsatisfying as the nail he fishes from his pocket when Ethel hints that he should marry her.

Brady, having failed with his son, moves to befriend strange children on street corners; this is the first step in a pattern in which the object of his love grows more and more abstract, shifting from a particular child, to children generally, and finally to humanity at large. The episode with the little girl who sells kisses for a quarter, still another prostitute figure, contains vestiges of Brady's earlier father-lover relationships, and his final incarnation as Santa Claus combines elements of his earlier platonic love of children and his mystical love for all of mankind. The hint of sexual deviance in the street-corner episodes combines with the growing abstraction of his love to form a developing portrait of Brady as a madman-saint.

Brady's ascension from platonic love into a final mystic love begins when his frustrated sexual desire for Ethel is sublimated into a disinterested pity: "He felt a certain wonder, what you might call pity . . . for this woman, his wife, who was . . . scared to death" (p. 55). As the story progresses, the widening circle of his love objects expands until it encompasses all of creation. In the rigorous schooling of the heart, a man must first suffer the predicament of human loneliness to understand and then pity it, must lose or bungle all his personal human connections to embrace the great impersonal abstraction—humanity. His identity refined almost out of existence, Brady becomes an archetype, the Blakean fool-madman-saint, like the Franciscan bum who wets bread crumbs with his own spittle and feeds it to the birds: "Very likely this old fool let himself think that in just such a manner he might fly himself, grow wings like an angel, and escape from the city and the world" (p. 205). The transcendence implied in this image is immediately qualified by a disembodied voice (a sign of now literal insanity? an objectification of hard-won wisdom?) which informs Brady that "there's no need . . . for great lovers in heaven. Pity is the great lover, and the great lovers are all on earth" (p. 206) because only life in this hell on earth needs to be pitied. Brady, the great lover who knows how to give but not receive, is like a second madman, "Teapot," a bottomless receptacle of pity, begging to be poured on all-suffering humanity. Pity is the one sort of love which is *all* giving, never receiving in return, thus Brady's final decision to become Santa Claus, a totally impersonal archetype and the world's greatest giver.

At first Brady chooses to remain suspended both in and out of this world, in the tower room where he works as a sorter of waybills. This stratagem allows him a degree of transcendence without making pity superfluous. From his vantage point, he can peer into a thousand lighted tenement rooms: "If he was more alive there than anywhere else—if he seemed to come to life when he faced this picture—it had something to do with the fact that he was cut off from it. Which was a very strange thing, since what the tower room made him feel was part of it" (pp. 238–39).

Even this much abstraction is not enough. Drawn from his post as Santa Claus by the light in the tower room and the smell of humanity, Brady achieves permanent transcendence in death. If one accepts Booth's stress on the positive side of transcendence, then conceivably this conclusion can be read as a final spiritual victory for mystic love in the face of previous, more personal defeats, and Brady, like Gatsby, can be absolved as having turned out all right at the end, in spite of the foul dust that floated in the wake of his dreams.[4] If one does not accept Booth's interpretation, Brady's final vision can be read as a supreme pipe dream growing from and contributing to the ruin of emotional connection in this world. I believe that the first reading can be accepted only by ignoring the dramatic context of the novel and its major images and further that the only thing that absolves Brady, and then just partially, is his ignorance. What actually happens in *The Works of Love* suggests that Morris has always been skeptical about the specific effects of transcendence, though perhaps fascinated by its power over the imagination.

In a meditation on the sleeping, moonlit town of Murdock, Brady comes to believe that the inhabitants dwell in a bizarre moonshine world of the heart. They are "poisoned" by "whatever it was . . . there in the house like a vapor . . . like an invisible hand. . . . This vapor made the people yellow in color, gave them fleshy bodies, and made their minds inert" (p. 136). The vapor is an emotional stupor born of the cruel conjunction between man's finite nature and infinite expectations. When earthbound relations fail to satisfy, man takes off into the "cloudland" of his dreams. As a result, a "journey to the moon" is less strange and remote a prospect than a journey into the hearts of these sleeping Nebraskans with their "out of this world" dreams: "Was it any wonder that men . . . traveled to the moon, so to speak, to get away from themselves? Were they all nearer to the moon . . . than they were to their neighbors, or the woman there in the house?" (p. 137).

Here transcendence has a negative connotation. It applies to man's flight from an unbearable present into either his heroic past or some fiction of his own making. For instance, Lockwood, the aging former miler, wants to relive his past stardom and remain one of the ageless wonders celebrated in the boyhood romances of Ralph Henry Barbour. Other instances are the girl's fantasy of true love for Francis X. Bushman and Brady's identification with the figure of a pagan lover glimpsed through a crack in the door of a movie theater. Morris's most complex image for the transcendent fantasy world is the hotel lobby; where night is day and day is night, sleep, waking and waking, sleep; where Brady can have himself paged to feel important; and where sex can be enjoyed in the lurid atmosphere of an illicit one-night stand. Only in the hotel lobby "does the lover meet the beloved. In the rented room is where men exceed themselves. . . . What you find in the lobby . . . is the other man and the other woman in your life. There in the lobby the other life is possible" (p. 174).

Significantly, these images are also associated with such locales as Los Angeles, which epitomizes the sterile unreality of the modern wasteland. With bows to T. S. Eliot, Brady sees Los Angeles as "This unreal city, this mammoth production full of strange, wacky people like himself. . . . Here, bigger than life, was Paradise on the American Plan. A hotel lobby, that is, as big as the great out-of-doors" (p. 191). The great escape into a dream positively goes to create the unreal present. In the imagination a place where dreams come true, the lobby is in reality a place of betrayal. Brady meets the girl, Gertrude, in a hotel lobby, and both times she deserts him she does so in lobbies—first of a movie theater, with its silver-screen fantasies of love, and then of a hotel. Brady's solution for the contradictions of reality is to get out of this world, but a solution which cannot exist in the real world is an escape from contradiction, not a resolution of it.

The conjoined figures of madman and saint, the fatuous Santa Claus image, and other details employed at the conclusion imply that Morris is at least ambivalent about Brady's final transcendence in death. The sunlamp which Brady buys for his instant ruddiness is tied to both the sunny, unreal city of Los Angeles, where one can get a tan the week before Christmas, and the singeing flame of illicit fantasy love mentioned in Gertrude's vaudeville skit. The climactic light image in the book, the sunlamp ends by blinding Brady and making him susceptible to the Pied Piper's enchantment, which he had earlier credited with leading Chicagoans out of this world into Lake Michigan, a submerged sea of illusion: "What they saw—or thought they saw—out on the water, cast a spell over them. Perhaps it had been the bright lights on a steamer. . . . But whatever it was . . . they had followed this Piper . . . and disappeared" (p. 242). Brady's Piper, the sewer-borne stink of humanity, is also the poisonous vapor he had earlier observed in sleeping Murdock.

If Adam Brady was the first man in the world, his son begins and ends as "the last man in the world" (p. 10), moving from the physical isolation of his Indian Bow childhood to the emotional isolation of his Chicago old age. Thus, the pilgrimage structure of *The Works of Love* is deliberately ironic, bringing Brady, in his tower room, "back—where he had started from" (p. 239). The feeling aroused by Brady's reiterated failures and the sterile circular pattern of his destiny is not transcendental ecstasy and triumph but overwhelming emotional frustration and futility. This frustration is evoked in the concluding image: "In the pockets [of Brady's coat] there were turtles and a post card to his son that had not been mailed" (p. 269). Turtles and an unmailed postcard—love Brady could not bring himself to receive and love he could not bring himself to declare.

Brady's aspiration to all-embracing mystic love is a form of flight (in both senses of the word) from the wasteland of the present, and flight, Morris came to believe, was a characteristic response of American civilization and American writing. As early as 1943, in an unpublished manuscript, he articulated one of the central judgments of *The Territory Ahead*: the great tradition of American writing is the "great American tradition of escape." Its representative figures are the likes of Henry Adams, Henry James, Melville, and above all Thoreau, who "advanced by walking backwards, the spine twisted, gently beckoning. . . . Here is the Epic, here is the gargantuan trek of the American mind . . ."[5]

This diagnosis clearly gains impetus from Morris's own personal and imaginative escapes, first into the undigested boyhood romance chronicled in *My Uncle Dudley*, and then into the imperfectly understood return to the home place in *The Man Who Was There* and the early photo-text books. In the novels from *Man and Boy* to *The Field of Vision*, the American impulse to flee the intolerable present is no longer the artist's problem, but a conscious theme worked out with growing intellectual subtlety and technical control. Morris's insight into the great American getaway was sharpened by D. H. Lawrence's landmark analysis in *Studies in Classic American Literature.*[6] In his introductory essay, "The Spirit of Place," Lawrence argues that the colonists first came to America "largely to get *away*—that most simple of motives. To get away. . . . away from themselves. . . . away from everything they are and have been" (pp. 13–14). And in getting away—from the old laws, the old continent, the old consciousness—the untethered Americans faced an unparalleled opportunity to begin a new life founded on entirely new principles. But "the world fears a new experience more than it fears anything. Because a new experience displaces so many old experiences. And it is like trying to use muscles that have perhaps never been used, or that have been going stiff for ages. It hurts horribly" (p. 11). Instead of building a new life from what they "*positively want[ed] to be*" (p. 14), Americans merely reacted against the old, forging a civilization of negative impulses. Nevertheless, "different places on the face of the earth have different vital effluence, different vibration" (p. 16). The spirit of the American place, redolent of new experiences and lessons, subtly impressed itself upon the sensibilities of her most representative authors, so that there is a telling duplicity between what they think they believe (in deference to or rejection of the old) and what they actually believe (as the new struggles to come out). While Crèvecoeur idealized nature because it is "absolutely the safest thing to get your emotional reactions over" (p. 33), he was compelled by the accuracy of his observation to write that "nothing exists but what has its enemy, one species pursue and live upon another" (p. 35). Following fast upon Crèvecoeur's romantic idealism, this recognition of the identity of each thing in all its attributes, is to Lawrence "the rudimentary American vision" (p. 35).

The same doubleness of vision permeates the fiction of Morris, the man from "God's country . . . a fiction inhabited by people with a love for the facts" (*God's Country and My People*, n. pag.), and the conflict between the change and growth required for life and the fear of new experiences is merely a restatement of the conflict in Morris's books between past and present. In the works examined so far the alternative to withdrawal and flight is not yet explicitly designated as organic vitalism, the alternative for Lawrence. However, in a 1969 story, "Drrdla," we find "the desire to open out, to confront what is new" identified with sexual adventurousness and "the fear which dictated withdrawal" identified with fear of sex.[7] The story also ties the desire to open out to evolutionary processes and represents it with animal imagery.

The novel in which the evolutionary theme and the animal imagery first occur is *The Huge Season*. In the same book, transcendence is more consciously presented as one manifestation of the great American getaway, and objections to transcendence are more fully spelled out than in *The Works of Love*. In fact *The Huge Season* is Morris's most philosophically ambitious work and in some ways the most ambitious in structure. In it, the value and limitations of transcendence are completely elaborated and related to theories of aesthetics and ontology.

The novel is divided into two distinct narratives presented in alternating sections. The "Captivity" sections, set in the past of the twenties, focus on the actions of Charles Lawrence, the hero-doer, and his relationship with his college roommates, Peter Foley and Jesse Proctor. They are narrated in the first person by Foley with a straightforward chronology and relatively little narrative commentary or stress on consciousness. The effect is to make the story vivid, gripping, and immediate in its impact. The "Foley" sections, set in the fifties, cover Foley's experiences during a single day of reminiscences about Lawrence. These sections constitute Morris's most direct and encyclopedic fictional statement of his ideas. Presented in the third person, the meditations of Foley, the witness-knower, are perhaps Morris's closest approach to Joycean stream of consciousness. Sentences are fragmented and crackle with literary allusions ranging as far afield from Morris's usual favorites as Housman and Dante. Connections between symbols, images, allusions, and ideas are complex, elliptical, and sometimes obscure. Foley's father, who bequeathed his watch to his son and who felt at home in his times, had a premodern sense of time as an orderly sequence of uniform moments dispassionately measured on the watch's face. But for Foley himself, who looks "at the watch without seeing the time" (p. 3), time is subjective and post-Bergsonian. Since he feels "the times *are* out of joint, and. . . . I was more alive . . . thirty years ago" (pp. 3–4), his present is a chaotic jumble of past memories and present impressions.

The present-time sections of *The Huge Season* are constructed around Foley's round-trip excursion from Philadelphia to New York. The physical journey suggests Foley's psychological return to his past, into which he apparently gets new insights designed to break the spell of his "captivity" and free him for a return to the present at the end.

Many of the major themes and situations in *The Huge Season* have been extensively dealt with by previous critics. The novel dramatizes the theme of nostalgia[8] by showing how the "huge season" of the twenties, in the person of its real and fictional heroes, cast its baleful spell over the Americans who, like Proctor, tried to strike its romantic postures in the more deadly serious era that followed or, like Foley, were unable to perform any meaningful action because the past made such action seem prosaic and superfluous. The hero figure, Lawrence, personifies the inimitable style of the decade, the "habit of perfection, [which] united George Herman Ruth and Charles A. Lindbergh, Albie Booth and Jack Dempsey, Juan Belmonte and Jay Gatsby, and every man, anywhere, who stood alone with his own symbolic bull. He had his gesture, his moment of truth, or his early death in the afternoon" (p. 105).

The novel analyzes where this habit came from and where it leads. Lawrence is driven from both within and without. From his grandfather, who invented barbed wire, he has inherited a predisposition toward a rugged individualism and independence characteristic of frontier America, but ironically he has inherited a fortune along with it. As Muncy saw in *The World in the Attic*, pioneer hardihood produced the great soft life of contemporary America, and the great soft life makes hardihood an anachronism, depriving the hero of constructive outlets for his energies and leaving him "disinherited" of his heroic opportunities. The frontiers that remain to be conquered are the frontiers of imagination. Thus, Lawrence is like a Gatsby who has always had his Daisy, trying to fulfill his platonic conception of himself without any tangible object to which that conception can be attached. Like a Jacob wrestling with an angel which is a projection of himself, he seems alone and locked in some obscure inner combat even on a tennis court. At the same time, the scrutiny of his witnesses brings home to Lawrence his heroic obligations and outlines his gestures in red. For instance, Proctor's attendance at tennis practices embarrasses Lawrence into revealing that one of his arms is shorter than the other. As the adulation of the witnesses spurs him to more and more flamboyant acts of heroism, he becomes a tennis champ with a deliberately unorthodox playing style, the first boy in his dorm suite to get the clap, and like Hemingway, whom he resembles, an amateur bullfighter in Spain. Although he is chiefly a man of action, his models come from the archetypal books he has never read; his epithet "old man" is a version of

Gatsby's "old sport," and the groin wound he receives in a *novillada* recalls Jake Barnes (Morris parodies Hemingway in the passage discussing the wound [p. 86]).

To the witnesses, Lawrence is something of a Daisy to their Gatsby, one of the careless, glittering rich, complete with his own Tom Buchanan in Dickie Livingston. He is variously their green light, "the man in whom the sun rose and set" (p. 14), and the figure of perishable breath to whom is wedded their unutterable vision of heroism. Unlike Gatsby, the witnesses physically survive the final setting of their sun and pay the penalty for having lived too long with a single dream: "With the passing of Lawrence a constellation had blacked out. One seldom . . . heard from such bright suns as Proctor and Lou Baker . . . and Peter Foley himself. . . . leaving no trace, casting no light, emitting no radiation" (p. 14). With Lawrence's suicide, they too are disinherited, bereft of their heroic model and inspiration. Proctor "erodes" into a Jewish martyr and ineffectual freedom fighter rescuing cockroaches from his bathtub, his struggle to bring people a "good society" instead of a "goods society" (p. 241) a conspicuous failure. The one woman in the group, Lou Baker, erodes into a bush-league Gertrude Stein trading in the cultural stock of the twenties and, like Foley, perpetually at work on a book about the period. Foley still wears the jacket given him by Lawrence's family twenty years earlier. "The single shot that killed Lawrence had crippled all of them" (p. 18), making the "lone eagles" of yesterday the "dead ducks" of today.

This human drama is sometimes inexplicable without the larger metaphysical drama of which it is a part. In his manuscript, Foley writes, "Young men are a corn dance, a rite of spring" (p. 104). The dance image, extremely important in later Morris works, is borrowed from "The Dance" section of Hart Crane's *The Bridge*, which looms in the metaphysical life of the novel in the same way the actual Brooklyn Bridge towers over the neighborhood where Lou Baker lives. Speaking of Crane's poem, Lou tells Foley that "the Brooklyn

Bridge was America. A span of art, that is, between the dream and the reality. A bird's wing, no more, across the broken gap of memory. . . . a modern corn-dance ceremony for making rain" (p. 191). Lawrence also aspires to realize the dream ideal of heroism in the real world. His habit of perfection is the means by which he seeks to transcend the "bullshit" he discerns in the snobbery of his rich family, the academic and social scramble of undergraduate life, and the pretensions of expatriates in Paris. The bull he faces is a mythic bull who "don't shit in the ring" (p. 12), who is free of the shit that encumbers the real.

This, at least, is the idea. As things actually work out in the novel, however, Lawrence constructs more of a launching pad for a total escape from the real than a bridge uniting it with the ideal. For perfection is impossible in an imperfect world; this is why Lawrence says at one point, "Nobody ever wins" (p. 200). Nobody who tries to do the impossible, to him the only thing worth doing, ever wins because by definition the impossible cannot be done. Yet Lawrence believes of Proctor, "What he admires won't let him down" (p. 202), and as Foley points out, what he admires is Lawrence, of whom Proctor expects impossible heroics. The conclusive test that one has tried the impossible is to push his humanity until it breaks, and not one to let his witnesses down, Lawrence does exactly this.

Lawrence is a transcendent hero in the sense I have earlier defined. The status of Proctor is more problematic. Marcus Klein argues that Lawrence and Proctor represent opposing heroic models—the former striving to get out of the world and the latter, "to get all the way into it" (Klein, p. 229)—and further, that Foley, about to be summoned before the McCarthy committee at the end of the novel, is saved by gradually moving toward Proctor's kind of engagement. There is some reason for seeing Lawrence and Proctor as opposites—Lawrence as the man in whom the sun rose and Proctor as the man in whom it set, Lawrence as Jay Gatsby and Proctor as James Gatz, Lawrence as a young Boyd and Proctor as an aging Boyd, Lawrence, in Dudley's words, as "the big fella you can't keep down" and Proctor as "the little guy you can't keep up" (*My Uncle Dudley*, p. 97). Nevertheless, Proctor is repeatedly characterized with images of transcendence (a planet in its orbit, the martyr-saint-madman), and his wounded heel and scarred face certainly class him with Lawrence's other crippled witnesses. Moreover, the critique of transcendence which emerges in the novel pointedly applies to him as well as Lawrence. As sure as Jake Barnes metamorphosed into Robert Jordan, the nihilistic, disillusioned bohemianism of Lawrence in the twenties spawned the left-wing political activism of Proctor in the thirties. Both are unfavorably contrasted with another force in the novel.

The Huge Season teems with animal life, and the most important animal is a chipmunk Foley observes dancing wildly to keep from being killed by a cat.[9] Perhaps, Foley reasons, man developed through a "creative evolution. . . . founded on audacity. The unpredictable behavior that lit up the darkness with something new. That in some audacious moment of the lunar past, at the mouth of some cave, resulted in man" (p. 167). This would be "the Origin of a species based on charm, on audacity, on the powers of the dance, and the music that soothed whatever needed soothing in the savage breast" (p. 168).

The evolutionary impulse embodies the ethical value of survival, and it is this ethic in the book, not Proctor's, against which Lawrence is tested and, to a considerable extent, found wanting. While the chipmunk dances to save his life, Lawrence's gestures are compulsively suicidal: he wrecks his Bugatti, thrusts his hand into burning smudge pot to prove his audacity, has himself beaten up to avoid a physical exam which would expose his venereal disease, is seriously gored in an amateur bullfight, and finally shoots himself. "The steady erosion of the liberal mind," at work in Foley, Proctor, and distinguished suicides like "Winant, Matthiessen, Forrestal" (pp. 290–91) is destructive dissolution, the antithesis of creative evolution. Leaving behind either "fossils," residuals of the past, or bones "chirping in a time that had stopped" (p. 306), erosion produces the transcendent hero. Evolution will produce an immanent hero, a type not realized in *The Huge Season*.

Morris himself has said, "Brady seems to point toward an intolerable future . . ."[10] and Foley and Proctor, if not Lawrence, find themselves in it, a technological hell decked out in allusions to Dante and Eliot. Morris's most stringent criticism of Lawrence, the grandson of the inventor of barbed wire, is to link him to the growth of the machine culture. Lawrence's belief in the American myth of unlimited potential for personal success is a blood relation to the public faith in a glorious future secured through technological progress. Both imply a belief in an inhuman perfection and finality which cannot survive in this evolving world, and thus have death as their inevitable issue.

Morris's criticism of technology has received little attention, although it is not peripheral to his work. The depth of his antagonism to the machine culture can be measured by the savagery of his attack on it in *The Huge Season* and in the book of essays *A Bill of Rites, A Bill of Wrongs, A Bill of Goods* (1968), which echoes many of the criticisms in *The Huge Season*. Basically, Morris fears a future of "high octane and low imagination" (*The Territory Ahead*, p. 3), a future in which what is humanly meaningful and valuable is obliterated by a proliferation of things. The spread of a mass-produced culture robs life of its old style of imaginative individualism; advertising obscures the object with its image; insurance policies and drugs deaden pain and humanity at the same time; information drives out consciousness; man's supposedly rational powers are devoted to developing new weapons and justifying their use with mind-boggling computations which effectively strip nuclear war of its enormity. Through a progress that travesties evolution, Foley sees man superseded by the "new man, the cybernetic marvel, [who] opened his plastic jaws and said, *I am a fact finder*" (p. 189).

In a complex allusive passage, Foley goes to the heart of Morris's disgust with progress. Quoting the list of rules for self-improvement which young James Gatz set down for himself (p. 188), Foley attacks the American dream of success through material progress. In this dream, "the brooks too broad for leaping were easily leaped in the Elevator shoes. A little rough at the start, even a little sordid, but one fine day—as advertised in *Life*—that brook too broad for leaping would be lapping at the door" (p. 189). With the help of elevator shoes, quintessential image of modern man's faith in the power of trivial gadgets, even Housman's brook (death) may be overcome. Technology may vanquish death itself, or so *Life* argues. But the fate of Gatsby and Western society mocks *Life* and life. When Foley goes to see the Disney nature film *God's Half Acre*,[11] he watches a newsreel of an atomic blast. This "man-made sun," a triumph of technology, is linked to Lawrence, the sun of the planet-witnesses (as well as Brady's sunlamp mysticism), and suggests that both technological perfection and Lawrence's transcendence can come only at the expense of life as process, the life of nature. The "symbolic zero of Hiroshima, the surrealist's nightmare of man-made dissolution and vacuity" (p. 169) is the void where nature no longer is, the point where the material is made immaterial with a vengeance. Foley wonders if Mother Nature is experimenting with the chipmunk because of her notable failure with man: "If what Nature had in mind was survival, Man had ceased to be at the heart of Nature and had gone off on a suicidal impulse of his own" (p. 168).[12]

When it does not contribute directly to the inferno of the modern present, transcendence is at least a spectacular manifestation of the great American getaway. Viewed in this light, Lawrence's compulsive quest for an impossible perfection, like Brady's substitution of abstract pity for personal love, is a tacit confession of defeat in the realm of the possible. What Morris wrote of Thomas Wolfe pertains here: "An insatiable hunger, an insatiable desire, is not the sign of life but of impotence. Impotence, indeed, is part of the romantic agony. If one desires what one cannot have, if one must do only what cannot be done, the agony in the garden is of self-induced helplessness" (*The Territory Ahead*, p. 32). The signs of Lawrence's impotence—first his short arm, then the groin wound, and finally the setting of his sun not to rise again—identify him as a Fisher King whose lands cannot be restored because he has willfully absented himself from the scene. His subject-witnesses become fossils or corpses prematurely planted in the resulting moral desert where they do not "sprout" (p. 130), or at least not until the end of the novel.

As for Proctor, his lifelong struggle against fascism is equivalent to Dudley's quixotic defiance of Cupid in the same cause. Both represent an evasion of "sivilized" life, an attempt to prolong the shoot-out at high noon into an era when the real enemy of humanity is less obviously villainous than fascism, but more imposing—technological man with his vision of an inhuman future. Proctor and Lou together are like the lovers in a Kokoschka painting, "sleeping through the tempest that. . . . the current Prince of Darkness," Senator McCarthy, whips up around them (p. 161). In contrast to the figures in an old photo, whose blurred appearance evidences that life, time, and motion were present even in the instant of the shutter's flash, the lovers repose, serenely transcendent, above time. In the narrator of the newsreel, Foley recognizes "the everlasting disaster-hungry prophet, since men would rather die, in a righteous foxhole, than come and face the battle of daily life. . . . Foley could see the saintly, luminous face of Proctor, the quiet smile radiating a power like the doom itself. The power to transform, the raw material made immaterial, heavenly. There seemed to be a law that when faced with evil man turned this power upon himself . . ." (p. 169). The failure of Proctor, who has spent twenty years in one embattled foxhole or another, is clear. His moral suicide is the equivalent of Lawrence's physical one: both amount to the ultimate self-transformation.

Placed for emphasis near the end of the novel is Foley's recollection of the episode which most dramatically establishes his failure—his "nightmare" medical examination in the induction center. Although, Thoreau-like, he has planned to refuse induction as a pacifist, his first moral stand turns out to be his last. The heart murmur which causes him to be rejected is symbolic of the moral wound inflicted on him by Lawrence, for a pacifist does not act at all, merely protests by passively being what he is. In the induction center Foley comes face to face with man, the thing itself, the poor, bare, forked animal of this contingent world. Rejected, he feels "nothing that he thought he should feel"; he feels, instead, "*Nothing*" (p. 297), the nothing at the heart of a "hellish" universe. In this moment, he becomes, like Fitzgerald in *The Crack-Up*, "the first of his generation to know that life was *absurd*" (*The Territory Ahead*, p. 160). Such a world requires an active commitment which Foley lacks the moral heart to make. The man who would protest merely through passively being finds himself mocked and betrayed by his own being, his defective heart. At the end he judges Lawrence, Proctor, Lou, and himself: "Did they lack conviction? No. . . . What they lacked was intention. They could shoot off guns, at themselves. . . . But they would not carry this war to the enemy. That led to action, action to evil, blood on the escutcheon of lily-white Goodness, and to the temporal kingdom rather than the eternal heavenly one. That led . . . where they had no intention of ending up. The world of men here below" (pp. 299–300). Like actual suicide, such moral suicide leaves a mess behind for the rest of mankind to clean up.

For Crane, in *The Bridge*, technology and material progress were the physical expression of a positive spiritual principle, thus the metaphors of the harp and the altar applied to the bridge. In repudiating technology, Morris repudiates Crane's positive spiritual force and makes the goal of building a "span of art between the dream and the reality" very problematic. In *The Huge Season*, the realms of dream and reality are doomed to remain absolutely separate. Nevertheless, there is a sense in which Lawrence's "corn dance" can bring rain to the technological wasteland which it helped to create by abandoning the field to the enemy. As *The Territory Ahead* makes clear, Morris fears not so much the ultimate zero of Hiroshima as the spiritual zero of a society which dispenses with imagination. In the machine culture Foley confronts, one place a man can still pick up the imaginative charge is with figures like Lawrence who fly in the face of the facts. At the conclusion of *The Huge Season*, radioactivity, one of the deadly effects of the bomb, becomes an image of the imaginative charge: "How explain that Lawrence, in whom the sun rose, and Proctor, in whom it set, were now alive in Foley, a man scarcely alive himself. . . . Impermanent himself, he had picked up this permanent thing. He was hot, he was radioactive, and the bones of Peter Foley would go on chirping in a time that had stopped" (p. 306). The wasteland flowers in man's creative heart, and the sun rises again in the witnesses.

In *The Crack-Up*, an essay much admired by Morris, Fitzgerald wrote, "The test of a first-rate intelligence is the ability to hold two opposed ideas in the mind at the same time, and still retain the ability to function."[13] In regard to Lawrence and transcendence, Morris seems to be in just this frame of mind: we cannot live with Lawrence, but we cannot live without him, for after all he is responsible for such humanity as we find in the book. At times in *The Huge Season* Morris's ambivalence seems to give way to out-and-out confusion, especially near the end. Morris describes Foley: "Destination unknown, resolution uncertain, purpose unclear, source undetermined, but [Foley was] a slit in the darkness where the eye of the chipmunk might peer out. A crack in the armor where the bugler sounded a wild, carefree note" (p. 303). The implications of immanence and creative evolution in the chipmunk image do not square with the contrary implications of transcendence in the radioactive image and of teleological confusion in this passage. After all, the rest of the book clearly shows that one cannot at the same time engage in the chipmunk's dance of life and the dance of death which produces Lawrence's suicide and the bomb. By the time he finishes his next novel, *The Field of Vision*, Morris will have carefully worked out his distinctions between the transcendent and immanent heroes, but he has not reached that degree of clarity here.

More than that, the very wealth of Morris's philosophical speculations in *The Huge Season*, the intellectual weight he heaps on the drama, accentuates the thinness and poverty of the drama itself, especially the sections that deal with the present. Lawrence's imaginative crippling of his witnesses turns out to be more plausible as a metaphor for the overshadowing of contemporary art by the potent art of the twenties than as an exposition of actual psychological hang-ups. In fact, the most convincing demonstration of Lawrence's psychological power is the failure of Foley and Lou as writers. This is part of a general defect in the story: the characterization hinges on symbolic details rather than on the drama or on convincing psychological portraits. The defect is most evident at the end. Proctor deliberately shoots the pistol, apparently to prove once and for all that he can defy his own self-destructive nature and renounce suicide, but it is not clear what in the meager present-time action of the novel makes him do what he does. The talky party scene, with its largely aimless horseplay, does pass a judgment on the witnesses—Mrs. Pierce's exasperated admonition, "Children! Children!" (p. 247)—but this hardly seems a strong enough catalyst to provoke a major change. The most important psychological development in *The Huge Season*, Foley's release into the present at the end, is partially justified by his reexamination of the past throughout the day and is certainly signalled by his disposal of the pistol, a symbol of the destructive elements in Lawrence's heroism. Nevertheless, the scenes set in the present are often more of an occasion for reviewing insights he already has than stimuli to new insights, and the book leaves us with a feeling that we are being asked to take his release largely on faith.

Although *Cause for Wonder* (1963) is a later novel than *The Works of Love* and *The Huge Season*, the picture of transcendence that emerges from it is the same. My comments in the introduction (see pp. 6–9) are sufficient to demonstrate its similarities to *The Huge Season*: like Lawrence, Dulac is the slightly mad transcendent hero casting his spell over the half-reluctant witnesses even after thirty years. Howe is Dulac's Foley, from his bungled love affair with Katherine, the Lou Baker figure, to his unfinished novel about Castle Riva. The psychological return to the past which Foley makes in his meditations is, for Howe, a literal return to the scene of past enchantments. Once there, Howe repeatedly superimposes past memories on present impressions producing a nonlinear, Bergsonian sense of time. Indeed, Riva itself recalls the mind in the process of perceiving a duration made possible by indelible memories of the past: "What, after all, was this Riva . . . but a symbol, suitably haunted, of the mind? A looted ruin crowded with ghosts" (p. 269). The present Howe temporarily abandons resembles the wasteland of *The Huge Season*: it is morally upside down, a place where people dig holes in the backyard for fall*out* rather than to fall *in*. A new element in the novel is the idea that this world's topsy-turvy moral insanity will be righted by the madman's topsy-turvy literal insanity (in the way the image in a camera's view finder is inverted and then righted in the finished photo). Like R. D. Laing, Morris suggests that insanity is a sane response to a crazy world.

In returning to Riva, Howe manages to recapture an "impersonal, salvageable" past, a past abstracted to the point of being an archetype and thus "out of this world." Emblems of that stripped-down, archetypal past are the castle, a shell emptied of its perishable artifacts, and Dulac himself, also a mere shell, with only a small repertoire of audacious gestures to establish his power over the witnesses. As in *The Huge Season*, Morris pays tribute to the castle and its host; they are cause for wonder, "an ark" in a world rapidly being inundated with things and threatened by the demythologizing power of science and information. Again the benefit of transcendence is spiritual inviolability, but again transcendence also adds up to an evasion of the world here below: Riva is "a place to hide" (p. 29), where Dulac flees to "beat the game" (p. 8). Again the efficacy of such evasion is questioned: When the Jewish refugees who fled to Riva to escape the Nazis are cornered there, the castle turns out to be more of a "booby trap" than a haven (p. 163). The title of Howe's unfinished manuscript, "Run For Your Life," drives home his feeling of ambivalence when he left the castle earlier: "Was I running *for* my life, or was I running away?" (p. 8). Was he trying to escape an enchantment fatal to life or dodging an imaginative vitality so powerful it frightened him?

Since one of its major themes is the mind's annihilation of time, *Cause for Wonder* omits traditional plot development, which requires a beginning and an end, narrative conventions disavowed in the first and last paragraphs of the book. In their place, it substitutes "a new music in the making" (p. 175), a musical structure based on juxtaposed and counterpointed images: Riva past and Riva present; Castle Riva and its Western Hemisphere counterpart, the Texas ranch; Horney, the man of the present, and Osborn, the man of the past; the Old World hero Dulac and the New World hero Osborn. The opening pages describing Howe's visit to his boyhood Kansas are not a digression, but an overture introducing images, allusions, and themes developed at greater length in the body of the novel. The allusion to the "Rosebud" sled in Orson

Welles's film *Citizen Kane* is a particularly rich example, casting light on several of the characters, as well as Morris himself. Like Kane, Morris tries to repossess the past through objects (as in the photo-text books), an impulse also detectable in Howe, Dulac, and Spiegel. Like Kane, these three characters seek refuge from an alienated and loveless present in an idealized past, and like Kane, Howe takes as his symbol of the past the snow-filled glass ball, which he associates with the immortal recollection of his first winter at Riva. This association prepares the way for the novel's pervasive ice-and-snow imagery, and the reference to *Citizen Kane* looks toward the book's motion-picture imagery. The return to Kansas foreshadows Howe's return to Austria.

The protracted period of composition of *Cause for Wonder*, perhaps explains why it harks back to an earlier book, *The Huge Season*, and recapitulates its themes and character types without adding much that is new. The repetitions and the many revisions (five complete drafts over twenty-six years) testify to the difficulty Morris had in coming to terms with his material, which had a personal fascination for him that never comes across in the art. Writing ruefully of the actual experience on which the novel was based, he admits that it took on in his imagination "a tremendous and resonant infatuation. Nothing could equal the glow of my dispersed impressions. In actual fact, there was a paucity of substance" (Cohn, p. 73). It is exactly this sense of paucity, of significance claimed disproportionate to the true value of events, that one gets from *Cause for Wonder*, the weakest novel of his maturity. The musical structure was a daring idea, but it never really works, and the effect is of almost no unifying principle at all. With no strong central metaphor, such as the bullring in *The Field of Vision*, and no dramatic power, as in *The Deep Sleep*, *Cause for Wonder* comes across as a random series of illustrations of its chief idea that "it's all in the mind." This effect is heightened by overly explicit commentary, by characters who are ciphers for attitudes—for example, Horney, standing for an obsession with the present—and by heavy-handed symbols and allusions—such as "Gatz-A and Gatz-B," as the schizoid face of America. Other characters, like George and Dulac, have all the mannerisms of Morris heroes with little of the magic.

The tardy reversion to earlier material also places Morris in a position of rehashing the value of transcendence after he had exhausted the subject in *The Works of Love* and *The Huge Season* and solidified his reservations about it in *The Field of Vision*. *Cause for Wonder*, like its immediate predecessor, *What a Way to Go*, is retracing old ground, and Morris has never been good at merely repeating himself. But history was about to take a hand. As *One Day* would show, the Kennedy assassination would never again let Morris see the great American getaway in quite the same tolerant light as in *Cause for Wonder*. One form of that getaway—transcendence—we have looked at. Now we must return to the early fifties to see the getaway in a somewhat different form and context—the getaway from the great American home.

5

The Getaway: The Flight from Aunt Sally in Man and Boy *and* The Deep Sleep

Man and Boy (1951) and *The Deep Sleep* (1953) deal with the theme of escape prominent in *The Works of Love* and *The Huge Season*. Here too the ultimate escape is through transcendence, but there is less emphasis on transcendence itself and more on what the hero is escaping—in both novels a repressive, female-dominated home. In depicting the hero's home life, *Man and Boy* and *The Deep Sleep* put the final touches to the portrait of the American family begun in *The Works of Love*. The father of Warren Ormsby, the protagonist of *Man and Boy*, has supplied eggs for dining cars just as Will Brady had done, and Ormsby is the son who would have resulted if Brady's marriage to Ethel Bassett had produced children. The novel, then, examines the emotional dysfunction of the marriage relationship in a new generation.[1]

Man and Boy recounts the events of a single day during World War II when Ormsby and Mrs. Ormsby travel to New York to christen a destroyer to be named for their son, Virgil, who has been killed in action. Like Dudley, Brady, and Lawrence, Ormsby is a "westerner," descended from the rough-and-ready cowboys and dirt farmers who tamed the American West. When he meets the future Mrs. Ormsby's grandmother, a crusty matriarch tested in the fire of frontier hardship, she warms to him only after he mentions how his grandfather "used to eat three rabbits a meal on the Western Reserve" (p. 106). The hickory log chopped by the old lady's husband represents the pioneer heritage, which the grandmother now bequeaths to Ormsby because he is to become the next male in the family line through marriage. But the protestant ethic of the pioneers has both a masculine and a feminine aspect. For Ormsby as for Charles Lawrence, the pioneer past has become a soft and complacent present where the need for the male pioneer virtues—endurance, courage, daring, independence—is sharply circumscribed. In the resulting void, those pioneer virtues largely the property of the female—abstinence, self-denial, sobriety, moral purity—come into the ascendancy and woman herself with them. The true blood-descendant of that hickory-tough grandfather is Violet Ames Ormsby, two-thirds her own woman (as her name suggests) and called "Mother" by her intimidated husband. She is the most "suitable" of all suitable mates, an Ethel Bassett with the aggressiveness and will to rule the household and make the age over into her image.

Mother is so dedicated to protestant sobriety that she has lost her humanity. Pathologically fastidious about dirt and bodily functions, she covers the floors and furniture with newspapers six days a week and runs the shower to drown out sounds from the bathroom. Emotions quickly go the way of other human frailties. She reverses the usual conditions of human intercourse: her warmest and most open conversations are long distance on the telephone, while inside the house she communicates with her husband and son through telegraphically worded memos. Like Brady, she habitually speaks from a distance and from "*behind* something" (p. 44). Her work as a community leader and lobbyist for conservation laws has the effect of Brady's mysticism; it insulates her from genuine emotional give-and-take between individuals by diffusing her emotional energies into abstract humanitarian causes.

Mother's conservation activities, especially on behalf of birds, obviously relate to the novel's pervasive bird imagery and help to define the differences between Mother's response to nature and Ormsby's. Ormsby's feelings for animals are natural and unforced, but Mother, moved by an abstract code of right action, cares little for the creatures themselves. To

Ormsby, feeding the birds has been a "religious" act, a "Eucharist" (p. 169),[2] but Mother has destroyed his natural feeling for birds by making him overaware of them intellectually by pointing out their distinguishing traits and harping on their Latin names: "He had always liked birds . . . until the summer Mother got him to spying on them" (p. 22). This alienating process explains the association of the bird imagery with her unloved son Virgil. In one of his father's nightmares, Virgil appears with "a crown of bright, exotic plumage" and "the face of a bird" (p. 3). At one with nature, the dream figure indicates its direct, passional relation to the birds by summoning them with a wooing call and feeding them from an upraised palm as Ormsby had done in his youth. But when the father beckons to the birds, they attack him, a dream symbol reflecting his unconscious conviction that Mother has destroyed his natural relation to the boy and twisted the boy's instincts toward love into aggression. In the waking world, Ormsby provokes an analogous hostility when, in the humane spirit of what Mother calls a "visitation," he offers a bum a five-dollar bill only to have it flung back in his face because such an extravagant gift insults the bum's dignity: "He kept yelling that he was a man, and could give it, too" (p. 134).

The female's ascendancy over the pioneer heritage leads to a modern confusion of traditional sexual roles and to male-female conflict. Mother's moral outrage when Ormsby gives the boy his first air rifle, her theft of Ormsby's pocketknife, and her insistence that the hickory log be kept in the basement represent an obvious repression of the male phallus and a repudiation of the female social function ironically implied by her own name. She is eventually so successful in destroying Ormsby's manhood that the boy always seems surprised to hear he is Ormsby's son. An earlier version of *Man and Boy*'s first few chapters, published as a short story, suggests that the sexual side of the Ormsbys' married life has lasted only long enough for the boy to be conceived: "As a precaution Mother had slept . . . in her corset—as a precaution and as an aid to self-control. In the fall they had ordered twin beds."[3]

Mrs. Ormsby first asserts her moral dominance over the male during a visit to a Texas ranch when she was ten. The locale is ripe with natural, elemental associations—"Anything good, or unusually bad, anything that took on enormous proportions . . . made her think of Texas, or Mother Nature, automatically" (p. 126)—and stands for the habitat of man's most primitive instinctual drives. When Violet slaps one of her boy cousins who rushes at her "hooting" like an "Indian" and waving a phallic shard of glass, she establishes the characteristic pattern of her life: "In dealing with the male, use the element of surprise. All the time she was there . . . that boy never took his eyes off of her, nor did he ever again brandish his knife, or anything else. Right off the bat he was quite a bit the same as Warren had been" (pp. 129–30). Texas, in the nineteenth century the setting for the male's conquest of the Indians and fulfillment of the pioneer myth, becomes, in the twentieth century, the setting for the female's appropriation of masculine power and authority to herself.

When a little boy in Yellowstone Park once asked Mrs. Ormsby why Old Faithful erupts, she had answered, "Son, that's Mother Nature" (pp. 209–10). Mother's sexual drive, its creative expression inhibited by the protestant ethic, explodes like Old Faithful, its potentially constructive energy squandered for the sake of a colorful spectacle. It is Mother's nature to have twisted her sexual drive into a campaign of terror against males of every species. Her chief antagonist and victim is her son Virgil, who refused to nurse with her even as a baby and registered unspoken contempt for her aphorisms by refusing to understand them. His alienation from the home is nicely suggested when he sleeps under the newspapers spread on the furniture like a bum on a park bench.

Eventually Virgil's rebellion takes the form of a flight from Mother's domain out into untamed nature where, as a hunter, he is soon at one with his environment. For all her interest in conservation, "Mother had . . . never left the back yard because there were no trails there to take. The boy came and went without breaking one. . . . in the summer the grass was back as soon as he passed" (p. 166). In making the getaway from the civilizing reach of his own personal Aunt Sally, the boy follows the classic pattern of freedom-seeking American heroes, from Huck to McMurphy in Ken Kesey's *One Flew Over the Cuckoo's Nest*. But the getaway has its drawbacks, as D. H. Lawrence wrote in *Studies in Classic American Literature*: "Men are free when they are in a living homeland, not when they are straying and breaking away. Men are free when they are obeying some deep, inward voice of religious belief. . . . when they belong to a living, organic, *believing*, community, active in fulfilling some unfulfilled, perhaps unrealized purpose" (pp. 16–17). Because the boy never manages the transition from rebelling against Mother to following some positive, "inward voice of belief," all his acts, like those of Charles Lawrence, are infected with a willful destructiveness. D. H. Lawrence's description of Natty Bumppo, the great fictional hunter, fits the boy: "He is a man with a gun. He is a killer, a slayer. . . . Self-effacing, self-forgetting, still he is a killer" (p. 69).

For Lawrence, Natty especially personifies the homicidal destructiveness of American culture, homicidal and, at bottom, suicidal, compelled by subterranean instincts to kill the old world and the old self so a new may be born out of them. Like Virgil in his father's dream, Natty "will bring the bird of the spirit out of the high air" (p. 69), to fuse it with the raw, realistic earth. But because his heritage is impotence and emasculation, Virgil's death mocks the creative death and rebirth essential for growth of the self. When the war comes, his rebellion is transferred to the struggle against fascism, again in the typical American style of Dudley, Proctor, and Robert Jordan: "He wanted to shoot at something or other so badly that he just ran off" (p. 12). Although Mother opposes guns and killing, she is indirectly responsible for Virgil's death as a war hero. This explains why the Navy asks her rather than Ormsby to christen the ship named after the boy. Virgil *is* slain and resurrected, but as a naval destroyer, a mechanical monster which will continue to follow the murderous course Mother has set for him. Mothers turn out to be prime movers of war. Mrs. Dinardo, "an armored Amazon" (p. 197) in her sequined dress, has four sons in the war, and Mrs. Sudcliffe looks forward to the day when a ship will be named for her unborn son and he will therefore be dead. Ironically, Mother's own pronouncement is confirmed; the home is "*even more than the battlefield . . . the most dangerous place in the world*" (p. 38).

In death, Virgil becomes a transcendent hero through Mother's ability to get "the best out of everyone" (p. 8). As Madden shows,[4] the chief beneficiary is Ormsby, who possesses the boy in his imagination, where Virgil is "safe from the weather, the air and. . . . from time itself" (p. 77). The growing abstraction in Ormsby's perception of the boy is evident in his comparison of Virgil to Floyd Collins. Ormsby remembers the effort to save Collins while forgetting whether it was successful because the man's personal existence was less important than his role as the archetypal man in trouble, a fellow caught in a hole he couldn't get out of.

For Madden, Virgil's transcendence is ultimately good because of the imaginative transformations it inspires in Mother and Ormsby. Yet the imaginative spectacle, though impressive in its way, has been costly in human terms, and the rhetoric of *Man and Boy* offers a complex and ambiguous moral evaluation of the boy's death and, by extension, of Mother. The ambiguity comes at least partly from the fact that several standards of moral judgment are possible. Taking fidelity to nature as a standard, Ormsby decides that he had never "known anything righter, more natural . . . than that the boy would be killed" (p. 8), a verdict consistent with the dark, irrational, destructive side of nature represented by Old Faithful and by the bird Ormsby observes killing worms in the yard without eating them. On the other hand, Ormsby's feeling that Virgil was "*nipped in the bud*" suggests that in his case natural processes were thwarted, and that, as Ormsby thinks, the boy missed "the very reasons for being alive" and was "not quite alive" (p. 70). This feeling implies a condemnation of Mother for poisoning what little life Virgil had.

Judged for her conformity to the pioneer tradition, Mother is a positive figure for having produced a male offspring whose feats against the Japanese are the equivalent of subduing the Indians and mastering the continent. The question remains whether the pioneers, like Proctor, won the battle with the wilderness at the cost of forsaking the battle that really mattered, the battle of daily life. *Man and Boy* does not answer yes as explicitly as *The Huge Season*, but the epithet *boy* suggests that Virgil, for all his heroics, fails to become a man. The title of the book makes his failure to grow up a central issue, and Ormsby's habit of calling his wife "Mother" is meant to show that he too has never grown up. There is something childish about mere physical courage. Nevertheless, Virgil's fulfillment of the pioneer tradition establishes Mother as a hero, but of a different kind from her son. As in *The Huge Season*, Morris uses the Brooklyn Bridge as a symbol of heroic aspiration. The bridge, looking "like a great bow drawn taut and about to release something" (p. 187), connotes the suppressed violence of Mother Nature and its convulsive release in Virgil's war experience, which catapults him out of this world. Morris preserves the duality set up in *The Man Who Was There*, where the male creative impulse is satisfied through imagination and the female through procreation. Mother says to Mrs. Dinardo and Mrs. Sudcliffe, "A boat is a bridge to span the oceans and a street is a bridge to span the land. . . . we are bridges too, I am a bridge—" (p. 187). While Virgil spans the gap between earth and heaven, Mother spans the earthbound gap between generations. She is the gateway through which her grandfather's toughness is passed to her son. Hers is a heroism inseparable from time and nature, thus her repeated association with nature images. Mother is Morris's first fully realized immanent hero, not just Mr. Ormsby's wife, but "Mother," the very essence of American motherhood itself.

Conforming to the open-road structure, *Man and Boy* is built around a trip from Philadelphia and the home where Virgil's life began, to New York and the ship where his life ended. The journey in effect recapitulates Virgil's life, or rather the forces which shaped it, and also stimulates a recognition of Mother's heroic status by her witnesses, Ormsby and Lipido. During the composition of the novel, however, Morris's own feelings toward Mother shifted from guarded dislike of her tyranny to admiration for her imaginative power as a creation. He has admitted that "I had hardly introduced her to the story . . . before she took control and began to talk back."[5] In another place he speaks of her "blood-curdling roar" but concedes, "She is our own invention . . . and there is some indication that she serves us better than we deserve."[6] In Lipido's changing attitude especially, we can see reflected Morris's own growing respect for Mother. At first Lipido seems expressly designed to question Mother's values and challenge her influence over Ormsby: he comes from Texas, the land of suppressed male potency and the western myth of masculine heroism; his name obviously puns on libido; and his stunted size indicates the effectiveness of Mother's sexual repression and mocks the tall Texan of tradition. Moreover, Lipido is identified with Virgil, whose open belligerence to Mother he voices.

What reconciles Lipido, Ormsby's substitute son, to Mother is her brassy self-confidence, which allows her to remain self-possessed in the most trying situations and even to turn them to her own ends. When Lipido jabs her from the rear on the train platform, she weathers the shock with hardly an eyelid's flutter, and her panache in humbling the Navy wrings from him the tribute that closes the novel: "She'll surprise you, won't she?" (p. 212). This talent for audacity and improvisation is the very quality Morris added to his initial conception of the character. In the *Harper's Bazaar* story, the boy, at age seven, brings one of the mouldy jars from Mother's icebox into a room full of guests. "When one of the ladies asked the boy where in the world he had found it, he naturally said—in the *ice box*. Mother had never forgiven him" (p. 187). In the novel, on the other hand, Mother has developed her heroic aplomb to the point that she can stay on top of the situation: "Any other woman . . . would have died on the spot, but Mother just sat there with a charming smile on her face. . . . By her not saying a word every woman in the room got the impression that this was something the boy was growing for himself. . . . There was simply no accounting for the way Mother could turn a blow like that . . ." (pp. 34–35).

Apparently we are supposed to judge Mother by her power over the imagination, as a spectacular natural phenomenon, if you will. Her power is demonstrated by a contrast of images: goddesslike Mother turns on a lamp while pronouncing the command "*Fiat Lux*" (p. 37), but Ormsby produces only faint glimmerings by striking matches. The disparity in candlepower distinguishes a hero from a witness. Unfortunately, when Morris has Mother send the boy's dogs to the pound, outlaw Christmas, and bang on the pipes in order to enjoy the sight of Ormsby scrambling to answer her signal, he goes beyond what is needed to prove her a hero and makes it hard to resist making normative judgments about her. The moral repugnance this behavior excites overshadows any admiration we feel for her imaginative power. Mother's brassiness in front of Mrs. Dinardo's tenement and her composure when Lipido jabs her are just too trivial to justify the impression they make on Lipido or to kill the bad taste left in our mouths by her treatment of her family. In this sense the novel is a failure, but an instructive one. Next to *Love Among the Cannibals*, *Man and Boy* is Morris's most broadly comic satire, and the exaggeration required to achieve the comic effect makes the figure of Mother abstract in more than the archetypal sense: she has the bold, simple outline we find in cartoon caricature. Such a figure and the satirical effect it aims for do not lend themselves to producing the ambivalent responses evoked by characters in high comedy or tragedy and therefore cannot accommodate Morris's ambivalence about Mother. We cannot have the same complex reaction to Uriah Heep that we have to Iago.

This explains, I think, why Morris wrote *The Deep Sleep*, a book so similar to *Man and Boy* in subject, setting, and incident, and yet displaying great growth in technical sophistication and depth of insight into material. I suggest that *The Deep Sleep* is a deliberate rewriting of *Man and Boy* specifically seeking to produce the sort of carefully weighed, ambiguous moral judgment impossible in the earlier novel. Because making such a judgment requires a more complicated narrative technique than that in *Man and Boy*, Morris recasts his material to fit the still-point structure. In *Man and Boy*, short sections seen from Mother's perspective alternate with sections seen from Ormsby's. Although he is limited in insight and intellect, Ormsby is more sensitive than Brady and convincingly analyzes the meaning of Virgil's death. Mother's sections are much less introspective and largely supply exposition about the marriage. In contrast, *The Deep Sleep* has more complex characters and a more intricate set of character relationships. Its drama (it hardly has a plot) is contained in the characters' slowly evolving awareness of what the central marriage must have been like, and the action is largely retrospective. The book has five centers of consciousness: Judge Porter's mother (called the Grandmother), his son-in-law Webb, his daughter Katherine, Parsons (the handyman), and Mrs. Porter. Alternating almost regularly as they circle the activities on the day before the funeral of the Judge, they can develop a more complex picture of marriage than is possible with just two centers of consciousness.

In this way the failure of *Man and Boy* is instrumental in Morris's development of the still-point structure, which appears in *The Deep Sleep* without the suggestion present in *The Field of Vision* that a single event appears differently to various eyes. Though *The Deep Sleep* lacks this epistemological observation, it also lacks the later book's slight air of contrivance; it is one of Morris's most forceful and yet unforced books. Instead of the bullring, the novel has the Porter house as its center. The house, with its "sober protestant colors, the air of summer leisure, the *Saturday Evening Post* look of innocence and promise" (p. 16), epitomizes the moral and psychological ambience of American life. With his painter's eye, the son-in-law Webb perceives in a mirror reflection of the Porter's bedroom a succinct and telling portrait of America: "He had been led through the house, room by room, so that this room had come as a symbolic climax, as if the house had gathered itself together in the lens of the mirror. . . . each room seemed to open on a wider vista, a deeper, more ambitious prospect of American life" (pp. 6–7).

The success of *The Deep Sleep* comes largely from the interplay of characters' meditations and from Morris's ability to suggest the quality as well as substance of vision in each (an example is Webb's tendency to visualize the world as a series of scenes viewed from a definite physical perspective). As a maverick accustomed to resisting female intimidation, Webb is inclined to appraise Mrs. Porter harshly, but as a sensitive painter, he is more objective, bent on "getting the picture" of the marriage, but a full and balanced picture even if that means seeing the good too. As an intellectual, he is able to place his picture in a conceptual framework beyond the psychological grasp of an Ormsby.

Because Webb is a sensitive and persuasive artist, the reader is tempted to think of him as Morris's mouthpiece, but Katherine's compassionate feminine insight is a counterweight to Webb's feelings about people. It is clear that Webb underestimates Katherine's ability to see her mother's faults, while Katherine, for her part, does not believe him capable of the sympathy toward Mrs. Porter he eventually shows.[7] The balanced interplay of feelings makes their relationship seem real and their judgments seem truthful and fully tested. Since they both come to the same conclusion about the Porters, they are closer than the antagonisms aroused during their running debate about the marriage would suggest.

Parsons is important because he loves Mrs. Porter in his way and, as a kind of man around the house, probably comes as close as anyone could to articulating the Judge's feelings about her. The Grandmother, another avatar of the pioneer tradition, is limited in her understanding of others because sensitivity and compassion are not qualities on which this tradition has placed value. In keeping with her unemotional and undemonstrative character, Mrs. Porter is depicted largely through her habits and gestures and not through intimate glimpses of her heart and mind; thus she remains throughout the novel something of a mystery to be unraveled, like the marriage itself.

The element of mystery makes *The Deep Sleep* one of Morris's most successful books in portraying developing consciousness. Although Webb thinks in static, pictorial terms, his inquiry is structured like a detective story in which he gradually collects and sifts the clues to get a fuller and sharper picture of the truth. He is a Hamlet to Mrs. Porter's Gertrude (p. 279) trying to solve the "murder" of the Judge, a father figure who haunts his memory throughout the day. Like Hamlet, Webb is impeded somewhat by his own emotional hangups about mothers. Whenever "the case of the Judge . . . seemed to be closed," Webb reopens it (p. 15). The day after the Judge's death, when his case would seem to be closed for all time, develops instead into a representative day in his life, as Webb finds himself in the Judge's shoes, going through his father-in-law's customary rituals in connection with the home—including anger at the women, flight to various hideaways, and shopping for the groceries. His identification with the Judge brings Webb to a full realization of the marriage's compromises and culpabilities, but most of all to the very experience of the marriage itself. Although in a sense the Judge's wife and mother turn out to be the culprits, the victim himself is not totally innocent. Thus, Webb's final solution to the puzzle partially absolves the wife but acknowledges the larger guilt of human nature.

The portrait of the fallen American family which takes shape in *The Deep Sleep* is influenced by Henry James. Replying to a question about the place of women in society, Morris has asserted: "My opinions on this subject have been formulated, with my problem in mind, by Henry James. (Vide: *The American Scene.*) Betrayed by Man (deprived of him, that is), woman is taking her abiding revenge on him . . . she inherits, by default, the world man should be running. Since only man will deeply gratify her, the Vote and the Station Wagon leave something to be desired."[8] The pertinent passages in *The Amerian Scene*—also quoted by Morris in *The Territory Ahead* as part of a chapter (pp. 187–214) on James's book—elaborate on this diagnosis. To James, the acquisitive ethic of American life has so narrowed the outlook of the average male that he can focus on nothing but business, while woman is left to rule the rest of life. The world the male abdicates instead of running is "the lonely waste, the boundless, gaping void of 'society'; which is but a name for all the other so numerous relations with the world he lives in that are imputable to a civilized being."[9] As a result, the husband becomes a "sleeping partner" in the marriage—best known to his wife as "having yielded what she would have clutched to death" (p. 202), that is, culture, manners, morals, and personal relationships.

James's analysis is more accurately borne out in *The Deep Sleep* than in *Man and Boy*. Here it is the husband who is "the national figure," a successful professional man unselfishly devoting his life to labor for the public good. In this way, he is given a larger share of the responsibility for the family's problems than he had in *Man and Boy*, for Judge Porter's public dedication amounts to a private desertion. He is the recumbent Adam whose "deep sleep" of public service makes possible Eve's ascendancy in the private sphere. The reason the Judge is the big bird watcher in the family is that, as Mrs. Porter says, "Only men can find time for such things" (p. 96); the women are too busy at the unending job of managing the house and setting the tone of American life. Highly respected by those whom he deals with in his public life, the Judge is nevertheless a prophet without honor or authority in his own house, where, as Parsons says, "he left it up to the Missus" (p. 85). Mrs. Porter's imposing rule covers every activity conceivably falling under the shadow of the house: she corrects Parsons's enunciation, criticizes Katherine's clothes, oversees the Grandmother's diet, and bans Webb's paintings. She deftly "handles" the nosy Mrs. Erskine when she pries into Porter affairs, unobtrusively straightens the rug when the Erskines pay their sympathy call, dismisses Katherine's allergies as merely "fashionable," and leaves the blinds up to prove the Porters have nothing to hide.

Although lacking Mother's heroic flair for improvisation, Mrs. Porter is more sympathetic and human than her predecessor because she has none of Mother's calculated malice and compulsion to emasculate the male. Nevertheless, her composed self-sufficiency, rigidly ordered domestic routines, and intimidating air of unruffled competence seem a tacit criticism of all lesser mortals. Parsons says admiringly, " 'She's got no *human* failings'. . . . As that sounded a little strange he added, 'Mrs. Porter has her rules, and she sticks by 'em' " (pp. 86–87). Her almost *in*human perfection may have hounded the all-too-mortal Judge to his grave. When he credits Mrs. Porter's diet with prolonging his life, Parsons speaks better than he knows: "If I'm alive right now, and the Judge isn't, you can put it all down to Mrs. Porter" (p. 87). Having no human failings, Mrs. Porter just misses the characteristic failing of goddesses—having no humanity. Just when we expect this verdict to be delivered on Mrs. Porter as it had been on Mother, Morris convincingly represents her as human at last. Therein lies her greater fascination as a literary character and the greater relevance of her situation. Instead of flat-out inhumanity, Morris sees in Mrs. Porter an extraordinary emotional reserve, a sense of self-containment so profound that, enclosed in a phone booth, she seems to Katherine to be on her characteristic footing with the world: "Her mother appeared to be in a private, undisturbed world of her own. . . . she never faced the telephone or anyone else to whom she was speaking. . . . she was *not* really talking to people, but while they were present she talked to herself, aloud" (p. 148).

Much more tragically than in *Man and Boy*, the capital offense in the house finally boils down to the refusal of the inhabitants to acknowledge and express their feelings. As in Tolstoy's "The Death of Ivan Ilych," a story Morris much admires, the Judge's face-to-face encounter with death brings home to him passionate realities of existence lost sight of during an inauthentic life terribly lived too much on the surface. Three months before his death he had shouted suddenly for Webb with what "had been a command and a cry of woe at the same time. By the time Webb got to the room the Judge's front had collapsed, his guard was down, and he looked like a figure seated at the very bottom of hell" (p. 21). Because of its rich compassion for all the characters, *The Deep Sleep* has none of the satirical savagery in Tolstoy's novella, but the Judge's cry, like Ivan Ilych's three days of uninterrupted screaming, gives desperate vent to suppressed despair at a terrifying moral insight: as horrible as it is to die, it is more horrible to realize that one has never truly lived. His despair at life and fear of death is "superseded, by an even greater fear—the fear of showing how he really felt" (p. 21), and the Judge retreats once more into his reserve. He keeps Parsons at his bedside because "it was easier for the Judge to know that Parsons was just sitting there, watching him dying, than to know that he was lying there in that bed and dying alone. It had been a pretty awful truth for Parsons to bear. If this great man . . . was afraid to be alone and die in his sick room, what would Carl Weber Parsons do when his own number popped up?" (p. 121). But after all the Judge is "broken . . . on the wheel of his choice" (p. 14), self-tortured in his terror at feeling and acquiescence to his wife's authority.

The children are also victims of Mrs. Porter's cold punctiliousness. Under the constant barrage of their Mother's faultfinding, they had felt like "orphans of the storm" (pp. 111–12) who would be more at home, at peace, with Mrs. Erskine across the street: "They were said to be bright, attractive children from an outsider's point of view, but nothing they ever did on the inside was good enough" (p. 111). Although the pressure of this steady assault on her self-esteem had driven Katherine, while still a young girl, to try "to take what she referred to as her own life" (p. 23), her brother Roger was even more of a casualty. Roger is the Virgil of the novel, but more explicitly than Virgil, he is bereft of a father's affectionate support. This is established when, as a child, he runs away wearing a World War I helmet "like a little monster" (p. 25) and carrying a rucksack containing, he says, "everything that belonged to him" (p. 26). The sack actually contains the Judge's things, including his "fine Swiss watch," a revered, almost talismanic, object in the house. Roger, like Citizen Kane, greedily hoards objects as attempted compensations for missing love, and these particular objects represent to him his father's love, which he must commandeer in the no-man's-land of the house. The Judge, like Mrs. Porter, is known "through the orphans that he left" (p. 224) and the children that he wounded. As much as his wife, he is accountable for Roger's being turned into a psychic monster, a "GENIUS BURNING" (p. 28) whose sole release from emotional torment is death in the war.

The Judge's suppression of feeling in the face of death and Roger's retreat to the garage conform to the familiar pattern of flight from civilized life personified by the female. The Judge's life is punctuated by such escapes. Like Brady's tower, his island hideaway is both a dream refuge and an emblem of his spiritual isolation. Ensconced in another of the Judge's favorite sanctuaries, the attic, Webb delivers Morris's fullest indictment of the upright wife in the form of "commandments" for protestant right living: "Thou shalt not give a particle of gratification. Thou shalt drive from the Temple the man who smokes, and he shall live in a tent behind the two-car garage, and thou shalt drive from the bed the man who lusts, and he shall lie in tourist camps with interstate whores, and thou shalt drive from the bathroom the man who farts, and he shall sit in a dark cubbyhole in the basement, and thou shalt drive from the parlor the man who feels, and he shall make himself an island in the midst of the waters, for the man who feels undermines the Law of the House!" (p. 279).

Morris uses the figure of the Grandmother to place Webb's indictment in a historical context. Like Tom Scanlon after her, the Grandmother casts a baleful eye on what the world has been coming to, especially in the example of her own offspring: "An everlasting judgment, had been passed on them all. . . . it sent them all to hell, to an everlasting fire. . . . this judgment . . . came from that point anchored in time where the Grandmother weighed the world and found it wanting" (pp. 20–21). The Grandmother's anchor is secured in an immutable past, and from this vantage point, the members of the present generation, surrounded by the great soft life, can never live up to rigorous pioneer standards even if, as in the Judge's case, they die trying. For she too is almost superhuman, a "Rock of Ages" vigorously surviving her aging son and asking after his health each day as he grows weaker.

The Grandmother and Mrs. Porter form a composite figure in Morris's tableau of the American household. In making the female the chief repository and guardian of moral values, the protestant tradition decrees that she cannot be sexually aroused. Although Parsons finds Mrs. Porter attractive, "there was nothing you might call sexy about her." Both he and the Judge agree, "Mrs. Porter had never in her life had such an idea in mind" (p. 122). In consequence, she is not a sexually aroused partner to her husband, but a morally superior mother scolding her naughty husband-son, who, in keeping with the ageless myth propagated by Twain, is still a boy at heart. The Judge keeps a bottle of cheap moonshine in his office because, Webb decides, "so long as he had it he knew he could pass for one of the boys" (p. 142). He surreptitiously nibbles his banana candy and imbibes the forbidden fruit of the bottle because both he and Mrs. Porter expect him to misbehave like the bad boy he is. This explains why Parsons, who would seem to make a perfect husband since he follows all the female rules, is not married: he lacks the rebelliousness to be a convincing bad boy. The Grandmother, who helped write the script, and the husband and wife, who read the lines, are all parties to the moral charade. If the Grandmother consigns the present to hell, the protestant ethic she personifies has already created the modern hell by its emotional dishonesty.

The Deep Sleep stands as the culmination of Morris's disenchantment with the pioneer ethic, and his conclusion about it is spelled out once and for all in Webb's judgment on the Grandmother: "Her simple-minded world no longer held any charms for him" (p. 20), and she herself is only a "third-class set of brains . . . in first-class shape" (p. 130). The spirit of the pioneer past has always been long on endurance but short on brains, unable to see that the world needs more feeling, not more austerity.

This much has already been implied in *Man and Boy*, but *The Deep Sleep* makes it more explicit and hints at a way out of the dishonesty which will become important in subsequent novels. Webb believes that "a woman would settle, when the time came, for the worst of all possible worlds," because women regard the perpetuation of life as a matter-of-fact biological business in which death plays a necessary and undramatic part; if death strikes, the female attitude is "have another child, another man, another lover, and get on with it" (p. 15). A young mother Webb notices during the day seems to worship her baby son, or rather the image of her own moral aspirations, which she projects onto him: "She searched him like a map for some key word, some familiar sign . . . some likeness of a lover or some conception of her better self." Between them flow the mysterious and vital impulses of nature, "the same force that drew the salmon up the river" (p. 183). Morris, like Yeats, believes that mothers worship images, impose normative visions on their children. If the Grandmother and Mrs. Porter oppress their children with their stern and exacting expectations, they are only fulfilling the mother's inescapable role. If the child dies trying to meet them, their sorrow is brief, for his increasing age severs him from his mother's love and compassion, the only qualities which might have mitigated her uncompromising standards: "Once the male . . . broke away from the saddle on the hip . . . he was free, and he was also more or less detached from *life*." The real pain for the biologically oriented mother came when the "only bond that mattered, the only cord that bled, had been cut many years before" (p. 184).

The evidence of Morris's later books suggests that the biological self-sufficiency which Webb perceives in the female is an illusion created by the protestant ethic. The only close physical bond between man and woman which that ethic permits is that between mother and son because only it respects protestant sexual sanctions. As a result, the female is limited to the physical fulfillment of motherhood because she is debarred from experiencing the adult male's imaginative power, and the male, whose sole contact with physical life is through her, is cut off from physical fulfillment. But a marriage bond between man and woman secured through the sexual act could lead the male out of the modern wasteland and back to the springs of vital life in the female. An authentic husband-wife relation would replace the false mother-son relation imposed by the past and would reestablish the trinity described in *The Man Who Was There*. In the imagery of *The Deep Sleep*, the failure of the adult relationship causes the house to resemble another curiously American dwelling in the novel, the house Earl Parsons built with homemade bricks to face toward Valley Forge: there is no stairway, only a ladder, between the first and second floors. Metaphorically, there exists only a tenuous connection between the physical and emotional lives as well as the inner and outer lives of the inhabitants.

The importance of sex to a successful marriage, requiring the acknowledgement of the husband as a lover rather than a son, is only implied in *The Deep Sleep*, where the still-point structure throws the emphasis on the witnesses' insights into the Porter marriage as it actually was, rather than on possible solutions to the problems within the marriage. In spite of separate experiences, the two chief witnesses, Katherine and Webb, arrive at the same conclusion that there was something in the relation of the Porters that was after all worth having, and the imagery ties that something to sex, at least indirectly. Katherine comes to believe that her mother has a personal integrity and self-sufficiency inherited from her pioneer ancestors: "She lost touch with her family, but she seemed to keep in touch with something else. . . . Like the Grandmother, her mother was not beholden to *any*one" (p. 150). This integrity forms the basis for an obscure concord between her parents: "They each had been true to some sort of conscience, they had each made some sort of peace with their souls . . . "(p. 219). Katherine comes to understand that what she had always supposed was drudgery—washing the nightly dishes—is really a ritual obeisance to the protestant God, for whom cleanliness is next to godliness. On this and other rituals the rule of the house has securely rested. Her mother has loved the washing, and her father, in helping with this chore, has made himself a place in the home after all: "Your father and I," says her mother, "always found the time to run our own house" (p. 299). For the only time, Mrs. Porter admits to a real sense of loss: "I'm going to miss your father" (p. 302). For his part, the Judge showed his affection for his wife when he asked Parsons to help him over to the twin bed which, after forty years, bears Mrs. Porter's imprint: "He wanted it where he could reach and touch it with his hand. . . . Mrs. Porter had left her permanent print on that bed. She wasn't in it anymore, but the Judge didn't want to be alone" (p. 123).

Katherine believes that "a family, nearly any family" is one of the things Webb could "never understand" because "he had never had a family himself, he had almost been an orphan" (p. 32). However, being an actual orphan frees Webb from an unthinking acceptance of the mother figure's claim to moral infallibility. As a result, he is a naturally anarchic spirit fit to carry out the bad boy Roger's rebellion against Mrs. Porter, and yet, unlike the emotional orphan Roger, he is not psychologically crippled in such a way as to be compelled to express his rebellion in negative, destructive ways. Rather his revolt carries him toward greater compassion and understanding. Webb's retreat to the attic and his smoking of the forbidden cigar complete his identification with the insubordinate son and the naughty husband and prepare the way for the climactic event of the novel—his placing the Judge's gold watch where Mrs. Porter will be sure to find it. Like Foley's disposal of Lawrence's pistol, Webb's gesture is a symbolic resolution to the story; what distinguishes it from Foley's gesture is, first, that it is more richly suggestive, and, second, that it confirms character development already rendered in the drama instead of offering an inadequate substitute for such development. Webb's gesture demonstrates that he has learned to understand families in spite of Katherine's prediction and proves him capable of a compassion which makes him worthy of her love.

The loud ticking of the Judge's cheap dollar watch stands for the conspicuous outer face of the Porter marriage, the emotional frigidity and divided life which are the measure of its failure, and the gold watch symbolizes its precious inner core associated with their moment of greatest sexual fulfillment, their grand tour of the continent where "things came to a head" (p. 270) and their first child was conceived. Mrs. Porter proves the gold watch's importance to her by recovering it when the Judge lost it and by searching for it at the end of the novel after the others have gone to bed. The Judge has proved its importance to him by putting it in a "safe place." In bringing the watch down from the attic, Webb is like Roger, who returned the stolen watch after deciding not to run away, and like the Judge, who preserved it and the memories it evokes in the attic, a realm of inviolable romance. Thus, Webb's gesture symbolically reconciles Mrs. Porter to both husband and son and acknowledges the partial success of the Porter marriage. An earthly trinity is symbolically reconstructed: the orphaned son Webb becomes a son of the Porters, the mother recovers a memento of the husband as imaginative lover, and the husband, reborn in his son-in-law, salutes the wife of his bone and flesh.

In addition to qualifying each other's views, Katherine and Webb achieve a relationship which in some respects parallels and in others contrasts with that of the Porters, thereby supplying a dramatic commentary on it. Webb's commitment to painting corresponds to the Judge's devotion to public service. It leaves Katherine with only the private half of his life to call hers: "It often crossed her mind that she had given a whole life, or almost a whole one, for his half." The difference between this relation and the Porters' is that Webb, a stronger figure than the Judge, is a hero of the imagination and is not afraid of feeling. For this reason, Katherine tolerates the unequal division of emotional labor "rather than not have him at all" (p. 31), and Katherine's tolerance perhaps hints at a similar strength of undeclared love in Mrs. Porter.

The contrast between Katherine's love for Webb and her girlhood infatuation with Dr. Barr illustrates an important point about both the Porters and Webbs. With his wife, Barr always looks "like a man who was dying"; without her, like a man who was "getting well" (p. 243). The reason seems to be that his emotional attachments are incurably idealistic, full of "the silliness in books, poems, and music about the notion that love was out of this world" (p. 245), whereas Katherine has now "outgrown" that kind of infatuation for a more mature, down-to-earth affection for Paul. Like Barr and Brady earlier, the Judge is "poisoned" by his marriage because he cannot completely reconcile the idealized dream wife in the attic with the imposingly competent woman who runs the house.

Years earlier when Katherine showed off her mastery of classical piano for Dr. Barr, she felt she was "playing two kinds of music" simultaneously, one for her former lover, with his romantic illusions intact, and one for her more skeptical husband. Only the mixture of the two is "true to what Paul called life" (p. 244). Like the two watches, the two lovers, and the attic-house duality, these two kinds of music stand for opposed sides of life—its spiritualized romance and its more physical reality, the person one marries in imagination and the person one marries in fact. Paul the husband joins the gold watch to the silver and bridges the chasm between the attic and the house because only a unity involving both is true to what Webb the painter calls life. The Porters and the Webbs have preserved in their relationships something of both the romance and the reality, although the Webbs have a more satisfying balance of the two because they are freer of the moral unreality of the protestant ethic.

It is tempting to read the house-attic duality as representing very rigidly Booth's real-ideal duality.[10] In my view, however, *The Deep Sleep* of all Morris's novels lends itself the least to discussion in terms of abstract categories. It is the moving humanity of Webb's closing gesture that strikes us in the reading and stays with us later, not any metaphysical meaning it might have. The complex design and explicit philosophical speculation of *The Huge Season* are overshadowed in *The Deep Sleep* by the very quality *The Huge Season* often lacks—a simple dramatic force, a sense of felt life, of real, dramatically compelling people grappling with meaningful human problems. This quality can best be experienced in reading, not in a critical analysis. A reading reveals *The Deep Sleep* for what it surely is—one of the best novels ever written about the American family.

With *Man and Boy* and *The Deep Sleep*, Morris finished spelling out his objections to the protestant ethic and showed the connection between the great American getaway and the flight from the home. In *Man and Boy*, *The Huge Season*, and *The Deep Sleep*, he begins to present these problems as related to man's disinheritance from his biological roots. He was now ready to consider some alternatives.

6

At the Center: The Field of Vision *and* Love Among the Cannibals

Gordon Boyd, the unsuccessful writer of *The Field of Vision* and *Ceremony in Lone Tree*, has suffered the fate of American authors from Melville to Wolfe: his early promise is unfulfilled. The same cannot be said of Morris. His promise, sometimes completely lost sight of in a protracted apprenticeship, is beautifully realized in the remarkable series of books from *The Deep Sleep* to *Ceremony in Lone Tree*. At the center of this series and of Morris's career is *The Field of Vision* (1956), his most honored novel and one which brings to fruition the major seeds of his art up to that time. In accepting the National Book Award for the work, Morris admits that he is attempting to combine important elements of his previous works and give them their definitive expression: "Fragments . . . [of his own distinctive experience] are held up to the light in the book. . . . They are segments of a jigsaw, fragments of a larger picture, seeking a pattern in which they can rest. . . . To put them finally to rest, indeed, is what the author had in mind."[1]

It is less clear but no less important that Morris's next novel, *Love Among the Cannibals* (1957), also fits into the puzzle and fills out the emerging pattern. In a way it is a complete departure from what has gone before; it is simple and direct, with a straightforward narrative drive, while *The Field of Vision* is complex, convoluted, oblique. Nevertheless, in another way, *Love Among the Cannibals* brings to an apex forces felt through and growing out of its predecessor. The two novels occupy a position in Morris's career like that of *The Tower* and *The Winding Stair* in Yeats: they are not just divergent, but complementary. Their themes, structures, and imagery together contain the two opposing poles of Morris's art. Consequently, I discuss them together and defer until the next chapter the examination of *Ceremony in Lone Tree*, which in a sense is a sequel to both.

The Field of Vision forms the best and most representative example of Morris's still-point structure. The third person narration moves serially to each of five characters perched on the curving rim of the bullring—McKee, Mrs. McKee (Lois), Boyd, Scanlon, and Lehmann. Through their eyes the action in the center takes shape, and the narration returns to each several times in order until Lois, Scanlon, and Lehmann are phased out near the end.[2] Although vestiges of this structure are detectable in other works, only here is it totally functional; only here could there be no novel without it. Of all the books, this one alone limits the spectators to such a narrow range of common experience—the action in the ring, sometimes presented through overlapping views—and thus it alone illustrates how the same event can not only mean, but *be* something different to each observer.

In *The Deep Sleep*, the center of the novel, the American Home, furnished plausible opportunities for examining its subject, the American Heart. In *The Field of Vision*, this dramatic aptness is replaced by the extraordinary symbolic and allusive richness of the bullfight. It looks backward to the bullfighting of Charles Lawrence and the bullslinging of Dudley and beyond them to the tradition of American heroism exemplified by Hemingway. The hot sand of the arena unifies the novel through a wide range of metaphorical and symbolic associations: the sand pit where Boyd tried to walk on water, the desert hell where Scanlon lost his soul, the dream-haunted expanses of Nebraska, the wasteland of the present, and the aridity of fact unwatered by the imagination. The dry heat of the sand also forms an antithesis to the novel's pervasive imagery of water (with its paradoxical implications of vision, fertility, and psychological drowning) and cold (with its suggestions of sexual frigidity, timelessness, and lifeless fixity). The relation between the audience and the sport encapsulates the larger issues and structure of the novel, with the hero in the center courting death, the witnesses on the sidelines drinking it all in with their soda pop, and the "riffraff," the ring functionaries, behind the barricades waiting to clean up the mess.

With an ingenuity worthy of the School of Donne, Morris develops action in the arena into a highly particularized metaphorical commentary on the novel's central issues—vision, heroism, character, the nature of the creative act, the tyranny of the past and how to escape it. The spectators' contemplation of the still point, incarnated in the center of the bullring, transports them into the very origin of life itself. The still point, the mystic world axis, the Word, God, the Logos, the Life Force—call it what we will, it is all these and more. Bergson perceives something like it in "Organization," the principle by which organic bodies generate themselves and by which life as a whole has developed: "Organization . . . works from the center to the periphery. It begins in a point that is almost a mathematical point, and spreads around this point by concentric waves which go on enlarging. . . . The organizing act . . . has something explosive about it: it needs at the beginning the smallest possible place. . . . The spermatozoon, which sets in motion the evolutionary process of the embryonic life, is one of the smallest cells of the organism . . ." (*Creative Evolution*, p. 103). At the center of the ring is the bullfight ritual, and at the center of the ritual is the mysterious creative impulse which, as physical conception, separates nature from inanimate things and, as imaginative conception, separates men from dumb beasts.

As a ritual, the bullfight represents an attempt to impose order upon the chaos of existence and serves as a concrete model for imaginative action. For Boyd, the moment of truth in the ring comes at the instant when the action of the cape brings the astonished bull to a standstill. This moment is a sign that man, unlike the beasts, has the power of transcendence, which is the power to imagine, and in imagining to produce a condition of stillness alien to the process of life in time: "The bull could understand movement, but not its absence, the man could understand both movement and its absence, and in controlling this impulse to move, the still point, he dominated the bull. Except for the still point there would be no dance. . . . The moment of truth was at that moment . . ." (pp. 192–93). Through the power of imagination, emanating from the creative center, brute reality is "transformed into a frieze of permanence. . . . the double transformation had taken place. Word into flesh, and the flesh itself into myth" (p. 111). The creative impulse expresses itself in the man, and the man responds to this inner music with a bizarre dance of his own. Like the still point, the image of the dance has ancient and far-flung provenance: "There is a universal belief that, in so far as it is a rhythmic art form, it [the dance] is a symbol of the act of creation. . . . This is why the dance is one of the most ancient forms of magic."[3] In fact, the series of transformations has only just begun, for the spectators transform the dance they see into the dance they imagine in ever widening circles reaching out to Morris, the penultimate magician, and through the necromancy of his words, to the reader himself: "Words wheeling around the still point, the dance, the way the bull wheeled around the bullfighter, the way the mind wheeled around the still point on the sand. Each man his own bullfighter, with his own center, a circle overlapped by countless other circles, like the pattern of expanding rings rain made on the surface of a pond" (p. 193).

The bullfight is a potent metaphor, but it has another advantage. The action in the ring comprises almost all of the significant present-time action in the novel, and precisely because its relationship to the characters is symbolic rather than dramatic, Morris is left free to focus on the consciousness of the spectators. Although the title *The Field of Vision* signifies something like the photographer's "angle of vision," it also signifies "the field, the mystical clearing, upon which one can project his visions." In a passage that may have specifically influenced Morris's technique, Henry James uses the term *field* in describing each artist's peculiar window in the house of fiction: "The spreading field, the human scene, is the 'choice of subject'; the pierced aperture . . . is the 'literary form'; but they are, singly or together, as nothing without . . . the consciousness of the artist. Tell me what the artist is, and I will tell you of what he has *been* conscious."[4] And conversely, for the characters in *The Field of Vision*, what each sees, what each is conscious of, is the key unlocking what he is. When peering down into the round bullring, the tourist detects what he sees in the stolen hub caps for sale on the boulevard—a distorted reflection of himself. In such a novel the process of arriving at insights is the action; consciousness itself is the drama.

The five narrators, along with Paula Kahler, whose view is represented through Lehmann's imaginative identification, form a complicated set of interrelated foils. McKee, a witness, illustrates convention, with failure of passion and imagination; Lois, a second witness, illustrates passion repressed into convention and the female's distrust of imagination; Boyd embodies personal heroism, with personal passion and imagination expressed and then squandered. All three are trapped in a romanticized personal past. In contrast, Scanlon, who possesses no passion but much imagination, embodies the impersonal heroism of the national past and is a witness and prisoner of the pioneer myth. Paula is an impersonal hero trapped in a self-created fantasy of the present; and Lehmann, both witness and hero, alone among all the characters lives in the present without losing touch with the past. Although both he and Boyd come to understand the forces at work within and around them, Lehmann is detached where Boyd is involved, impersonal where Boyd is personal, a man of intellect where Boyd is a man of feeling, compassionate where Boyd is passionate.

The homely quotidian from which the others diverge, a moral mean as flat as the Nebraska plains, is Walter McKee. Superior to Morris's portrait of Brady, his picture of McKee as Mr. Average American is sympathetic without being sentimental and critical without making McKee seem slow-witted instead of insensitive. Although basically unselfish and good, McKee never sees more of his wife of forty years than "whether she had . . . goose pimples on her arms or not" (p. 36). He and Lois "*couldn't be happier*" (p. 11) because his insights are only skin deep, and that is why he is never jealous, even of Boyd, his most formidable rival. McKee's monumentally commonplace sensibility is established by the fact that he likes to walk around "anything in a circle . . . since they always brought him back where he started from" (p. 171), just as the bullring takes him back to the Lincoln Library basement and the bullfight takes him back to his own antiheroic showdown with the hog. While the bull is making it hot for heroes in the ring, McKee shivers in the *sombra* and reflects on a life that Boyd, the constant protagonist of his memories, has lived for him. Gored though he is by life, Boyd is the authentic hero and the symbolic father of McKee's son, while McKee is the symbolic cuckold, left at the end holding a bull's horns (with the bull safely detached) and banished from the car until Lois and his grandson Gordon decide to let him back into their exclusive relationship. It is a colorful portrait of colorlessness, and in fiction there is nothing harder. Indeed, McKee seems to me about the best portrait of the ordinary in our literature. The thread that ties him to Boyd is also his most quintessentially American trait: "McKee was a believer. Having settled on something he kept the faith" (p. 57).

Lois is simpler but just as believable. Frozen into the protestant stereotype of the pure woman, she has let the fire of her instinctive passion die out. Her purity is willed, not natural. The original tranquility of the American Eden, the seemingly eternal innocence of fresh adolescent faces in the summer twilight on the front porch, was shattered by the serpent Boyd, whose kiss meant more than all her years with McKee. But after tasting the candied apple, Lois turned back to McKee, the safe man of no feeling, and away from Boyd, the daemon lover who visited her dream. For above all, like the chicken who ate the fermented laying mash, Lois "didn't trust her own senses" (p. 31). What is left of her passion is sublimated into the overprotective maternal fussiness she showers on her grandson.

Although Boyd, the McKees, and Scanlon are trapped in dreams of the past, it is a mistake to assume that nostalgia, the most prominent predicament in *The Field of Vision*, is therefore its major subject.[5] As the bullfight suggests, a more accurate conception of the subject is the American tradition of heroism in all its ramifications. The problem of nostalgia is only one aspect of this broader issue.

Scanlon's dream of the western passage, perhaps the single most powerful narrative thread in *The Field of Vision*, is another version of the failure of commitment Morris earlier examined in Brady and Lawrence. It is a colorful getaway into a transcendent dream of heroism with the purpose of evading "what the world had been coming to" (p. 49), the present and all the demands it makes. Morris loads the old man's reminiscences with irony. Although at the bullfight Scanlon "couldn't believe his eyes—the ones he had" (p. 41), he believes the ones he does not have quickly enough. They belong to his father, Tim Scanlon, who, like Tom himself, "was mad as a coot" (p. 44). The mythic past is doubly illusory, the mad Tom's recollection of the mad Tim's tall tale, spun again to fire the lurid imagination of a six-year-old boy. The account of Scanlon's trek west leads him into a symbolically resonant vision of hell, where all normal human expectations are upended and reversed. Here things last longer than people, the heat seems to last forever, the Devil-vulture circles on high, and the paradoxical image of water signifies that Scanlon is drowned in a fantasy-spell so deep as to be unbreakable. The vulture, the desert, the hint of cannibalism, and the sky that seems to go up forever fall into Northrop Frye's category of demonic images,[6] and the wheeling vulture, "drawing this circle like a kid would do with a stick on water" (p. 97), represents a demonic inversion of the creative circle of the bullring.

Scanlon's scouting mission climaxes with the discovery of a dead man in the middle of a dry sea—himself: "There were two men within him, and he knew for sure that one of them had died. The better man. . . . had died because he knew where he was, and had died of it" (p. 187). The desert where Scanlon found himself was the intolerable wasteland of the twentieth-century present, but in refusing to face it, he has died to the present and has not known where he was since. Attaching cosmic value to his westering experience, Scanlon has coached young Gordon that the "shortest way to heaven's right smack through hell" (p. 56). The shortest way to heaven, a mythic transcendence, is through the hell of heroic testing. But permanent transcendence like this perpetual sleep amounts to moral death; thus the corpse of the real, morally responsible Scanlon has been left behind in Death Valley with no footprints to show that he got out. The Scanlon who has come through, "the mummified effigy of the real thing" (p. 101), has defied the predictions that he will soon die because he has not been truly alive for years. He survives in a hell here and now, which he, like Brady, has made by evading the emotional commitments required in the unexciting, domestic world of the present. His failure is evident when his wife dies and his only reaction is "what'll the hens do?" (p. 41).

Similarly, Boyd had taken his foul ball to get it signed by Ty Cobb and thereby transformed from fact into fiction and removed from time. As this often quoted passage on Boyd's nostalgia indicates, his own fate has been such transcendence: "A stranger transformation. . . . had occurred. Not merely a foul ball into a pocket, but a pocket into a winding sheet where the hero lay, cocoonlike, for the next twenty years. Out of this world, in the deep freeze of his adolescent dreams" (p. 109). This passage is only one of many indictments the novel levels at Boyd's tradition of heroism. The next few lines, seldom quoted, get to the real point about nostalgia: "There was not one bull, but many, each transformation called for another . . ." (pp. 109–10). This statement can best be understood in existential terms. In *Nausea*, Jean-Paul Sartre chronicles the development of his protagonist Roquentin from unthinking automatism to a full realization of his existential condition. The novel concludes with Roquentin's understanding that, as a result of his personal choices, "I might succeed—in the past, nothing but the past—in accepting myself."[7] For Sartre, heroism comes from accepting the responsibility for choosing one's essence in a contingent world and from anxiety about whether one has chosen right. Since contingency exists only in the present, only in the present can the responsibility for selfhood be exercised and the anxiety of selfhood be suffered. The past contains only the essence, the sum of one's choices up to the present moment, the dance but not the dancer.

In *The Field of Vision*, Boyd comes to endorse a logical extension of this principle. The bullfighter has an obligation to kill "according to the rules. That is to say, according to the risks" (pp. 104–5), but the past contains only the memory of risk. In the present, Da Silva is gored the moment after he brings the bull to a standstill; the suspension of motion is not permanent, and the presence of risk is confirmed. There is indeed not one bull but many, a new one every minute for those with the will to live in the present.

The necessity of risk and the example of the bullfight call into question the ultimate social and moral value of this heroic tradition. Existentialism, as propounded by Sartre, took much of its historical impetus from the struggle against fascism. As a result, existentialism tends to portray heroism in what Nietzsche called a "borderline" situation, a situation requiring overt physical action to resolve a life-and-death confrontation. Such heroism not only involves risk, it courts risk. Even when the hero is successful, he partakes of the murderous, suicidal impulses of Virgil Ormsby and Charles Lawrence. Viewed from this angle, the bullfight becomes a highly ritualized form of the hunt, with the matador stalking the bull while inviting death from his horns. Lehmann speaks of "the anguished dilemma," the tragic fact that man rises above his animal nature by virtue of an imagination that demands risk and can lead away from life: "Bull into Man was followed, too often, by Man into Ghost, the horn of the dilemma . . . was that it led to flight" (p. 114). Too often. This is perhaps a normative judgment, but in *The Field of Vision* overall, Morris employs a tone of detached observation rather than active censure. Nevertheless, his stress on the childlike appeal of physical heroism may be meant as a criticism. When Boyd asks young Gordon if he wants to get to heaven by going through hell, the boy replies in the spirit of American heroes such as Ahab and Robert Jordan: "I do if I can go to hell *first*" (p. 56). It is the *hell* he wants, and it is the boy in the man who wants it. It is a boy who dares the bull with a red flag tied to a stick; it is children like Gordon who made a song about Davy Crockett and fake coonskins caps (symbols in the novel of a now debased heroic tradition) a national craze.

In Boyd's case, his heroic gestures—ripping the pocket from Ty Cobb's baseball uniform, upsetting the proprieties with the sexually disturbing kiss, walking on water, and squirting pop at the bull—are the antics of an adolescent. The origin of his naughtiness and the direction it takes in his life are a part of his heritage from another American boy hero, Huck Finn. Ty Cobb's pocket, "the portable raft on which he floated, anchored to his childhood" (p. 68), and the style of heroism with which it is identified are the perennial bad boy's refuge from Aunt Sally—Boyd's tough pioneer mother, who tried to "sivilize" him by making him a conventional success. She holds up as an example to emulate a small-town boy who made good, Ashley Crete, but Boyd's audacious gestures repudiate his mother's respectable dreams and the spirit of Ashley's conscientious go-getting. He sheds Ashley's hand-me-down clothes before the walk on water, leaving the naked, essential Boyd to take the risks.

The vigor of Boyd's rejection actually testifies to the force of his mother's influence, which continues to be manifested indirectly in his destructive desire for transcendence. To walk on water is to do the impossible, and it is only the impossible which requires transcendence to a more perfect world. As an artist, Boyd has carried Charles Lawrence's compulsive hunger for the impossible over into aesthetics. The American myth espoused by Boyd's mother that each man's potential for material success is unlimited, has fostered a second myth, pilloried by Morris in his remarks on Thomas Wolfe in *The Territory Ahead*, that American art must try the impossible in order to do justice to the impossible greatness of the American experience, the spiritual equivalent of her wide open spaces. Of course, he who tries the impossible must fail; it is only by failing that he knows what he has tried is impossible. Morris's allusions define his judgment of Boyd. It is the central judgment toward which both *The Field of Vision* and the author's career to this point are moving. The thread from Ty Cobb's pocket has led Boyd into the labyrinth of the past, the spectre of Ashley Crete's success, but unlike Theseus's thread, it does not lead him out. Trapped in the labyrinth, Boyd is vanquished by his personal Minotaur, the impossible myth of the impossible. The labyrinth, another of Frye's demonic images (Frye, p. 150), comprises the hell this modern Huck has chosen for himself. The image of drowning connected with his failure to walk on water identifies Boyd with Icarus, who flew too close to the sun, the transcendent, when he tried to escape the Cretan labyrinth. In contrast, the authentic heroics of the bullfight, which also have "*Art*" as their end, remain an earthbound phenomenon, not a "miracle," but "an everyday fact" (p. 105). True art and heroism come from the highest creative acts that are possible. Not coincidentally this is a major conclusion of *The Territory Ahead*, published two years after *The Field of Vision*.

The problem with transcendence is the problem with nostalgia: the indispensable requirement of true selfhood, Boyd decides, is growth, "to keep it open, to keep the puzzle puzzling, the pattern changing and alive" (p. 155). Growth and life are viable only with the possible and in what D. H. Lawrence called "the immediate present" where "there is no perfection, no consummation, nothing finished."[8] Again a comparison with a work by Sartre is revealing. The hell of *No Exit*, like that of Scanlon and Boyd, consists precisely in its being outside of time and therefore finished. The characters are trapped in essences they no longer have the power to change. Morris's further conclusion that Boyd's attempt to fail is a cliché "borrowed from the wings, from the costume rack" (p. 70) amounts to the same judgment in somewhat different terms. Since a cliché, strictly speaking, is a pattern from the past inappropriately continued into the present, it precludes spontaneity and originality, impedes growth, and falsifies one's true nature at any given moment. The sign of Boyd's inability to fail on a level of the self deeper than the surface cliché is that he does not drown in the attempt to walk on water and that he does not die of a heart attack when squirting pop at the bull.

Paul-Paula Kahler, the last of Morris's transcendent heroes in *The Field of Vision*, opens up new perspectives on the phenomenon. Paula exemplifies one of the major themes in contemporary fiction—the theme of self-transformation. In changing from a man into a woman, Paula, unlike Boyd, has failed according to his own fundamental nature, for as Lehmann says, Paula has "a nature that refused to acknowledge the aggressive elements. Maleness, that is. Maleness being at the heart of it" (p. 115). In works like *Pale Fire* and *Slaughter-house-Five*, self-transformation is a means of overcoming life's pain, for the imaginative power of such a fiction, if it cannot change the drab, tormenting world of fact, at least reduces it to unimportance. However, the solipsism of Shade-Kinbote[9] in *Pale Fire* is not possible in *The Field of Vision*, with its five narrators. A reality external to the viewer must be taken into account, and in this objective realm, Paula cannot expunge his aggression any more than he can change his sex. Thus, he strangles a man who threatens his illusion by attempting a sexual assault. And when Paula cries for help in his sleep, it is the not-quite-buried male who wants out. The power of imagination to transform the world is limited: "Saint Paula Kahler, who had changed one world, still burned with need in the world she had changed" (p. 202).

An earlier version of Paula's story, the novel *War Games*, makes the same point and also makes a connection between Paula's illusion and the characteristic illusions and dreams of America. Written in 1951–52 but not published until 1971, this book contains material which was later reworked in the characters of Boyd, Lehmann, and Paula and in several novels besides *The Field of Vision*.[10] The war games of the title are the imaginative strategies adopted by the characters to make their lives tolerable on the battlefield of a contingent world. The novel traces a growing relationship between the protagonist, the Colonel, and Mrs. Tabori, the Paul-Paula character. The Colonel is introduced to Paul's story through Paul's dying brother Hyman Kopfman, who recounts their experiences as Viennese immigrants in Chicago. His story is a Morris reprise of *The Great Gatsby*. The Kopfmans exemplify an idealistic faith in the promise of America, a foolish vision of unfounded hope which leads Hyman to send out "both of his shoes to be polished" (p. 15), even though one of his feet has been amputated. Hyman, with his wasting disease, brings together the hopeful dream of America and the hopelessness of its actual condition or reality. It is in this sense that the Colonel, when looking at Hyman, is "seeing America first!" (p. 11).

Hyman's story of how he and Paul visited a garden for the blind dressed in their parents' clothes again shows the limitations of a subjective optimism that does not conform to the facts. An "out of this world place," the garden symbolizes their transcendent vision of an unfallen America, where "there were always flowers, because nobody picked them. There were birds and butterflies, because nobody killed them. There were no small boys with rocks and sticks, nor big boys with guns. There was only peace . . ." (p. 15). In such a world, Paul can dress like a woman if he wants to because the blind cannot see him anyway. In actuality, Paul and Hyman are morally blind themselves because there is no peace, only the battle of life, and everybody sooner or later becomes a casualty, if only to disease, old age, death, and the terrible irrationality of the human heart. The Colonel's eventual acquiescence in Mrs. Tabori's sex makes the same point again. He accepts her as the woman in his life, a kind of symbolic mate, even though he suspects her of having murdered two people and permanently paralyzing his real wife. An "odd couple," the Colonel and Mrs. Tabori flee from the doom impending for all things existing in time into "the ark," symbol of a transcendence that is more than a little mad.

Like Scanlon, the Paul of *War Games*, in his fading Viennese finery, lives in the past; in contrast, the Paul of *The Field of Vision* lives totally in the present, for in rejecting maleness, he also rejects the masculine world of his past, associated with his four brothers, the YMCA, and his treasured ideal of "brotherly love" (p. 162). This change from the original Paul emphasizes another requisite for true selfhood. Man, to remain man, must also remain a part of nature. Although Paula Kahler follows his psychological nature in transforming himself into a woman, he denies nature in the larger sense, the forces of physical generation which made him inescapably male. To live in the mind alone, he has sacrificed his connection with the organic pole of the human creative impulse. Organic creation may be thought of as moving from the center outward, but it can also be thought of as moving in a straight line from past to present. The "word made flesh" then becomes the "word from the past." Lehmann astutely diagnoses the trouble with Paul's condition: "If that pipe line to the lower quarters was broken . . . *all* thinking ceased. . . . Some connection with the *first* cell had been destroyed, the cable that carried . . . the word from the past, and without this word there was no mind. . . . There was no mind. . . . if the mind, that is, was nothing but itself" (p. 204).

The Field of Vision includes a character whose function it is to supply a commentary on all forms of heroism and a model for a kind of heroism free of the shortcomings of transcendence. That character, the fraudulent psychiatrist Lehmann, belies his name and his nonprofessional status in having a legitimate "arrangement of sorts with the soul" (p. 66). The elements of caricature in the portrayal of Lehmann, such as his broken dialect and red mittens, are part of a calculated mask of character which he deliberately assumes. His ability to put on such a mask specifically demonstrates his command over his imagination and more broadly helps to establish his authority as a spokesman for life's shaping forces. A man who had "other people's problems, but few of his own" (p. 65), Lehmann also remains outside the circle of Nebraska characters, thus achieving a detachment impossible for them, enabling him to correctly diagnose the part played by the failure cliché in Boyd's case.

Lehmann's insight into Paula has a subtle and complex origin. Of the story he tells about an acquaintance whose corpse was sold to dissectors, Lehmann's patients have asked, "Was it fiction, this fable, or was it fact?" (p. 67). In truth the fable lies not in the story, but in the telling; it is fact transformed into fiction, an adaptation to Lehmann's biography of the event that drove Paul mad. Even Lehmann's key axiom that man develops "each accordink to hiss nachur" (p. 155) is originally Paul's pronouncement (p. 164), the psychiatrist's dialect having made it his own. This willed identification with Paul verifies that Lehmann has imaginatively mastered Paul's experience and the larger phenomenon of transformation without being psychologically crippled for life himself. The identification becomes most intense and profound in a seedy Chicago hotel room where Lehmann has an intimation of universal compassion. The room, where "time . . . seemed to have stopped," unmistakably stands for transcendence, an "eternal moment in the shifting tides of life." As another confrontation "at the heart of the labyrinth" (p. 120), it parallels Boyd's transcendence. When the groggy fly falls helpless on Lehmann's chest, he, like Paula, denies nature. It is the fly's nature to make man miserable and man's nature to swat such pests, except in those rare moments when it is even more in keeping with his nature to spare life out of a universal compassion. Recalling Dmitri Karamazov's dream of the Russian babe freezing on the steppes, Lehmann is brought to feel "the pity life seemed to feel in the presence of such a fugitive thing as life" (p. 123). Lehmann's transcendent pity is superior to Paula's "sainthood" because it includes the male as well as the female, both Paula and Paul, and without destroying his capacity for change. At the end of this recollection Lehmann applauds, not for the bull just killed in the ring, "but for Lehmann, who muss go on lifink" (p. 124). Although he has demonstrated an insight into transcendence, he remains immanent like those still living in the ring.

The concluding Lehmann section, with its strategic position as the last strictly contemplative section in the novel, sets forth a comprehensive philosophy of immanence. The lights of a Mexican city at night suggest to Lehmann the light of human understanding and imagination coming on in man's mind and touch off a meditation on the course and meaning of the human experiment. The end of life, Lehmann decides, is to seek a more perfect understanding of itself through the agency of the mind, which "in order to think had to begin at the beginning" (p. 203). This end is realized through a creative evolution linking all life, "in a jeweled chain of being, with that first cell, and the inscrutable impulse it seemed to feel to multiply" (pp. 203–4). A man "with pronounced Neanderthal connections," hairy all over except for the top of his head, but resembling in his stereo earphones a "Flying Saucer pilot, or a Space Cadet" (p. 65), Lehmann himself symbolically incarnates the entire course of evolution and both imaginative and organic poles of the creative impulse.

Lehmann responds to the goring of the matador with an analogous image, which counters the Minotaur of transcendence with the "living centaur" of the immanent hero. Gored from behind and lifted on the bull's horns, Da Silva is transformed into "an archetypal man growing out of the beast" (p. 114); he personifies the dual nature of man and the chain of evolution that has culminated in his imaginative audacity: "Out of the shoulders of the bull, on the horns of this dilemma, against the current that must always determine his direction, in reaching for more light man would have to risk such light as he had" (p. 205). The centaur, prefigured in Furman, is fully realized in Da Silva and Lehmann, whose success is the reverse of Boyd's failure just as the centaur is the reverse of the Minotaur. The dance in the ring is thus "a pantomime of metamorphosis . . . which seeks to change the dancer into a god. . . . [an] incarnation of eternal energy" realized in "the union of space and time within evolution" (Cirlot, p. 73).

The Field of Vision attempts to show why immanence offers the most valid engagement with life. Unfortunately, because of its shortened time span and introspective focus, the still-point structure does not lend itself well to dramatizing action in time, or life as an organic continuum, or even convincing character development. Perhaps for this reason, Boyd, not Lehmann, remains the dramatic center of *The Field of Vision*, and as with Foley, though much less seriously, Morris has trouble making Boyd's movement from ignorance to insight and his resulting release from transcendence understandable and believable. While a detailed look at each Boyd section reveals some progression of insights leading through the book to the major one, it does not answer questions raised by the fact that so many of these insights are inspired by past events. The most important of these, positioned in the penultimate Boyd section, is the playground scene I quoted from in chapter 1. It is immediately preceded by a portentous present-time announcement: "Boyd detected a change in himself. A big one. The real change-over in his life" (p. 197). There follows the passage where the little girl is said to have "run up the blind on his true *self*" and Boyd is said to have been "able to see. . . . behind appearances, such as the one he made himself" (p. 198). What he sees apparently is the cliché quality of his own heroic agony when contrasted with the genuine, intense feeling of children: "Only children led passionate lives. The life . . . that Boyd—once a prodigy of action—no longer lived himself. . . . They represented the forces he felt submerged in life. All the powers that convention concealed. . . . the flow of current that kept . . . the lights burning, and the desires that made peace impossible in the world" (p. 197).

On the conceptual level, the point of this scene is clear. But why does this event have such an effect now, at the bullfight, instead of when it first happened? And if we have *this* event for Boyd's enlightenment, why do we need the bullfight at all? Why does this revelation in the playground strike so much more forcefully than Lehmann's even earlier explanation to Boyd of his problem? For strike it does. In the following Boyd section, he unleashes the passion stored in the child Gordon by throwing the cap into the ring, an action that becomes a catalyst leading to his touching bottom. Symbolically, he finally fails all the way, that is, drowns in order to be reborn. Certainly the boy is changed by Boyd's influence; he moves from valuing his cap for its cost to refusing a paper bull from

McKee because "It's not a bull if you buy it" (p. 249). Nevertheless, Boyd's conversion comes across as an arbitrary symbolic resolution of his conflicts, not as a compelling dramatic change.

Morris apparently felt the same since *Ceremony in Lone Tree* returns to Boyd's problem for another try at solving it. More immediately in *Love Among the Canibals*, he tackled the problem of how to dramatize, through action, the condition of immanence, which in Lehmann was depicted through reflection. Although *Love Among the Cannibals* may seem an incongruous departure from his previous books, Morris's own comments have stressed the continuity of his work and the novel's place in it. His feelings about the past began with "infatuation, a conviction that the past was real and desirable, and should be the way life is" and concluded in *The Field of Vision* with "a serious questioning of the past." After that, he was ready for *Love Among the Cannibals*, "an effort to come to terms with the present, in terms of only the present."[11] To put it another way, having confronted the Minotaur of transcendence, Morris turned to the centaur of immanence, or rather returned to it since *Love Among the Cannibals* is similar to *My Uncle Dudley*.

Love Among the Cannibals uses the open-road structure in an effort to dramatize the organic connection between an immanent hero and the physical pole of the creative impulse as embodied in an evolving cosmos. It traces the adventures of a Hollywood songwriting team, Mac and Horter, as they travel to Mexico with their girl friends, Billie and Eva Baum (called the Greek). The carrier of the physically creative charge is the Greek; as a female, she is the fictional descendent of Gussie Newcomb and Mother, but without the destructive inhibitions and distortions produced in them by the protestant myth of female purity. The open-road structure gives tangible form to the evolution of life from the remotest past to the immediate present, and the freewheeling motion on the road, with its unexpected encounters from moment to moment, suggests the characters' efforts to confront the perpetual novelty and unpredictability of the present.

With nostalgia and transcendence routed in *The Field of Vision*, the major obstacle to creative action in the present is the cliché—the formularized and thus false emotional response, the object from which the originality has been drained by overexposure, the past insight dulled by being prolonged into the present, the once spontaneous gesture deadeningly reiterated. In a sense we live too late; the "raw material" of our world takes its structure in our eyes from a culture saturated with clichés, and thus nothing totally new is possible. For Morris, then, "Our first problem, [as artists and men] surgically speaking, is to remove the encrusted cliché from the subject,"[12] that is, to revitalize the cliché by placing it in a new context and thereby wringing from it a new meaning. Ironically, a major criticism leveled at *Love Among the Cannibals* by critics and reviewers is "that the primitivism it opposes to the cliché is itself a cliché, a literary sentiment exhausted and more than exhausted by D. H. Lawrence. The girl of the songwriter's dreams, who is no better than she should be, is an appropriate symbol after all: this raw material has been processed and overprocessed before."[13] This articulate summary of detractors' views cuts in several directions at once. First, it suggests that once anything has been done well by one artist, it can only be botched by others. Second, the phrase "literary sentiment" hints that Morris mindlessly parroted Lawrence without really believing in "primitivism," and last, because he did not believe in it, the primitivism is not convincing in the novel.

Love Among the Cannibals admittedly has neither the originality of conception and complexity of structure found in *The Field of Vision* nor the rich humanity of *The Deep Sleep*. Yet few of Morris's other novels do, and they are not what he attempted here. What he aims at, he gets, and that is no small accomplishment. As for Lawrence's influence on *Love Among the Cannibals*, it is both more and less than critics say. His impact is felt in far more varied, subtle, and extensive ways throughout Morris than in the mere borrowing of themes in this work, but Morris is not simply duplicating his predecessor. For one thing, this novel, unlike any of Lawrence's, is a farce, Morris's funniest book. For another, it is more of a satire on contemporary manners than any of Lawrence's novels; and finally, the concept of the cliché opens up subject areas not found anywhere in them. The criticism that Morris does not really believe in primitivism is refuted by the fact that *Love Among the Cannibals* fits into a pattern developing in Morris's novels from the very first. The concerns of the novel are among the author's characteristic concerns, and they do not disappear in later books but return in new forms and combinations with other elements. The real answer to these criticisms, however, and the real test of the novel's success is the skill with which Morris makes use of Laurentian materials to realize his own distinctive ends in dramatically compelling ways. The novel is one of his most fully realized works dramatically, both in developing characters through meaningful action and in making significant use of setting and detail.

Because *Love Among the Cannibals* takes place in a conceptual present, everything—settings, people, objects—is in a state of flux. The Los Angeles beach where much of the first half of the book is set is both a contemporary wasteland and the transitional zone where evolving creatures from our ancestral past crawled from sea to land; it is redolent of beginnings and endings, the spot "where we came in, and where we'll go out" (p. 13). The villa in Acapulco where the characters stay is a partially completed shell which will have electricity and water "any day now" (p. 156); the studio car is stripped down and rebuilt by thieves; and Horter constantly revises both the song he composes and his life to fit his developing relationship with the Greek.

This perpetual destruction and creation, the death of one instant in the birth of the next, has social as well as cosmic relevance. Morris points out a distinguishing trait of America in "Made in U.S.A.": "Nowhere else in the world, and at no other time, has a culture so massive remained as a *process*, changing its shape, and its nature, daily, before the world's eyes" (p. 494). For Morris, California particularly typifies a nightmarishly fluid culture bereft of the artifacts, traditions, and values of the past. The decaying farmhouses, the cane-bottomed chairs, and the rusting cultivators of his Nebraska youth are superseded by swim caps with artificial hair, packs of Parliaments, and portable record players. The people are rootless, in aimless transit from an undistinguished past to a nameless future: "Everyone in California is from somewhere else" (p. 9). The prologue strikes this special note. On the beach, Horter meets a girl originally from Iowa, and she complains with candor of men who are "so perverse they always had to be on *top*" (p. 10) in the sex act. His first instinctive reaction is fearful and bewildered: "Things can change in twenty years. . . . When I was her age I didn't know beans. She knows too much" (p. 11). The reaction expressed in the title of Horter's song, "What Next?" is more balanced. The question is disturbingly American, expressing the pragmatic pioneer's mixture of admiration at the latest thing and dismay at things which are too newfangled.

In order to survive morally in this present, Horter must discover for himself a form of permanence which is consistent with, rather than a reaction against, change. That permanence is defined by a pair of structural contrasts in the novel which dramatize the difference between the quick and the dead, the real thing and the cliché. The first half of the novel in California balances the second half in Mexico, and the love affair of Horter and the Greek is systematically counterpointed with that between Mac and Billie. The story is a deliberate cliché, the stuff of a hundred bad movie musicals like the one the partners are purportedly writing. The song-writing team meet two girls, one nice and one, in Klein's words, "no better than she should be," and their romantic excursion to Mexico ends with one marrying his nice girl and the other being jilted. In Morris's telling, conventional moral valuations are upset.

Southern California—with its streets named after cities on the Riviera, its predictable parties at mansions sporting borrowed hunting trophies, its performers for whom "everything is in the sales talk and nothing in what they sell" (p. 41), its songs deliberately imitative of better songs, and its voyeuristic and commercialized exploitation of sex—exemplifies all that is superficial, frivolous, emotionally empty, and fundamentally unreal about contemporary life.

Mexico, on the other hand, impresses Morris with its honesty. In an article called "Mexican Journey," he writes of having a Mexican boy wash his car, thus "removing the protective finish I labored to put on back where I come from. . . . It is for that, above all, that I am back."[14] With this protective finish gone, he can be "rubbed, supported, pressed" by the crowds without shrinking away; he can "take life in through my eyes, my lungs and my pores" (p. 13). In Morris's moral geography, Mexico stands for a place where one's guard is down, the defenses and evasions of civilized convention are dropped, and one confronts the naked realities of one's self and one's condition. This point is brought home more compellingly here than in *The Field of Vision* because the open-road structure allows for a sustained contrast between the authenticity of Mexico and the meretriciousness of California. Significantly, Mexico brings to the fore traits and motives which each of the characters has kept camouflaged in California, each of the characters, that is, except the Greek, who is always honestly herself in any situation. Thus, she is the one who is tanned all over, while Horter is white around the loins, where he is used to wearing bathing trunks. Morris suggests a fleeting identity between Mexico and California; the beach dominates both, the California mansion is decorated with Mexican artifacts. These similarities and the fact that the Greek is at home in either locale stress that the reality exposed in Mexico is present, but masked, in California. The trip to

Mexico, less a country than a condition of the soul, is a rite of passage emblematic of a psychological transformation in the protagonist Horter.

The Greek, immanent hero and nature goddess, is the agent of this transformation. To dismiss her as a conventional sexpot is to ignore both the philosophical implications developed through the character and the concrete details of imagery and behavior with which she is depicted. In her brush with death at fourteen, the Greek has died and been reborn, like Lawrence's man who died or the pagan Persephone. She stands for the irrepressible continuity of life from one generation, from one moment, to the next, and her constant association with the sea, the source of life in the novel, establishes her communion with the physical powers of nature.

The Greek's narrow escape from death explains her complete seriousness about things that count—in contrast to Horter, she is a student of classical music—and total disregard for things that do not, such as propriety, money, toilet paper, and Horter's male vanity. But seriousness is not solemnity, and like such fictional precursors as Agee and Dudley, she has a robust and infectious sense of humor. Her gesture of kicking off her shoes[15] as a prelude to sex expresses an irrepressible exuberance that affirms life. This sense of earthly comedy matches the cosmic comedy of life's persistence in the face of death, which she personifies.

In a larger sense, the Greek, unlike a *Playboy* bunny, is never frivolous or indiscriminate in her relations with men. Again like Agee, she is a life-bringer, for her lovers benefit by renewing, through her, their own ties to the evolving universe. Toward men she expresses a missionary zeal, "This life I have is a gift. . . . Why should I hoard it?" (p. 79). Her maternal aspect reinforces her life-giving function. Pregnant at fourteen, a madonnalike nurse at twenty-four, the Greek even asks Horter if he wants a child at his age, a question suggesting that her interest in him is sincere, at least during the period of their involvement.

The Greek exemplifies the state of psychic health to which she restores her lovers. It takes two forms: a sense of organic wholeness within the self and a condition of what D. H. Lawrence called "living relatedness" toward the myriad and various living things of the cosmos.[16] The first of these is reflected in her assertion that "the mind is in the body" (p. 80). Or rather the body has a mind of its own. Its wisdom cannot be "known" with the reason or sought through a narrowly rational process. When Horter marvels, "I *haven't* known you for one whole week" (p. 188), she responds, "What is there to know?" (p. 189). For Horter, as he admits (p. 131), development of the self has always come through books because he is a mind-centered person, but the Greek's "development" proceeds through her experiences with various lovers. It is not the personal ego gratification which Horter, his pride damaged by being one of a series, tries to make it: "You . . . think a lover is a bar-bell exerciser for your soul, a set of Indian clubs for your inner development" (p. 125). Rather, it is a process of natural growth which she maintains cannot be rationally "planned" (p. 81), only directed, in Horter's words, by "the flow of my desire, and in return, the flow of hers" (p. 249).

The Greek's affairs with her lovers, established by following the flow of desire, comprise "living relatedness," which is another version of the instinctive democracy of the soul practiced by Dudley and described by Lawrence in his Whitman essay. Her development amounts to a "morality of actual living, not of salvation" (*Studies in Classic American Literature*, p. 185), and her response to people is based on instinctive attraction or antipathy between her self and theirs. For this reason she is consistently discriminating in her choice of lovers. She slaps Mac when he makes a pass at her on the assumption that, since she does not fit his cliché conception of a nice girl, she must therefore fit his equally cliché conception of a slut. It is not all men and not this man her development requires. The Greek's love for the marine biologist Leggett, on the other hand, ignores his "ridiculous" surface for a deeper, and finally more sexual, appeal; what fires her passion is his "passion for a bottle of sea-green ooze" (p. 206), a specimen of sea water and algae constituting the "primeval ooze of life" (p. 205).

Similarly, it is necessary to realize that her attraction to Horter testifies to the presence of certain positive qualities in him. He earns the Greek's interest with his sensitivity, which is evidenced in his recognition of the hollowness of California life, his desire for the fulfillment he is missing, and his instinctive appreciation of her heroic vitality. Narrating the story from Horter's point of view allows Morris to give us an inside view of Horter's gradual conversion by the Greek, while at the same time making use of his sophistication in the book's commentary. The very fact that Horter, unlike the Kid, is influenced by the hero in a palpable, dramatic way measures how far Morris has come in mastering narrative technique since *My Uncle Dudley*. *Love Among the Cannibals* also goes *My Uncle Dudley* one better in design, for in addition to being well-developed characters, Horter and the Greek take on a symbolic dimension because they represent the imaginative and organic poles of the creative impulse.

A serious poet before becoming a writer of trashy songs, Horter has retained the critical intelligence to understand Mac's bondage to clichés and to recognize in a plush Los Angeles suburb "the pathos of a beautiful world in which nobody . . . knows how to live" (p. 95). At the beginning of the novel, "nobody" includes himself. He has thrown in his lot with the cliché world of Los Angeles, having been unable to translate his understanding into action. Still, he is spiritually healthier than Mac because he acknowledges his sellout, and after glimpsing the Greek the first time, he is moved to long for "Just One More Chance" (p. 41) at the authentic life he is missing. Horter's initial impression of the Greek strikes deeper than her physical beauty or sex appeal: "I didn't *know* how she looked—I would only recognize her by how I felt. . . . The way I often feel in elevators" (p. 39). He abruptly turns away as one would from "Paradise, the one with long white shadows" (p. 162), for "if the sight really moves you, the first thing you do is turn away. That's how . . . we know that it's beautiful." When we try to look at it directly, "the mind lights up, then blacks out," leaving only a stereoptican slide view in the memory (p. 40). His problem is how to go beyond the eye and with it the mind that abstracts, fixes, falsifies, decks out the object in clichés—how to go beyond to an immediate felt experience of the thing itself in all its living evanescence: in Bergson's terms, how to go beyond knowledge to *intuition* of the living reality. The interesting thing is that the Greek makes Horter want to try. The open road, with the Greek as guide, will convey him away from the critical intelligence he already has back to an integration of intelligence with the total self.

Horter's affair with the Greek shows promise when, on their first date, he feels like "Adam . . . without shame or embarrassment" (p. 74), in spite of the conventional motel surroundings. But Horter's mind is his master, and as in Lawrence, the mind is an egoist. Horter wants to impress the girl with his songwriting and his youthfulness. He applies a double standard of morality and resents her former lovers, and above all else he wants "to keep what I had found all to myself" (p. 79). When she admits to other affairs and says that she has slept with Horter, not because of his person or accomplishments, but because "you arouse my desire" (p. 82), he judges her by a popular cliché. Since she cannot be a nice girl (she slept with him on the first date), she must be on the make. He checks his wallet to see if he has been rolled.

The remainder of the novel is given over to erasing Horter's predispositions to jealousy and to distrust of the Greek's motives. This double process involves a gradual mortification of his ego and a growing conviction of the girl's disinterestedness. He is humbled when she gigglingly hides him in her closet, when he realizes that "she could take me or leave me" (p. 149), and when she finally does leave. His new selflessness is manifested at the conclusion when he contemplates the thought of her new lover without jealousy: "I did not burn in the hell of who . . . might share . . . [her desire] now. I blessed his luck" (p. 249). At the same time, the running contrast with the mercenary coyness of Billie, brings home to Horter the disinterestedness of the Greek's sexuality. He responds to her openness with honesty of his own when he does not lie about the trip to Mexico as he had planned. By the end, when Billie insinuates the Greek is sleeping with Horter to advance her career, there is never any question of his believing the charge. It is interesting to note too that the Greek leaves not just out of fickleness, but also to prove Billie wrong.

Horter's twofold shift in attitude signifies a deeper conversion. On the morning after his last Edenic night in Acapulco with the Greek, he awakes to find himself "pretty much as God made me, with a few minor alterations" (p. 212). He has returned, stripped to the essentials, to a natural state, but without sacrificing the alterations effected by the Greek. These include a return to a wholeness where the ego does not dominate (achieved through renewed contact with the physical), an understanding that passion is impersonal because it is transpersonal, and a conviction that there are more important things than a career. He says, "I possessed nothing . . . but my past. That much I could take with me" (p. 249); this is not only memory, but man's entire evolutionary history. Bergson explains it this way, "Doubtless we think with only a small part of our past, but it is with our entire past . . . that we desire, will and act. Our past, then, as a whole, is made manifest to us in its impulse; it is felt in the form of tendency, although a small part of it only is known in the form of idea" (*Creative Evolution*, p. 8). Horter's acquisition of the real thing consists in arriving at this state of soul, not in getting the Greek permanently, as some critics expected. In this regard, *Love Among the Cannibals* is more satisfying than *What a Way to Go*, in which Soby does get the girl, because this ending compels Morris to establish the fact of Horter's change through internal character development rather than plot.

The cannibal imagery in the novel underscores, of course, the idea that man does not live by bread alone. A "canny-belle" like the Greek initiates the male into a psychologically nourishing love affair, a function that again ties her to the life-giving, food-giving Mother. Just as the savage ritualistically assimilates his slain enemy's strength and courage by eating his flesh, Horter acquires the Greek's sense of life by metaphorically "bolting" her. The eating also symbolizes a process of reduction back to a prerational order of being. After stripping to the flesh, one strips to the bone. Morris makes the process analogous to the withering of the temporal self in Eliot's *Ash Wednesday*. Horter says, "You've been living on my heart, my lungs, and my liver. . . . If and when you get around to the hollow of my skull, I'll serve it up. If anybody asks us if these bones live . . . we can say yes, thanks to . . . the essential business of love" (pp. 227–28).

With a contrasting cannibalism, the cliché-ridden Mac is spiritually devoured by his predatory nice girl, Billie. Mac's imagination, conversation, and dress are the standard uniform of a Hollywood writer. His view of women is another version of the American cultural cliché Morris examined in *The Works of Love*: there are only two types of women—the sexy and therefore sluttish ones who sleep with Mac to promote their careers and the nice, pure ones who can be found, bursting with amateur talent, in the most unexpected places, and who have their origin in a popular song he never quite got over. Toward this second type Mac feels only "the loftiest Father's Day sentiments. . . . His Million-Dollar Babies are left untouched. They are all heart, having nothing in common with the chicks . . . who need a little practical push along" (p. 23).

This cliché, violated by both Billie and the Greek, leaves Mac prey to Billie, who uses her spurious innocence to manipulate him. To preserve her fresh-scrubbed image, she consults the spiritual uplift of a "book by Norman Vincent Peale on the 44 Practical Ways to Happier and Healthier Living" (p. 140), the antithesis of the Greek's unplanned development. Although she operates within limits of conventional morality, Billie is clearly the true prostitute in the story. Her virtue is merely a ploy to extract the highest price from Mac—marriage and a boost for her singing career. Her charges against the Greek, relayed to Horter by Mac, are a projection of her own motives: "She says this chick's fulla designs. Bein' a woman herself, she knows how this chick's mind works" (p. 238).

Like Horter, Mac has his ego obliterated by his love affair, though only in the sense that Billie is able to substitute her ego for his. On the morning after the wedding, Mac, shaved and washed for the first time in Mexico, his conversation purged of four-letter words, picks out "Love for Sale" on the piano (p. 230). But Mac is unable to feel even his disillusionment at being trapped genuinely; his cliché gin binge leaves him at the end in the men's room of a hotel, only slightly more unconscious than he has been throughout, not quite having transformed himself into F. Scott Fitzgerald.

The Field of Vision and *Love Among the Cannibals* at last fully define the major polarities which give Morris's work its distinctive character: still point and open road, transcendent hero and immanent hero, past and present, meditation and action, reason and intuition, division and wholeness, stasis and movement, imagination and organic vitalism, stagnation and growth, male and female. The two novels do, however, leave Morris with an immediate problem. Since *Love Among the Cannibals* stands in an antithetical relation to *The Field of Vision*, it cannot resolve the dilemmas faced by the characters in its predecessor. The worlds of the two novels do not seem to touch one another at any point. The problem of the cliché and the problem of transcendence are related only indirectly and only in a theoretical way. Morris embarks on a series of novels intended to bring the worlds of these two central works more closely together. The first and most ambitious of these is *Ceremony in Lone Tree*.

7

Wedding the Past and Present: Ceremony in Lone Tree *and* What a Way to Go

Ceremony in Lone Tree (1960) should be Morris's best novel since it fits together even more pieces from the jigsaw of Morris's art than *The Field of Vision*. No sooner had he addressed himself to the drama of the present in *Love Among the Cannibals*, than he felt a need to bring the materials of this creative present into a relation with the materials of the past he had tried to put finally to rest in *The Field of Vision*. Moreover, in 1958, nineteen-year-old Charles Starkweather went on a murderous rampage through the author's native Nebraska, leaving eleven people dead before being caught. The episode brought home to Morris the existence of a destructive present growing out of conditions depicted in *Man and Boy* and *The Huge Season*, and this material too found a place in the new novel. The Nebraska setting also allowed for the introduction of materials from the story of Will Brady. As a result, *Ceremony in Lone Tree* contains more of Morris's ideas, structures, character types, and images than any of his other novels.

The familiar characters include Boyd, McKee, Lois, little Gordon, and Scanlon, all from *The Field of Vision*, while Etoile, Lois's niece, resembles the Greek, from *Love Among the Cannibals*. These characters join other members of the Scanlon clan to celebrate the old man's ninetieth birthday in the now archetypal setting of Lone Tree. Because it follows *The*

Field of Vision and *Love Among the Cannibals*, *Ceremony in Lone Tree* makes use of their materials in a special way. Since the bullfight subordinated action to reflection, *The Field of Vision* is very much a novel of ideas; it offers a thoroughly worked out theoretical philosophy about such subjects as the relation of essence to existence, the nature and varieties of creative being, the requirements of heroism, and man's relation to time and an evolving universe. Although it contains more action, *Love Among the Cannibals* does much the same thing for such subjects as the traits of an immanent hero and the quality of her relationship to the world around her. On the other hand, because it grows out of these predecessors, *Ceremony in Lone Tree* can take the theories they propound as givens. For instance, *Ceremony in Lone Tree* leans heavily on *The Field of Vision* to establish the character and importance of Scanlon, who hardly speaks in the later book but who is nevertheless a key character. In the same way, Etoile's similarities to the Greek are sufficient to establish that she represents the same relation to the world, and the allusions to Brady bring the total experience of *The Works of Love* to bear on the world of Lone Tree.

Its relationship to the earlier books allows *Ceremony in Lone Tree* to be much more a novel of situations than *The Field of Vision*. It examines the earlier novel's concept of heroism in a concrete personal and social context. *The Field of Vision* answers the question, "What is heroism ontologically?" *Ceremony in Lone Tree* answers the question, "What is it about modern life as lived in America that has caused heroism to take the form it has?" The greater focus on dramatic action also makes *Ceremony in Lone Tree* different in other ways. The pressure of external reality proves too great for the dream, and the present overwhelms and drowns out the siren songs of the past. Because the most important event of the present is the violence of Charlie Munger, the Starkweather figure, and his spiritual double, Lee Roy Momeyer, *Ceremony in Lone Tree* has greater gloom and urgency than *The Field of Vision*. The guilt for this violence eventually touches all the major characters: though none have killed, all have been capable of it. Moreover, the violence of the two killers, together with other elements, makes heroism seem more destructive in *Ceremony in Lone Tree*. Lehmann, the chief spokesman for a positive, immanent heroism is gone, and the fact that Scanlon is seen completely from without robs his heroism of the authority derived from its imaginative power. In Boyd's case there is less importance given to his heroic successes and more to his failures.

The net result is that *Ceremony in Lone Tree* stresses American heroism as a source of psychological and social trauma rather than an object of awe or wonder. The trauma is not presented as a matter of transcendence or seeking the impossible, even though Morris's previous images of transcendence—moonshine and space travel (*The Works of Love*), freezing (*The Field of Vision*), and the bomb (*The Huge Season*)—are abundantly in evidence. Since Morris had just linked healthy, creative selfhood to impersonal sexuality in *Love Among the Cannibals*, he makes the root of the trauma sexual repression[1] and, a related aspect of the same problem, the flight from Aunt Sally. Both emphasize the boyishness of the American heroic tradition, a quality more fully dramatized here than anywhere else in Morris. *Man and Boy*, *The Works of Love*, and *The Deep Sleep* traced both repression and the flight from the home to the protestant ethic of the pure woman, and although that connection is never explicitly made in *Ceremony in Lone Tree*, this is another of the givens that have to be granted for the novel to make complete sense. The burden of nostalgia in the novel amounts to the influence of this ethic,[2] and, for once, nostalgia has the importance critics claim for it. For instance, it accounts for the novel's pervasive western imagery, determines its major setting in the Lone Tree past, and dictates the nature of the novel's structure.

The ridiculous figure cut by McKee's grandson, Calvin, illustrates the predominant impulse of most of the males in

Ceremony in Lone Tree. They want to relive the heroic trials of the cowboy: Lee Roy wields his grease gun and echoes the TV cowboy Paladin with the motto, "HAVE GUNS—WILL LUBRICATE" (p. 50); Jennings writes western stories; Bud stalks animals with bow and arrow; Colonel Ewing claims Cherokee blood and an acquaintance with Will Rogers; little Gordon packs Scanlon's pistols. In *The Field of Vision* Morris implied that the value of this cowboy archetype depended on its spontaneity and recklessness. In Scanlon it was bad because it precluded change and risk, but when Gordon scampered around the ring in a modern imitation of the authentic Davy Crockett spirit, it was a proper engagement with the present because its impulse was fresh and the danger was real. Yet it is hard to read *Ceremony in Lone Tree* without feeling the archetype itself has been found wanting. Because the western myth placed men in isolation from women, the males of the novel are unable to establish a relationship with a female like Horter's love affair with the Greek; that is, an adult sexual relationship based on emotional equality and give-and-take. Rather, the males are either in flight from women, or are mothered by them, or are dominated by them and are resisting the domination. For instance, Calvin wants Etoile, when he wants her at all, as a fishing buddy, and Bud, who "never grew old . . . [because] first he would have to grow up" (p. 75), is another of his wife Maxine's children.

For Lee Roy, the unnatural male-female relation leads to murder. He is a typical child of the present, physically and psychosexually stunted like Lipido, of *Man and Boy*, by the intimidating women around him (his mother, who tries to force him into the ministry, and the sexy Etoile) and naturally attracted to machines, which he can fix by instinct without knowing anything about them. Eventually Lee Roy's car, like Virgil's gun, becomes an extension of himself with which he relieves his mixture of repressed sexuality and hostility toward women by running down three boys dressed in female clothes: " 'F—k the bastards,' he had said, and that was just what he had done" (p. 127).

For their part, the women seem either to have seized male prerogatives for themselves or to have inherited them by default. The brassy and outspoken Eileen steals words from Calvin's mouth. The warmth of Maxine, an unpretentious and long-suffering mother figure, is wasted on the childish Bud, while her icy sister Lois has to settle for her grandson as a surrogate lover. Etoile combines Lois's looks and Maxine's warmth, but she is forced to be aggressive in order to land the reluctant Calvin. The very fact that Lois fires Scanlon's pistol and that Eileen, not her husband, attends the ceremony underscores that the women are the true descendants of Scanlon's pioneer stock, at least in these two generations.

Lois's relationship with little Gordon gives the fullest picture of the sexual dynamics at work in Lone Tree. Lois experiences her most intense love affair with Gordon because, since he is her grandchild, the sexuality of the relationship is veiled. Yet sexual it is: "He knew exactly how to make her suffer like those lovers in the oriental operas where they screamed, swooned, took draughts of poison, or fell on knives" (pp. 242–43). After the trip to Mexico, where he identifies with the rambunctious maleness of Boyd, Gordon follows the lead of Huck and Virgil Ormsby. Declaring his independence from females, he announces he wants to play with himself rather than with girls. The preference is intrinsically masturbatory, with all the dissipation and misdirection of energy that implies. It is expressed, as so often in Morris, in the desire to kill others—as when Gordon tries to shoot Maxine—or oneself—as when a Mexican boy shoots himself in the eye to punish his mother. In this way, the heroic charge which was transmitted to Gordon by Boyd in *The Field of Vision* and which there seemed creative, now begins to appear destructive and self-defeating.

Ceremony in Lone Tree embarks on a similar revisionist interpretation of Boyd and McKee as characters. Boyd's stature is diminished as the motive force behind his heroism is changed. In *The Field of Vision* he became a hero to defy his mother, while as a lover he was presented as too rich for Lois's blood. But here, associating various sorts of failure with sexual failure, Morris places Boyd along with Brady in the ranks of his unsuccessful lovers. Opening *Ceremony in Lone Tree* with Boyd in Acapulco creates a contrast with Horter. Unlike Horter, Boyd is unable to recognize the real thing when he finds it in Mexico. His image of his Mexican mistress is loaded with literary clichés—"marble faun," "flower of evil" (p. 26)—and he is surprised when a mirror shows no signs of the cliché moral deterioration he expects. Just as the affair with the Mexican girl parallels Brady's liaisons with prostitutes, Boyd's experience with "Daughter," the young woman he picks up on the road, parallels Brady's flawed marriage to the girl. Since Daughter resembles the Greek in her instinct for the truth and her lack of reservations about speaking it, Boyd's failure with her forms another ironic contrast to Horter.

Ceremony in Lone Tree also shifts the blame for Lois's marriage from Lois herself to Boyd. After Boyd castigates the McKees for a lack of feeling in their marriage, Lois rebuts him by asking if even he knows why he did not "speak for himself" (p. 184), forty years earlier if his own feeling was so strong. The answer is suggested by the blank letter Boyd sent to Lois after first meeting her: "Speechless. For the first and last time in his life. Clever, very clever, and while waiting for an answer he had heard from McKee [about the wedding plans]. . . . Would Boyd be the best man? My God, wasn't he? The irony of it seemed to justify his loss" (p. 228). Like Judge Porter, Boyd has "the talent for sleep" (p. 228); it takes the form of an infatuation with striking poses—first, the clever suitor wittily speechless with admiration, and second, the rejected lover who pines forever for the only woman in his life. Daughter's experience with her ex-husband Irwin qualifies her as an expert on Boyd, who is "just like him" (p. 35). She accuses Boyd of being "friggin scared of everything" (p. 36), and says the only woman in his life "wouldn't be in it" (p. 39) because he is so wrapped up in himself.

The fact is that Boyd has no business accusing others of suppression of feeling even if he is right about them. The blank letter is the symbol of his undeclared love for Lois. With his fear of connection, he becomes a Prufrockian figure who parts his hair behind (p. 210) and "who merely thought, and thought, and thought" (p. 253) instead of popping the overwhelming question. Also like Prufrock, Boyd comes across in *Ceremony in Lone Tree* as full of high sentence but at times almost the Fool, especially when Daughter deflates his pretensions. A certain amount of foolishness was apparent in *The Field of Vision*, but here it undercuts the hard truths Boyd speaks by hinting that his only motive for speaking is to show off. When Boyd appears at the door of the hotel, McKee thinks he has "never before . . . seen him so speechless" (p. 149). Never before and never again. McKee has missed the speechless letter to Lois, but all Boyd needs is an audience to start making up for his reticence then by a self-conscious and smart-alecky monologue now. Like his decision to bring Daughter to the ceremony, Boyd's speeches seem more calculated to make a scene than an impression. To Lois, Boyd is like Bud, Scanlon, and the others, "little boys at heart. They would live if they could arrange it in rooms full of other people's clothes which they would slip on, then run downstairs and startle the grownups" (p. 235). At their worst, Boyd's outbursts are symptoms of spiritual arrogance. This point is made after his diatribe about the insensibility of the others, when Daughter says, "His friggin feelings are hurt. He's the one who has them" (p. 197). Nevertheless, Boyd is redeemed by the fact that he is his own worst critic. He admits Lois did not marry him because "I didn't ask her" (p. 38), classifies himself as a "completely self-unmade man" (p. 145), and fears the others may turn out to be "realer than I am" (p. 43).

Boyd, of course, displays the characteristic failings of American heroes as laid down in Morris's other books. His extended recital of his unpublished story about "Morgenstern

Boyd" draws heavily from the opening pages of *War Games*. Morgenstern (the morning star of hope) corresponds to the Colonel, hopelessly pessimistic about life yet surviving in spite of himself. Hyman Kopfman is again the hopeful American, blind to his hopeless condition. If Kopfman resembles Gatsby, Morgenstern resembles Fitzgerald, who eventually recognized life's radical absurdity. And yet, as Boyd concedes, his two characters become more alike in the telling; the major change from the *War Games* version is that the Colonel's eventual escape into transcendence is dropped and both men die in the hospital. Although he identifies himself with Morgenstern, Boyd lives on and in other respects dramatizes the insights of Fitzgerald in *The Crack-Up*, as interpreted by Morris: "Where others merely lost themselves, Fitzgerald knew where he was lost. . . . It was . . . the paralysis of will that grew out of the knowledge that the past was dead, and that the present had no future. The Good, that is . . . might not prevail" (*The Territory Ahead*, p. 163). The pessimistic note struck here is precisely the change in tone which sets *Ceremony in Lone Tree* apart from its two immediate predecessors.

In *The Field of Vision*, McKee resembled Kopfman-Gatsby. He was the self-made man with confidence in America, the kind who hopes "for the best when the worst was happening" (p. 149). But like Kopfman and Morgenstern, McKee and Boyd come to resemble one another in *Ceremony in Lone Tree*. With more sensitivity and insight than he had shown previously, McKee begins to recognize the radical absurdity of existence. The death of his friend in a collision of airplanes brings home to him man's subjection to accident: "It was like two gnats . . . colliding with each other over the state of Texas. It was just that unlikely, and yet it had happened" (p. 245). McKee also has begun to lose his faith in man's ability to affect the human condition. Like Morris himself in *A Bill of Rites, A Bill of Wrongs, A Bill of Goods* (1968), McKee feels that things like insurance which are designed to make life easier merely underscore man's helplessness in a finite world and add a further degree of unreality to his situation. Social standards of value touch the human reality at no discernible point: "One man's eye was worth fifteen hundred dollars [in insurance], no matter what he saw through it; whereas one that people liked to look at was said to be worth several hundred thousand. . . . McKee would like to know if there was anything in this world, except insurance policies, that claimed to make any sense out of life" (pp. 246–47). As in *The Field of Vision*, "Citizen McKee" (p. 231) is a portrait of the American norm, but this time suffering from that sense of bewilderment and loss of confidence that has swept the nation in recent years. Marking the shift, McKee alters from Gatsby to Fitzgerald, for the disconcerting realization that young hoodlums have "more life" than he does also makes him think the good might not prevail: "If McKee represented Good, like the Gray Ladies on the war posters, then the forces of Evil would carry the day" (p. 51).

On a more down-to-earth level, *Ceremony in Lone Tree* provides several opportunities for McKee to get the reader on his side. We share his impatience with Bud, his dislike of Ewing, and his affection for Maxine. We approve his cordiality to Jennings and concur in his belief that "nature [would] take its course" (p. 51) with Calvin and Etoile. When he finds Boyd's unopened letter to Lois, we sympathize with his dilemma: "A stranger had approached him with a letter on which was written *To whom it may concern*. . . . Was it better to open the letter . . . or to slip it in your pocket" (p. 252). It may concern him, but when he declines to read the letter, he shows more respect for the privacy of the human heart than Boyd, with his public avowals of feeling. Whatever we may think of America's McKees, they are the practical doers who pick up the pieces after the explosions, just as McKee builds a fire for coffee and drives away with the wagon with Scanlon's body in it at the end. The shift to this constructive image from the ludicrous cuckold image at the end of *The Field of Vision* measures the overall shift in sympathy toward McKee in *Ceremony in Lone Tree*.

The ceremony of the novel is partly a ritual release from a killing thralldom to the past. It includes not only Boyd, imperfectly liberated in *The Field of Vision*, but also Scanlon and the McKees. Although this release is represented by several metaphors, Morris tries, with a very ambitious structure, to develop all these metaphors in a single series of events leading to a climax of great symbolic resonance. The shortness of the book's first section, "The Scene," belies its importance. Like everything else in *Ceremony in Lone Tree*, the details of the scene take on added meaning in light of earlier books. Lone Tree, where the dreams of past and future cross, is the West Egg on Morris's spiritual map of America. As in *The Works of Love*, the Lone Tree hotel stands for the great hotel lobby of America where the inhabitants rub elbows with dreams, yet never seem to touch each other. The prairie outside is the battlefield of our contingent world, as in *War Games*, and from it "there is no place to hide" (p. 3). No place to hide, but a non-place to hide, the dreamscape in the mind's eye. The battle is lost and lost sight of when the sea of imagination in the eye of the beholder, Tom Scanlon, inundates the plain of fact.

The meaning of the sea image is enlarged by Morris's essay on Melville in *The Territory Ahead*: "The plains call men, but it seems to be the sea, real or imaginary, that speaks to them in such a metaphysical voice" (p. 68), metaphysical because a man sets to sea to find "some notion of himself" (p. 69). In a passage owing much to Lawrence's essay "The Spirit of Place," Morris articulates a principle of great relevance to Scanlon's case and to much of what I have been saying about Morris's picture of the American experience: "*Flight* always cuts two ways; it is both toward something and away from something—but perhaps the sea, the symbol of unknowing, is the ideal field of action for both impulses. In getting away from it all, from all that is not the self, that is not real-seeming, that is not real living, man is obliged to confront the lonely facts of self-awareness, the true-false image of himself the mirror of the sea affords" (pp. 69–70). On the blank spaces of the plains, on the sea that exists only in his mind, the lone Scanlon projects the objectively false but subjectively true image of himself, the pioneer looking west at the fresh green breast of the new world flowering with promise.

The flaw in the glass of the hotel window represents Scanlon's distorted private vision of a pioneer past. Miles to the east in Lincoln, the East Egg of *Ceremony in Lone Tree*, Walter McKee lives in his glass house, which stands for a more official American dream, the faith in unlimited prospects for material success and technological progress in the future. Scanlon's dream lives in the hearts of Americans; McKee's is publicly professed by the Chamber of Commerce. Together they make up the true "Spirit of St. Louis," which is actually the spirit of America—the faith in technology, the courage of lonely accomplishment, the satisfaction of conquering a new frontier, the impulse to transcendence. All America, like Charles Lindbergh, is still, in a sense, suspended over the Atlantic.

The movement from West to East in "The Scene" signifies a movement in time from past to present. Lone Tree has led to Lincoln, with its electric egg-timers and automatic garage doors, its mailmen more at home with other families than their own, and its desperate suppressed passions likely to erupt in violence. "The Scene" then returns to Lone Tree, as the characters must and will return to break the death grip of the past. "The Scene" concludes just where the novel will conclude, in the present once more, now menaced by Charlie Munger and Lee Roy Momeyer. They are the ugly reflex of the dream: Charlie Munger kills because "he wanted to be somebody" (p. 21). His impulse is a perversion of American go-getting and a flight from self like that of Gordon, Scanlon, and above all Boyd: "He wanted to be somebody. Didn't everybody? Almost anybody . . . but who he happened to be" (p. 21).

"The Roundup" section takes place in a largely daylight world where the past is felt through its calamitous effect on the present. The life of this present is permeated by what Auden called "the unmentionable odor of death"—the murders of Munger and Lee Roy, the spectacle of the bomb wrought by progress, and the emotional ruin of the American family as represented by Scanlon's descendants. The apparent life is death; the apparent waking world is actually sunk in Judge Porter's deep sleep of sexual repression and blunted feeling. It leads to a hellish nightmare peopled with grotesque boy-men who kill rather than communicate.

The roundup that draws the characters together is a literal roundup, the first and last chapters ending on the train carrying Boyd and Jennings to Lone Tree. In one sense the train moves from life to death, in another from death to life. It earlier transported a woman accompanying her husband's coffin to a funeral. For her, as for Morris, the train becomes "an instrument of God's will and man's destiny," and from the "ceremony of death" to which it carried her "she would salvage something for the living" (p. 130). The train conveys Boyd to his deliverance from a past that has been killing him for years, but it brings death in the person of Jennings. As an author of western stories, Jennings certifies the pastness of the past by the very fact that he can write about it. It becomes his lot to kill the dream. As Scanlon's westering in *The Field of Vision* showed, there are two men in every man, the fancied and the real. Having learned from the experience of his father, Will Brady, Jennings is able to penetrate the fancy, like the man who sees the Santa Claus on the corner but recognizes the bum Conley underneath: "Did every man wear another man's outfit and walk around in another man's shoes until the voice cried out 'That you, Jennings?' and he knew who he was?" (pp. 276–77). When Jennings thus addresses Scanlon, the pioneer of the dream disappears as if he "had vanished into thin air" (p. 277), and only the real Scanlon, a corpse for most of his adult life, is left.

"The Roundup" conforms to the open-road structure, gathering the far-flung characters in the present and taking them back to their origin and center in Lone Tree. The action of Bergson's organization is, in effect, reversed. "The Ceremony" situates the characters around the still point as they reflect on the meaning of Lone Tree. The ceremony was to have been Scanlon's birthday; instead it becomes the *re*-birth day of the others by becoming the occasion for at least a brief insight into their condition. But that moment of dawn at the end of the book is preceded by the long night of "The Ceremony," which counters the daylight world of "The Roundup." Here the past is seen directly as the past; the deep sleep of the present is represented by Scanlon's sleep, which lasts up to the moment just before dawn when he symbolically awakens to the present and then dies. The night stands for death, a return to one's beginnings in nonbeing, in preparation for the waking or spiritual rebirth.

The waking is accomplished by the detonation of the emotional bomb impending throughout the story. The bomb image is first introduced along with some other important images as Boyd ponders in a Nevada motel about an H-bomb test: "Back in Polk and Lone Tree no bomb was expected. . . . because everybody slept. The old man in the past, the young ones in the future, McKee in his cocoon, and Lois, the . . . ever-chaste Penelope, busy at her looming. WAKE BEFORE BOMB? How did one do it? . . . The past, whether one liked it or not, was all that one actually possessed: the green stuff, the gilt-edge securities. The present was that moment of exchange—when all might be lost" (p. 32). As in existentialism, the present is fearful because the meaning it contains and the selfhood expressed in it remain as yet uncreated and thus still require a man's choices. The secure, created selfhood of the past is perpetually risked and man's courage to risk it is perpetually tested in the exacting crucible of the present. The bomb is creatively destructive since it symbolically illuminates the dark night of Lone Tree with a flash of imaginative insight and annihilates the deadening past so that the present can be born from the ruins: "Where no heat was thrown off, there was no light—where it [the past] failed to ignite the present, it was dead. The phoenix, that strange bird of the ashes, rose each day from the embers where the past had died and the future was at stake" (p. 32). Both here and in *What a Way to Go*, the phoenix (as in Lawrence) stands for time's unending renewal and the creative self's unending responsibility for renewal.

The dawn that breaks at the end of *Ceremony in Lone Tree* signifies such a renewal. The birthday ceremony becomes a funeral and wake for the past, and the wagon with which Calvin planned to recapture Scanlon's golden past becomes the hearse where it is laid to rest. The arrival of the wagon and the death of Scanlon are signalled by a minibomb, the discharge of the pistol. Three generations collaborate in the firing, thus maintaining a continuous heroic heritage: Scanlon supplies the pistol, Gordon the bullet, and Lois the will to pull the trigger.

The discharge of the gun is the climactic event of *Ceremony in Lone Tree*, and all the strands of story, image, and theme dovetail into it. What saves this climax from seeming too pat and contrived is that Morris chooses to leave both Lois's motive and the ultimate effect complex and uncertain. Throughout the novel, Lois's disapproval of guns has reflected both a praiseworthy moral objection to killing and an unconscious fear of their phallic character: "If she could have one wish in the world it would be to live where there were no guns, nor anything that you could point at anyone. . . . The pointed finger, like the water gun, could kill something in a person that would never recover . . ." (p. 58). Lois's ambivalent feeling about guns makes her shooting of the pistol morally ambiguous. It could be a constructive short-circuiting of Gordon's swing toward cowboy heroics, or it could be an unconscious compulsion to emasculate the male by disarming him.[3] Beyond this, her gesture expresses her frustration at the folly paraded through the novel and, on a more profound level, her anxiety that she may never rise above her quotidian existence. Like her mother, who lay awake for years afraid of the fire that never broke out, Lois explodes, not out of terror "that something might happen, but [that] after waiting so long it might not" (p. 264). Shooting the gun is a purely existential protest against the very structure of experience and a bid to be somehow, at least for a moment, a shaper of destiny, not a slave to it. It is analogous to Lee Roy's desire to be "in control for once in his life" (p. 127).

The firing of the gun has the therapeutic effect of clearing the air and waking the characters to "a brief moment in the present, that one moment later joined the past" (p. 32). For that moment, they forsake the security of insentient being for the terrible anxiety of becoming, but apparently only for a moment. The bomb flash endures but for an instant. The past outlives its particular historical occasions just as the institution of monarchy outlives particular kings: "The past is dead," Boyd announces, "Long live the past" (p. 284). The last word in the novel is *asleep*; the last picture is of Boyd and Daughter dozing in the wagon; the last reflection is that the hell of the contingent world resists amelioration by technological progress. One day irrigation may make the desert around Lone Tree flower, but for now, McKee says, "It's going to be a hot one" (p. 304).

At the instant of what should be release, the whole possibility of release is deliberately made problematic. This effect is in keeping with two shifts in focus that make *Ceremony in Lone Tree* more somber in tone than its two predecessors. In *Love Among the Cannibals*, Morris was chiefly concerned with what might be called the aesthetics of behavior in the present, what served the cause of imagination and what did not, but Charles Starkweather's violence impelled Morris to a more explicit concern with the morality of behavior in the present, its right and wrong measured by good and bad effects on others. With the moral interest comes a certain earnestness. Moreover, in *The Field of Vision* and *Love Among the Cannibals* organic life was examined in the context of an overall teleological development from lower to higher forms. It had a discernible direction and a meaning. In *Ceremony in Lone Tree*, however, life is regarded in the context of the frequently blind irrationality of individual cases. It is a grotesque and intimidating kind of life which causes the fatally injured sparrow McKee tries to put out of its misery to struggle fiercely for survival, even though its condition is hopeless.

Morris's increased pessimism about life extends even to the Etoile-Calvin love affair. This one positive thread in *Ceremony in Lone Tree*, modeled as might be expected on *Love Among the Cannibals*, concludes on a questioning note. The portrait of Calvin parodies the western hero as he might appear at the movies on Saturday afternoon. As handsome as Gary Cooper, he is the strong, silent type only because he stutters from fear of the aggressive women around him, and because of his fear he would prefer never to kiss the girl. During his adventure as a prospector, he follows traces of gold like lines on a map in search of the Golden West of Scanlon's yarns. When that romantic quest for "his grandfather's country" (p. 99) becomes polluted by uranium hunters, figures from the present, he shifts the object of his quest to Miss Samantha, "*the Girl of the Golden West*" (p. 88), personified by Etoile. Miss Samantha represents the mythic past to be reborn on Scanlon's birthday, but Etoile, the only child of the creative present in the novel, has other ideas. She discards the past when she tosses away Calvin's cowboy hat, and her gesture of throwing water on him has multiple significance; it suggests regeneration, waking him from his futile dream, and shocking him out of destructive, childish behavior (earlier the adults throw water on Gordon to stop him from holding his breath). When Etoile draws Calvin into an adult sexual relationship, the only one in the book, she destroys his plan to have the West reborn in her. Instead, the arrival of the wagon puts the seal on the death of the past through a final ceremony—the literal wedding of Calvin and Etoile and the symbolic wedding of past and present.

The marriage would seem to affirm the persistence of life in the face of death and to ensure the continuance of heroic qualities from the past. These qualities would combine the best of the Scanlon line with Etoile's vitality, the imagination and the body. Nevertheless, the spectacle of the wagon's arrival causes Lois to shoot the pistol and Maxine to wonder, "Had Etoile just *married* something like that? With her father dead, was it all to start over again?" (p. 292). This is the problematic note; it is not, after all, certain that heroism will continue in a constructive form. Does life in the novel develop in a straight line or turn back on itself in a sterile, frustrating circle of reiterated mistakes? Morris gives no final answer.

I began by saying that *Ceremony in Lone Tree* should be Morris's best novel, but I do not think that it is. One of the best maybe, but not the best. The technique of using multiple centers of consciousness is not as functional here as in *The Field of Vision*, nor does the center of action, Lone Tree, allow for the variety of insights and effects the bullring did. Though the physical angles of vision differ, the psychological angles do not. At times, as in the last Maxine chapter, the narration is virtually omniscient. Because the emphasis on what is objectively viewed is greater than that on subjective vision, Morris is able to stress action more, and *Ceremony in Lone Tree* does mark an advance in his handling of significant action, though some readers may feel that too many plot strands fall neatly into place at the end. In addition, there are no individual passages that have the narrative power of Scanlon's wagon-train sequence or Lehmann's hotel scene.

The very abundance of material in *Ceremony in Lone Tree* in some ways acts against it. The fairly simple, boldly drawn conflict between the mother's dominance and the son's desire for independence (or between sexual repression and free expression of sexuality) works well in a novel with a single plot line like *Man and Boy*. In *Ceremony in Lone Tree* so many problems and relationships are traced back to these two basic conflicts that at the end the issues seem to be dealt with simplistically; in my judgment *One Day* does a better job treating the complex causes of violence. Moreover, Jennings does not contribute much to the book, especially since he is not a memorable character and many of his insights could plausibly be attributed to Boyd or McKee, who have had similar ideas. Finally, Boyd spends a lot of time talking about his relationships to McKee and Lois, and what he says is too much of a rehash of what was brought out in *The Field of Vision*.

The tendency to repeat himself, still a minor flaw in *Ceremony in Lone Tree*, balloons to major proportions in Morris's next two books—*What a Way to Go* (1962) and *Cause for Wonder* (1963), the two weakest works of his maturity. Compounding the problem, both novels seem to be worrying their major ideas to death; this, not their European setting, does the books in.

Cause for Wonder has been discussed in chapters 1 and 4. *What a Way to Go*, which I think the better of the two, recounts the sea voyage of a middle-aged college professor, Arnold Soby, to Venice and the Isles of Greece and his wooing of a fellow traveler, a seventeen-year-old beauty named Cynthia Pomeroy. Thus, *What a Way to Go* resembles *Love Among the Cannibals* in its use of the open-road structure and its focus on a love affair between an imaginative male and a female closely attuned to organic forces. The difference is that Soby's courtship and marriage of Cynthia is a controlling metaphor for the joining of several sets of opposites in the novel. There is, for instance, a conscious, concerted attempt to wed the theme of self-transformation and transforming vision, found in *The Field of Vision*, with the theme of sex as a means to a state of healthy becoming, found in *Love Among the Cannibals*. Since both Soby and Cynthia, in different senses, embody the past and present, their marriage also weds these opposites. Soby embodies the present in that his imagination occupies the vanguard of time, making each new moment comprehensible to man, and he also embodies the past in that as a teacher he serves as a source and interpreter of past knowledge. Being in an unfinished state, Cynthia represents the novelty of the present, yet her sexuality expresses the life impulse from man's darkest past. In the novel's special terms, their marriage also joins the mind's eye and the eye's mind, the wisdom of the mind and the wisdom of the body, the personal and the impersonal (Soby and Cynthia on the one hand and the archetypal poles of the self they stand for on the other), and finally, in a sense, the Laurentian and Jamesian currents of Morris's art. The disparity in age between Cynthia and Soby and their student-teacher roles recall the frustrating father-daughter relationships of Brady and Boyd, but in this case sexual compatibility leads to a satisfying love relationship.

Instead of the structure contrasting locales as in *Love Among the Cannibals*, *What a Way to Go* employs a structure in which each stage of the journey by "Parsifal Soby, currently in quest of he knew-not-what" (p. 71) stands for a state of consciousness peculiar to developing the psyche. The goal of the quest may be defined as the acquisition of something resembling D. H. Lawrence's "prehistoric present," that is, those forces originating in prehistory but, because they are truly living forces, manifested even now.[4] In *What a Way to Go*, the prehistoric present is at first embodied in classical culture and thus the forces seem to be imaginative, but when later embodied in Cynthia, the forces become organic, as of course they were for Lawrence. For Soby, the tour to Greece turns into an ordeal of initiation and testing in which he outlasts several other aspirants to win the grail, that is, the girl. Because transpersonal forces work through him, he feels a sense of fatality, of something bigger than himself, guiding his destiny. Near the end, he boards the boat to join Cynthia "propelled from behind . . . the smile of the anointed on his sweaty face" (p. 289). "What a way to go" is a fitting travel slogan, exclaiming at both the style and direction of the trip; it also points to the need for the old self to die. When Cynthia says she wants to be "so beautiful that everybody who saw me would just fall down *dead*," Soby thinks, "*some* people. . . . fell down dead—in order to arise, like the phoenix, from their own ashes" (p. 258). The initiation rite facillitates psychological change, the dying or discarding of the old self to make way for a new. The symbolic death of the old Soby comes when he is briefly knocked unconscious as the storm-tossed ship pitches. He rises to consummate his love for Cynthia.

The sea in *What a Way to Go* represents the fluid quality of the present, that perilous zone where "a sea change" in the psyche is possible. In effect, Morris exploits the connotations of the sea image found in both *Love Among the Cannibals* and *The Field of Vision*: it is the primal life source and the place where, in Miss Kollwitz's quote from Marvell, "*each kind / Does streight its own resemblance find*" (p. 57), that is, where one is left alone to confront some mind-born image of himself in the mirror of the sea. For the tourists, the ocean passage offers a freedom from past restraints conducive to change and, in the Bal Masque, gives them a chance to try on other selves while reviving ancient fertility rites. Metaphorically, the novel chronicles a gradual immersion in the sea, emblem of the unconscious, and a gradual return to the ancestral past embodied in archetypes from the unconscious.

Morris's treatment of Venice, the intermediate stage of the trip, enlarges the images of submersion—the city appears "sunken" (p. 72)—and masquerade—it seems a vast Bal Masque.[5] The city also evokes allusions to Mann's *Death in Venice* which go to the heart of the novel's theme. *Death in Venice* is really about life in Venice, life in Morris's special sense. Like Paula Kahler, Gustave Aschenbach undergoes an extraordinary transformation, from distinguished novelist to be-rouged homosexual and would-be sybarite. As Morris discusses it in his essay "The Lunatic, the Lover, and the Poet," Aschenbach's change is "grotesque," and the grotesque is nothing more than "the rejected version of ourselves."[6] The seeds of the second Aschenbach, like the plague germs, were incubating in the body of the first all along; for his change ultimately comes from a physical source. As Morris says, "the grotesque suggests that man is still a piece of nature. The forces at play in his personality are more natural than social, and more super-natural than natural" (p. 728).

The transformation begins with the sexual impulse, the natural, but it often concludes with the imagination and its power to turn a boy into an old man's archetypal image of beauty. The image, resplendent with the gleam that never was on sea or land, stands above nature in the transforming vision of the beholder. In this process the two connotations which the sea has in Morris come together, and the marriage of material body and immaterial imagination is consummated. In Aschenbach, Soby says, "Another man, an Ur-mensch, asserted his rights. . . . A buried life, much of it horrifying, but he recognized its wisdom. . . . One might suggest it was less of the mind than the spinal chord" (p. 138). The brain becomes a secondary and tardy appurtenance developed to serve the larger ends of life and the body. It is in and through the eye itself, a part of the body in all its wisdom, that fiction is made manifest: "The mind merely ratified a choice already made. Free will? Did any smitten lover ever feel he was free to choose? He was chosen" (p. 139).

The lunatic, the lover, and the poet are important figures in Morris's work, and the allusion to Shakespeare in the title of his essay throws light into many corners of his fiction. It also points up his kinship with Nabokov, whose major novels develop the implications of the proposition that the lunatic, the lover, and the poet are of imagination all compact. *Lolita*, which is both alluded to and parodied in *What a Way to Go*, offers a transformation of the love object similar to Aschenbach's, and both stories erect immense barriers to passion in order to demonstrate the power of the imagination which can surmount them.

In transforming what he sees, Aschenbach transforms himself. The characters of *What a Way to Go* are judged by the degree to which they can accomplish either or both of these transformations and by the manner in which they do it. Soby's rivals, Pignata and Hodler, try to transform Cynthia into Botticelli's Primavera and Homer's Nausicaa. The central question in the book is why Soby succeeds in courtship when they fail. Several times in the novel Morris speaks of an archetypal, "impersonal reality" behind the personal toward which the lovers aspire. It is tempting to say that Pignata and Hodler view Cynthia through a screen of clichés and therefore fail to achieve a truly archetypal vision of her. But what is Nausicaa, if not an archetype, and what is Soby's vision of Cynthia as a mermaid but a cliché (and not a particularly distinguished one)? If we think of the impersonal as a kind of platonic reality, or ideal form, which each individual only roughly approximates, then surely the images of all three lovers are impersonal. The reason for Soby's success and the others' failure is more complicated than freedom from or bondage to clichés, possibly so complicated as to be confused. In several ways Pignata's painting fails to capture the true essence of Cynthia: he uses the Primavera as a model when Botticelli's foam-born Venus would seem more fitting; the idealism suggested by Pignata's use of gold leaf does not fit the wise-cracking teenager. The biggest trouble may be trying to capture Cynthia as a painting at all. The reality of Cynthia, like that of all things which live, is multifaceted and ever changing. It cannot be fixed or pinned down to suit the beholder. Even Pignata's series of pictures cannot do that. The only way to give a painting the warm pliability of life is to stick your head through it, as Cynthia finally does. In other words, the painting and the girl express a Bergsonian dualism between concept and life. The brain abstracts; the wisdom of the body experiences. There are really two different kinds of impersonality in *What a Way to Go*—that which is real in the platonic sense and is known as a fixed image in the mind and that which is real in the Bergsonian sense and can only be intuited in all its dynamic livingness by the whole man. The latter is impersonal in that it expresses the transpersonal "vital impetus." The first kind of impersonality consists of "extinct fossils," transcendent archetypes such as the Primavera or Nausicaa, and the second are "non-extinct fossils" (p. 46), archetypes such as the mermaid, which, like the centaur, denotes a condition of immanence.

Cynthia has donned the various roles imposed by the men like costumes on a rack, and all to please Soby: "Don't you like *any* of them?" she asks (p. 302). But the secret of his success is that he prefers the "somewhat elusive, still evolving, indeterminate type" (p. 112), and regards her as a real person morally responsible for her own character. The lunatic, the lover and the poet *are* of imagination all compact. Shakespeare was right about that, but their fictions may serve differing ends. Aschenbach contemplates, he does not enjoy, his beloved. The impersonality he possesses is a platonic image of the abstraction beauty, however primitive the roots of the image. Moreover, the homosexual character of his passion frustrates the process of reproduction, the end which the body originally intended passion to serve. There are "two poles of his [man's] nature—to materialize or to spiritualize" (p. 185); the artist Pignata must spiritualize or find his art imperfectly abstracted from the desires of the flesh, but the lover Soby must materialize if the love object is ever to be possessed in the flesh. Significantly, Cynthia is physically more suitable as a mate for Soby than Tadzio or Lolita are for their admirers.

Soby thinks of love as "a curious knowing—with unknowing at its base" (p. 29) because it is knowing with the body. At the end the disembodied voice of Aschenbach, speaking through Soby's imagination, gives this advice: "If it's something immortal you're after look behind the eyes, not at them. . . . However, if it's something mortal you're after—and I take it that it is—what you see before your eyes can be good enough. . . . the beloved is both named and nameless, a charming Oberlin freshman, a Nausicaa . . . a Lolita. . . . *Im*-persons, rather than persons. . . . We have no name for what is fish below the thighs. Could that be why it is the lasting personality?" (pp. 307–8). "What is fish below the thighs" is the sexual Cynthia, the momentary avatar of the life that lasts. It takes over in the climactic storm at sea, which annihilates consciousness and transports the lovers back to primal emotions such as a "terror so free of complications it had no name" (p. 299). Of course, one does not live entirely on this level. Life is experienced only through its historical manifestations; one can find the impersonal wisdom of the body only through personal conjunction with a particular body. Thus, the last stage of Soby and Cynthia's journey is a return to a daylight world, now domesticated by their marriage.

The subplot of *What a Way to Go*, involving the Jew Perkheimer's bating of German tourists, and one of its major patterns of symbols and allusions, posits an analogous Dionysian-Apollonian dualism. The Germans in the novel flock to Greece "to gaze into the Grecian mirror for the one perfect German" (p. 242). This imagined paragon of perfection, actually impossible in an imperfect world, would give form to their exalted conception of German culture as characterized by Apollonian intellectual control and self-containment. Goethe, the figure most representative of this conception, is poles apart from Aschenbach, a German who succumbed to irrational passions and gave allegiance to a "*stranger* God" than Apollo (p. 12). His dream fantasy depicts a Dionysian rout where ego is obliterated in the darker transpersonal forces of the cosmos and self is scattered to the winds like a god rent to pieces. Perkheimer, who taunts the Germans like Lear's fool, is "not German enough" to be taken in by the Apollonian vision. His very blood, three-sevenths Jewish, repudiates it with reminders of Auschwitz and the perverse eruption of the darker side of the German psyche in World War II. His Jewish body stripped to the flesh drives the Germans from the salon by threatening them with the spectacle of imperfect becoming, of the thing itself, of man's inescapably animal nature exposed for all to see.

Ironically, *What a Way to Go* looks better as a carefully laid out plan for a novel than as a novel. Several factors work against the success of the quest structure. For one thing, the stages in the development of Soby's character are unclear. Morris gives him a former wife who has schooled him in the wisdom of the body, apparently with the idea that Cynthia's attraction to him will be more plausible if he is supposed to be an expert on the imagination and its physical roots. But if he is already an expert, why does he require the initiation? In fact, Soby remains so much the passive and detached commentator through most of the story, that he hardly comes alive as a character at all until the last one-sixth of the novel, when he finally is convinced that Cynthia has her eye on him and not one of the others. Cynthia herself is not a bad comic character, although she seems less substantial than the Greek because so many of her mannerisms are adolescent. Another reason for the failure of the quest is that each of its stages—the Atlantic passage, Venice, and finally Greece—really represents about the same thing, the trying on of rejected selves: there is no real development in the tour itself. Similarly, although *What a Way to Go* is rife with images, the range of imagery is narrow and its meaning is too cut-and-dried. Most of the images involve the sea, fish, cats,[7] or a masquerade, and these are all used so much that they finally seem perfunctory. Perhaps the real trouble is that since the number of ways to dramatize uninhibited sexuality is limited, it is not completely satisfying as a fictional representation of immanence. This limitation may explain why *Cause for Wonder* turns back to transcendence as its major focus.

With *What a Way to Go* and *Cause for Wonder* the long record of sustained growth in Morris's mastery of material seemed to have come to an end. In actuality, he was on the threshold of finding a new way to dramatize immanence and of writing three very fine short books. Before he got to them, however, the assassination of John F. Kennedy sent Morris off on a somewhat different track and to a masterwork of a different kind.

8

How Things Are: One Day *and* In Orbit

Ceremony in Lone Tree and *One Day* comprise complementary views of the same subject. *Ceremony in Lone Tree* examines how the cultural and historical traditions of America's past, as expressed in such figures as Virgil, Lawrence, Scanlon, and Boyd, eventually culminated in violent rebels like Charlie Munger. *One Day* (1965) is Morris's most effective picture of what in the American present and in the nature of human experience arouses Munger's kind of violence, as well as his most comprehensive study of the psychological forces behind it. As in the case of the Starkweather killings, Morris attempts to integrate a historical event into a fictional action, with this difference: even were Munger left out, *Ceremony in Lone Tree* would have the ceremony as its central drama, but the major action of *One Day* is the *re*action of Escondido to President Kennedy's assassination, an event which stands in somewhat the same relation to this novel as the bullfight does to *The Field of Vision*. For a writer like Morris, for whom the relation between raw fact and reality processed and made significant by the imagination has long been an overriding concern, *One Day* represents a radical experiment in adapting fact to fictional ends.

Years ago, Morris zeroed in on the pertinent aesthetic issue raised by this experiment: "Anything that takes us back to realism as the *real* thing is a retrogression." Settings, characters, events, and details in a work of fiction are chosen not for verisimilitude alone, but for "the depth and wider meaning of the subject or the experience."[1] They are not convincing because they have happened but because they have meaning and inevitability in relation to the theme and structure of the work. Moreover, finding the meaning of an event with the magnitude of the assassination presents an author with special difficulties. For one, the murder of a recent president, as a naked fact, threatens to speak more stridently than any interpretation of it. As Morris says of the assassination in an essay on *One Day*, "Its impact . . . had overpowered my fiction and paralyzed my imagination. How could the writer match the news on the hour?"[2] Paradoxically, a second problem is that such a murder may yield too many possible meanings, which at the same time are too obvious and accessible. How could any one writer find his meaning, that which takes its power and conviction from the larger currents of his art, while avoiding the easy cliché?

As his essay records, Morris was already at work on the novel when the assassination occurred (p. 14), and he audaciously chose to assimilate the fact to the fiction. The reason was simple; the theme of the projected novel was to be "nothing less than how things are" (p. 15), and on November 22, 1963, America was gauging how things are from the news on the hour. The decision is brilliantly vindicated, for the assassination turns out to be one of the most effective central actions in any Morris novel. It makes dramatic sense within the world of the fiction because Morris is able to make moral sense of the event within the context of the American experience. It is the same sense he has been making all along. If Lone Tree was the moral crossroads of the nation's past, Escondido, California, is the moral crossroads of her present: "Dropped off here a small-town man would feel right at home" (p. 8). The narration adapts a loose version of the still-point structure to the hours of this one momentous day. The national tragedy parallels and comments upon a local drama, Alec Cartwright's abandonment of her illegitimate baby at the City Pound, and the personal recollections of the citizens provide new perspectives on the events in Dallas. At the intersection of this point in space with this point in time, the conditions which made Lee Harvey Oswald inevitable are illuminated as in the flash of a gun. The characters situated around the square either gaze into the center at their own complicity or turn away.

The chief reflective consciousness of *One Day* is Harold Cowie, whose "natural tendency to see everything from the sidelines" (p. 65) amounts to a withdrawal from active engagement with life. The roots of Cowie's character type lie deep in our national life, as it has been pictured in Morris's fiction. Cowie's father, who was "ill at ease with women in general, speechless with the one he had married" (p. 73), resembles Brady. The aunt who was a mother to him is, like Mrs. Porter, a staunch proponent of the puritan ethic, perpetually on guard against the demoralizing influence of boys who wear their caps over one ear and grow up to marry waitresses. These antecedents and the middle-American connotations of Des Moines, where he grew up, are part of a portrait of Cowie as a representative American intellectual. In a nation which idolizes the doer over the thinker, Cowie's insights are never translated into action. From his earliest youth he feels confined on middle earth between the heaven of his mother and the "nether world" where his uncle works as a pressman. When Cowie sets out to fly from middle earth toward heaven, he ends up, like Scanlon, in a hell on earth.

The nature of middle earth is established for Cowie by two episodes associated with his childhood and a third occurring during a trip to Mexico as a young man. Cowie had lost a cigar box full of marbles and had found it twenty years later with his name still burned on the lid, empty. And at fifteen he had accidentally lost his pet chameleon in a pile of sand. For the adult Cowie, the marbles were to be the key unlocking the seemingly inviolable past, but his search for them yielded only an empty shell of what once was, the box without the marbles. Like so many Morris characters, Cowie learns that while memories are imperishable, realities are not, the disparity forming a cogent demonstration of the mutability of life in time. The incident with the chameleon teaches the related lessons that life is fragile and man is helpless before the thousands of accidents occurring every day: "An accident took the life of the child in the home, the driver on the highway . . . and the poor devil idly passing the building going up, or the one coming down. . . . The man in the street . . . mortgaged away his peace to appease this monster, as men in the past sacrificed maidens to appease the Gods. And those appeasable Gods had disappeared to be replaced by a new one. The accident. The meaningless event" (p. 170).

Cowie's interlude in Mexico is the occasion for Morris's most powerful evocation of that country as the place where the compromises and mendacities of civilization give way before the primal facts of existence. Even man's weakness for dreaming is made tangible in the figure of the young mother who carries her dead baby around believing it to be alive. She epitomizes the living death of middle earth and contrasts with Alec, in her later abandonment of her living child. On the trip Cowie again encounters chance at work when in a car wreck he kills two road workers. What follows establishes the pattern of moral flight in his character. The natives of Matamoros, where Cowie convalesces, try to ease his guilt with this comfort: "The word for what must happen is *accident*. Let him be thankful that what happened had not been *worse*" (p. 178). It is just this—the rule of chance and the cruel consolation that things could be worse but not better—which Cowie refuses to face. He repudiates the brute, objective time of an amoral material universe, the time which can be recorded by a clock: "No true sense could be made of human events if one accepted the illusion traced on the clock's face. . . . Cowie preferred to believe in a time wherein it was clear, and in no way accidental, that he would round a predictable corner and responsibly wipe out the lives of two men" (p. 189). His insomnia comes to signify that he follows a time of his own.

Cowie assumes the role of matchmaker between Dr. Carillo and Concepción, his landlady's daughter, to sustain the illusion that this is an orderly universe; bringing them together would prove there was a preordained cosmic purpose behind his apparently senseless accident. When Cowie discovers that Concepción really loves him, his comfortable illusion is destroyed, and he turns from intellectual evasion to literal flight. Unprepared to accept love in a world where human connections are subject to the conditions of finitude, he chooses to remain a bachelor, ultimately deciding that "meaningful events *are* accidents" (p. 21); they are inherent in the condition of finitude and their meaning is to confirm the world's contingency.

Strategically placed near the end of *One Day*, the account of how the barber Luigi Boni fed a pack of trapped cats forms a highly suggestive parable bearing upon the world view advanced in the novel. Luigi has always accepted the direction of those who think they know better than he does, as when he follows the suggestion of Alec's mother, Evelina, to continue living at the dock, and his reaction to the assassination projects his passive acceptance of direction by an outside intelligence to a cosmic level: "To the extent that anything defied explanation the hand of God could be seen behind it. . . . If the meaning . . . escaped Luigi, it was clear to God" (p. 360). The incident with the cats, however, disposes of this consolation. When the mother cat has kittens, Luigi faces an insoluble moral dilemma characteristic of a contingent world: "What did it all add up to but just more hungry mouths to feed? In place of the one she had, there were now five. And if he fed them, and they lived, and if he went on feeding her. . . . What would it prove to be but worse?" (p. 351). When Luigi's problem is solved by an illness that keeps him from feeding the cats, he decides, "For the cats in the cage Luigi was God. If he fed them, they lived. If not they died" (p. 351). To the cats, the disappearance of Luigi must have seemed a collossal and inscrutable catastrophe. What is explicable to man was inexplicable to the cats; the accidents which make sense to God make no sense, and offer no comfort, to questioning man.

Although, like Cowie, Escondido "doesn't go by clocks" (p. 6), the references to clocks, chimes, and timed stoplights and the book's division into sections entitled "Morning," "Afternoon," and "Evening" confirm that the town's escape from time and chance events is an illusion. Morris calls these events "the news on the hour," and most of the news is bad: "With the fog coming in the news on the hour is often the same. A man has leaped off the bridge, a car has leaped off the highway, the fog along the coast is stretching inland" (p. 4). Suggesting the staggering pace at which bad news is announced in contemporary America, the news on the hour also ticks off relentlessly the march of time.

The bad news reaching Escondido on this day contains a more urgent reminder of man's finitude; death can come unexpectedly, as it did to the late husband of Cowie's housekeeper, who dropped dead on a driving range with his bucket of golf balls half full, and as it does to the young president. In his essay on *One Day*, Morris describes the section "Holmes, Speaking," nominally presented by a mortician as a commercial for the noon news, as "a devotion on the larger subject of Death itself" (p. 20). Falling near the exact center of the novel and at high noon of the day, this strangely moving section is not what one might expect—a conventional elegy on the president's death or an ironic attack on the American way of death (a favorite Morris target). Morris makes no effort to create the consistent illusion that the monologue is spoken by a real undertaker in a real broadcast. Instead, he gives a highly stylized impression of what a mortician might sound like if he were delivering a sales pitch under the guise of a sophisticated tribute to his profession. At the same time, a line like "I detect in myself a profound respect for the bones that still live" (p. 256), with its glancing allusion to a favorite quotation of the author's, and serious observations on subjects like euthanasia call deliberate attention to the presence of Morris himself behind the Holmes persona. As a result, the speculations on death in the monologue are perceived as Morris's own and carry the authority of omniscient authorial commentary. What would seem satirical if taken at face value is imbued with a deeper significance, and there is a curious interplay of mocking tone and essentially serious meditation. I know of no effect quite like this anywhere else in fiction.

Holmes's most somber comments acknowledge death as the universal fate of things in time. When King Tutankhamen was buried, "Some danger threatened. Just as it does today. Any moment and we all might return to dust" (p. 246). Sitting at the wheel of his hearse, Holmes recognizes that the corpse has a message for us all: "When the body dies it is death that is born" (p. 250)—when one man dies, the inevitability of death is brought home to the survivors. To avoid facing the fact of death, the survivors demean death with a cheap burial which "*dispenses* with death, as it *disposes* of the body" (p. 248). Although Holmes ostensibly intends this argument to sell more expensive funerals, it actually affirms the importance Morris gives to death as the one incontrovertible proof of life. When Medicare is joined by Morti-corpse and bodies are launched into space or ground into garbage, an essential proof of humanity is lost, and men are reduced to the animal level of scavengers with no moral being.

At day's end the meditations of the dogcatcher Chavez return to many of Holmes's reflections, endowing them with elegiac grandeur. As a Mexican, Chavez is the one character to engage the fallen world on its own terms. A quester after faith, he has been disillusioned by the flaws in the official representatives of established religion, but he has developed for himself an instinctive, elemental faith based on personal integrity. Instead of giving up on the flesh, as Cowie does by living in a dream and Alec does by abandoning her child at the City Pound, Chavez refuses to allow pariah dogs to devour the corpse of his stillborn son. He stands against the scavengers mentioned by Holmes because a certain dignity is due the flesh as well as the soul: "It was dead that every *body* would be for the longest time. This being so it deserved more respect." His massive and robust wife Conchita has reality for him only in the flesh which will one day die: "To reduce her to ashes was to do just that: reduce her. She was not ashes, she was not spirit, and when it came time for her to die it would have to be said that an awful lot of woman lay dead" (p. 375). Only by acknowledging the reality of the living flesh can man grasp the full enormity of what has happened in Dallas.

The shift toward depicting individual specimens of nature as bizarrely irrational, noted earlier in *Ceremony in Lone Tree*, is more concerted in *One Day*, where life itself seems absurd. The protective coloration of Cowie's chameleon ensures that he will not find it and it will die; the cats Luigi feeds proliferate and make inroads on their meager supplies of food. When Evelina Cartwright is savagely stung by bees, she seems "possessed by some nameless evil" (p. 330); the life in the bees produces the grotesque eruption of thoughtless, swarming, killing forces. A similar "possession" in Ruth Elyot, Alec's roommate, shows that human beings may turn such forces against their own blood, so that there is not even the justification of self-preservation. To save the honor of her family, Ruth finds the superhuman strength to bear and throttle her illegitimate child. The act "was not pretty," Alec decides, "But it was what one meant by that culprit life" (p. 407).

The world view is again existential; it emphasizes human finitude, sees man as existing in a field of contingencies which confront him with the need to make difficult moral choices, and implies that conscious anxiety about finitude, often aroused by an encounter with nothingness, is preferable to an automatism in which one's consciousness is caught in the unthinking routines of ordinary life. On the other hand, Morris, unlike doctrinaire existentialists, emphasizes the consciousness that comes in existential moments more than the choice which goes with and stimulates it. Moreover, he regards consciousness as of less value in itself than in producing such conventional proofs of humanity as passion and compassion. In effect, this means that he goes beyond describing the process of choice, the classic existential concern, to prescribing what that choice should be.

To Morris, man's existential predicament is the first link in a complicated and not always clear chain of motives leading to the assassination. As Cowie's case illustrates, man's response to the ontological fact of life's contingency constitutes a significant social fact. After Cowie tried for hours to find his lost chameleon, Mr. Ahearn asked him a question which was to "echo" through his adult life, "For chrissakes, kid . . . when will you give up?" (p. 83). From that moment, "the phrase *I give up* might be found, like a tariff stamp, on Cowie's bottom" (p. 170): he gives up Concepción for bachelorhood, medicine for veterinary work, people for animals, and consciousness for a kind of moral sleeping sickness. Concepción's name suggests that he thereby rejects life itself, just as her lovely body and acne-pitted face suggest life's ambiguous combination of beauty and ugliness.

Cowie comes to see giving up as the major "Bill of Wrongs" accompanying America's Bill of Rights: "In each man's weary pursuit of happiness this right to give up loomed larger and larger. . . . numberless lovers had given up love, and increasing numbers had given up their conscious lives. A non-conscious life they still lived. . . . But to be fully conscious was to be fully exposed. . . . As a matter of survival one gave it up" (p. 365). Faced with conditions he can do nothing about—time, death, chance—man is drained of the will and courage to cope with those he can do something about—his human relationships. Seeking to avoid the pain of being human, he forsakes humanity itself.

Cowie's behavior is particularly American because the belief in human perfectibility implicit in our institutions and our laudable belief in man's right to the pursuit of happiness have spawned the popular myth that man has a right to happiness itself. After the assassination, Cowie decides that life has "an infinite capacity for corruption, a finite capacity for perfection" (p. 286). This conclusion, which flies in the face of the American dream, also condemns the very act of dreaming. While our middle earth remains intractably finite, the boundless heaven of our dreams seduces us away from engagement with life. In the abandonment of finite earth lies the infinite corruption of dreams. That Morris substantially agrees with Cowie is clear when he writes in his own character in *A Bill of Rites, A Bill of Wrongs, A Bill of Goods* (1968), "We are a generous people, and our gift to the world is flight. It needs no apology. It is our best face to the world. Behind it we daily accumulate the arrears that defy reparation and exceed accounting" (p. 177).

When the American faith in the infinite capacity of life to delight and satisfy runs hard up against the facts of man's finite nature, the citizen either takes refuge in nonessentials which can be perfected and improved, such as technology, business, and social institutions, or explodes in frustrated aggression against others or himself. The most painless way to give up is to cover up the resulting emotional void with a shiny surface of superfluous objects and sterile social conventions, or in the words of the novel, "with a polish that would stick without waxing, an enamel so pretty hell itself would look good reflected in it" (p. 156). *One Day*, along with *A Bill of Rites, A Bill of Wrongs, A Bill of Goods*, contains Morris's fullest denunciation of our consumer culture, particularly our hunger for possessions. In his book of essays, Morris writes of a "black child woman, eight months pregnant" who says "what she wants for her child is more *things*, that's all, *more things*. Her brain has been washed of the horror of her condition. Her nature has been drained of its human nature. She is not quite human" (p. 175). The episode in which Luigi's mother pilfers articles from her employer illustrates the potential moral and psychological destructiveness of an obsession with objects.

In *The Crack-Up* Fitzgerald wrote, "In a real dark night of the soul it is always three o'clock in the morning, day after day. At that hour the tendency is to refuse to face things as long as possible by retiring into an infantile dream—but one is continually startled out of this by various contacts with the world."[3] In *One Day*, where infantile dreams and adult nightmares are all too durable, the recurrent image of sleep connotes a profound narcosis of sensibility. Parallel images are the fog enveloping Escondido with the bad news on the hour and connoting an emotional blindness which transforms the town into an "asphalt cemetery" (p. 7) for the spiritually dead, and the TV snow, connoting an emotional rigor mortis. Adele Skopje, "the Madame Sosostris of this wasteland,"[4] resembles Eliot's seer in speaking better than she knows. She pronounces authoritative judgment on Escondido—"Attachment to things is death. Attachment to non-things is life" (p. 90)—but fears death by water—"To get wet all over was to dangerously threaten the spark of life" (p. 109) because wetness "chills the blood"—when the chill cast by an obsession with objects is the real threat. In Adele's case the threat is literally realized when the ice machine goes berserk causing the car wreck that takes her life.

As evidenced by the Horlick and Cartwright families, those who accept personal relationships, instead of dodging them, have these relationships poisoned by selfishness, insensitivity, or reserve. Wendell Horlick particularly emerges as a savagely funny portrait in black of an indigenous American type. While himself fulfilling the masculine ideal as soldier, hunter, and athlete, Wendell is disappointed in his effeminate son Irving, who uses his father's shot put for cracking open rocks to see if they contain gold. Irving's success as a scrounger of junk is the reductio ad absurdum of the national passion for things and an implied criticism of Wendell, a poor provider, who hates him. Wendell also despises his ugly wife Miriam, whom he married because he was intimidated by pretty women, and looks forward to the pain she will suffer when Irving finally leaves home. Wendell's gradual withdrawal into feigned deafness epitomizes the barriers modern man erects to insulate himself from any sympathy with others. Ironically it means that Wendell himself deserves the misanthropic sentence he passes on the rest of humanity: "People are no damn good . . . but hell, that ain't news" (p. 54). For her part, Miriam wallows in an imaginary love for Cowie and compares people unfavorably with vegetables. In her masochistic self-pity, she comes up with an image for her condition which fits the whole town: "A cold day in hell was just a perfectly normal day in her life" (p. 340).

The relationship of Evelina Cartwright with her daughter Alec has been "twenty years of war" (p. 161). Evelina finds abstract love of the collective, expressed in her work on public-spirited projects, more comfortable than concrete love of the individual: "It was not children she did not care for—just her own" (p. 143). Although she makes a great show of loving babies, she avoids the personal commitment implied by the smell of diapers, which she hates to get on her clothes.

The strongest positive emotions of Escondido's citizens are reserved for pets. If human love is complicated and flawed, a dog loves his owner perfectly, and in love for pets, as in Evelina's love for the abstraction humanity, there is little real giving of the self. The cartons supplied for taking new pets from the pound read "FREE LOVE" (p. 365)—love which one gets for nothing, for no emotional expenditure. Cowie admits his own failure: "Lacking in passion . . . the problem of keeping up the connections [with people] was simply too much for Cowie. . . . He had settled for connections not so easily broken. . . . The raccoon waiting in the darkness, the cat in the doorway, dispensed with the mockery of understanding: the lines of give and take were always up" (p. 365). In this emotional cop-out, there is a confusion of love objects. Where pets are loved more than people, people become less than human, thus the transference of animal imagery to humans and human imagery to pets.

Like Huck Finn, Morris has been there before. The world of Escondido corresponds to the respectable Aunt Sally world of Mrs. Ormsby, though Morris's perception of it has deepened and taken on a metaphysical dimension not present in *Man and Boy*. Like *Man and Boy* and *Huckleberry Finn*, *One Day* has its rebels and its runaways. Just as the literal fog in Escondido makes a neon light resemble a smoldering fire, so the symbolic fog of insensibility harbors a fire of social unrest (represented by the civil-rights protests of the period), which is a moral descendant of Virgil's heroics and, more ominously, of Huck's flight. For protest too betokens an escape from feeling, and one the assassination reflects on directly. The chief protester, Alec Cartwright, is like a child "found in ruins; indifferent, if not actually alien, to the idea of parents" (p. 168); she is a casualty in life's war, a representative of an entire generation morally orphaned by the lack of any decent values in her parents' generation.

Alec's protest against the shiny "surface" of Escondido is expressed through her love affair with "Protest" Jackson, the black freedom-rider. She finally breaks with him when she sees that her revolution is more radical than his. Impressed by Ralph Ellison's novel, he wants to be a "visible" man, but his protest has nothing for the invisible man, the man beneath the surface. Instead of more and deeper feeling, he wants more of what the people of Escondido already have, things and status. Against this background Alec gives birth to her ultimate protest—the illegitimate son who bears as a real name what had been only his father's nickname to indicate the greater essential legitimacy of this protest. As the novel was planned before the assassination, the major moral revelations were to be caused by Alec's depositing her baby in the Escondido Pound, which stands as a corrosive testament to the highest love of which the town is capable. The animal images in *One*

Day lend their accumulated moral weight to this gesture: in a world gone to the dogs, the only place for a real human being is the Pound.

But Alec's gesture fails to shock the nation as it was supposed to because in Dallas frustration very like hers explodes with more violent results. On the opposite side of the same coin from protest is impotence, a sense of helplessness toward a loveless world of accident, and violence, its convulsive release. In *One Day*, Oswald's murderous impotence becomes the common property of men who can form no lasting connection in the face of a meaningless universe: of Mr. Ahearn, who demolishes with an axe the car he has been trying for two years to assemble, of Horlick, whose only pleasure is to shoot something, and of Cowie, the thoughtful loner in flight from life. In Oswald, impotence finds its ultimate perverted protest; he kills "the one man with the power to act as he could not" (p. 366), a man who has made connections. If anything, this killing is even more negative than those of Charlie Munger and Lee Roy. They killed to secure for themselves a sense of power over life; Oswald seems to kill merely to destroy that power, lost to himself, in others.

The assassination therefore has a clear lesson for the characters of *One Day*. It teaches Alec that placing her child in the Pound is only one more way of giving up, not only on the baby, but also on the whole human race. Like Ruth Elyot's murder of her baby, Alec's gesture amounts to a wish to murder what is human in herself. The citizens of Escondido are accomplices before the fact to the murder for having shared Oswald's impotence and contributed to its causes. As Alec says, "We all killed him" (p. 237), a judgment supported by Morris's images—the fog-wrapped square emits "the eerie spectral glow of a scene awaiting its crime" (p. 7)—and by a series of allusions to *Macbeth*.

In his essay on *One Day*, Morris says that its theme before and after the murder of President Kennedy was to be "man's inhumanity to man, his fall, and his second chance" (p. 14). In view of this, the murder seems positively fortunate for the novel; besides being a powerful example of man's inhumanity to man, it is the one imaginable event with the requisite shock value to cause the characters to take a second look at themselves, the necessary first step toward a "second chance." As it is, even the murder is not terrible enough to reach some inhabitants of Escondido. Luigi is too willing to accept the most comfortable reflections about life, and the Horlicks are too self-involved to be permanently touched by it. Evelina denies Alec's confession of guilt for the murder and even tries to give away her grandson, the emblem of her consanguinity with Alec. Above all, the assassination has no special moral significance for Evelina; it represents merely the fulfillment of Adele's prophecy that this day spells bad luck for travelers.

Although the murder teaches much about himself to Cowie, who accepts his guilt when he acknowledges his similarity to Oswald, it is not clear whether the knowledge will make a real difference in his life. Only Alec gets a clear-cut second chance, which she takes in refusing to give up her baby a second time when Evelina tries to get rid of him. Although she felt pity rather than love for him before, she now believes "that love might well emerge from what she was feeling" (p. 332). The child who had been called Protest, Alec renames Friday in tribute to this special Friday when love replaces protest in her heart and she finds "the future in her hands" (p. 433). One reason Alec can change is that the assassination so dramatically dwarfs her own small protest and, in the example of Oswald, exposes its dark underside. It is hard to imagine how any other predictable aftermath to the abandonment could have had the same effect, and thus hard to imagine *One Day* without the assassination. This is why it is so effective as a significant dramatic action.

This hopeful reading of *One Day* is qualified somewhat by the book's structure. The time inversion, with "Eleven P.M. Friday" coming first and the final section concluding the day before the murder, suggests the tragic irrevocability of time.

Like "The Scene" in *Ceremony in Lone Tree*, "Eleven P.M. Friday" uses the description of the square to sketch the moral ruin of Escondido; thus the characters start where the reader does, after the fact. It is the tragedy of life in time that appraisals can come only after some damage has been done. By concluding section 1 with a reminder that the wheel of time has come full circle and by ending the novel with the events leading up to Alec's abandonment of her child, Morris heightens the effect of time returning on itself in a frustrating circle.

The problematic note helps to answer the possible charge that both Morris's cry of universal responsibility and his larger judgment that materialism has made Americans unfeeling are simplistic clichés. Another answer is that there are few works which do not sound simplistic when their themes are summarized in a sentence. I have tried to give some sense of the complex reasoning behind Morris's overall conclusion as well as the intricate interrelationships of the novel's images. Virtually all its details (such as the fog, Cowie's insomnia, Jackson's reading) not only provide verisimilitude, but also contribute to the novel's design and meaning. They are not merely facts, not realism for its own sake, but facts made aesthetically significant by the imagination. More important is what an abstract analysis like this one cannot give a sense of: the solidity of felt experience behind *One Day* and the rich suggestiveness and complexity of its drama. Cowie, Chavez, Wendell, and Alec, at least in the last section, are among Morris's finest characters, and the Holmes chapter is a tour de force in the management of tone, a place where the author's distinctive voice overwhelmingly emerges. As with all good art, these constitute the novel's true value.

For Morris, human nature has never seemed so intractably fallen as it does in *One Day*. In an essay published not long after in *A Bill of Rites, A Bill of Wrongs, A Bill of Goods*, Morris again ponders what a piece of work is man: "He is a killer who murders, he is a poet who dreams, he is a saint who abstains, he is a lover who loves, he is a fool in his folly, he is a thinker who thinks like a man." This exhaustive catalogue of Morris's heroic types reflects the ambivalence about man he displays in his work as a whole: "We are exalted and appalled, we are cleansed and debased, with the news on the hour. It is how things are" (p. 171).

Although there is precious little to exalt us in *One Day*, that deficiency is made up for in the novel *In Orbit* (1967), which depicts how some of the same things are in a decidedly more upbeat way. The story concerns how the small town of Pickett, Indiana, reacts to a high school dropout who roars through assaulting its citizens and to a tornado which follows close on his heels, enabling him to escape the police. For all his violence, the dropout, Jubal E. Gainer, is, in Morris's deliberate pun (p. 81), a jubilee, a cause for rejoicing. The mood of rejoicing is reconciled with the destructive action because *In Orbit* is Morris's most detached contemplation of the amoral forces that run man and our universe.[5] These forces, like the boys on motorcycles, "don't mean no meanness . . . and . . . don't mean no goodness either. They just couldn't care less" (p. 110).

As expressed through Jubal, the powers that shape our lives are destructive and creative; individual and cultural; social, historical, metaphysical, and natural. He joins in one person the organic and imaginative poles of the creative impulse; the powers of time, contingency, fate, and weather; the urge to get away from something and the urge to get together with something. Thus, better than *Ceremony in Lone Tree*, *In Orbit* unifies the divergent tendencies of Morris's art, and better than *Love Among the Cannibals* it sets off the metaphysical fireworks of the present—the breakneck speed, the perpetual motion, the unpredictability and surprise, the destructiveness, and the contingency.

In Orbit takes place in a present personified in a type indigenous to America in the sixties—the motorcycle freak with black-leather jacket who keeps in motion in an implied rejection of the straight society through which he moves. Like Lee Roy, the members of this fraternity have become one with their machines: "Gas percolates in their veins. Batteries light up their eyes" (p. 42). Like the twister and the cowboy, they do not "like fenced-in situations. They needed space to twist in, hop, skip and jump in, room to pull up, to tear down, to raise hell in" (p. 118). Through these identifications, Jubal comes to stand for America's entire self-destructing culture, a culture all energy and no form, where nothing is sacred because all is consumed in process: "On Hodler's troubled mind's eye it [American culture] seems a mindless force, like the dipping, dancing funnel of a twister. . . . It is like nothing so much as the dreams of men on the launching pad. Or those boys who come riding, nameless as elemental forces . . ." (p. 15). Although Pickett seems a throwback to a simpler, pastoral America, its historic elm, symbol of the past, "falls to give this day its meaning" (p. 75). As surely as the glass balls on Hodler's ancient lightning rods are being chipped away by the rifles of college boys, Pickett's village culture is eroded by the encroaching present, as evidenced in crop-dusting planes, discarded beer cans, and automatic doors at the supermarket. On this day the boy on the run and the tornado will definitively blast Pickett out of the past for good.

Just as the American culture's disposition toward process survives throughout its history, so Jubal reflects an entire range of American heroic archetypes; that is, he embodies a principle or force continuous throughout time and ineradicable. The force partakes of the imaginative and the organic. The image of orbiting brings together both transcendence (being out of this world) and immanence (being in motion through space-time), and the book's structure—nine brief chapters following Jubal's frenetic rampage through Pickett—suggests the motion of the open road, while opening and closing the book with almost identical framing passages suggests the completion of an orbit. Jubal displays an imaginative flourish in tying his duffle to a parking meter and inserting a coin. Yet his near rape of Holly affirms his connection with the "spine curve below": "he has the impression that his head is severed from a tail that wags and thrusts" (p. 69). The novel articulates the paradox dramatized in *The Field of Vision* and *What a Way to Go* of physical impulses inspiring imaginative vision. In "doing no more than what comes naturally," Jubal creates a timeless impression that stands above nature: "The supernatural is his natural way of life" (p. 10).

In the series of similes used in the opening description (p. 9), Jubal epitomizes the perfection of physical skill ("a diver just before he hits the water"), the aspiration toward transcendence ("a Moslem prayer-borne toward Mecca"), and America's heroic past ("a cowpoke hanging to the steer's horns"). Along with the images of motorcycle rider and spaceman, *In Orbit*'s pervasive western imagery confirms that Jubal fulfills heroic archetypes of America's past, present, and future. As part of his pioneer credentials, he springs from the hardheaded rural stock Morris dealt with in the photo-text books. His father chews tobacco and wears shirts with detachable celluloid collars; his mother starts fires with corncobs in their unpainted house. But as Morris writes in *God's Country and My People* (1968). "The land-locked plainsman was the first man to orbit" (n. pag.). Whether to settle the earth or conquer the sky, the impulse and the hero are the same. Since his creative flair promotes Jubal to the level of a fiction, he resembles least the bare fact of what he is, a dropout fleeing the draft, and since he is an archetype, we can add details to make him into any particular boy we know.

Jubal's natural field of action is a contingent world represented through interwoven motifs of war, chance, news, and weather. *In Orbit*'s erratic structure suggests that the world runs, in the story's repeated phrase, "as luck would have it." The book's episodes grow from a tissue of chance conjunctions in time and space, of lucky or unlucky breaks, of opportunities realized or missed. Miss Holly, Jubal's first victim, would be normal "if the needle hadn't skipped" in her making (p. 19), and Haffner, his second, might have been a successful court jester "at another time and another place" (p. 37). At this time and this place he luckily survives his unlucky assault by Jubal. The vagaries of chance are evidenced in the unpredictability of weather. Although the front page of Hodler's newspaper sets the odds for rain at 80 percent, Haffner loves the weather, as he loves music, when it is most surprising: "Is it weather, he asks, if you can forecast it?" (p. 39). Although at the outset Pauline Bergdahl's hot news tip for the day is the boy on the loose, the major news story turns out to be the weather, the twister produced by "unpredictable mixtures" and above all "the element of chance, that dissolved it in vapor, or brought it to perfection" (p. 122).

What keeps Jubal's getaway from the Muncie draft board and the war from being the sort of evasion represented earlier in Scanlon and Paula is that he remains subject to chance and weather. That is, Jubal's escape, like the suicidal heroics of the bullfight, remains in space-time and triggers a continuing series of existential encounters with life. The "important detail" about Jubal in the opening description is "he is in motion. . . . If you pin him down in time, he is lost in space. Between where he is from and where he is going he wheels in an unpredictable orbit. To that extent he is free. Any moment it might cost him his life" (pp. 9–10). The freedom is both Bergsonian and existential. Bergson denied determinism and affirmed free will by arguing that since each moment is eternally new, it was also unpredictable; what cannot be predicted—Jubal's orbit—cannot be determined. Moreover, in following his natural impulse toward motion, Jubal remains within a contingent world, a fact confirmed by the abiding risk of death. He achieves existential freedom by asserting his selfhood against external determinants.

The point is made again in the novella's drama. When William Holden's plane runs out of gas over North Korea in the movie *The Bridges at Toko-Ri*, Jubal decides that war is not for him; he had always known that "war was hell, but nobody had told him it was crazy" (p. 23). Holden is undone, not by the enemy, but by simple bad luck. Yet the war Jubal runs from is no crazier than the world he runs through. For a man on this earth, every place is alien soil ruled by chance. Thus, during his escape Jubal finds himself, like William Holden, out of gas and left to run for his life. The attacks his flight precipitates are a series of unfortunate mischances and bungled attempts to do the right thing with a group of zanies. He admits himself, "You run into some awful nutty people" (p. 83). As the violent events of the day multiply behind him, "he has come too far to ever turn back" (p. 87), and the last bit of luck, the twister, actually prevents a tragic conclusion to his adventure by giving him the chance to escape.

What makes the escape morally palatable to the reader is that Jubal brings to his victims "the peace, or the folly, that passeth understanding" (p. 103) by exposing them to a direct experience of the creative-destructive mystery. The parking meter which Jubal transforms ticks off "the time before the dead will arise" (p. 80), and these dead include inhabitants of Pickett who are made new and reborn through his imaginative charge. Jubal's "visitation" (p. 62) of Holly becomes an annunciation in which Jubal as "space-man" is the transcendent Word visiting His creative power upon Holly's virgin flesh. As in the religious print on Holly's wall, he is "God speaking . . . out of the whirlwind" (p. 61), the twister. The victims are the very inhabitants of Pickett who are likely to be susceptible to Jubal's spell. Being feebleminded, Miss Holly is earthy like the Greek, while Haffner (who loves unpredictable musical performances) and the storekeeper Kashpearl (who likes books with their titles missing) both relish the element of surprise attendant on living for the moment. To bystanders like the newspaperman Hodler and Avery, Holly's guardian, Jubal brings the satisfaction of having their suppressed fantasies acted out.[6] Placing the section giving Hodler and Avery's reaction to the attack on Holly before the section showing the attack from Jubal's perspective ironically underscores that his actual behavior fails to live up to their lurid expectations.

The major observer of Jubal's rampage is Hodler, another of Morris's passive intellectuals. A bachelor who rents out most of his house to others and a reporter rather than a maker of news, Hodler lives vicariously through events reported in the paper. He is obsessed with the need to keep things orderly, especially the news itself. His fetish for remembering dates expresses his psychological need for a detachment and distance from events created by placing them within an orderly and completed historical continuum. Nevertheless, Hodler has a suppressed affinity for anarchy: "He likes the sporting of nature. He likes the idea of a world ruled by nature's Gods" (p. 117). In running down the story of Jubal, he is led to express his previously unacknowledged approval of impulsive behavior, to forget the date, and to attempt his only active effort to make news himself when he tries to warn Jubal of the approaching twister. He is compelled, however, to observe the twister from a totally passive position, buoyed up by his air-filled slicker and swept against a drain in a creek. His position during the storm epitomizes mankind's subjection to the creative and destructive forces of the cosmos.

Three-fourths of the way through *In Orbit*, Jubal's course and impetus shift: "All this time he has been on the run from something: what he feels now is the pull of something" (p. 116). Charlotte Hatfield, who exerts the pull, is perhaps Morris's most effective portrait of the sexually liberated female living by instinct and attuned to organic impulses. Because she lives by instinct, Charlotte is inept in handling machines, skillful in handling cats. Much of the portrait's overall effectiveness comes from Morris's counterpointing of Charlotte with her husband Alan, a poet who represents reflective male imagination. While he looks far ahead, seeing things in an orderly historical perspective, Charlotte is emotionally nearsighted. She sees only what is immediate and only what she wants to see. While he is rational, she scorns reason for feeling. While, as a teacher, he imparts knowledge, she deprecates mental knowing. While "anything at all might interest" the reflective Alan, "it has to be *alive* to interest Charlotte" (p. 134). She is not reminded of anything when he wonders aloud what the tornado's destruction may resemble; the poet's hunger for making connections has no charms for one who directly experiences. She also sneers at Alan's desire to "harness" the twister's power (p. 147).

In Orbit climaxes with a scene, an admitted "allegory" (p. 125), where all the disparate elements of the story merge in a single explosive instant. For metaphorical virtuosity and unity of design, it rivals the climactic scene in *Ceremony in Lone Tree*. The spinning twister unites in one image the still point of the turning world and straight-line motion on the open road. This unification becomes a paradigm for an extraordinary conjunction of opposites: the passive reporter Hodler and the active newsmaker Jubal, the detached Apollonian vision of Alan as he reflects on Charlotte's dance and the Dionysian possession of Charlotte by the creative impulse expressed in the dance, the whirling human dance and the whirling inhuman tornado. The parallelism extends even to minor details: the funnel-shaped trumpet on the record and the revolving record itself point toward two features of the twister. In a passage recalling Lehmann's meditations, Alan relates Charlotte's improvised dance to the larger organic forces of the cosmos. The dance and the "pointless, mindless" kicking of the baby next door remind him of a picture of life in *Life* magazine, an x-ray photo of a foetus in the womb sucking its thumb (a reflex earlier displayed by Miss Holly): "Before it knew the pleasures and purposes of sucking this womb-trapped infant suckled. Before it heard music, there was a tingling dance along the nerves. In the blood that coursed the veins . . . a blueprint for the wondrous work of man, music coursed before the ear had been shaped to hear. What had not been *given*? What could not be described as an inheritance?" (pp. 139–40). The allusion to *Finnegans Wake* that follows affirms the presence of a circle which inevitably ties the behavior of the present to the biological, historical, and cultural givens of the past. Extended to the situation of the artist, the circle links his art back to the total givens of his past experience, from which it springs.

For all the impressive imagistic fireworks, the dramatic significance of this scene for the characters and in the overall structure of the work is less explicit than the release from the past effected at the end of *Ceremony in Lone Tree.* The meaning is best approached through Morris's allusion (p. 137) to Yeats's "Among School Children." In Charlotte's performance, Alan decides, the dancer and the dance become one. In *A Bill of Rites, A Bill of Wrongs, A Bill of Goods*, Morris wrote that our chief problem as artists and men is "to make . . . a distinction [between dancer and dance] impossible" (p. 131), that is, to join our essence and our existence. The prescription is the same we have encountered earlier in *The Field of Vision*, but the effect in this scene reaches beyond the prose sense of the idea. For Yeats, the last stanza of "Among School Children" accomplished a wedding of opposites which he had struggled toward through much of his career. The realization that labor in this world was blossoming in another healed the terrible schism between flesh and spirit, time and eternity, flux and permanence, reality and justice. It disposed of the problem of mutability by showing that change was really growth. It unified what had seemed divided, reconciled Yeats to the predicament of a fallen human nature, and made an almost Hindu-like resignation to contraries possible.

The climax of *In Orbit* creates the same effect of cosmic acceptance which accounts for the novella's tone of exuberant equanimity in the face of disaster and is captured in Pauline's statement that a twister is "lovely"—not the "shambles" it makes, but the "will to do it" (p. 111). The powerful sense of fulfillment implied in the acceptance is shared by the actors in the scene. Alan has his vision of life; Charlotte is fulfilled in the dance; Hodler gets a remarkable news story; and Jubal finally blasts off as the twister picks him up and carries him off for a brief ride in a literal orbit. In the final description, Jubal, a diver about to hit the water at the beginning, now may have "gone too deep and too long without air" (p. 153). His prospects for the future are limited and problematic. In a material sense he is no better off than before. But the portrait of Bach on his sweatshirt smiles in a salute to the joy of complete self-realization, when the essence of the self is totally expressed in action and the painful contraries of life are reconciled in the majesty of being.

In Orbit may be regarded as a distillation of the significant themes, images, and relationships of Morris's entire canon in a single, quintessential poetic statement. The richness and resonance of Jubal as a character and of the action he careens through give *In Orbit* a sense of intention fully and satisfyingly carried out. In this way Morris himself manages to wed the dancer and the dance. In *A Bill of Rites, A Bill of Wrongs, A Bill of Goods*, he says, "When the writing is good everything is symbolic, but symbolic writing is seldom good" (p. 83). Virtually every detail of *In Orbit*, however realistic in itself, takes on greater meaning in terms of the work's aesthetic design. Even the movie playing at the theatre—the Beatles in *Help*! (p. 110)—enunciates the universal human need first expressed in Paula Kahler's nightmare cry in *The Field of Vision*. Because *One Day* is much longer, there is more room for mistakes, and it has a few—over-insistence on animal imagery, for instance. Nevertheless, it too must stand as one of Morris's most effective fictions.

Morris has written that the contemporary artist "must become that paradox, both a visionary and a realist" (*The Territory Ahead*, p. 218). In *One Day*, Morris the realist stares unflinchingly at how things are, at the givens of our condition. When a president dies in Dallas, that is how things are in Escondidos all across the continent. In *In Orbit*, Morris the visionary draws from how things are a plausible affirmation. To paraphrase *The Territory Ahead*, "Through the window of his fiction we breathe the air of his brave new world" (p. 231).

9

Journey's End: Fire Sermon *and* A Life

In spite of its brevity, *In Orbit* has one of the most complicated designs to be found in Morris's fiction. After such a stylistic tour de force, the reader may well wonder where Morris can go from there. The answer is that the very triumph of complexity in *In Orbit* has the effect of making simplicity possible for him. By the strange alchemy of the imagination, what had seemed difficult now became easy; what had required an elaborate and convoluted design and plot now could be executed with a single plot line, few characters, omniscient narration, and a straightforward simplicity absent in Morris since *The World in the Attic*. The directness of *Fire Sermon* and *A Life*, really two installments of the same story, is matched by their subtlety and depth. The single luminous story line, ripe with associations from Morris's previous work, allows a wisdom hard won in a lifetime of writing to come through. In *Fire Sermon* and *A Life* the characters come to full dramatic life like those in *The Deep Sleep*, and the story follows their evolving consciousness in episodes both dramatically meaningful and humanly powerful.

Using the open-road structure, *Fire Sermon* (1971) recounts the trip of Floyd Warner and "the boy," his grandnephew Kermit, from California to the Nebraska home place. It is no accident that this now familiar passage from West to East recalls *My Uncle Dudley*; Warner and the boy are really Dudley and the Kid, the meaning of their adventure enriched and qualified in Morris's thirty years of writing. Warner's mobile home in a California trailer park, though a bit of an antique, is a beautifully suggestive symbol of modern culture—attenuated, cramped, doomed to early obsolescence, a little crass but in its way a technological triumph, and not permanently anchored in any one location. It epitomizes the rootless, nervous, traditionless California civilization. Almost a mansion by comparison, the family farmhouse on the home place epitomizes the slower, more expansive, more heroic traditions of the pioneer past—the endurance in the face of nature and of time's ravages, the frugality that could never stand to throw anything away, the sense of family, the roots in one spot. To travel from the one to the other is to reexamine and repossess one's past as a preparation for throwing off its influence. Concommitantly, the journey proves beyond any further doubt, even to Warner, that you can't go home again and, like seeing an old girl friend after twenty years with three children by another man, brings home the irrevocable pastness of the past. In this sense the journey takes Warner and the boy from the past to a present in which the boy must be a man and the man, an aging fossil unnaturally preserved from change, no longer has any place.

The exorcism of the past is only one of several rituals enacted in this single journey. It completes the prolonged funeral of Viola and effects a symbolic one for Warner. Because the journey becomes Scanlon's ceremony reenacted with Scanlon conscious and aware of its purport, *Fire Sermon*'s break with the past is more dramatically and psychologically convincing than that portrayed in *Ceremony in Lone Tree*. In a larger sense what happens to Warner represents the final stage in any man's moral development, his resignation to the hard facts of time, change, and death. For the boy, *Fire Sermon* dramatizes initiation into manhood. In effect, the ceremonial cremation of the past with which the story concludes allows the present, as particularly represented in the boy's newly acquired manhood, to be resurrected from the ashes. The experiences of the old man and the boy are complementary and fall together in the son's destruction of the father. As *The Golden Bough* shows, a central ritual of human culture is the slaying, either real or symbolic, of the aging god or king, to make way for the youth who will take his place. On the psychological level such rites reflect the need for the son to kill the father's psychological authority and assume responsibility for his own life. To be a man, the boy must cast off Warner's symbolic paternity, and for Warner, that necessitates an acknowledgement of his own fathering of the despised younger generation. That done, *A Life* completes the ritual of Warner's giving himself up to death.

Part of the power and suggestiveness of Warner's character derives from his position in the line of Dudley and a whole series of Morris pioneers. His creation of the Dust Bowl, his several wives, his history of boom and bust, and his cherishing of the mysterious crystals are by now familiar marks of a single archetypal attitude toward life. Dudley originally took to the open road to discover in himself those heroic qualities conducive to continuing life in the present, but Morris eventually came to regard the impulse behind Dudley's escapades as akin to Huck's fear of Aunt Sally and Twain's own romanticizing of the past. In Fremont Osborn, of *Cause for Wonder*, the Dudley-Warner character has become the classic American "aginner" outraged by the shenanigans of the present and an intransigent opponent of change. A slightly more active version of Scanlon, Fremont, as a young man, had been a progressive maverick who flew "in the teeth of custom" (p. 46) to raise wheat where men had never dared to before and an iconoclastic freethinker who ridiculed his father's piety with "Pecos diamonds" testifying "to the subtle craftsmanship of the Devil" (p. 34). Although he still fancies himself an advanced thinker, time has transmuted the forward-looking rebel to a backward-looking old coot as life has caught up with and surpassed his rebellion. The Medusa's head of time has petrified him as surely as the petrified wood he shows to Howe. The historical anomaly of the aging rebel, imagining himself focused on the future when he is solidly situated in the past, produces an older version of Gatsby's duplicitous dream.

In the same way and with much the same biography, Floyd Warner, a school-crossing guard with STOP and GO stenciled on his helmet, shows to the world the Janus-like face of this native American type. As a youth he shared with each new generation of Americans the rage to destroy the old world in order to mold a new one nearer to the heart's desire. This variation on the American impulse to get away is a form of patricide, a killing of the father's power over oneself in the form of institutions and opinions of the past. When Warner rebelled against the conventional pieties of his father, "the first great hate of his life" (p. 20), he followed the characteristic American pattern of revolt established when the Pilgrims settled in Salem to escape the patriarchal authority of the Anglican church and continued when the colonials overthrew their king and father, George III. The central tragedy of America's tumultuous history is that, in a sense, the cost of freedom must always be murder. This aspect of the American spirit is expressed in the words Warner reads from Harold Bell Wright: ours is a land where "*every man is—by divine right—his own king; he is his own jury, his own counsel, his own judge, and—if it must be—his own executioner*" (p. 40).

Warner's militant agnosticism—the murder of his father's God—leads him, like Huck and so many Morris heroes, to choose hell over the heaven of his saintly sister Viola. He shouts that he will see his dead friends again "only if they all burn in hell!" (p. 41), absolutely the only place he plans to go if there is an afterlife. Warner's continued rebellion has meaning only in relation to a piety as anachronistic as his own reverence for Robert Ingersoll as a prophet of advanced thought. He reads Viola's devout letters to the boy because they satisfy his need for a target to oppose. The irony of history has transformed Warner himself into the protective patriarch and incarnation of the past, standing on the world's street corner to warn heedless youth against the dangers of crossing into the uncertain future. He will never, as he supposes, find a new lock that the old keys he carries will fit because the old answers simply do not fit the new questions. If he only knew it, he is as outdated as his almost useless Maxwell.

Although Kermit is generally known as the "*old man's boy*" (p. 4), in a larger sense, both refuse to admit that the old man's past has spawned the boy's present. Warner vows to live long enough to spoil the greedy plans of those who want to inherit his trailer, but the hippies he abhors are already in possession of the present which the trailer symbolizes. Being of the opinion, with Colonel Ingersoll, that "no man on whom the snow did not fall was worth a hill of beans" (p. 74), Warner plans to transport the boy back to Nebraska, where the testing rigors of climate have not been tamed by civilization, and once on the road, he scorns travelers like Sympson, for whom modern conveniences have removed the hardships attendant on travel. But it is the hardheaded pragmatism, the daring to try the new, and the gift of know-how displayed in Warner's generation that has made these conveniences possible and has created the soft modern world represented by California's temperate climate.

Warner plans the Nebraska trip to teach the boy "who you are" (p. 65) through rediscovery of his roots and to initiate him through the ordeals of the road. In this Warner succeeds, but in a way and at a cost he never expected. To achieve manhood and self-knowledge, the boy must recognize the old man as his "next of kin," but that also means seeing him as old, as part of a past which must now give way to the new. Similarly, the major effect of the trip is to bring home to Warner himself the folly of trying to arrest time and the fact of his own obsolescence. The ordeals of the journey—popping ears and nosebleed—not only mark the boy's perilous entry into the zone of trials where he must earn his manhood, but also enforce the lesson that Warner is not the man he once was any more than the Maxwell is a serviceable car. His decision to let Kermit drive, while a further test of the boy's maturity, is also a concession to his own advancing years. The episode in which the old man is almost borne away by the mindless animal horde of sheep is an image central to all of Morris's work. Against the ongoing flow of immanent life, the transcendent Warner stands, "a single buffeted figure, a snag in the river that flowed wide and fast" (p. 89). Warner would like to think himself in the vanguard of time, but no matter how far he travels, the real present, in the figures of the hitchhikers, Stanley and Joy, always ends up ahead of him.

Kermit and eventually Warner come to comprehend the root of the boy's instinctive alliance with Stanley and Joy: "They were all young, and he was old. They were on the one side, and he was on the other" (p. 110). The naturalness of this division robs it of any enmity for the boy, and the old man must also learn to accept the naturalness in order for the proper relation of age and youth, past and present, to be restored. Near the end, when Warner answers the question about how many "kids" he has by saying, "Three in all" (p. 127), he in effect acknowledges Stanley and Joy as his next of kin too, as the young who must inherit the world he has made. The sense of his paternity is enhanced when he bangs on the trailer for them to be quiet and they obey.

The last step in Warner's resignation to change is played out on the stage of the home place, where he comes face to face with his own advanced age. The dying community with its decaying house full of artifacts is Morris's last long look at the past of his own father's generation, the past preserved in the photo-text books but eclipsed in time. When Warner and Kermit enter the house, the red rug on the stairs "glows as if the carpet were burning" (p. 135), already half ablaze with a Heraclitan fire symbolizing, like the bomb in *Ceremony in*

Lone Tree, the perpetual destructiveness of flux. Kermit recognizes the artifacts may have value as antiques, but to the pragmatic old man, for whom value has always been equated with utility, the uselessness of Viola's hoard passes judgment on himself; he too is merely "another object preserved from the past" (p. 137).

Although the house is crowded with objects, the description of the village and the home place is dominated by images of emptiness and vacancy; it moves from two basements that have been dug for stores that were never built to the photo of Warner's father with a child on his knee holding an empty bird cage. The bird, the life, is "the only thing that ever got away!" (p. 133). The evocation of the void signifies transcendence; Warner and everything else that defies time is out of this world, "far out," in Stanley's words (p. 138). The condition of transcendence is underscored by Morris's use of the present tense in passages describing the life in California and the home place and the past tense in contrasting narrative passages. Both the home place and the uneventful routine of California seem to defy time, but action, the journey to Nebraska, establishes the characters' orientation in time.

Warner "sags" in the poisoned air of the past. His statement that he feels only "as good as might be expected" (p. 140) amounts to an impressive admission of his age and prepares for the ritual purification of the present when the house is consumed in the fire of change. He enters the present himself in using the fashionable swearword—*fucking* (p. 146)—one of the few curses previously banned from his own vocabulary. After the home place burns and Warner drives off leaving the trailer behind to his legatees, it is for Joy to deliver the fire sermon: when birds grow old, she says, "and their time has come, they just go off alone in the woods and die" (p. 153). This is what the old man has done; "It's nature's way . . . and people should live according to nature. Some people really do" (p. 154). This is Morris's most Bergsonian vision. The preserving ice of the timeless dream melts in the fire of change and flux necessary for life. Warner has moved from transcendence to immanence and then departed the stage of life, leaving youth and the present in possession of their heritage.

In spite of this break with the past and the nearness of death at the end, the overwhelming impression created by *Fire Sermon* is one of life and continuity. Warner may see Stanley and Joy as spoilers of the American dream, and Stanley may denounce the dream as a fraud, but actually Stanley and Joy are updated versions of Warner and Viola. Stanley "looked familiar" (p. 76) the first time they see him on the road because he resembles Warner in wanting to kill the influence of the father over himself. "You're lucky," he tells Kermit about his dead parents and aging guardian. "I had to fight 'em. All *you* got to do is let them die off" (p. 117). A "Weatherman" in active revolutionary struggle against a sick American society, Stanley scorns Kermit's affection for Warner, whom he sees as the personification of that society. It is "kid stuff," evidence that the boy has not matured enough to judge things by his own values instead of his uncle's: "When you grow up you'll see it different" (p. 116).

Warner's description of Viola as "a silly child and a saintly woman" (p. 40) fits Joy, with her "warm smile" and childlike need for supervision to keep from blundering into patches of cockleburs. Joy's role as the chief commentator on the book's ending emphasizes her importance in it. Joseph Campbell's explanation of the mystic word "Aum," a variation of which is chanted by Joy at the end of the story (p. 154), goes to the heart of Morris's conception of life in *Fire Sermon*: "As in the actual experience of every living being, so in the grandiose figure of the living cosmos . . . the life of the universe runs down and must be renewed."[1] This mystery of dissolution and generation, so often seen in the death-rebirth imagery in Morris's fiction, is represented for Hindus "in the holy syllable AUM. . . . The syllable itself is God as creator-preserver-destroyer, but the silence [around the syllable] is God Eternal, absolutely uninvolved in all the opening-and-closings of the round" (pp. 266–67). As the girl's name suggests, the chanting of the word affirms that all of life's pains, divisions, and contraries are mystically subsumed in an all-pervading, all-accepting joy at the triumphant mystery of being. Such joy is the descendant of Viola's gentle, unswerving faith in the goodness of people and the universe, a faith strong enough, even in the opinion of the skeptical Warner, "to save half the people in hell" (p. 11).

For Joy the sacred word is heard "in the fire," which "transforms" (p. 154) and "purifies" (p. 155). The resident deity of *Fire Sermon* would seem to be Shiva, the destroyer, but the novel finds room for preserving forces as well. Although how the fire starts is not spelled out, Stanley's facetious remark that it is ignited by the friction of sexual intercourse between himself and Joy (p. 152) seems at least half right. He is correct when he says, "All the non-fuckers are sick" (p. 109), but in the special sense that loss of sexual viability denotes old age and approaching death, while "Them f—king goddam kids!" (p. 146) possess the true title to the present because their sexuality can extend life into the next generation.

The ritual of initiation, of course, also implies continuity. Because Kermit's parents have been killed in a fiery car accident (which foreshadows the later transformation of the house), the normal discontinuity between generations is magnified by the age difference between himself and the old man, whom the boy loves but shies away from as "his *next* of kin" (p. 9), thus adding to the ordinary problems of growing up. The pronunciation of Kermit's last name—"Oil-sleekle" (p. 4)—suggests the fluid and slippery nature of his self as he hovers between boy and man. His predisposition toward the values of youth is suggested by his desire to be called "man" by hippies, his denial of Warner's paternity when Stanley and Joy join them, and his role of interpreter between the old man and the young people. In addition to an ordeal testing maturity, the Nebraska journey allows Kermit the opportunity to associate with the youth of Stanley and Joy, but the eventual manhood he acquires runs several layers deeper than Stanley's. By the end he has already grown into a wise and sensitive observer of life. He grasps the distinction, lost on Warner and Stanley, between value and use, and he appreciates that not all questions have answers and not all significance can be articulated. He wonders why the 1879 coin he has found should have survived the ravages of time: "The meaning of this escaped him in a manner he found satisfying. Already he was old enough to gaze in wonder at life" (p. 142). To gaze in wonder. In a sense this is the ultimate mark of maturity aimed at in all of Morris's fiction. With the artist's sensitivity to the intangible and the spiritual, Kermit senses the eyes of Aunt Viola "on him right at this moment" (p. 149). The alternate heat and cold and the feeling of being almost dead he experiences after the fire signify Kermit's passage through the last ordeal into manhood. Having emerged from under the protective umbrella of the father's authority, he can accept a legacy without its implying dependence. A last artifact survives, bequeathed by Warner's ghost to Kermit, his next of kin—the ox shoe in the earth, a talisman to bring the luck "he's going to need" (p. 155) in this crazy world of ours.

Fire Sermon is Morris's most poetic and moving argument for the need to change with a changing life. The theoretical defense of immanence as a way of life is not worked out as explicitly as in *The Field of Vision*, but the urgency of the need for it is felt more strongly here than in any other Morris work. Lawrence said it best. With the past behind him where it should be, the boy is free to follow his natural bent; the soul "is to go down the open road . . . keeping company with those whose soul draws them near to her, accomplishing nothing save the journey . . . in the long life-travel into the unknown, the soul in her subtle sympathies accomplishing herself by the way" (*Studies in Classic American Literature*, p. 186). The sense of commitment to change may well be reinforced by the fact that Morris himself, as a man and as a novelist, effects his own most final and convincing severance from the past in *Fire Sermon*. It is as if he had deliberately loaded up Viola's home place with every artifact out of every one of his books and photos for one last grand conflagration before moving on. But when the time for departure comes, he pauses for a moment with Floyd Warner. The Dudley-Fremont-Warner character has survived too long and meant too much in Morris's life and fiction to let him go driving off into the sunset unremarked. And besides, this soul, in motion after forty years of stubborn resistance to time, now faces the greatest unknown of all—death.

In *A Life* (1973), Morris dramatizes Warner's approach to death through three interrelated psychological processes—growing self-knowledge, growing resignation to human finitude, and growing abstraction of the total self into transcendent spirit. As in the past, Morris uses the open-road structure to dramatize immanence, which is implied in the second of these processes. But in *A Life*, the journey from the Nebraska home place to his former ranch on the Pecos carries Warner beyond the still recognizably Dionysian mysticism of *Fire Sermon* to a more spiritual mysticism at the end.

The title *A Life* is appropriate in that the book depicts "a life," Warner's, in its entirety. After the fire he discovers that, "the wheel of his life having come full circle, the past was now coming toward him as the present mysteriously receded" (p. 26). Warner is a short man, and "the shorter the grass, the longer the roots" (p. 2). His roots stretch back to the Pecos country, and his trip there is more than physical as he sees important episodes of his life flash before his eyes throughout the journey. Just as "the center of a town was something people knew and not something to be decided by a crew of surveyors" (p. 46), so too the moral center of a man's life is located by how he feels about it. Warner's return to the Pecos, his center, resembles the pilgrimage in Robert Frost's "Directive," except that the wholeness Warner achieves at the end grows out of the new insight which his nearness to death prepares him to bring to past memories. Not by chance, the episodes from his past Warner recalls are central chapters in his moral history: his revolt against his father and his father's God, his experience of gratuitous human evil in the boy Vance Fry and of equally gratuitous good in Viola, his taste of woman's love with Muriel, his struggle with nature on the ranch. Like Viola, the old man feels himself "unraveling like a ball of yarn" (p. 32–33), and once on the Pecos, he can see his life whole and unclouded by the immediate demands of living. It seems completely unrolled, "mapped out before him . . . its reassuring but somewhat monotonous pattern like that of wallpaper he had lived with" (p. 16). The process and the image recall Yeats's concept of "dreaming back," the unwinding of the mummy's sheath, the unwinding of experience from the spindle of the self accomplished between death and reincarnation. It also inverts Bergson's organization. For Warner, as for Yeats, dreaming back tempers the soul, producing a deepening wisdom and an ever growing spiritualization.

A Life depicts Warner's gradual submission to death's inevitability with subtlety and compassion. He begins by feeling "he had lost in last few days a part of himself, measurable as weight" (p. 8), his illusions of usefulness and viability. As with everything he owns, he has used his body until it has worn out, and now he faces the desolating yet finally comforting conclusion that "there's nothing can happen that hasn't already happened" (p. 14), nothing, that is, in life. To accept that the one thing left to happen is death is the first step toward accepting death as the fitting conclusion to life. To attain complete acceptance, Warner must suffer that mortification of the ego that comes to all men who realize that they are subject to the power of something larger than themselves. In effect, this is a reconciliation with and submission to the father, whether God or nature; occurring in the last half of life, it balances the killing of the father necessary for manhood in the first half of life. The moral devaluation of the self parallels the slow physical dissolution of the body in the death process; in both cases the personal one is dissolved in the impersonal all.

As a young man, Warner, stiff-necked with pride and self-absorption, tried to reduce everything to the measure of himself. Even God, both as a discrete being and a presence expressed in nature, was a personal possession which only he could have and whose truth only he could interpret. He hated his father's "monstrous love of God, and God's love of him" (p. 43) because, as Viola decided, both Warner and his father wanted God all to themselves. Later Warner abandoned his father's God for a struggle with nature, embodied in the fierce, unending wind of the Pecos. Like Warner perched on the privy with "the plain empty and rolling as far as you can see it, the sky topless as far as you can feel it, the wind howling like a ghost in the uncovered hole at his side" (p. 55), a man contemplating his own littleness in relation to the wind might feel that he is face to face with the void. For one who takes the self as the measure of all, all that is not the self is nothing, is empty. Even as a young man on the Pecos, Warner knew better than that. The wind he engages in a "battle of wills" (p. 41) is an almost personal adversary, "a force in nature to match his own stubborn fury" (p. 40). Being unable to preempt devotion, he has instead preempted opposition. The wind suggests both the Holy Spirit and the natural forces, visible and invisible, that govern the cosmos. Eventually Warner had decided "it seemed wiser to live with it" (p. 126) than to fight it, and as an old man on the Pecos, he acknowledges the wind's dominion: "The wind's invisible will had blown him away, and blown him back. Given time it would work its will on everything it touched, as surely as fire: the works of man disappeared into thin air or went up in smoke" (p. 126).

To the invisible forces common in the earlier Morris, such as time, *A Life* adds something new; the concepts of accident and luck prominent in *One Day* and *In Orbit* have developed into a sense of destiny or providence ruling human life and capable of planning and willing certain specific ends. Part of this fatalism may arise inadvertently out of the need to objectify the inevitability of death for one who is old; a sense of anthropomorphism is created by the choice of a human agent to carry out the inevitable destiny of old age. Nevertheless, even in the first scene, when Warner is cautioned that "it's bad luck" to let Effie Mae "get a grip on you" (pp. 12–13), an impression of willed design figures in his story. It is later reinforced by his identification with Ivy Holtorfer, "the last white man in the county to be killed by Indians" (p. 20) and, like Warner, a late representative of the pioneer experience. It is as if Warner had lived his eighty-two years for Ivy too, slain at seventeen, as if the circle described in his journey carries him back to that moment when "the bullet or the arrow" had found Ivy (p. 21) and his own suspended destiny to be the last white man killed by Indians is finally accomplished.

The Indian Blackbird functions perfectly well as a realistic creation, the disaffected Vietnam veteran forced by white man's law to kill a white man's enemy when his brother has been jailed for killing according to Indian law, but from the first he also takes on symbolic dimensions. Through his association with the color black, the bullet holes in his coat, and his disposal of the dead cat as "more surplus" (p. 94), he personifies death, which in the natural course of things destroys all that has outlived its usefulness and become surplus in life. While there is no need to find a source for the character outside Morris's imagination, both Blackbird and the author's treatment of him may have been suggested by a passage from an essay by Morris's friend Loren Eiseley. In it Eiseley relates seeing a blackbird kill a nestling of other birds: "He was a bird of death." Although other birds raised a cry of protest, "he, the murderer, the black bird at the heart of life, sat on there, glistening in the common light, formidable, unmoving, unperturbed, untouchable."[2] The same aura of implacable will attaches to Morris's "impersonal" (p. 100) character, who was "a presence . . . a force, outside of his [Warner's] experience" (p. 101), and yet Blackbird clearly serves a still larger force himself. He saves the old man from being run over by a diesel, so that the rightness of the death which finally comes will not be marred by an accident, and even in killing, "Blackbird, too, has been shaped to this moment" (p. 152).

For Warner, who has generally entertained the illusion of control over his own life, a major conclusion drawn from his last journey is that in the affairs of men "one thing always led to another" in an unbreakable and sometimes obscure chain of causality. The existential freedom Morris has postulated so often, which resides in the fact that man creates his own essence by a continuing series of free choices, is valid only so long as one pictures life as occurring in a fleeting instant in a perpetual present. But the moment one pictures life as a continuum of instants extending in time from past to future, patterns of causality and tendency appear which operate outside one's particular choices. A man's most trivial acts today can have momentous and unseen consequences tomorrow.

Thus in *A Life*, Warner's sense of freedom is drastically curtailed. Unseen forces contrive to direct him to the diner: "Since morning, one thing had led to another, and they had all led to this seat at the counter" (p. 74). Here Warner is faced with one of the crucial decisions of his life, whether to accept the bum as a rider (and, by implication, to go back to California, the bum's destination, and pick up the life he has renounced earlier) or to take on Blackbird, who has not asked for a ride, and head for the Pecos and whatever lies ahead of him. The freedom of the choice is diminished by the fact that Warner cannot consciously appreciate its future significance, and that, although he does the inviting, Blackbird has already taken the initiative by slamming the door in the bum's face. Thus, Warner "had not been free to choose one or the other—he had been chosen" (p. 142). Looking back on his life at the end, Warner realizes for the first time that it has often been so, in spite of the inflexible will be fancied he possessed: "He saw that the crucial decisions, the meaningful choices, had invariably been made by others; his choice had been in conceding that their choice had been right. . . . his own will had been challenged; and lost. In losing he had hoped to hold on to something he valued more highly than his will. The love of Viola; the affection and respect of the boy" (pp. 142–43). Whether or not this is an accurate assessment of the past, it demonstrates Warner's present willingness to downgrade the claims of the will in favor of finer and more disinterested emotions. The loss is redeemed in the willingness to lose.

In the same spirit, Warner conspires in his own murder; he himself points out the sharpness of the can lid Blackbird uses to slash the old man's wrists, a method with appropriate overtones of suicide. Warner's choice is in accepting the inevitable "dead end" of his life's journey, which is preferable at least to his old friend Pauline Deeter's senility. To the imagined question, "Old man, what do you want?" Warner can answer "help," help to die: "Everything had happened according to a plan that would prove to be his as much as Blackbird's, so that what he wanted . . . was what he had got" (p. 150). Like Hamlet, Warner, the truculent pioneer and willful rebel against time, his father, and his father's God, finds his greatest fulfillment in aligning his will with the larger will which plots his fate. Death will come when it will come. The readiness is all.

Early in his adventure, Warner poses to himself a question, "What gain could come from a loss of life" (p. 34), and it might be paraphrased, "What gain could come from a loss of will, of self?" Both might be answered, "A sense of larger destiny satisfyingly accomplished." As Warner's long day wanes, he feels increasingly surrounded by a spiritual deep out of which speak the voices of the past and a special voice posing many such eschatological questions. The voice objectifies the hard-won wisdom of Warner's spiritual travail. This spirituality Morris represents with many of his characteristic images of transcendence (such as being airborne, in the early prayer-circle scene). Following his usual practice, he identifies physical sight with imaginative vision, but here he also identifies imagination, or the consciousness, with the soul. At the home place, Warner's transcendent consciousness is manifested as a pair of all-seeing eyes detached from the mortal, aging flesh of the old man. The eyes hover before him, like the gaze of Beatrice before Dante (*Purgatorio*, XXX), signalling his passage through the purging fire of change into a more refined form. Later Warner wryly speculates that the failing of physical sight may be "a cunning way to discourage work," to encourage passive meditation, and, since "out of sight was out of mind" (p. 133), to purify the inner vision of all mortal concerns so that it can turn to immortality. When the moon rises near sunset, Morris inverts the usual symbolic connotation he attaches to moonshine; instead of the deceptive, will-o'-the-wisp fancies of men who evade commitment, the moonlight here connotes a higher spiritual vision accessible when earthly vision fails. By the moon's half-light, Warner is able to see better and to "judge distance" (p. 140), like the distance of eighty-two years between the beginning of his life and its end. As the last blood trickles from his veins, he undergoes a spiritual apotheosis, an impression like an optical illusion "that he was outside, not inside his own body. . . . One seemed as real to him as the other: to be outside, perhaps, even realer." The familiar Morris images of sleep and waking are used to distinguish ordinary existence from Warner's present transcendent state of being: "*I have been walking in my sleep, and now I am awake*" (p. 151). His fading sight catches a final tableau, itself frozen like a timeless "painting" of which he himself is now a part (p. 152); the consciousness has left the man, the soul has transcended time.

With this conclusion, Morris accomplishes his most successful reconciliation of the impulses to immanence and transcendence. For the immanent self that has reached the end of its life in this world, transcendence, the immersion of the self in the all, represents the last available stage of growth. Thus, Morris concludes with an image of immanence. Warner "had lived in the manner he believed he had chosen, not knowing that he had been one of those chosen not merely to grow old, but to grow ripe" (p. 152).

Although both *Fire Sermon* and *A Life* are extremely accomplished fictions in their own right, an indisputable part of their appeal lies in the special place they fill in Morris's canon. For him, as for Warner, things have come full circle in these books, back to the figure of Uncle Dudley on his long life-travel into the unknown, back to the real-life prototype of Dudley, Uncle Verne, back to the author's formative boyhood adventure when he helped to create the Dust Bowl. *Fire Sermon* and *A Life* cap a long struggle a good deal more complicated and exciting in its way than that active boyhood encounter with the wind and dust—Morris's lifelong aesthetic struggle to process the raw material of his experience and transform it into lasting art. This may explain why more than any other novels I know of, these books, and especially *A Life*, put us inside their major subject—ripeness, life fully lived out to its end—to communicate what existence at this extremity is truly like. Morris is able to catch this sense of ripeness because, in substantial measure, the ripeness is his own. *Fire Sermon* and *A Life* not only take ripeness as their subject; they are an impressive demonstration of ripeness in Morris's art.

In a way, Morris resembles Yeats. In the careers of both, the growth in their understanding of the human predicament forms an archetypal pattern of human growth—from youth disillusioned by our grey, impermanent world and longing for fixity in the land of the heart's desire, to a maturity engaged in complex ways with the complex conditions of our chaotic, divided world, to a serene old age where complexity gives way to a final simplicity accepting and affirming life in all its pains and divisions. It is the path that every man must pursue from youth to old age. That their art treats this path as a subject while recording their own journey in its stately, formal progress, may be the true legacy of the poet and the novelist.

10

Wright Morris: The Man in the Middle

Standing on the caboose platform in *Ceremony in Lone Tree*, Boyd asks himself, "Why . . . did things coming toward him seem to break into pieces, and things that receded into the past seem to make sense?" (p. 46). One of the corollaries of existential thought is that the present can never be understood because, until the hero gives it shape and meaning with his free choices, until it becomes the past, there is nothing to understand. The literature of the present is also very much in the making, and for the critic too, the past seems to make more sense than the present. Time makes a lot of things clear, if only because the memory blurs so much that is unimportant and cushions so much that is painful, and usually the more time a critic puts between his criticism and its texts, the sharper, if not better, his vision is likely to be. For this reason, any judgments one might make about contemporary American fiction must be tentative. Nevertheless, Wright Morris has been writing for thirty years, during which time he has become a full and accomplished artist and has secured for himself a definite place in American fiction. It is therefore possible and useful to offer some generalizations about where postwar American fiction has been, where it seems to be going, and where Morris fits in to the overall trends.

The nature of my generalizations is qualified by my particular approach, and certainly many other descriptions of the period are possible. Critics like John Aldridge, in *After the Lost Generation* (1951) and *In Search of Heresy* (1956), Ihab Hassan, in *Radical Innocence* (1961), and Marcus Klein, in *After Alienation* (1964), characterize postwar fiction in terms of its "values," its themes and visions, and the nature of its heroes. Their formulations are the sort which chiefly arise out of the writing once it has been finished. I want to consider fiction as a writer might when he sits down at his typewriter—from the perspective of what fiction is conceived to be, what its relation is to those elements of writing we call experience, and what, if any, human importance it might have. These are some of the very matters Morris himself considers in his criticism, and they are also important to many of his contemporaries.

Since I have already examined Morris's novels, my chief interest here is in the recent book of criticism *About Fiction* (1975). Although there is no necessary relation between an author's stated theories and the actual character of his work, Morris's criticism, of which *About Fiction* is representative, is remarkably consistent both with his general aims as a writer and with the thematic materials of his novels. It therefore serves to define the special qualities of his work and to place it in relation to that of his fellow postwar writers. As the subtitle (*Reverent Reflections on the Nature of Fiction with Irreverent Observations on Writers, Readers, & Other Abuses*) suggests, *About Fiction* is a loosely organized series of "reflections" on the nature of writing, especially at the present in America. In spite of the apparent randomness, however, a number of clearly defined concerns of the author emerge. By the time he has finished, Morris has addressed himself to two divergent streams in contemporary writing which represent diametrically opposed ideas of the relation between fiction and reality and which therefore lay down two extreme boundaries within which the novels of the time will be contained. The rigidity of the dualism is mine, deliberately imposed out of the need to achieve some order in dealing with amorphous historical materials.

The first of the two streams in contemporary writing is characterized by the feeling that the purpose of fiction is to give the audience reality as directly and in as unmediated a form as possible. The audience for serious fiction proved particularly responsive to this feeling, especially before 1960, a fact which accounts in part for the success of such realistic works as James Jones's *From Here to Eternity* (1951), J. D. Salinger's *The Catcher in the Rye* (1951), Norman Mailer's *The Naked and the Dead* (1948), John Updike's *Rabbit, Run* (1960), William Styron's *Lie Down in Darkness* (1951), and Robert Penn Warren's *All the King's Men* (1946)—these last two fairly conventional examples of realism beneath surfaces that owe something to Faulkner's heightened, almost expressionistic style. Realism is, of course, a loose designation, not revealing much about such matters as a particular writer's aims or subjects; the list of works I have just given testifies to the variety of postwar realism. Further, what the author perceives as fidelity to reality may be perceived by the reader as distortion. Flannery O'Connor's statement that she did not know she was writing about grotesques until she read reviews of her work illustrates this phenomenon. Nevertheless, the artists working in this tradition set out, perhaps unconsciously, to be truthful in a general way to some external reality. Philip Roth, who wrote one of the best realistic novellas of the period, *Goodbye Columbus* (1959), voices the passion for the thing itself when he says that it is "the tug of reality, its mystery and magnetism, that leads one to the writing of fiction" and complains about contemporary writers who spurn "life as it is lived in this world, in this reality."[1] Through these remarks breathes the cold breath of the red-eyed elders in Wallace Stevens's "Peter Quince at the Clavier," who gazed on Susanna and lusted after the woman, not the vision. In its most extreme form the desire to get the facts is expressed in the "non-fiction novel," the "new genre" bruited in the sixties at the appearance of Truman Capote's *In Cold Blood* (1965) and Norman Mailer's *Armies of the Night* (1968).

In *About Fiction*, Morris touches on many causes for turning toward the real. For one, man, plagued by a hunger for the real in the platonic sense used by Booth, goes to the facts in a mistaken belief that the real is to be found in them. For another, in the expanding America of the nineteenth century, the artist who had exhausted the raw materials of one region could revitalize his art by changing his region, by changing the facts about which he was writing. This experience fostered the notion that art resided in the facts themselves. In the twentieth century, Morris further argues, the development of photography has made it seem that one can get closer to the facts than ever, while at the same time the pressure of facts in the environment has grown. The massed life of the cities declares itself to our consciousness through the polluted air we breathe, and we watch the shooting of an assassin from our living rooms. Such immediacy promotes the superstition that reality can be known in itself: "With the aggressive *thereness* of our environment . . . the presentiment grows that facts will be found wherever we peel away the encrustations of fiction." Even the writer "came to feel that with a little more effort life could be grasped without the intervention of fiction" (*About Fiction*, pp. 40–41).

For Morris, the most insidious cause of the hunger for the real among novelists themselves has been the growing use of the vernacular as *the* literary language of American fiction. The language of "real life" persuades us that real life is what we are getting in fiction: "The daily use and abuse of the 'vernacular tongue' . . . has blurred the once clear-cut distinction between life and its mirrored reflection. The world and its image are seen as one. The 'style' that gives us this assurance is a craft achievement so invisible it appears to be absent, persuading the reader that life and the lifelike . . . will appear as one" (ibid., p. 46). The trouble with this persuasion is not just that four-letter words tend to lead the artist to an exclusive preoccupation with four-letter truths, or that the artist who "perceives" must ultimately mean more to us than one who merely "observes," although Morris points out both these problems. As he said in the interview about his photography cited in chapter 3, the final difficulty is that reality is never attained in art without being filtered through some subjective vision, and no art exists that does not mediate between the audience and the experience. Hemingway's use of the vernacular may have made it appear "that the 'gap' between literature and life had narrowed," but "in point of fact, the true-to-life can only be true to the prevailing reality concept. No ultimate reality will be evoked by cracking barriers or talking plainer" (ibid., p. 30). The Bergsonian dualism I discussed in chapter 1 applies here; however successful the work of art may be in evoking the sense of life, art and life are two different things. For Morris, the sense of life is indispensable in fiction, but it is not something that is a given in the artist's materials, the automatic product of fidelity to facts; it is achieved through his style, not through the elimination of style.

The best realistic fiction testifies to the mediating function of art rather than invalidating it. Norman Mailer, says Morris, "will be able to read [Saul] Bellow, because he feels that he's getting less fiction through Bellow than he gets through other writers," yet Bellow "knows, as any writer knows, that you provide one illusion of reality over another . . . but both are fictions."[2] This is the point Morris makes in *About Fiction* by comparing a "true-to-life" example of the vernacular from a newspaper (p. 44), and the "life-like" vernacular of a passage from *The Catcher in the Rye* (p. 45). The difference is a sense of life created by the imagination. Nevertheless, because Morris is so strongly committed to the idea that fiction must process reality, there are differences between his novels and those of more conventional realists. Most of the novels of Saul Bellow illustrate the realistic mode and record the pressures of reality in the contemporary environment. In *Mr. Sammler's Planet* (1970), the milieu is typical of postwar America—the hell of the city where facts impinge on the self from every side. One critic has pointed out Bellow's fondness for images of weight and pressure,[3] reflecting a feeling that there is too much life, too much reality, for the imagination to take it all in. It hangs heavy on the spirit, and Bellow's hero struggles with the problem of moral survival in the face of the "thereness" Morris speaks of. Sammler, trying to keep his intellect clear amidst all this experience, is oppressed by "the multiplication of facts and sensations," which deprive him, "because of volume, of mass, of the power to impart design."[4]

The very quality of Bellow's realism suggests that Sammler's feeling about his world is Bellow's own. John Aldridge and Wright Morris have briefly discussed the element of the "idiosyncratic" and "grotesque" in Bellow's handling of characters (*Conversations*, pp. 16–17). In *Mr. Sammler's Planet*, this element is evident, for instance, in the exaggerated lubricity of Angela Gruner, letting "that twerp in Mexico ball her fore and aft in front of Wharton, with who-knows-what-else thrown in free by her" (p. 171). It sometimes governs Bellow's choice of metaphors, as when the two sexes, with their fencing for advantage, are described as "like two different savage tribes. In full paint. Surprising and shocking each other in the bush" (p. 189). The extravagance of outward gesture suggested by this comparison points to a Dickensian strain in Bellow, but the exaggeration also registers the shock of a sensibility affronted by the outrageousness of reality, and, more particularly, of an intellect affronted by the rise of the primitive and irrational in human behavior. In *Mr. Sammler's Planet*, the irrational is manifested in "the peculiar aim of sexual niggerhood for everyone" (p. 149) and symbolized by the spectre of growing black crime. In the figure of the black pickpocket who exposes his penis in order to intimidate Sammler, Bellow portrays how sex, in its most reductive physical form, has become the sole measure of value and worth, the sole grounds of human discourse. The brutally physical exults over reason, law, and conscience.

Sammler eventually decides that the root of the irrational "madness" in modern society is an inflated sense of individualism and an exaggeration of the human potential for triumphing over limitations. The road to sanity lies in accepting one's limitations while "trying to live with a civil heart. With disinterested charity" (p. 125). Sammler's debate with the Indian, Dr. Lal, on the advisability of going to the moon focuses on this central issue in the novel. Lal sees space travel as an antidote to man's sense of frustration at impinging reality on earth: "We are crowded in, packed in, now, and human beings must feel that there is a way out, and that the intellectual power and skill of their own species opens this way" (p. 200). Sammler counters that the moon shot is but another of man's attempts "to transcend his unsatisfactory humanity," an effort doomed to failure because "mankind cannot be something else. It cannot get rid of itself" (p. 215). The earth is still Mr. Sammler's planet, and the episodes where Sammler falls wounded into the mass grave prepared by the Nazis and hides "in the mud, under scum" (p. 129) from the Poles are emblems of his inescapable immersion in an earthbound, existential reality in all its thereness. The character who best exemplifies a heroic engagement with the facts of human nature and the human environment is Sammler's nephew, Elya Gruner, who faces the ultimate fact of human mortality, but in his life manages to remain true to an instinctive sense of God's will. Elya's example teaches Sammler that each man feels in his heart an ethical imperative, "the terms of his contract" with God, terms that "we all know, God, that we know, that we know, we know, we know" (p. 286).

In his stress on the acceptance of human limits and the active commitment to life here and now, Bellow resembles Morris writing in novels like *The Huge Season* and *The Field of Vision*, but there are differences in the way Bellow and Morris treat the commitment theme. For one thing, Morris's treatment, though less learned, specifically ties the need for commitment to the theory of creative evolution and opposes to it the impulse to transcendence. Sammler's ethical imperative is finally irrational, what we know, we know, we know. As in *Herzog* (1964), the hero's learning brings many of the best insights of the past to bear upon the human dilemma, but the final affirmation is made possible by going beyond learning to consult the heart.[5] Bellow is also direct and explicit in dealing with the contemporary scene and its issues; *Mr. Sammler's Planet* alludes to

Karl Marx, Herbert Marcuse, Norman O. Brown, Dean Rusk, Richard Nixon, and Che Guevara, among others. Morris tends to treat contemporary issues more obliquely and by implication. He is less interested in the issues as issues and more interested in them as occasions for examining the American scene and character.

Another major difference between the two authors is that in such novels as *The Field of Vision* the theme of engagement with this world has an explicit aesthetic dimension, the result of Morris's concern with the nature of fiction. Bellow, the child of the teeming cities, records in his fiction the pressures of an external, material reality. Morris, the child of the empty plains, sees material reality as a chaotic void upon which must be projected some inner vision. This intimation of the need to impose an internally derived pattern accounts for the strong sense of structural design in Morris's best fiction. Details must not only be realistic, but also fit into a pattern of imagery. Indeed, one danger in Morris's mature fiction is too much design. Imagery sometimes becomes overinsistent; structure threatens to resolve issues that should be resolved through character development. On the other hand, in books like *The Adventures of Augie March* (1953), Bellow needs more of a sense of structure. Morris's use of the vernacular again involves a concern with signification and design not found in more conventional realists. The overwhelming authenticity captured in Morris's portraits of middle-American types like the McKees relies substantially on his ear for their manner of speaking (even McKee's reflections are full of colloquial expressions which reveal facets of his character). McKee, in telling Lois and Mr. Clokey to enjoy Cuernavaca says, "You two go ahead and fool around" (*The Field of Vision*, p. 137). This speech is pure midwestern tourist, but it contains an unconscious pun which reveals to Lois that McKee is oblivious to her sexual feelings. It never occurs to him that "fool around" may mean more than see the sights. In *One Day*, to pick a different sort of example, Miriam Horlick's use of the proverbial expression about "a cold day in hell" fits in to the novel's pattern of freezing and inferno images.[6]

Morris's remarks in *About Fiction* bear on a second important group of contemporary novelists who stand at the opposite extreme from those who seek to capture reality itself. The writers in this second group feel that fiction is to be prized for its very fictiveness, prized because it is not reality. One characteristic of "radical innocence" which Ihab Hassan discusses in his book of that title[7] is a "recoil" into the self and away from the world. This impulse is evident in *Mr. Sammler's Planet* and *The Field of Vision*, with their focus on meditation and consciousness. In an extreme form, the recoil into the self can lead to the projection of a distorted inner vision upon the materials of external reality. When the projected vision is regarded as having an autonomous reality and when this principle of autonomy is made the central tenet in a consciously articulated theory of fiction, then there arises the tradition in postwar fiction which Robert Scholes, in a 1967 book, called "fabulation." For Scholes, the development of cinema sounded the death knell of fictional realism: "Realism purports . . . to subordinate the words themselves to their referents, the things the words point to. Realism exalts Life and diminishes Art, exalts things and diminishes words. But when it comes to representing *things*, one picture *is* worth a thousand words."[8] Therefore, "fiction must abandon its attempt to 'represent reality' and rely more on the power of words to stimulate the imagination" (pp. 11–12). The result will be fabulation, "a more verbal kind of fiction. . . . a more fictional kind. . . . a less realistic and more artistic kind of narrative: more shapely, more evocative; more concerned with ideas and ideals, less concerned with things" (p. 12).

Scholes makes it clear that fabulation is neither an exclusively American nor an exclusively modern phenomenon. His definition seems broad enough to encompass examples of what Richard Chase, speaking of nineteenth-century American fiction, has called the "romance novel," but Scholes discusses three contemporary Americans at length—John Barth, John Hawkes, and Kurt Vonnegut, Jr.—and his definition would especially apply to others whose work relies heavily on fantasy elements—such as Donald Barthelme, Vladimir Nabokov, and Thomas Pynchon. The fabulators themselves have described their fictional aims in various ways. Hawkes, for instance, is very much in the surrealist tradition of André Breton; he views fiction as "an exclamation of psychic materials which come to the writer all readily distorted, prefigured in that nightly inner schism between the rational and the absurd."[9] Others such as Barth, Vonnegut, and Nabokov have been concerned, even in the conscious themes of their novels, with the issue articulated by Scholes, the relation of imagination and reality; they have set out to dramatize how the imagination functions to process the reality in which man finds himself. As part of their pursuit of this aim, they deliberately, in Scholes's words, take a "delight in design" which "asserts the authority of the shaper, the fabulator behind the fable" (p. 10). Specifically, many fabulations underline the artificiality of fiction by employing conspicuous devices like frame tales or allegorical structures and by substituting for the invisible vernacular style of realism a style which contains a lot of what Tony Tanner calls "foreground," that is, a "use of language in such a way that it draws attention to itself—often by its originality."[10]

Whereas realism dominated postwar American fiction between 1945 and 1960, fabulation has since assumed growing importance. The shift toward fabulation can sometimes be observed in the career of a single writer; it is marked by John Barth's decision to write *The Sot-Weed Factor* (1960), an imitation of the eighteenth-century novel, after his earlier, more realistic imitations of life, *The Floating Opera* (1956) and *The End of the Road* (1958). Many fabulist fictions center around a key moment when a character turns away from the real world toward a fantasy world of unlimited imaginative possibilities. Herbert Stencil's discovery of his father's diary entry about V in Thomas Pynchon's *V.* (1963) is such a moment, and

Pynchon's *The Crying of Lot 49* (1966) is structured around a whole series of these moments, from Pierce Inverarity's phone call before the book's opening, to the crying of lot 49, which will take place right after the book ends. In one of the central texts of the fabulist tradition, Vladimir Nabokov's *Pale Fire* (1962), the poet John Shade has occupied a limiting world of material reality external to himself and replete with all the contingencies to which man on this earth is subject. Faced, like Elya Gruner, with death, Shade decides that the way to immortality lies through the imagination, in the creation of a timeless work of art. As with Paula Kahler in *The Field of Vision*, the inner vision is represented in the image of a madman's transforming hallucination. A lunatic is really an artificer, Shade says, "a person who deliberately peels off a drab and unhappy past and replaces it with a brilliant invention."[11] At the moment when he would complete his poem with the word *slain*, Shade chooses instead to slay himself in his imagination. The unfinished poem about a real New England becomes a wacky prose commentary about the fantasy realm of Zembla; the aging but sane poet becomes the vigorous but insane king and commentator Kinbote. Although as a poet Shade may well be "one oozy footstep" behind Frost (p. 34), his supreme creations, Kinbote and the "distant northern land" of Zembla (p. 224), stand for the highest crystallizations of timeless art.

A similar moment of turning from fact to fiction is portrayed in Kurt Vonnegut's *Slaughterhouse-Five* (1969), a book which contrasts both with *Mr. Sammler's Planet* and with such Morris works as *The Field of Vision* and *In Orbit*. Like Sammler, Billy Pilgrim is subject to the pressures of external reality on the self in the form of metaphysical and historical evils, which are epitomized by the Dresden fire bombing. Indeed, a major Vonnegut theme is that external pressures can obliterate the self by imposing unsatisfactory social roles on the individual. Billy's civilian life—an incongruous success story in which he marries the boss's daughter out of expediency—does not square with the naive and ineffectual character he is shown to have. Where there is no self that can truly be said to act on its own and not in conformity to some socially imposed role, there is no question of man's affecting external reality as Sammler would with his ethical imperative. Man is totally determined: "Among the things Billy Pilgrim could not change were the past, the present, and the future."[12]

Nevertheless, Billy can still change himself, embracing an insane vision which transforms the world from within. Billy's story, as we have it, is not what actually happened to him, but what he imagines his life has been like after having gone mad. The onset of his madness becomes evident shortly before he goes on a New York radio show to break the news about his trip to the planet Tralfamadore. Billy stares in the window of a pornographic book store while "the news of the day . . . was being written in a ribbon of lights on a building" (p. 173) at his back. At the moment he enters the store to look at science-fiction novels, he rejects the external reality embodied in the news of the day and "re-invents" his life from the materials of erotic daydreams and science fiction. His imagined trip to Tralfamadore is really a flight into the imagination and a fitting symbol for the rejection of earthbound reality. On Tralfamadore, man's helplessness in a material universe is transformed into a virtue; nothing can be changed because all time exists simultaneously and always will. To observe this fact about time, one must transcend it, rise above time to the eternal realm of the imagination.

The idea that one can do nothing to affect life, the withdrawal into imagination, and the image of flight from earth are the converse of the earthbound commitment in *Mr. Sammler's Planet* and *The Field of Vision*. In addition, *Slaughterhouse-Five* discards realism and offers an explicit defense of a nonrealistic aesthetic. Fellow mental patient Eliot Rosewater tells Billy that *The Brothers Karamazov*, by Feodor Dostoyevsky, contains "everything there was to know about life," but he adds, "that isn't *enough* any more" (p. 87). Any realistic work, even the greatest masterpiece, will be inadequate precisely because it is limited to dealing with what there is to know about life, about the unalterable facts, about the reality that Billy and Eliot cannot face. Writing in his own voice, Vonnegut confides that he had originally felt realism could do justice to his own Dresden experience. The terrifying facts would speak for themselves. But as Morris has often said and Vonnegut discovered after years of wrestling with his subject, the facts never speak for themselves; they must be processed by the imagination. The first and last chapters of the novel bring in the Vonnegut persona to focus on the act of processing and to establish a parallel between the author and his hero. Just as Billy survived the holocaust of life on earth by piecing together fragments of his experience for his Tralfamadore vision, so Vonnegut mastered the trauma of Dresden by piecing together fragments of fact and fancy for *Slaughterhouse-Five*. The novel's fluid movement backward and forward in time (actually movement in Billy's disordered imagination) suggests life as seen from Tralfamadore, from outside of time; that is, life as imagined in a transcendental fiction. Further, the book's interweaving of the real with the fanciful creates a nightmare effect not possible with realism alone.

The qualities which set Morris's work apart from that of more conventional realists like Bellow align him with the fabulators. These qualities include an emphasis on design which "asserts the authority of the shaper," a heavy reliance on image and symbol, and often an explicit theme examining the nature of art. The major difference between Morris and the fabulators is that his fiction is representational, an imitation of "real life." It is a difference that bears looking at in detail. Although both *Pale Fire* and *Slaughterhouse-Five* express rejections of material reality, the reality survives in both as that which the vision turns away from, whether represented by Shade's concern with mortality or Vonnegut's concept of a society inimical to the self. Nevertheless, if the road of the vernacular, as Morris says, leads downhill into a sordid materialism, the road of fabulation often leads out of this world to an autonomous realm of fantasy. It proves to be a short jump from writing fiction that imitates works of fiction to writing fiction that is about little else but fiction. Vonnegut moves on to *Breakfast of Champions* (1973), Barth to *Chimera* (1972). Moreover, the principle that reality in art can be known only through a subjective vision can lead to the belief that vision is the only reality, and when reality as a separate entity disappears, the function of representation in fiction becomes meaningless.[13] This process is observable as *Pale Fire* and *Slaughterhouse-Five* give way to Nabokov's *Ada* (1969) and Vonnegut's *Slapstick* (1976), where the free play of the authors' memories and fancies is imitated.

Behind much of fabulation's drive toward the nonrepresentational is the familiar feeling, a legacy of the Romantic age, that art must constantly change in order to remain vital. The fiction of today, so the argument goes, cannot be nourished by the exhausted materials and modes of yesterday, those of realism. An important statement of this position has been made by Barth. He concedes, "with reservations and hedges," that "the novel . . . has by this hour of the world just about shot its bolt," and praises the intricate fictions of Jorge Luis Borges (and *Pale Fire*) as illustrating ways of producing art out of such a "felt ultimacy" at the end of a tradition. Barth also lets the idea come through that any fiction good enough to care about requires a sense of newness: "I sympathize with a remark attributed to Bellow, that to be technically up to date is the least important attribute of a writer, though I would have to add that this least important attribute may be nevertheless essential. In any case, to be technically *out* of date is likely to be a genuine defect."[14] One has the feeling that, judged in the light of such statements and compared with works like *Ada*, Morris's representational art would not be innovative enough or contain enough of the element of "story" or fancy to be thought good by most fabulators. The impulses of fabulation thus raise serious historical questions about the importance of representational writers like Morris and Bellow and about whether the nonrepresentational mode will eventually come to dominate fiction as it has the visual arts. These questions are related to the deeper philosophical issue of the place of "life" or reality in fiction. Does the imperative to "make it new," a central tenet in Morris's own artistic creed, pronounce a negative verdict on his representational art? The facts supplied us by the world are, after all, finite. Has the time come, or indeed passed, when to make it new the writer must abandon the finite world of facts for the infinite and inexhaustible world of the imagination?

In remarks spread throughout *About Fiction*, Morris answers such questions. Although the materials of reality may be theoretically finite, they are rich enough, indeed at times all too rich, and the true challenge to the imagination is to release that richness. Even if the raw material could be exhausted, the ways of seeing it cannot. Writing of *The Brothers Karamazov*, Morris says, "Nothing is more common to the Russian scene than starving peasants and indifferent landlords. They are facts of life. The writer must make of this life what it failed to make of itself," and in the scene where Mitya observes "the babe" freezing on the steppes, Dostoyevsky does just that: "The commonplace is made uncommon" (*About Fiction*, p. 74). There could hardly be a better description of the transfiguring power of art. Further, it is only necessary for the writer to know that a sense of life must be achieved through the mediating power of art and for that knowledge to be reflected *in some way* in the processing of his materials. It is not necessary to parade that knowledge by making his work an imitation of a novel or putting it in a frame tale or using a conspicuous style. If the writer has the talent to realize his vision, whatever it may be, then the creative act will yield a sense of life and design as a matter of course. The reader's experience bears this out: *Slaughterhouse-Five* has both more art and more life than Vonnegut's other novels partly because the sense of Vonnegut's struggle to process his own Dresden adventure comes through. What Morris says about science fiction applies as well to all kinds of nonrepresentational fiction: "When the . . . writer turns to science fiction he will write one more good or bad novel, not one of a type. The distinction lies in the writer, not the genre" (ibid., p. 76).

Newness, too, is a matter of the man, not the style or artistic program. The point is to "make it good, or make it sound, or make it true" (ibid., p. 80), and newness is a by-product of these aims. Beyond this general principle, Morris raises practical objections to an overinsistence on newness. For one thing, he feels that the imagination should not be arbitrarily limited to any one course: "Newness has its place in the house of fiction . . . but the windows face in all directions. . . . It is new enough if the craft is adequate to the inspiration" (p. 83). In addition, writers need traditions, what Morris calls "ruts," in which to write. The exclusive concern with newness makes the rejection of tradition the lone criterion of art and has not usually produced the kind of art from which subsequent writers can learn. In the last analysis, Morris concludes, "Over several centuries good novels have proved how *alike* they are, rather than how different" (p. 115).

The sensible, empirical character of this last observation typifies *About Fiction* as a whole. The more dogmatic assertion in the sentences immediately preceding it—novels cannot change too much because "novels are about people. People are not made new yearly" (p. 115)—reflects assumptions about the fundamental nature of words, as opposed to other art media, and about the value of fiction for man. Implicit in *About Fiction* is the recognition that there is a difference between words and music or paint, and explicit is the belief that literature has human value. Music is, by its nature, abstract; the visual arts may provide the viewer with pleasurable visual experiences without representing anything. But words refer to ideas and things outside themselves. Words without referents, fictions that do not point beyond themselves to some recognizable inner or outer reality, are of interest only as glossolalia. Even more important is Morris's supreme conviction, shining forth from almost every page of *About Fiction* and animating his novels, that fiction, though "remarkably useless in the world of events" (p. 8), nevertheless has one unimpeachable value: it speaks to and expands the consciousness of man in a manner that is "life-enhancing." For to be more conscious is, in a way, to be more human, "an estate that the great talents of fiction have long given their fullest attention" (p. 134). Billy Pilgrim finds himself on an earth where he feels he has no choice, but for Morris, great fiction, like Tolstoy's "The Death of Ivan Ilych," can still be life-enhancing precisely because it offers the reader the one choice Billy lacked the courage to make—the choice to face the truth.

The concept of a life-enhancing fiction springs from Morris's fidelity to the spirits of Henry James and D. H. Lawrence. For, as Morris's fiction shows, the artist's struggle to perfect his art and the man's struggle to live creatively are analogous. In expanding the consciousness of man, like the fiction of James, Morris's novels make "life possible in the modern world," like the fiction of Lawrence (*The Territory Ahead*, p. 225). This is the true meaning, importance, and explanation of the shift toward immanence in his novels. Paula Kahler's transformed vision is an impressive imaginative spectacle, but only Lehmann's vision makes life possible because only his vision encompasses both the imaginative and material reality. Boyd the artist's problem is how *in* the world to create a work of art, but that is just one aspect of Boyd the man's problem, the problem of us all—how *in* the world to live.

John Aldridge has written that Morris has not received the attention he deserves partly because of his unfashionable subject. Jewish novels have an extraliterary appeal to Jewish critics, for instance, but no group in our largely urban intelligentsia has any special interest in novels about the plains.[15] Ironically, beneath the superficial level of subject, Morris's concerns are central to the writing of the immediate present. It probably gives secret delight to the man from Central City, Nebraska, with his relish for the fact that has been processed and given symbolic meaning, to realize that he stands directly in the middle of the two major streams of postwar American fiction and to know that, perhaps better than any other novelist writing today, he has reconciled the conflicting claims of reality and imagination. For Bellow, in *Mr. Sammler's Planet*, the American effort to reach the moon in 1969 is chiefly a real datum of contemporary life, one that requires analysis and comment because of its very realness. It serves to contrast, in a relatively straightforward way, our technological expertise, which can conquer space, and our inadequacy in personal relationships, which cannot make life livable here on earth (Morris has also noted this contrast in *A Bill of Rites, A Bill of Wrongs, A Bill of Goods*). For Vonnegut, the flight to Tralfamadore has no realistic dimension; it is a symbol only, an emblem of getting away from an unbearable reality. In a novel like *In Orbit*, Morris introduces the subject of space flight indirectly through the title in order to allude to a real phenomenon of current American life, with the implication it carries about our obsession with technology. But in Morris's processing of that phenomenon, it has become something more. He places the space flight within the broader context of our history, recognizing it as the expression of some powerful buried impulse in the American psyche that subdued a savage continent and now gazes longingly back on that adventure (indeed, because he recognized the impulse, he was able to use the image of space flight in books like *The Works of Love*, which precedes the fact of space flight). He links it to other expressions of that impulse in Americans like Jubal. This subtle and complex analysis is not presented in an expository form, but emerges through the interrelationship of the novel's themes, characters, and images. The prospect of space travel relates to many other images in *In Orbit* and to the images of transcendence, with all that has come to imply, in Morris's other fiction. Finally, it has suggested to Morris the orbital structure of his novel.

Such exceptional acts of the imagination can be found throughout the best works of Wright Morris. His artist's sense of the need to process experience leads him to anticipate major fabulist themes and to make the fabulator's strong sense of design an earmark of his fiction. His moralist's insight into the American scene has enabled him almost to predict some of the traumatic episodes of our recent history, seeing in the heroic Virgil Ormsbys of the forties the potential assassins of the sixties. Thus, in another sense too, Morris is in the middle. In his art, he mediates between the bizarre, bewildering, and often wondrous life on this planet and our necessary yet hard-won consciousness of what that life means. Through his lifelong struggle to process the raw material of his experience into art, the regenerative powers of his imagination have redeemed the wasteland of our national life. His work is truly life-enhancing.

Notes

CHAPTER 1

1. "Introduction," *Wright Morris: A Reader*, p. ix.

2. See Bibliography for the list of editions of Morris's full-length works cited. All further references to works by Wright Morris will be cited in the text.

3. "The Alone Generation," *Contemporaries* (Boston: Little, Brown, 1962), pp. 213–14.

4. *Contemporary American Literature, 1945–1972: An Introduction* (New York: Ungar, 1973), p. 36.

5. Morris was first interested in fiction. See his comments in "Interview," in *Wright Morris: Structures and Artifacts: Photographs 1933–1954*, p. 111.

6. Gerald Nemanic, "A Ripening Eye: Wright Morris and the Field of Vision," *MidAmerica I: The Yearbook of the Society for the Study of Midwestern Literature* (1974), p. 126.

7. "The Poetry of W. B. Yeats," in James Hall and Martin Steinmann, eds., *The Permanence of Yeats* (1950; rptd. New York: Collier Books, 1961), p. 305.

8. "The Two Worlds in the Fiction of Wright Morris," *Sewanee Review* 65 (Summer 1957): 375–99.

9. Jack Rice Cohn, "Wright Morris: The Design of the Midwestern Fiction" (Ph.D. diss., University of California, Berkeley, 1970), p. 72. Further references will be cited in the text as Cohn.

10. "The Hero and the Witness in Wright Morris' Field of Vision," *Prairie Schooner* 34 (Fall 1960): 263–78; "The Great Plains in the Novels of Wright Morris," *Critique* 4 (Winter 1961–62): 5–23; "Wright Morris' *In Orbit*: An Unbroken Series of Poetic Gestures," *Critique* 10 (Fall 1968): 102–19; "Morris' *Cannibals*, Cain's *Serenade*: The Dynamics of Style and Technique," *Journal of Popular Culture* 8 (Summer 1974): 59–70; portions of the first two articles are included in condensed form in his book *Wright Morris*, Twayne United States Authors Series (New York: Twayne Publishers, 1964). Unless otherwise specified, further references to Madden will be to the book and will be carried in the text.

11. W. B. Yeats to Lady Elizabeth Pelham, 4 January 1939. Quoted in Joseph Hone, *W. B. Yeats: 1865–1939* (New York: MacMillan, 1943), p. 510.

12. Neither Booth nor Madden can be included among the critics who ignore the nonmidwestern fiction. Madden's book is the best synthesis of Morris's career yet, and Booth argues for the comic European novels in "The Shaping of Prophecy: Craft and Idea in the Novels of Wright Morris," *American Scholar* 31 (Autumn 1962): 608–26.

13. *The Creative Mind*, trans. Mabelle L. Andison (New York: Philosophical Library, 1946), p. 22. Further references will be cited in the text.

14. *Creative Evolution*, trans. Arthur Mitchell (1911; rptd. New York: Modern Library, 1944), p. 295. Further references will be cited in the text.

15. Another striking similarity of imagery deserves to be noted. The motion-picture imagery of *Cause for Wonder*—still photographs projected twenty-four times per second so that they take on the appearance of movement—dramatizes the tension between organic mobility and conceptual stasis and is related to the snapshot imagery sprinkled throughout Morris's novels. In *Cause for Wonder*, the imagination of young Brian records and preserves the insane antics of his elders as if on celluloid: "For a moment they stood, without movement, as if the voice behind them had cried 'Camera!' and a scene that had long been in preparation was being shot. Behind them, shooting it, was the boy" (p. 262). Bergson employs the same "cinematograph" image to illustrate the abstracting power of intellect and to show how it creates a sense of mobile becoming by putting together a series of static percepts (*Creative Evolution*, pp. 331–34).

16. *The Immense Journey* (1957; rptd. New York: Time Reading Program, 1962), p. 87. Further references will be cited in the text.

17. "Letter to a Young Critic," *Massachusetts Review* 6 (Autumn–Winter 1965): 97. Further references will be cited in the text.

18. "Made in U.S.A.," *American Scholar* 29 (Autumn 1960): 483. Further references will be cited in the text.

19. Sam Bleufarb, "Point of View: An Interview with Wright Morris, July, 1958," *Accent* 19 (Winter 1959): 35. Further references will be cited in the text.

20. There is evidence that Lawrence knew Bergson's work early in his career (before 1913). Rose Marie Burwell, "A Catalogue of D. H. Lawrence's Reading from Early Childhood," *D. H. Lawrence Review* 3 (Fall 1970): 230.

21. *Apocalypse* (1931; rptd. New York: The Viking Press, 1960), p. 45. Further references will be cited in the text.

22. *Psychoanalysis and the Unconscious* and *Fantasia of the Unconscious* (1921, 1922; rptd. New York: The Viking Press, 1960), pp. 13–14. Further references will be cited in the text.

23. "Poetry of the Present," *The Complete Poems of D. H. Lawrence*, ed. Vivian de Sola Pinto and F. Warren Roberts (New York: The Viking Press, 1964), p. 182. See the last chapter of *The Territory Ahead* (pp. 217–31) for the full significance of the term to Morris.

24. "The Art of Fiction," in *Theory of Fiction: Henry James*, ed. James E. Miller, Jr. (Lincoln: University of Nebraska Press, 1972), pp. 34–35. Further references will be cited in the text.

25. Edith F. Cornwell, *The "Still Point": Theme and Variations in the Writings of T. S. Eliot, Coleridge, Yeats, Henry James, Virginia Woolf, and D. H. Lawrence* (New Brunswick, N.J.: Rutgers University Press, 1962), p. 156. Further references will be cited in the text.

26. "Preface to *The Portrait of a Lady*," in *Art of the Novel: Critical Prefaces by Henry James* (New York: Charles Scribner's Sons, 1934), p. 57. Further references will be cited in the text.

27. Friederich Nietzsche, *The Birth of Tragedy or: Hellenism and Pessimism*, in *Basic Writings of Nietzsche*, trans. Walter Kaufmann (New York: Modern Library, 1966), p. 37.

Chapter 2

1. "Made in U.S.A.," *American Scholar* 29 (Autumn 1960): 487. Further references will be cited in the text.

2. Wright Morris, "The Origin of a Species, 1942–1957," *Massachusetts Review* 7 (Winter 1966): 122. Further references will be cited in the text.

3. "Letter to a Young Critic," *Massachusetts Review* 6 (Autumn–Winter 1964–65): 95. Further references will be cited in the text.

4. David Madden, *Wright Morris*, pp. 32–41; John W. Hunt, Jr., "The Journey Back: The Early Novels of Wright Morris," *Critique* 5 (Spring–Summer 1962): 41–60.

5. Leon Howard, *Wright Morris*, p. 9.

6. Neither *The Inhabitants* nor *God's Country and My People* has page numbers. The speech by Dudley appears as part of two separate pages.

7. *Studies in Classic American Literature* (1923; rptd. Garden City, N.Y.: Doubleday Anchor Books, 1951), p. 190. All further references to this work will be cited in the text.

8. Harvey Breit, "Talk with Wright Morris," *New York Times Book Review*, 10 June 1951, p. 19.

9. An unpublished study of the manuscript indicates that the journey portions of *My Uncle Dudley* and the jail episode were originally two separate stories which were eventually spliced together. In tone and quality the splicing shows. Jack Rice Cohn, "Wright Morris: The Design of the Midwestern Fiction" (Ph.D. diss., University of California, Berkeley, 1970), p. 135.

Chapter 3

1. Sam Bleufarb, "Point of View: An Interview with Wright Morris, July 1958," *Accent* 19 (Winter 1959): 34–46; "Guest of Honour—No.

12—Wright Morris (U.S.A.)," *Photography* (London), July 1949, pp. 14–15; "The Inhabitants: *An Aspect of American Folkways*, A Note by Wright Morris," in James Laughlin, ed., *New Directions in Prose and Poetry, 1940* (Norfolk, Conn.: New Directions, 1940), pp. 147–48; "Letter to a Young Critic," *Massachusetts Review* 6 (Autumn–Winter 1965): 93–100; "The Origin of a Species, 1942–1957," *Massachusetts Review* 7 (Winter 1966): 121–35; "Privacy as a Subject for Photography," *Magazine of Art* 44 (February 1951): 51–55; "Interview," in *Wright Morris: Structures and Artifacts*, pp. 110–20. Further references will be cited in the text.

2. Chester E. Eisinger, "Wright Morris: The Artist in Search of America," *Fiction of the Forties*, pp. 328–41; Roger J. Guettinger, "The Problem with Jigsaw Puzzles: Form in the Fiction of Wright Moris," *Texas Quarterly* 11 (Spring 1968): 209–20; Leon Howard, *Wright Morris*; John W. Hunt, Jr., "The Journey Back: The Early Novels of Wright Morris," *Critique* 5 (Spring–Summer 1962): 41–60; David Madden, *Wright Morris*, pp. 48–56; Gerald Nemanic, "A Ripening Eye: Wright Morris and the Field of Vision," *MidAmerica I: The Yearbook of the Society for the Study of Midwestern Literature* (1974), pp. 120–31; Alan Trachtenberg, "The Craft of Vision," *Critique* 4 (Winter 1961–62): 41–55. Further references will be cited in the text.

3. Quoted in John K. Hutchens, "On an Author," *New York Herald Tribune Book Review*, 3 June 1951, p. 2.

4. Arthur E. Waterman, "The Novels of Wright Morris: An Escape from Nostalgia," *Critique* 4 (Winter 1961–62): 27.

Chapter 4

1. Jack Rice Cohn, "Wright Morris: The Design of the Midwestern Fiction," (Ph.D. diss., University of California, Berkeley, 1970), pp. 161 and 178–79 for MSS dates. His discussion of the developing texts provides information about the relation of *Man and Boy* to *The Works of Love*. Further references will be cited in the text.

2. The lack of clarity in chronology is made worse by Brady's rapid aging. He seems to be in his twenties when he meets Mickey Ahearn but has become very old before the boy reaches late adolescence. He is married to Ethel during World War I (p. 69).

3. In an essay published after I wrote this chapter, Wayne Booth stresses that Brady's perceptions become more visionary as his personal relationships deteriorate. See Wayne Booth, "Form in *The Works of Love*," in Robert E. Knoll, ed., *Conversations with Wright Morris*, pp. 35–73. See also Booth's discussion with Morris in the same book: "The Writing of Organic Fiction," pp. 74–100.

4. Madden seems to regard the transcendence as a final victory, although he stresses the corrupting power of Brady's struggle for material success as

well. See David Madden, *Wright Morris*, pp. 64–75. Marcus Klein, in *After Alienation*, pp. 219–20, sees *The Works of Love* as a major turning point in Morris's career because it brings home to him the futility of transcendence and subsequently causes him to choose "accommodation" to the nature of things: "The problem is how *in the world* to engage the Reality that is the definition of another world, and the end, simply, is that you can't. And at this point, then, the Real is to be obtained neither in the progressive present nor in the past. The road to it, in both directions, is out of this world. . . . Stories of more strenuous reconciling of the Real with the real can lead him . . . only to quicker suicides. And because this is the only possible ultimate resolution of the story he tells, Morris won't . . . try to come again to unifying, thoroughly tested solutions" (pp. 219–20). The problem with this interpretation is that it depends on accepting Booth's definition of "reality" as Platonic and therefore as timeless and transcendental. This acceptance leads Klein to dismiss the immanence of the later novels as so much wishful thinking and also implies that Morris found transcendence congenial before discovering its drawbacks in *The Works of Love*. Further references to Madden and Klein will be cited in the text.

5. From "Journal of the Plague Year," dated by Cohn as composed from 1940 to 1943. Quoted in Cohn, "Wright Morris: The Design of Midwestern Fiction," p. 114.

6. In a note to me on 6 December 1968, Morris suggested that Lawrence's view of American civilization and character in *Studies in Classic American Literature* was somewhat similar to his own. In a conversation with me on 18 October 1975, he indicated that he had first read *Studies* in the late forties or early fifties.

7. "Drrdla," *Esquire*, August 1969, pp. 87–90; rptd., *Green Grass, Blue Sky, White House* and *Real Losses, Imaginary Gains*.

8. Booth and Madden write on nostalgia, but the fullest treatment of the theme is in Arthur E. Waterman, "The Novels of Wright Morris: An Escape from Nostalgia," *Critique* 4 (Winter 1961–62): 24–40.

9. Although the account may seem contrived and farfetched, it was actually witnessed by Morris himself. See his essay "Nature Since Darwin," *Esquire*, November 1959, pp. 64–70.

10. "The Origin of a Species, 1942–57," *Massachusetts Review* 7 (Winter 1966): 127.

11. The actual title of the Disney film was *Nature's Half Acre*. Morris's title must surely be an inadvertence since the actual title would be more appropriate to his statements in this scene and to the patch of woods near Foley's home which he calls "God's Half Acre" (p. 25).

12. Another interesting work on the effects of technology on the modern mind is Morris's story "The Sound Tape," published in *Harper's Bazaar* 85 (May 1951): 125, 175–77. The setting of the story is that of *Man and Boy* and *The Deep Sleep*.

13. *The Crack-Up*, ed. Edmund Wilson (New York: New Directions, 1945), p. 69.

Chapter 5

1. Cohn points out similarities between Willy Brady, the boy, and Hapgee, a character in a manuscript who resembles Ormsby. Cohn further argues for an identification of Brady and Ormsby. Jack Rice Cohn, "Wright Morris: The Design of the Midwestern Fiction" (Ph.D. diss., University of California, Berkeley, 1970), pp. 162–63.

2. The love expressed by Ormsby in feeding the birds is less clearly mystical than in *The Works of Love* because the novel stresses natural forces at work in the world. The mystical element is present, however.

3. "The Ram in the Thicket," *Harper's Bazaar* 82 (May 1948): 181; rptd. *Real Losses, Imaginary Gains*. The story covers the action in the first sixty-one pages of the novel, but omits some material included in the finished work. Further references will be to the magazine and will be cited in the text.

4. David Madden, *Wright Morris*, pp. 85–89.

5. "Main Line Author of the Month: Wright Morris," *Main Line*, June 1951, p. 24.

6. Quoted in John K. Hutchens, "On an Author," *New York Herald Tribune Book Review*, 3 June 1951, p. 2.

7. See David Madden's excellent discussion of their differences in *Wright Morris*, pp. 96–100.

8. "Letter to a Young Critic," *Massachusetts Review* 6 (Autumn–Winter 1965): 99.

9. *The American Scene: Together with Three Essays from "Portraits of Places"* ed. W. H. Auden (New York: Charles Scribner's Sons, 1946), p. 345.

10. Marcus Klein, in *After Alienation*, discusses the novel in terms of Booth's real-ideal dualism; the life of the house is the "worldly time in which alone the Judge could have striven to escape to the timeless" (p. 225). In the novel as a whole, "There is still a radical discontinuity between exigent ordinary life and what is felt to be Real, and the dilemma [that the Real is attainable only through death] is of course in no way solved, but it comes to rest through being perceived in multiple instances, and it is accepted" (p. 220).

Chapter 6

1. "National Book Award Address, March 12, 1957," *Critique* 4 (Winter 1961–62): 74.

2. Ralph N. Miller, points out, however, that the third-person narration allows Morris's own persona to emerge at moments which require reliable authorial commentary. "The Fiction of Wright Morris: The Sense of

Ending," *MidAmerica III: The Yearbook of the Society for the Study of Midwestern Literature* (1976), p. 61.

3. J. E. Cirlot, *A Dictionary of Symbols*, trans. Jack Sage (New York: Philosophical Library, 1962), p. 73. Further references will be cited in the text.

4. "Preface to *The Portrait of a Lady*," in *The Art of the Novel: Critical Prefaces by Henry James* (New York: Charles Scribner's Sons, 1934), p. 46.

5. The critics who particularly focus on nostalgia are David Madden, *Wright Morris*, pp. 131–55, and Arthur E. Waterman, "The Novels of Wright Morris: An Escape from Nostalgia," *Critique* 4 (Winter 1961–62): 24–40.

6. *Anatomy of Criticism* (1957; rptd. New York: Atheneum, 1967), pp. 147–49. Further references will be cited in the text.

7. Jean-Paul Sartre, *Nausea*, trans. Lloyd Alexander (New York: New Directions, 1959), p. 238.

8. "Poetry of the Present," *The Complete Poems of D. H. Lawrence*, ed. Vivian de Sola Pinto and F. Warren Roberts (New York: The Viking Press, 1964), p. 182.

9. I accept Andrew Field's reading that Kinbote is Shade gone mad and achieving an immortal artifice in his madness. *Nabokov: His Life in Art* (Boston: Little, Brown and Co., 1967), pp. 291–322. See also Julia Bader, *Crystal Land: Artifice in Nabokov's English Novels* (Berkeley: University of California Press, 1972), pp. 31–56.

10. The basic story is repeated in *Ceremony in Lone Tree* (pp. 257–63). Another version is "The Safe Place," *Kenyon Review* 16 (Autumn 1954): 587–99; rptd. *Wright Morris: A Reader* and *Real Losses, Imaginary Gains*.

11. Sam Bleufarb, "Point of View: An Interview with Wright Morris, July 1958," *Accent* 19 (Winter 1959): 45.

12. "Made in U.S.A.," *American Scholar* 29 (Autumn 1960): 487. Further references will be cited in the text.

13. Marcus Klein, *After Alienation*, p. 234.

14. "Mexican Journey," *Holiday* 26 (November 1959): 52. Further references will be cited in the text.

15. This detail indirectly links her to Dudley and gives some insight into how Morris develops his material. Morris has attributed the same gesture to his Uncle Verne, the original of Dudley and a series of old men heroes. "The Origin of a Species, 1942–1957," *Massachusetts Review* 7 (Winter 1966): 122.

16. D. H. Lawrence, "Art and Morality," *Phoenix: The Posthumous Papers of D. H. Lawrence*, ed. Edward D. McDonald (1936; rptd. New York: The Viking Press, 1972), p. 520.

Chapter 7

1. I am indebted for many details of my interpretation to a very fine essay: Jonathan Baumbach, "Wake Before Bomb: *Ceremony in Lone Tree*,"

Critique 4 (Winter 1961–62): 56–71; rptd. in his *Landscape of Nightmare* (New York: New York University Press, 1965), pp. 152–69. He asserts, for example, that the acts of violence in the novel are "misdirected assertions of male potency in a society dominated, smothered, and emasculated by the female" (p. 159).

2. Arthur E. Waterman, "The Novels of Wright Morris: An Escape from Nostalgia," *Critique* 4 (Winter 1961–62), has a good summary of this point (p. 39).

3. David Madden argues the former in *Wright Morris* (p. 148) and Baumbach the latter (*Landscape of Nightmare*, p. 159).

4. Arthur E. Waterman ("The Novels of Wright Morris") first mentions Lawrence's concept of the prehistoric present in connection with Morris (p. 33). Whether Morris is consciously borrowing or not, the concept fits with the imagery of fossils beginning in his novels as early as *Man and Boy*. In some cases the concept is tied to evolution and organicism, but in others, it is associated with the imagination.

5. These impressions of Venice are typical of Morris's own, as evident in "Letter from Venice: Shooting the Works," *Partisan Review* 29 (Fall 1962): 578–86 and both the photos and text of *Love Affair: A Venetian Journal*.

6. "The Lunatic, the Lover, and the Poet," *Kenyon Review* 27 (Autumn 1965): 729. Further references will be cited in the text.

7. The cats Aschenbach and Winnie correspond to Mann's hero and Miss Throop except that their transformations are unequivocally animal in nature. Morris often uses the cat image for the instinctive, animal side of man's nature. See his stories, "The Cat in the Picture," *Esquire* 49 (May 1958): 90–94 and "Drrdla," *Esquire* 72 (August 1969): 87–90; rptd. *Blue Sky, Green Grass, White House* and *Real Losses, Imaginary Gains*. The former deals with the dichotomy of life and art, to life's advantage, and the latter stresses the need for continuing development of self. The sketch *The Cat's Meow* (1975; rptd. in *Real Losses, Imaginary Gains*) shows Morris's personal attitude about cats.

Chapter 8

1. Harvey Breit, "Talk with Wright Morris," *New York Times Book Review*, 10 June 1951, p. 19.

2. "*One Day*: November 22, 1963–November 22, 1967," in Thomas McCormack, ed., *Afterwords: Novelists on Their Novels*, p. 14. Further references will be cited in the text.

3. *The Crack-Up*, ed. Edmund Wilson (New York: New Directions, 1945), p. 75.

4. Arthur E. Waterman, "Wright Morris's *One Day*: The Novel of Revelation," *Furman Studies*, n.s. 15 (May 1968): 33.

5. On this point, Madden writes, "Just as weather becomes most visible when it condenses, shapes up into a twister, so we see ourselves, our town,

our national character most sharply when a violent catalyst gives shape to various impulses and makes them visible a moment before they disperse again," David Madden, "Wright Morris' *In Orbit*: An Unbroken Series of Poetic Gestures," *Critique* 10 (Fall 1968): 105. Madden's essay (pp. 102–19) is excellent and must be considered in any criticism of *In Orbit*.

6. See Madden's discussion in "Wright Morris' *In Orbit*," pp. 110–19.

CHAPTER 9

1. *The Hero with a Thousand Faces* (1949; rptd. New York: Meridian Books, 1956), p. 266.

2. *The Immense Journey* (1957; rptd. New York: Time Reading Program, 1962), p. 126.

CHAPTER 10

1. "Writing American Fiction," Marcus Klein, ed., in *The American Novel Since World War II* (Greenwich, Conn.: A Fawcett Premier Book, 1969), pp. 146, 150. Further references to this collection will be cited as Klein, *American Novel*.

2. "The American Novelist and the Contemporary Scene, A Conversation between John W. Aldridge and Wright Morris," in Robert E. Knoll, ed., *Conversations with Wright Morris*, p. 20. Further references to this collection will be cited as Knoll, *Conversations*. This book appeared after I had completed all but the last chapter of this study.

3. Irving Malin, "Seven Images," in Irving Malin, ed., *Saul Bellow and the Critics* (New York: New York University Press, 1967), pp. 142–46.

4. Saul Bellow, *Mr. Sammler's Planet* (1970; rptd. Greenwich, Conn.: A Fawcett Crest Book, 1970), pp. 8, 28. Further references will be cited in the text.

5. I am indebted to my colleague Professor Barbara Gitenstein for suggesting to me that Sammler's ethical imperative reflects the Jewish code of *mentshlekhkayt*. The code holds that man can sense his covenant with God in his heart and must go beyond intellect and learning to express his own innate goodness in action. For a discussion of the code, see Josephine Zadovsky Knopp, *The Trial of Judaism in Contemporary Jewish Writing* (Urbana: University of Illinois Press, 1975), pp. 6–29.

6. A somewhat different approach to Morris's use of the vernacular is touched on in a conversation between Morris and David Madden. See Knoll, *Conversations*, especially pp. 101–2 and pp. 108–13.

7. *Radical Innocence: Studies in the Contemporary American Novel* (Princeton, N.J.: Princeton University Press, 1961).

8. Robert Scholes, *The Fabulators* (New York: Oxford University Press, 1967), p. 11. Further references will be cited in the text.

9. "Notes on the Wild Goose Chase" (1962), in Klein, *American Novel*, p. 249.

10. *City of Words: American Fiction 1950–1970* (New York: Harper & Row, 1971), p. 20. Most of the figures Tanner discusses are fabulators, and his special focus in the study is the parallel between the author's search for a stylistic freedom and the hero's search for a freedom of self.

11. Vladimir Nabokov, *Pale Fire* (1962; rptd. New York: Berkley Medallion Books, 1968), p. 169. Further references will be cited in the text. My remarks are indebted to those by Andrew Field in *Nabokov: His Life in Art* (Boston: Little, Brown and Co., 1967), pp. 291–322.

12. Kurt Vonnegut, Jr., *Slaughterhouse-Five or the Children's Crusade, A Duty-Dance with Death* (New York: Delacorte Press, 1969), p. 52. Further references will be cited in the text.

13. Some basic assumptions of the fabulators are carried to extremes in a recent collection of essays. In the introduction, Raymond Federman argues that since "no meaning pre-exists language. . . . to write . . . is to *produce* meaning, and not *reproduce* a pre-existing meaning. . . . As such, fiction can no longer be reality, or a representation of reality, or an imitation, or even a recreation of reality; it can only be . . . autonomous reality." See Raymond Federman, ed., *Surfiction: Fiction Now . . . and Tomorrow* (Chicago: Swallow Press, 1975), p. 8.

14. "The Literature of Exhaustion" (1967), in Klein, *American Novel*, pp. 274, 269. Barth's own *Lost in the Fun House* (1968) illustrates the sort of fiction that might grow out of the convictions expressed in his essay.

15. "Wright Morris's Reputation," in John W. Aldridge, *The Devil in the Fire*, pp. 257–60.

Bibliography

The editions of Wright Morris's works that I have used in this study are all first editions, with the exception of *The Man Who Was There*. In this instance I have preferred the edition reprinted in 1977 by the University of Nebraska Press; it omits approximately fifteen lines (on page 219 of the first edition) in order to correct a printer's error in the original. For the convenience of students, I have listed paperback reprints currently available or announced for publication as this book goes to press. I have not listed reprints of uncollected articles and stories, but I have included essays later collected in revised form in *The Territory Ahead* and in *A Bill of Rites, A Bill of Wrongs, A Bill of Goods*. It should also be noted that the stories in *Green Grass, Blue Sky, White House*, in *Here is Einbaum*, and in *The Cat's Meow* are collected in *Real Losses, Imaginary Gains*.

I have listed only those critical works that I have found to be particularly helpful in writing this study. For a listing of book reviews, dissertations, and other materials, the reader is referred to "A Wright Morris Bibliography" compiled by Robert L. Boyce for *Conversations with Wright Morris* (see section V, below). Since the entries in the Boyce bibliography are arranged chronologically, my listing is alphabetical to provide the reader with two different ways of locating materials.

I. Books by Wright Morris

About Fiction: Reverent Reflections on the Nature of Fiction with Irreverent Observations on Writers, Readers, & Other Abuses. New York: Harper & Row, 1975.

A Bill of Rites, A Bill of Wrongs, A Bill of Goods. New York: New American Library, 1968.

The Cat's Meow. Los Angeles: Black Sparrow Press, 1975.

Cause for Wonder. New York: Atheneum, 1963. Reprint. Lincoln: University of Nebraska Press, 1978.

Ceremony in Lone Tree. New York: Atheneum, 1960. Reprint. Lincoln: University of Nebraska Press, 1973.

The Deep Sleep. New York: Charles Scribner's Sons, 1953. Reprint. Lincoln: University of Nebraska Press, 1975.

The Field of Vision. New York: Harcourt, Brace, and Co., 1956. Reprint. Lincoln: University of Nebraska Press, 1974.

Fire Sermon. New York: Harper & Row, 1971.

God's Country and My People. New York: Harper & Row, 1968.

Green Grass, Blue Sky, White House. Los Angeles: Black Sparrow Press, 1970.

Here is Einbaum. Los Angeles: Black Sparrow Press, 1973. Available in paperback.

The Home Place. New York: Charles Scribner's Sons, 1948. Reprint. Lincoln: University of Nebraska Press, 1968.

The Huge Season. New York: The Viking Press, 1954. Reprint. Lincoln: University of Nebraska Press, 1975.

The Inhabitants. New York: Charles Scribner's Sons, 1946.

In Orbit. New York: New American Library, 1967. Reprint. Lincoln: University of Nebraska Press, 1976.

A Life. New York: Harper & Row, 1973.

Love Affair: A Venetian Journal. New York: Harper & Row, 1972.

Love Among the Cannibals. New York: Harcourt, Brace and Co., 1957. Reprint. Lincoln: University of Nebraska Press, 1977.

Man and Boy. New York: Alfred A. Knopf, 1951. Reprint. Lincoln: University of Nebraska Press, 1974.

The Man Who Was There. New York: Charles Scribner's Sons, 1945. Reprint. Lincoln: University of Nebraska Press, 1977.

My Uncle Dudley. New York: Harcourt, Brace, and Co., 1942. Reprint. Lincoln: University of Nebraska Press, 1975.

One Day. New York: Atheneum, 1965. Reprint. Lincoln: University of Nebraska Press, 1976.

Real Losses, Imaginary Gains. New York: Harper & Row, 1976.

The Territory Ahead. New York: Harcourt, Brace, and Co., 1958. Reprint. Lincoln: University of Nebraska Press, 1978.

War Games. Los Angeles: Black Sparrow Press, 1972. Reprint. Lincoln: University of Nebraska Press, 1978.

What a Way to Go. New York: Atheneum, 1962. Reprint. Lincoln: University of Nebraska Press, forthcoming 1979.

The Works of Love. New York: Alfred A. Knopf, 1952. Reprint. Lincoln: University of Nebraska Press, 1972.

The World in the Attic. New York: Charles Scribner's Sons, 1949. Reprint. Lincoln: University of Nebraska Press, 1971.

Wright Morris: A Reader. Introduction by Granville Hicks. New York: Harper & Row, 1970. Reprint. New York: Avon, 1974.

II. UNCOLLECTED STORIES BY WRIGHT MORRIS

"The Cat in the Picture . . ." *Esquire* 49 (May 1958): 90–94.

"The Character of the Lover." *American Mercury* 73 (August 1951): 43–49.

"How I Met Joseph Mulligan Jr." *Harper's Magazine* 240 (February 1940): 82–85.

"The Lover." *Harper's Bazaar* 83 (May 1949): 118, 175–180.

"Lover, Is That You?" *Esquire* 65 (March 1966): 70, 132–136.

"A Man of Caliber." *Kenyon Review* 11 (Winter 1949): 101–7.

"The Scene." *The Noble Savage*, No. 1 (1960), pp. 60–75.

"The Sound Tape." *Harper's Bazaar* 85 (May 1951): 125, 175–177.

"Trick or Treat." *Quarterly Review of Literature* 18 (1973): 368–78.

"Wake Before Bomb." *Esquire* 52 (December 1959): 311–15.

"Where's Justice?" *Cross Section* 1948, edited by Edwin Seaver, pp. 221–30. New York: Simon and Schuster, 1948.

"The Word from Space—A Story." *Atlantic Monthly* 201 (April 1958): 38–42. Reprinted in *Magazine of Science Fiction* 15 (September 1958): 111–18.

III. UNCOLLECTED ARTICLES BY WRIGHT MORRIS

"The Ability to Function: A Reappraisal of Fitzgerald and Hemingway." *New World Writing*, No. 13, pp. 34–51.

Afterword to *Two Years before the Mast*, by Richard Henry Dana, pp. 376–83. New York: New American Library, Signet, 1964.

"An American in Paris." *New York Times Book Review*, 9 December 1951, p. 28.

"The Cars in My Life." *Holiday* 24 (December 1958): 45–53.

"Conversations in a Small Town." *Holiday* 30 (November 1961): 98, 100, 103, 107, 108.

"Death of the Reader." *Nation* 198 (13 January 1964): 53–54.

Foreword to *The Tragedy of Pudd'nhead Wilson*, by Mark Twain, pp. vii–xvii. New York: New American Library, Signet, 1964.

"Henry James's *The American Scene*." *Texas Quarterly* 1 (Summer–Autumn 1959): 27–42.

"How Come You Settled Down *Here*?" *Vogue* 119 (15 April 1952): 74, 117–19.

"How Things Are." In *Arts and the Public*, edited by James E. Miller and Paul D. Herring, pp. 33–52 and 230–53 (*passim*). Chicago: University of Chicago Press, 1967.

Introduction to *Windy McPherson's Son*, by Sherwood Anderson, pp. vii–xix. Chicago: University of Chicago Press, 1965.

"Letter from Venice: Shooting the Works." *Partisan Review* 29 (Fall 1962): 578–86.

"Letter to a Young Critic." *Massachusetts Review* 6 (Autumn–Winter 1964–65): 93–100.

"The Lunatic, the Lover, and the Poet." *Kenyon Review* 27 (Autumn 1965): 727–37.

"Made in U.S.A." *American Scholar* 29 (Autumn 1960): 483–94.

"Man on the Moon." *Partisan Review* 29 (Spring 1962): 241–49.

"Mexican Journey." *Holiday* 26 (November 1959): 50–63.

"National Book Award Address, March 12, 1957." *Critique* 4 (Winter 1961–62): 72–75.

"Nature Since Darwin." *Esquire* 52 (November 1959): 64–70.

"Norman Rockwell's America." *Atlantic Monthly* 200 (December 1957): 133–36, 138.

"*One Day*: November 22, 1963–November 22, 1967." In *Afterwords: Novelists on Their Novels*, edited by Thomas McCormack, pp. 10–27. New York: Harper & Row, 1969.

"One Law for the Lion." *Partisan Review* 28 (May–June 1961): 341–51. Reprinted in *The Territory Ahead* as a "Postscript." New York: Atheneum, 1963.

"The Open Road." *Esquire* 52 (June 1960): 98–99.

"The Origin of a Species, 1942–1957." *Massachusetts Review* 7 (Winter 1966): 121–35.

"Our Endless Plains." *Holiday* 24 (July 1958): 68–69, 138–42.

"The Territory Ahead." In *The Living Novel: A Symposium*, edited by Granville Hicks, pp. 120–56. New York: Macmillan, 1957.

"The Violent Land—Some Observations on the Faulkner Country." *Magazine of Art* 45 (March 1952): 99–103.

"What Was Missing in the Fireworks." *New York Times Book Review*, 1 September 1957, p. 3.

"The Word Between Them." In *Writers as Teachers/Teachers as Writers*, edited by Jonathan Baumbach, pp. 192–201. New York: Holt, Rinehart, and Winston, 1970.

IV. Selected Photo-text Material by Wright Morris

"The American Scene." *New York Times Magazine*, 4 July 1948, pp. 14–15.

"Built With More Than Hands." *New York Times Magazine*, 25 December 1949, pp. 12–13.

"Home Town Revisited." *New York Times Magazine*, 24 April 1949, pp. 24–25.

"Guest of Honour—No. 12—Wright Morris (U.S.A.)." *Photography* (London), July 1949, pp. 14–15.
"The Inhabitants." *Direction* 3 (November 1940): 12–13.
"The Inhabitants." In *New Directions in Prose and Poetry* 1940, edited by James Laughlin, pp. 145–80. Norfolk, Conn.: New Directions, 1940.
"The Inhabitants." *Photography* (London), July–August 1947, pp. 26–29.
"Landscape With Figures." In *New Directions in Prose and Poetry* 1941, edited by James Laughlin, pp. 253–77. Norfolk, Conn.: New Directions, 1941. Reprinted in *Spearhead: 10 Years' Experimental Writing in America*, pp. 191–201. New York: New Directions, 1947.
"Out of Shoes Come New Feet." *New York Times Magazine*, 11 June 1950, pp. 20–21.
"Privacy as a Subject for Photography." *Magazine of Art* 44 (February 1951): 51–55.
"Summer Encore." *New York Times Magazine*, 13 November 1949, pp. 26–27.
"The World in the Attic." *Photography* (London), September 1949, pp. 17–26.
Wright Morris: Structures and Artifacts: Photographs 1933–1954. Monographs on American Art, No. 4. Lincoln: University of Nebraska Press, 1975. P. 4: Wright Morris, "Statement." Pp. 110–21: Wright Morris interview with Jim Alinder.

V. Criticism about Wright Morris

Aldridge, John W. "*Wright Morris: A Reader*." (not a review) *New York Times Book Review*, 11 January 1970, pp. 4, 33. Reprinted as "Wright Morris's Reputation," in his *The Devil in the Fire: Retrospective Essays on American Literature and Culture*, 1951–71, pp. 257–60. New York: Harper's Magazine Press, 1972.
Baumbach, Jonathan. "Wake Before Bomb: *Ceremony in Lone Tree*." *Critique* 4 (Winter 1961–62): 56–71. Reprinted in his *Landscape of Nightmare: Studies in the Contemporary American Novel*, pp. 152–69. New York: New York University Press, 1965.
Bleufarb, Sam. "Point of View: An Interview with Wright Morris, July 1958." *Accent* 19 (Winter 1959): 34–46.
Booth, Wayne C. "The Shaping of Prophecy: Craft and Idea in the Novels of Wright Morris." *American Scholar* 31 (Autumn 1962): 608–26.
———. "The Two Worlds in the Fiction of Wright Morris." *Sewanee Review* 65 (Summer 1957): 375–99.
Breit, Harvey. "Talk with Wright Morris." *New York Times Book Review*, 10 June 1951, p. 19.
Eisinger, Chester E. "Wright Morris: The Artist in Search of America," in

his *Fiction of the Forties*, pp. 328–41. Chicago: University of Chicago Press, 1963.

Fiedler, Leslie A. *Love and Death in the American Novel*, pp. 323–24, 471–72. New York: Criterion Books, 1960.

Garrett, George. "Morris the Magician: A Look at *In Orbit*." *Hollins Critic* 4 (June 1967): 1–12. Reprinted in *The Sounder Few: Essays from the Hollins Critic*, edited by R. H. W. Dillard, George Garrett, and John R. Moore, pp. 263–280. Athens: University of Georgia Press, 1971.

Hicks, Granville. Introduction to *Wright Morris: A Reader*, pp. ix–xxxiii. New York: Harper & Row, 1970.

Howard, Leon. *Wright Morris*. Minnesota Pamphlets on American Writers, no. 69. Minneapolis: University of Minnesota Press, 1968.

Hunt, John W., Jr. "The Journey Back: The Early Novels of Wright Morris." *Critique* 5 (Spring–Summer 1962): 41–60.

Klein, Marcus. "Wright Morris: The American Territory," in his *After Alienation: American Novels in Mid-Century*, pp. 196–246. Cleveland: World Publishers, 1964.

Knoll, Robert E., ed. *Conversations with Wright Morris: Critical Views and Responses*. Lincoln: University of Nebraska Press, 1977.

Madden, David. "The Great Plains in the Novels of Wright Morris." *Critique* 4 (Winter 1961–62): 5–23.

———. "The Hero and the Witness in Wright Morris' Field of Vision." *Prairie Schooner* 34 (Fall 1960): 263–78.

———. *Wright Morris*. New York: Twayne Publishers, 1964.

———. "Wright Morris' *In Orbit*: An Unbroken Series of Poetic Gestures." *Critique* 10 (Fall 1968): 102–19. Reprinted in David Madden, *The Poetic Image in Six Genres*. Carbondale: Southern Illinois University Press, 1969.

Miller, Ralph N. "The Fiction of Wright Morris: The Sense of Ending." *MidAmerica III: The Yearbook of the Society for the Study of Midwestern Literature* (1976), pp. 56–76.

Nemanic, Gerald. "A Ripening Eye: Wright Morris and the Field of Vision." *MidAmerica I: The Yearbook of the Society for the Study of Midwestern Literature* (1974), pp. 120–31.

Trachtenberg, Alan. "The Craft of Vision." *Critique* 4 (Winter 1961–62): 41–55.

Waterman, Arthur E. "The Novels of Wright Morris: An Escape from Nostalgia." *Critique* 4 (Winter 1961–62): 24–40.

———. "Wright Morris' *One Day*: The Novel of Revelation." *Furman Studies*, n.s. 15 (May 1968): 29–36.

Wilson, J. C. "Wright Morris and the Search for the Still Point." *Prairie Schooner* 49 (Summer 1975): 154–63.

Acknowledgments

Part of the work on this study was financed by a summer stipend granted me in 1976 by the National Endowment for the Humanities. Aggregate quotations of over five hundred words from the works of Wright Morris are quoted by permission of the author. The three quotations from the manuscripts of Wright Morris are quoted by permission of the author, the Bancroft Library of the University of California, Berkeley, and Jack Rice Cohn, in whose dissertation the material is quoted. Portions of chapter 8 were first published in a different form in *MidAmerica III: The Yearbook of the Society for the Study of Midwestern Literature* (1976), and portions of chapter 6 were published in a different form in *The D. H. Lawrence Review* 10 (Summer 1977).

It gives me real pleasure to acknowledge the help of the following friends and colleagues who were kind enough to read and comment on parts of my manuscript: Larry Olpin, Norman Stafford, Tom Burtner, Norman and Renee Betz, Dean Hughes, Lee Newcomer, and Barbara Gitenstein. I also wish to acknowledge the help of Ben D. Kimpel, who directed my dissertation on Wright Morris, and James C. Cowan, who fired my interest in D. H. Lawrence. These early experiences were important in getting me started on this project.

G.B.C.

Index